"Have you noticed, Tanner, that we're alone here together? You and I. Nobody else is in this room with us."

He lifted her hands in his, slowly kissing first one, then the other as he looked down into her face. "If this room were filled to the rafters with other people, along with the shades of a thousand more, I would see only you. May I kiss you, Lydia?"

She swallowed, the action almost painful. Her mouth had gone suddenly dry. She could only look at him.

"I'm sorry. It's still too soon. I apologize—"

He didn't say anything else because she had gone up on her tiptoes and pressed her mouth to his.

His arms went around her, making her feel small but not fragile. Instead, she felt real, perhaps for the first time in her life knowing who she was. She was Lydia. She was a woman. She was *alive*....

KASEY MICHAELS

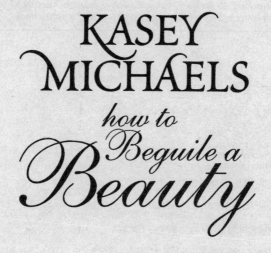

how to Beguile a Beauty

HQN™

Recycling programs
for this product may
not exist in your area.

ISBN-13: 978-0-373-77433-3

HOW TO BEGUILE A BEAUTY

Copyright © 2010 by Kathryn Seidick

This is a work of fiction. Names, characters, places and incidents are either the product of the author's imagination or are used fictitiously, and any resemblance to actual persons, living or dead, business establishments, events or locales is entirely coincidental.

This edition published by arrangement with Harlequin Books S.A.

For questions and comments about the quality of this book please contact us at Customer_eCare@Harlequin.ca.

® and TM are trademarks of the publisher. Trademarks indicated with ® are registered in the United States Patent and Trademark Office, the Canadian Trade Marks Office and in other countries.

www.HQNBooks.com

Printed in U.S.A.

To Jacob Edward Seidick

Welcome to the world, Jacob!

how to
Beguile a
Beauty

CHAPTER ONE

THE SUN SHONE BRIGHTLY as the traveling coach with the gold Basingstoke crest discreetly painted on its doors moved away from the flagway and out into Grosvenor Square. The magnificently liveried driver, a pair of similarly clad grooms hanging on to the rear rails for dear life, deftly swung the equipage about, and the team of fine black horses and the four accompanying outriders pranced their way toward the end of the Square, to the streets of London, and off to a great wide world of excitement and newfound love.

Harnesses jingled. The sharp sounds of iron-clad shoes striking the cobblestones sent up the message, *Farewell—fare thee well*.

The moment was a picture, really, a fine portrait set into motion. *Adventure Awaits* would make a fine title. Especially if the artist could capture the laughing Lady Nicole Daughtry, her bonnet discarded so that the sun fell fully on her face, as if the gods themselves had wished a closer look at her fresh, young beauty. Leaning rather precariously out the off-window, she continued to wave and blow exuberant kisses back toward the mansion until the coach reached the end of the Square and disappeared from sight.

And that was that. There was nothing more to see. Even the sun, which had deigned to appear amidst a Season noted most for damp and rain, withdrew behind a cloud, and the world turned grey once more.

Lady Lydia Daughtry pushed down the sash and backed away from the window on the second floor of Ashurst House to seat herself on the tufted light blue velvet padded bench in front of her bed. She sat with her back ramrod straight, her hands, else they tremble and betray her, neatly folded in her lap. Another portrait, yes, but one entirely without the fire and light she had just witnessed. After a few minutes of thus imitating a statue, she quietly sighed, her bosom rising and falling almost dramatically, before she resumed her quiet, even breathing.

To the casual observer, she was, as always, an island of calm. No one would think that her heart was pounding furiously, or that she felt perilously close to indulging in what her former governess would have condemned as a tantrum.

Not that the Lady Lydia ever had tantrums (if you threw something fragile against, for instance, a nearby wall, and it broke, you'd only have to clean up the pieces. So, really, what was the point?).

Her twin, however, the newly absent Lady Nicole, had manufactured any number of tantrums as a young child. The most memorable remained the last, the day their mother had wed her third husband and then im-

mediately shuffled off her three children once more to
Ashurst Hall. Children were not, it seemed, important
once there was a new man in Helen Daughtry's life. But
if Nicole wasn't to be deemed important, she would at
least be noticed, most especially when she'd loosed a
heavy silver vase at her new stepfather's head.

The man really should have ducked.

Lydia smiled at the memory. Nicole did, with such
marvelously dramatic flair, all the things the stick-in-
the-mud, cautious Lydia only dreamt of doing.

And now Nicole was gone. Her sister, her twin, her
heart-mate, was off on her way to meet the mother of her
fiancé, Lucas Paine, the Marquess of Basingstoke. And
life for neither Lydia nor Nicole would ever be the same.

Lydia had never in her eighteen years known a day
without Nicole by her side. The laughing Nicole. The
adventurous Nicole. Nicole, who could find excitement
anywhere, and manufacture some on her own if none
was to be found.

In the Ship of Life for the twins, Nicole had been the
wind in the sails. Lydia, as she often thought of herself,
had been the anchor. Her sister had pooh-poohed that,
saying Lydia was the rudder, the one who steered them
both along the straight and narrow and kept Nicole
from making an entire cake of herself with her mad
starts. But Lydia knew that Nicole was only being kind.

Because, as everyone else well knew, there wasn't
an ounce of excitement in Lady Lydia Daughtry's entire
body. She was quiet, pleasant, obeyed all the rules,
never caused anyone so much as a modicum of trouble.

To her own mind, she imagined doorstops were more adventuresome. And definitely more interesting, even if the only time anyone noticed one of them was when they tripped over them and stubbed their toes.

When Nicole was in the room, nobody noticed Lydia. Her sister's wide smile, glorious dark hair, shining eyes, infectious laugh and, well, rather luscious body, drew all attention. Even her freckles were exciting. Leaving the slim, blond, blue-eyed Lydia to rather fade into the wallpaper. And that was precisely how Lydia liked it.

But now her shield was gone.

She'd known this day would arrive at some point. But then steady, older, gentle Captain Swain Fitzgerald would have been her protector, her safe harbor.

Except that Captain Fitzgerald had perished at Quatre Bras a year earlier, his death devastating her because she'd loved Fitz with all of her young heart, yes, but also in ways her family would never understand. She'd thought that with her captain she'd found the answer to never having to leave her cocoon of shyness to face the world alone.

Proving to herself that she was something no one had ever suspected of her. She was extremely selfish. Perhaps she hadn't deserved the captain's love and devotion.

If she were a more dramatic sort, she might even believe that God had punished her selfishness by taking the captain from her. But Lydia was also intelligent, and she knew that God would not allow one person to die in order to teach another person a lesson.

Still, as time passed, nearly a year now since the captain's death, doubts about her love for the man had begun to creep into her brain during quiet moments. How much had she really loved him? How much had she loved the idea of love…of being always safe, protected? She'd been only seventeen. Even the captain, in his letters to her, had warned her of her youth, and promised that he would court her slowly once he'd "put Boney back in his cage."

For most of her young life she and Nicole and their brother, Rafe, had been shuffled back and forth between their home at Willowbrook to the late duke of Ashurst's estate—depending on their mother's mood and marital status. Nicole had made her feelings plain on the subject of their nomadic existence. Rafe had gone off to fight Napoleon, kicking the dust of both estates off his boots until finally returning home to learn that his uncle and cousins had died, and he was somehow now the duke himself.

And Lydia? She had never complained. She'd hidden in books, and behind Nicole's warming fire. But that didn't mean she hadn't felt the pain of being less than well-loved by her mother, and merely tolerated by her uncle and cousins.

So, yes, she had been drawn to the captain, Rafe's good friend and fellow soldier. He'd been older, wiser, tall and strong and solid, and he'd seen past her quiet exterior and found something about her that he'd liked. That he'd loved. It had been impossible not to love him back.

Together, they would have been happy for all of their lives.

She blinked away the tears that stung at her eyes. He'd loved her. She'd loved him. She could not, would not forget that one real truth, no matter how her mind sometimes plagued her. And she would never forget Captain Swain Fitzgerald, not ever. She may have learned to live without him over this past year, but then she'd had Nicole ever by her side, hadn't she?

Lydia didn't *want* the world the way Nicole did. She didn't smile easily, didn't trust often; she preferred to hide in books…and behind the effervescent Nicole, living vicariously through her outgoing twin.

Now she would face the world alone. It was a daunting, if not even terrifying thought for someone of Lydia's quiet sensibilities.

She longed to leave London, leave the Season, to escape back to Ashurst Hall and a quiet life. But Rafe was the duke now, and he still had business in the city, so they would not return to his estate until after the King's birthday in June at the earliest. He was much too busy to devote his precious free evenings to squiring her about Mayfair. His wife, Charlotte, carrying their first child, did not go into Society. Lydia's once-again widowed mother had set sail for Italy, fleeing from yet another of her romantic indiscretions…and now Nicole was lost to her.

How was she to go to balls and routs and musical evenings accompanied only by her chaperone? Mrs. Buttram would go off to natter with the other paid chaperones, and Lydia would be left to sit against the wall with all the other overlooked debutantes, all the desperate, reaching females tossed into the Marriage Mart with the mission of securing a rich or at least titled husband.

The heat, the cloying smell of too many hot-house blooms, too many unwashed or overly perfumed bodies. The ignominy of a nearly blank dance card, the occasional turn around the room with either some bored young lord on orders from his mama to squire a few of the wallflowers, or a crass inquisition from some adventurous fortune hunter who asked pointed questions about her dowry.

The thought alone was enough to make Lydia feel physically ill.

Of course, she could always count on Tanner Blake, the Duke of Malvern, to dance with her at least once an evening. It had been His Grace who had brought them the news about Captain Fitzgerald the preceding spring. It had been His Grace whom Lydia had condemned as a liar, his broad chest the one she had beat her fists upon in a terrifying burst of raw emotion, hating him for the words he spoke, struggling to be free of his strong arms, his attempts to comfort her as her world, all her dreams, shattered.

She hadn't been fair to the man. Lydia knew that. She had blamed him, blamed the messenger. Ever since that horrible day, ashamed of her unseemly hysterical outburst, she had tried her best to avoid the duke if at all possible. A return to Ashurst Hall had given her time and space, away from the duke. Long months during which she'd hoped he would forget her outburst, forget her.

Except that the man wouldn't go away. Ever since they'd all come back to town for another Season, even now, as he seemed to be mere days from announcing his betrothal to his third cousin, Jasmine Harburton, he remained a frequent visitor in Grosvenor Square.

And Lydia knew why.

The captain had been his friend; he'd said he wished for Lydia to be his friend. Tanner Blake's persistence had won out over her embarrassment, and her normal clear-headedness had replaced her irrational dislike for the man. For that alone, she was grateful to the healing powers of time and distance. But why hadn't he simply now told her the truth? That the captain, as he lay dying, had asked him to "take care of my Lyddie."

How terrible to force a man into agreeing to such an obligation. Yet how much worse it was to *be* that obligation. She believed the duke saw her as an object of charity, deserving of sympathy, which also forced her into the role of a young woman still daily, actively, grieving her lost love. Even as she hoped, prayed, she could leave this limbo she had existed in for the last year, with the captain still always alive in her heart, but as a cherished memory rather than a constant ache.

The Duke of Malvern was a good man. An honorable man. But did he ever see her as anything other than an obligation? And why was it becoming increasingly important to her that he think of her only as Lydia, and not some appendage to the past?

That was a question she couldn't even have asked of her twin.

There was a knock on Lydia's bedchamber door, and she quickly wiped at her damp cheeks as she called out, "Yes, please come in."

Charlotte Daughtry, Duchess of Ashurst, looking young and slightly flushed in the London heat as she carried around a belly that seemed to increase daily, entered the room, her head tipped to one side as she looked at Lydia. "I thought I'd give you some time by yourself. She's really happy, sweetheart. Be happy for her."

"I am," Lydia said sincerely, getting to her feet and accepting Charlotte's hug. "Lucas adores her, and she him. But I will miss her."

Charlotte idly rubbed at her perfectly round belly. "We'll all miss her, but it isn't as if she's gone to the ends of the earth. She and Lucas will be coming to Ashurst Hall in July, to see her new niece or nephew—please God, the babe will have arrived by then—and also so that we can make plans for the wedding. By the way, it will be your job to talk her out of arriving at the church on horseback, with some of the little girls from the village prancing along ahead of her, streamers in their hair, tossing rose petals. Lucas, I'm afraid, is so besotted he'd grant her anything."

Lydia smiled even as she blinked away fresh tears. She loathed feeling like a watering pot; she'd always been so careful to hide her emotions, especially the stronger ones, which tended to frighten her. "Actually, I think that would be very nice. Very…Nicole."

"Don't tell Rafe, but I agree. Oh, speaking of Rafe, he's downstairs with our friend Tanner, who has come to take you for a drive on this unusual warm day in dreary London. It's so lovely to see the sun, even when it plays hide-and-seek with us as it is today. Honestly, the only reason I came upstairs instead of leaving you some time to yourself was to tell you about Tanner's offer. Not only am I as big as two houses, I may be turning senile. At any rate, Tanner somehow knew Nicole was leaving today, and thought he'd bear you company. Such a wonderful friend, isn't he? So you go fetch your bonnet and pelisse, and I'll tell him you'll be down directly."

Lydia nodded, finding it difficult to speak, holding in her sigh until Charlotte had quit the room.

Was this to be her life for the remainder of the Season?

Charlotte and Rafe happily married; kind, caring, but also very much wrapped up in each other. Captain Fitzgerald, irrevocably lost to her. Nicole, her very best friend, off on a new adventure in her life.

And Tanner Blake, the man she'd initially taken in such dislike through no fault of his own, the man who still seemed so doggedly determined to live up to his promise to his friend Fitz, could soon be married as well, with a whole new set of obligations.

Why, were she the dramatic sort, she would say that she was alone in the midst of a multitude, which was not a very pleasant place to be.

"If the exercise weren't so fatiguing," she told herself, "I should most probably throw myself to the floor and drum my heels against the carpet. Nicole always vowed it made her feel better. But I'm much too polite and restrained and civilized. Much too dull and boring. No wonder I sit with the desperate wallflowers. I may as well be invisible. Then again, if my inside were on my outside, if I were to act as I think and damn the consequences, like Nicole, I should probably shock everyone to their cores, including myself."

Lydia allowed herself another deep sigh before she lifted her slightly pointed chin and dutifully went in search of her pelisse and bonnet. The bonnet with the sky blue ribbon Captain Fitzgerald had picked out for her last Season, saying it went so well with her eyes. Thus armed, she then headed for the staircase, having firmly decided that she was a Daughtry, not a mouse, and it was time she began acting like one.

CHAPTER TWO

"It will be a year soon," Tanner Blake, Duke of Malvern, remarked as he accepted a glass of claret from his friend Rafe. "Sometimes it all seems a lifetime ago, and then at others it feels like yesterday."

He knew he didn't have to say more than that for Rafe to understand to what he was referring. Last year's battle was a fact in all of their lives, one never to be forgotten.

"At least this time it looks as if Boney will be staying where we put him." Rafe took up a seat on the facing couch in the large drawing room, a handsome man with a firm jaw and intelligent eyes. He put forth his glass in a toast. "To Fitz. And to all the good and true men who died in that damned unnecessary battle."

Tanner solemnly clinked glasses with his friend. He wasn't the sort who indulged overmuch in spirits, but it was easier to trust the wine of France than it was the cloudy waters of London. He was much of an age with Rafe, but knew he looked younger, thanks to his dark blond hair with its tendency to wave when he neglected his barber, and to features his late mother had often cooed over as being "nearly Greek." It was only his eyes, seemingly turned a deeper green in the past year, which aged him beyond the schoolroom.

"They're calling it all Waterloo now, you know, because Wellington stayed at an inn there while he wrote his dispatch to Parliament after the battle. I suppose it's as good a name as any. A grand and glorious battle, they say now, a great victory for the Allies, destined to be one of the most memorable battles in history. All of these gushing fools forgetting that if they had just locked up the man more securely, none of it would have happened. To Fitz," Tanner said, raising his glass. "To Fitz, and to the rest—and to stout locks."

Both men drank, then fell silent for some moments, each of them lost in their memories of Captain Swain Fitzgerald and all the other good friends they had lost.

"I think she's doing much better," Tanner said at last, because it wasn't a far leap in his mind from the captain to Lady Lydia.

Rafe nodded his agreement. "To forget him would appall her, but Lydia knows that he'd want her to go on without him. You've been very good for her, Tanner."

"Have I? It's no secret that she saw me as a constant reminder of what she'd lost, at least at first. But our time apart may have taken some of the edge off the events of that day last spring. I'd like to think we've become friends this Season. It's what Fitz wanted."

"And you, being such an honorable man and all of that, also feel obligated to make good on your promise to a dying man. Tanner, I appreciate what you've done, what you're doing. Left on her own, especially now that Nicole has quit the city, it's no secret to either Charlie or me that Lydia would prefer to return to Ashurst Hall and a quiet life."

"I enjoy her company," Tanner said, his eyes shifting toward the carpet at his feet. "Taking her out for the occasional drive, visiting the Elgin Marbles. I certainly wouldn't say I've felt any of it a hardship." He lifted his gaze again. "Have there been any suitors? I should think you'd be knee-deep in them."

Rafe shook his head. "Oh, no, let me correct that. There has been one, but I sent him away. Damn near booted him down the stairs, as a matter of fact. One dance at Lady Hertford's ball, and the mushroom had the nerve to come propose marriage to Lydia's dowry, and then only after his plea for Nicole's dowry fell on deaf ears. It hasn't been easy, coming home from the war, falling into the dukedom, dealing with the twins who, to my shame, I barely remembered. Thank God for Charlie's steady common sense."

"Your wife is much too good for you, yes, but then you've always been a lucky bastard."

Rafe grinned, his eyes twinkling with mischief. "Don't tell her. She mistakenly believes I'm quite the grand catch."

Tanner sat back against the cushions, content to be with his friend, in this place, in this time. He enjoyed visiting Grosvenor Square, and would miss Rafe when the Season was over and they all deserted the city for their country estates. It probably would be another year until he saw Rafe again. Or Lydia.

"Rafe? Just because her sister isn't here, Lydia can't be allowed to shy away from Society for the remainder of the Season."

"I know. But Charlie is adamant in refusing to go into Society as she is. Women," Rafe said, his handsome features softening. "She's never looked more beautiful to me, but she has vowed that until she can see her own shoe-tops again, she is banning herself from all social engagements outside this house. And now that Mrs. Buttram is spending the majority of her time with her wrapped foot on a cushion—gout, she tells us—I imagine it's up to me to boost Lydia out of here from time to time."

"Not necessarily. My cousin is in town, and—"

"The one you're to be betrothed to at any moment, according to my wife, who may not go out in Society, but still manages to know every piece of gossip?"

Tanner once again took refuge in examining the fine Aubusson carpet. "Jasmine Harburton, my third cousin, yes. Her father seems to take the marriage as all but an accomplished fact, and he's a man not known for his reticence. The rumor has come back to me a dozen times, and I've been told at least two adventurous souls have written down a wager on the thing in the betting book at White's. Supposedly it was my father's death-bed wish that I marry Jasmine, you see, bringing their small estate into our holdings. She's an amenable enough young woman, but…"

"But, honorable man that you are, you're finding yourself growing rather weary of dead people planning out your life for you?" Rafe suggested, and then quickly took a sip from his glass, keeping his expression blank.

"Thank you for saying that for me. When I say it, or even think it, I feel rather cold and callous. Especially where Fitz is concerned. But, God, Rafe, the man was dying. Clinging to my hand with his last strength as the battle still raged a few miles away from that pitiful ruined barn where I'd found him. I would have agreed to anything he'd asked at that moment, to make his passing easier."

A flash of pain crossed Rafe's features. Fitz had been his closest friend during six years of war on the Peninsula. If he hadn't inherited the dukedom, hadn't been handed the responsibility for his sisters and mother and all of the Ashurst estates, he would have gone to Brussels with his friend for that last confrontation with Bonaparte. Instead, he had stayed behind, to work inside the War Office. Tanner knew what the man thought: Rafe could never know if his presence on the battlefield might have made a difference, to Fitz's future, to his own. "But now?"

Tanner saw Rafe's expression and mentally kicked himself for a fool, bringing up old pain. Yet fool he was, as he debated as to whether or not he should keep his own counsel. But this was Rafe, his good friend. "And now I'm here because I want to be here. I think I've known that from the moment I first pulled Lydia into my arms as she flailed at me in her grief."

Rafe shook his head ruefully as he slapped at his thigh. "Right again. Blast that Charlie, she's always right. She was right about Lucas, and now she's right about you. How do women do it?"

"I don't know," Tanner admitted, almost sighed... except that women sighed; men got themselves royally drunk. "Lydia no longer sees me as the enemy, her personal agent of death or whatever, but now I'm Fitz's good friend, probably a constant reminder of him. Hell of a turn, isn't it? He asks me to take care of her, watch over her...and I'm seeing myself as usurping his place in her life. I doubt that's what he had in mind."

"And now you're feeling guilty, disloyal? Don't do that. The past is the past, Tanner. It's gone."

"Is it? She loved him, Rafe. It's too soon. I need to give her more time."

"Don't wait too long, my friend. If Fitz's death taught us nothing else, it taught us that the luxury of time is just that. A luxury."

Tanner got to his feet, unable to sit still any longer. "Now that she's out from beneath Nicole's...well, shining star, I suppose...let me take her into Society, Rafe. My cousin's chaperone can easily handle them both. Lydia needs to understand that she is a beautiful young woman, inside and out. She always allowed Nicole to shine while she positioned herself in the background. If I'm to seriously pursue my suit, she needs to first find someone to compare me with other than Fitz."

"You want her to be courted by other men? Is that what you're saying?"

"God help me, yes, I suppose I am."

"You don't fear competition?"

"Not *live* competition, no, heartless as that sounds. A good man in life, in death I fear Fitz has been raised very nearly to sainthood by what was at the time a younger, very impressionable girl. She's known only his companionship and now, to a very small extent, mine. I want to win her, I won't lie about that, but not by default."

"Charlie has mentioned to me, and not all that kindly, that men in love all seem to have maggots in their heads. Once again, Tanner, you're proving the woman right. However, since you seem to be offering to take my place shepherding Lydia around Mayfair, who am I to argue, or to point out the obvious pitfalls? Although I will ask this, as I am Lydia's brother and protector. You aren't also using her to teach a lesson to Miss Harburton's father about his presumptions?"

Tanner didn't understand for a moment, and then smiled. "Well, now, Rafe, do you see that? I'm not as unselfish as you might think, am I. Even if I didn't realize it until you pointed it out to me. Thank you."

"You're welcome, I suppose. Ah, what tangled webs we weave, and all that rot."

"I'm not weaving a web. I'm being quite serious. I didn't even consider using Lydia to throw hints to Thomas Harburton and his assumption that I will wed his—" Tanner cut off his protest as he turned toward the foyer, to see Lydia walking toward the doorway to the drawing room.

Nicole, bless her energetic self, seemed to explode into a room, bringing her wide smile and dancing eyes with her, as if every moment was a party, an adventure. Lydia walked with such grace, almost floated, her posture the dream of any boarding school mistress, her movements never exaggerated as if trying to draw attention to herself. Both twins were magnificent, but when they were together, it was only natural for the eye to travel first to Nicole.

Men were so easily dazzled by the obvious, making straight for the glittering diamond, overlooking the perfect pearl.

What would the gentlemen of the *ton* see now, when Lydia made her appearances in the Park, in the ballrooms all across Mayfair? Would they see what he had seen from the very start?

Was he out of his mind, as Rafe fairly well suggested, to allow any other man within twenty feet of her when he already knew he wanted her for himself?

Probably.

"Lydia," Tanner said, bowing in her direction. "I thought some fresh air might be welcome after the past few days of rain. We should be just in time for the Promenade."

She gifted him with a small, elegant curtsy. "Good afternoon, Tanner. How nice of you to think of me. Hyde Park? I've only been there in the mornings, to take the air. I heard it is a sad crush at five in the afternoon. Are you sure you wish to dare it?"

"Oh, he'd dare anything. Wouldn't you, Tanner? He's

a very daring man," Rafe said, kissing his sister on the cheek. "And now, if you'll excuse me, I believe I have to go grovel at my brilliant wife's dainty feet—the ones she increasingly insists I tell her still exist. Tanner, were you planning to attend Lady Chalfont's ball this evening?"

Tanner looked at him, grateful for Rafe leading him so easily into the moment. "The invitation is among those stacked on my mantelpiece, yes. And I hear it may prove to be an entertaining evening."

"Wonderful. Lydia, do you hear that? You now have an escort, unless you wish my company instead. I really do need to work on my speech for Parliament, the one that will most probably earn me a few whistles and cat-calls when I again mention that it's time we began taking care of our poor soldiers."

Lydia looked from Rafe to Tanner, confusion clear in her eyes. "I shouldn't wish to take you away from such an important speech, just to squire me. But, Tanner, there is no reason for you to sacrifice yourself in the role of chaperone, either. I have no crushing desire to attend the ball in any case."

Tanner offered her his arm and walked her toward the foyer, throwing a silent *thank you* back over his shoulder at Rafe. "What? And miss out on those wonderful Gunther Ices I hear are to be served in the supper room? I've been looking forward to them all day, now that I think of it. And I also heard that her ladyship has commissioned an ice sculpture in the form of a pair of extremely long-necked swans. Ten feet high, I'm told. In this heat? We really should want to be there for the moment those long, delicate necks melt and the whole thing comes crashing down. Hugh Elliot has promised me he'll be there, watching, just so that he can shout *off with their heads* at just the correct moment."

Lydia looked up at him and smiled with those marvelous blue eyes of hers, clearly unaware that he immediately felt a figurative kick to his stomach. "You're making that up as you go along, aren't you, just so that I'll agree to the evening?"

They walked outside, to his waiting curricle. "Ah, and that you won't know unless you allow me to escort you to the ball, will you?"

"True. All right then, I accept your kind offer, sir. But there had better be swans."

"I admit I can't guarantee that, but at least I'm sure of the Gunther Ices. Lady Chalfont *always* has Gunther Ices, as they're her husband's favorite. Right after brandy, cigars, Faro banks and, rumor has it, a fiery redheaded opera dancer in Covent Garden. And here we are—up you go."

Tanner vaulted around the rear of the curricle once Lydia was seated, and climbed up, taking the reins from the groom.

"Rafe informed me that your chaperone is suffering from the gout," he said as they left Grosvenor Square for the short ride to Hyde Park. "And, as Nicole has left the city, I was thinking just now that you might miss her company at the ball."

"I miss her company at all times," Lydia corrected quietly. "But you're correct."

Tanner nodded, again, just as if he'd only this moment realized the problem, and the solution. "In that case, since my cousin is in town, and her chaperone is not suffering with the gout, what do you say I ask Jasmine if she wants to accompany us this evening, to bear you company now that Nicole is not here? I would not wish to have you feel alone in the ballroom."

Lydia turned her head to look toward a knot of ladies just then crossing the street, heading for the entrance to the park. Was she intrigued by them, or just avoiding his gaze? "I've never met your cousin. But, yes, that would be very nice, I'm sure."

If Lady Chalfont's swans could be kept in close proximity to Lydia this evening, there would be no danger of their necks melting through. The sudden unexpected chill in Lydia's voice was that evident, and strangely out of character. Lydia was never cross.

"Now I've upset you in some way," Tanner said as he deftly eased his curricle into the line of coaches, phaetons and other showy equipages all jockeying for position on the broad sandy track that wound through the park.

She shifted on the plank seat, to face him. "Oh, I'm sorry, Tanner. I'm—well, let me just say that it has been a rather strange day. It's not that I mean to be ungrateful. But it's also so…well, so *obvious*. You're being kind. Am I such a pitiful wreck, that people feel this need to be *kind* to me?"

"I wasn't being—"

"Oh, but you were, and I really should thank you,

even while in my heart I know I should not have to apologize for voicing my feelings in the matter," Lydia interrupted, her smooth pale cheeks taking on a hint of color, of fire. "So, please, allow me to say what I feel. Everyone is so kind to me. Be careful around Lydia, they must tell each other, tiptoe if at all possible. Poor Lydia, now that Nicole has gone away. Poor Lydia, the bluestocking, the *dull* one, who only dances when Nicole's card is already filled and the gentlemen hope to impress her by squiring her insipid, forgettable sister. Poor sad Lydia, still mourning her lost—"

She clamped her gloved hands to her mouth, her eyes now wide as saucers.

Tanner didn't know if he should apologize, or cheer. "Lydia? Are you all right?"

She slowly lowered her hands, to reveal a small but growing smile. "My goodness. I think I've just had a tantrum."

"Are you sure?" Tanner would have thought a tantrum involved a good deal more anger, some shouting, and possibly some general tossing and smashing of fragile china. But for a first effort, if that's what it had been, she had done rather well. She certainly had his attention.

"I am, yes. And Nicole's right. I *do* feel better. Tanner, since you say you are my friend, you will oblige me now by no longer treating me as if I should be packed up in cotton wool. Is that agreed? Wait, before you speak—and in turn, I will oblige you by not being such a…such a…well, whatever it is I was being that has had you all behaving as if I'm some delicate ice swan's neck apt to melt and topple at any moment."

Tanner felt a nearly overwhelming desire to pull her into his arms. But he was also aware that the opposite of coddling her in cotton wool was not an invitation for an all-out frontal assault and baring of his emotions.

"I'm sorry, Lydia, if we've all been tiptoeing around you. And, to prove it, I'll ask you this time, and not tell you or attempt to cajole you—would you care to accompany my cousin and myself to Lady Chalfont's ball this evening? Or would you much rather tell me to go find a pump and soak my head?"

"I would never say anything like that! At least I don't think I would." She then nodded her head twice, rather decisively. "Yes, thank you, I believe I should like very much attending the ball with you and Miss Harburton. And I'm certain I will enjoy meeting your cousin." Then she gave him another smile, and another figurative kick to the gut. "But you think it was a good tantrum?"

"Tolerable, yes. You might need a little more practice before you've perfected it, but it was a good beginning."

"I'm usually considered to be a good student. I'll apply myself. Oh…someone is attempting to get your attention. Over there," she said, pointing with her chin—how he delighted in the way she did that.

"Tanner Blake, it has been too long. How good to see you again," the man called out, waving his hand in the air as he approached on horseback. "It was one thing to be long-ago chums, and to crack a few bottles with you in Paris a few years ago, but now that you're the duke, I suppose I should take great care to cultivate your newly esteemed self."

Tanner quickly took in the finely set-up grey stallion and the even more perfectly set-up gentleman in the saddle, still doing his best not to appear shocked at his friend's sudden appearance. "Justin. Nobody told me you were in town. Did Vienna finally pall on you?"

Baron Justin Wilde, who had worn many hats during the last years in the fight against Bonaparte—many of them not known to any but the most highly-placed in the War Office—eased his mount around so that he was now riding alongside the curricle. The two men shook hands, no mean feat as both curricle and horse were still on the move.

Justin Wilde was now, as Tanner always remembered him to be, dressed in the first stare of fashion, the cut of his jacket accentuating the natural breadth of his shoulders, the buckskins molded to his strong thighs above high, close-fitting black Hessian boots sporting natty leather tassels and shined within an inch of their lives. But it was the lace at collar and cuffs that most firmly lifted him above the ordinary, as well as a face too handsome to allow anyone to feel threatened by him and his considerable muscles.

In fact, many would at first blush of meeting the Baron think him a smooth-speaking, faintly air-headed fop. They would look into those laughing green eyes beneath brows as dark as his boots and his hair, be disarmed by the frequent smile, and believe themselves in the company of a none-too-bright jewel of the *ton*. Which would be their mistake.

"I escaped Vienna nearly a month ago, slowly making my way home. Diplomacy can be boring, even when we're carving up empires like bakers cutting a cake." He half-stood in the stirrups as he tipped his curly-brimmed beaver at Lydia. "Forgive him, ma'am. The boy never did learn his manners. I am Justin Wilde, and you are the most delightful creature I've ever been privileged to see. Please tell me this scoundrel is only squiring you, and has no prior claim to your affections now that my heart hangs in the balance on your answer."

Tanner's laugh brought a small, hesitant smile to Lydia's face. "Lady Lydia Daughtry, please forgive me for being forced to introduce to you Baron Justin Wilde. Soldier and statesman, wit and fool. And he plays all of those roles better than most. I suggest you avoid him at all costs."

"Oh, foul, Tanner. Foul. You're twice the fool I am, and so I tell everyone. Lady Lydia, again, I implore you. Tell me your heart is not as yet bespoken, most especially to an unnamed rogue bearing a rather canny resemblance to the gentleman now looking so uncomfortable beside you, else mine own heart will surely break."

Tanner waited for Lydia's answer, realizing that he had no idea what she would say. Yesterday, he would have known she'd be polite, rather shy, and most definitely exceedingly proper. But today? He looked at her curiously, his heart jumping when she revealed a small, rather wry smile that made him see, perhaps for the first time, a resemblance to her mischievous twin.

"I most seriously doubt my words hold such power, sir," she said after a moment, "but if it eases your endangered heart at all, I will say that his Grace and I are friends out merely to enjoy the air and, of course, the present foolish company."

Wilde swiftly removed his hat and pressed it to his chest in mock admiration. "My God, Tanner, she speaks in complete sentences. And without simpering or stuttering or feigning light-headedness at my crude attempts at flattery." Once again he leaned his head forward, to look around Tanner. "Lady Lydia, please be so kind as to picture me figuratively at your feet. I had no idea beauty such as yours could exist, most especially in concert with a functioning mind."

Tanner put out his arm, pushing Wilde back on his saddle even as he maneuvered the reins and the curricle moved forward slowly, thanks to the crush of other vehicles. "You should take yourself back to Vienna, Justin, if your opinion of London ladies is so poor."

"Nonsense, Tanner. My opinion of *all* ladies is that they are delightful creatures. As long as one isn't so unfortunate as to have to engage them in conversation for more than a few minutes, of course. Which, fortunately, I usually don't. But Lady Lydia seems to be a wonderful exception to the rule."

Now it seemed to be Lydia's turn to push—politely—Tanner back on his seat as she leaned forward to question the Baron. "Exception though you have deemed me, I feel I must now ask you a question. Are you then a misogynist, sir? Or perhaps a misanthrope, and your distaste extends to all creatures who are not you? Are you Alceste?"

Tanner now sat back on the bench seat all by himself, without further direction from either Wilde or Lydia. He figured it was safer.

"Alceste, you say? That woeful cynic? Then you are familiar with Molière and his masterpiece, *Le Misanthrope?* Tanner, did you hear that? Wait, wait, this can't be. Lady Lydia, indulge me by completing this line. *He's a wonderful talker, who has the art…?"*

Tanner laughed out loud. "God's teeth, Justin, you'd quiz her?"

"No, no, it's all right. Shall I?" Lydia looked to Tanner, who merely nodded. "Very well, then. *He's a wonderful talker, who has the art of telling you nothing in a great harangue."*

"Ha! I can see why that line is one of your favorites, Justin. Sounds just like you. Are we done now? I brought Lady Lydia here to see the sights, not to amuse you. Although I'll admit to being quite well amused myself."

"I'll leave you now, yes," Wilde said, his considering gaze still on Lydia, who seemed to have suddenly remembered that she was the shy twin, the one who never put herself forward. "But perhaps we can meet again later, Tanner? It has been too long."

Tanner agreed, because he did truly enjoy Justin

Wilde. He told him that he and Lydia would be attending Lady Chalfont's ball later in the evening, and then finally watched as Wilde rode off, probably already planning on whom he would next harass with his perfect—and yet unexpected, almost bizarrely so—presence.

"What a strange man," Lydia said as Tanner moved the curricle forward only a few feet, the crush of equipages now reaching a multitude on this rare sunny afternoon. "Does he really think women are so... useless?"

"I'd say I wouldn't know, except that I like the man, and feel he may have made a rather odd first impression. Justin was once married to an extraordinarily beautiful young woman, Lydia, and it ended badly. He has told me that he chose her for her beauty, which, again, according to him, is a mistake made too often by vain and foolish gentlemen."

"I believe that particular mistaken and short-sighted conclusion is shared by both genders."

Tanner looked at her curiously. "Really?"

"You're surprised?"

"I suppose not. And we men probably spend nearly as much time in front of the mirror or with our tailors as do women. Thank you for that insight."

"You're welcome," she said, her smile once again shy. But, then, he treasured all of Lydia's smiles, which had been far too infrequent since he'd first met her. "Now tell me the rest. I'm sure there's more to the story."

"Oh, there most definitely is. Justin was bored with

his beauty within a fortnight, as her conversations veered from demands that he compliment her every outfit to reciting endless minutiae about the outfits of other women of their acquaintance. He said—and I remember it well because he was so very serious at the time, if a bit in his cups—that she could probably recite the names of every fabric, gee-gaw and thingamabob known to man with much more ease than she could the alphabet."

"Poor man. Poor wife."

"She found solace," Tanner said, deciding it was time he took advantage of a break in the endless train of vehicles, and turned his curricle toward a nearby exit to the street. Seeing Justin again had been a shock, albeit a good one. "From what I've heard, not from Justin, who would never have allowed such an indiscretion, she found a variety of ways to comfort herself. Gowns, jewels…a long line of other men more than willing to keep reassuring her she was beautiful."

"Was beautiful? Does that mean—?"

"Yes, it does, but not soon enough to save Justin, I'm afraid, even though that sounds callous. A month before Danielle met an unfortunate end tripping down a length of marble stairs at Carlton House after catching a heel on the outrageously flounced hem of her gown—the Prince of Wales had to take to his bed for a week after the accident—one of her lovers made the mistake of bragging about his latest conquest. Justin felt bound to call the man out, defending the honor of his dishonorable wife."

"He killed the man?"

"He hadn't planned to, but yes. I served as one of Justin's seconds, so I saw it all. His fool opponent turned to fire on the count of two. We called out to warn Justin. He turned at once, and fired in self-defense. But the man was still dead, and Justin had to flee the country. It's only his valuable service to the Crown, I imagine, and the passing of years that has allowed him to return to England. I wonder how he'll be received now, eight long years later. The man he killed was the second son of an earl, you understand. There's always a new bit of gossip to keep the *ton* happy, but that old gossip couldn't be so far beneath the surface of many memories. Not with Justin showing himself so boldly in the Park. It's as if he's encouraging everyone to talk about him."

"But you'll stand by him."

Tanner looked at her. She hadn't framed her words as a question. "Yes, I will. Even though—no, especially because the old hurts don't seem so far beneath Justin's own surface now that he's returned to England. He may have been teasing with you, but the wounds of his failed marriage and the consequences seem to have served to jade his opinion toward women."

"Or perhaps served to undermine his faith in his own judgment when it comes to women," Lydia said, causing Tanner to look at her sharply.

"Justin Wilde? Unsure of himself? I wouldn't think that possible."

"'Doubts are more cruel than the worst of truths,'"

Lydia said quietly. "After making what he has admitted to you was a terrible mistake on the part of his heart so many years ago, how can he now trust his own judgment?"

Tanner turned his pair of bays into Grosvenor Square, wishing he hadn't chosen to desert the park so soon, for now he had no excuse to continue this unsettling conversation. "Molière again. And, again, from *Le Misanthrope*. He needs a friend, doesn't he? For all his appearance of being so secure and confident."

"He has a friend," Lydia said, putting her gloved hand on Tanner's arm. "And I know from personal experience that you make a very good friend."

Tanner thanked her, feeling as if he'd just heard a death knell. Another quote, this one not from Molière, slid into his head. Something about friendship being love without wings...

CHAPTER THREE

Dearest Nicole,

You've been gone less than a day, and yet I find I have so many things I wish to tell you. At the moment, I should be dressing for Lady Chalfont's ball, but you know I will put off that chore as long as possible in any event, as I find I loathe little in life, but balls definitely are near the top of that short list.

You'd be so proud of me. I had a tantrum today, nearly in the middle of Hyde Park during the Promenade (such a sad crush of mostly sad people). I believe I startled Tanner with my outburst, perhaps as much as I startled myself, but I will confess I get so weary of being coddled. Not that you have ever coddled me! I shall miss your forthrightness, so I have decided I must be forthright myself, for myself. After all, I am a Daughtry. Surely there must be fiery blood somewhere inside me? To that end, this afternoon I informed Tanner that I would rather he not feel obligated to me because of some promise to Captain Fitzgerald.

He seemed taken by surprise to think I should know that. I didn't tell him about the captain's last letter to me, the one Tanner himself unwittingly delivered that fateful day last spring. Perhaps one day I will. Suffice it for now that he knows I consider him a friend, and that I wish he would do me the same honor, rather than as the burden of a promise.

Oh, but there's more! I met the most interesting man today, one Baron Justin Wilde. He has a Tragic Past, as you would certainly term it, and he seems to joke of it, even as his eyes clearly reveal his pain. Meeting him so soon after my tantrum, I fear I may have been more than a bit forward with the man, but he didn't seem to be appalled by my amazingly blunt speech. Indeed, if you can imagine the thing, I made him smile. The Baron is a friend of Tanner's, and we will see him again this evening at Lady Chalfont's. It's lovely to have something to look forward to besides sitting with my back against the wall, watching everyone else dance, offering up prayers no one will ask me to participate. You know something, Nicole? I just realized I perhaps do not fade into the wallpaper so much as I might intimidate the gentlemen who mistake my shyness and boredom for aloofness and haughty ways. My goodness, but that's a thought to ponder!

I hope that by the time this letter reaches you, you are happily settled at Basingstoke, and am confident you have already charmed everyone there. I will save this letter until tomorrow, at which time I will report to you the happenings of this evening, as I know you will worry otherwise, and I promise I shall do my best to enjoy myself.

LYDIA READ WHAT she had written, frowned over the last line, and then crossed it out. Taking up her pen once more, she wrote:

And I know I will enjoy myself, most especially if there are swans.

Yes, that was better. If her evening was at all remarkable her letter would run to at least two sheets. But her brother was a duke, and he would frank her for the postage. How delightful! She had always been careful to keep her letters short, or to cross her lines in an attempt at economy, even if that made her letters difficult for the recipient to read. Well, that was just another silly, sensible habit she would dispense with as of today. This rather momentous day.

She slipped the page into the drawer of her dressing table before examining her reflection in the mirror. She liked what Sarah had done to her hair, sweeping it all severely back from her forehead and then massing long curls behind her left ear. When she moved, the shining blond curls tickled at her shoulder, making her feel very…female.

She looked most closely at her eyes, wondering if others could see sadness in them, as she had done when she'd looked into Baron Wilde's eyes. Nicole would say they'd both been disappointed in love, although for quite different reasons.

"But at least you were not *betrayed* by love," she told her reflection. "You have happy memories no one can take from you. You were not exiled from your own country for eight terrible years, so that you have become jaded or distrusting."

She propped her elbow on the dressing table and rested her chin on her palm, continuing to examine her reflection until she'd come to a decision. "And you are going to stop feeling sorry for yourself *right now*. There are many worse things in life than having been loved, than having family and friends who care for you and wish you to be happy."

"My lady? Were you wanting something? I've finished pressing off your gown."

Lydia turned away from the mirror. "Oh, no, Sarah, I didn't want anything. I'm afraid you caught me out scolding myself." She got to her feet, smoothing down her silken undergarments. "And doesn't that gown look nice. You've done a wonderful job with the crimping iron."

Sarah curtsied. "Thank you, my lady, I do try. Only burned myself the once this time. Her Grace said to tell you that His Grace the Duke of Malvern is waiting on you downstairs in the drawing room. Such a well set up gentleman, my lady. I've always favored the blond ones. What a pair the two of you make, if you don't mind my saying so."

Lydia became at once uneasy. Had she somehow

betrayed her feelings to her maid? And if she had, who else knew? She really had to be more careful. After all, the man was going to marry his cousin. "The duke is my friend, Sarah."

"Yes, miss, he certainly is. But mayhap he wants to be more than a friend? Not that it's my place to say so, but Maisie and I just happened to be looking out the front window from the attics as you went off with His Grace this afternoon, and he had quite the spring in his step, Maisie said, if you take m'meaning. Now if you'll just duck yourself down and lift up your arms, my lady, we'll have this gown on you without so much as mussing a hair on your head. Ah, that's the trick. And are you sure you wouldn't be wanting just a quick whisper of a touch from the rouge pot?"

Lydia emerged from the yards of palest blue watered silk, about to tell the maid that she would rather not color her cheeks. She would have liked to ask what Maisie had meant by Tanner having a spring in his step, but she was certain that wasn't a proper question.

"Ah, never mind, my lady," the maid said, motioning for Lydia to turn around so that she could do up the covered buttons. "You've got lovely color now, all on your own. And why would that be, I wonder? There you are, all done. Now I'll just fetch your wrap whilst you tug on these gloves, and you'll be all nice and tight."

Lydia smiled weakly as Sarah skipped off to the dressing room, and then quickly returned to the dressing table, bending forward to check her reflection one more time. Goodness. Her cheeks *were* rather flushed, weren't they? And were her eyes brighter? All because Tanner supposedly had a spring in his step?

She leaned in closer, and suddenly realized that the neckline of her gown—lovely with its fluted and crimped flounce that ran completely around the neckline and the off-the-shoulder design—was rather lower than she'd remembered it the day of her final fitting in Bond Street. A good two inches lower, in fact.

How could the seamstress have made such a—but wait! Hadn't Nicole taken the woman to one side for a private chat that day? And then winked at her twin and told her that she was sure the watered silk would be quite the stunner?

"If I lean forward too far, it most certainly will be," Lydia said, holding her hand to her neckline as she leaned forward, stood back, leaned forward once more, this time without pressing a hand to her bodice. Her eyes went as wide as saucers. "Oh, dear Lord, I—Sarah? *Sarah!*"

The maid reappeared with a fringed ivory cashmere shawl threaded through with silver draped over her arm. "My lady?"

"Sarah, I need to change my gown. The bodice is all wrong. It doesn't fit."

Sarah tipped her head to one side, running her gaze up and down Lydia's length. "It doesn't? I'd say it fits you a treat, my lady. Besides, Lady Nicole made sure that all of your party gowns were—well, she's a good sister to you, my lady, and that's a fact."

The door to the hallway opened and Charlotte entered, carrying a dark blue velvet case. "Tanner's waiting, Lydia, but I just remembered that Nicole had asked me to be certain to please lend you my sapphires if you were to wear the—*oh, my.*"

Sarah curtsied, beaming. "Yes, Your Grace. Just as I was telling her. Fits her a treat, don't it?"

"A treat? Yes, I can see where that word comes first to mind," Charlotte said rather tongue-in-cheek, approaching Lydia and then walking fully around her. "You may go, Sarah, thank you."

"Oh, but I want her to—"

"Lydia, let her go. You look beautiful. You *are* beautiful."

Would nobody listen to her? Couldn't they see what she saw? "I'm...I'm *hanging out,* just like Mama!"

Charlotte giggled. "Darling, your mama would sacrifice an entire herd of goats to look like you do tonight. But, yes, the resemblance is rather startling. And Helen Daughtry was, and still is, an extraordinarily beautiful woman. Your beauty, however, is more refined. Which doesn't mean that you should hide it."

"I don't think it means that I should *flaunt*—do you really think the gown is, well, *proper?*"

Charlotte opened the velvet case and withdrew a stunning diamond and sapphire necklace. "Proper is perhaps not the word I'd use. Not precisely, no. I would rather say the gown is stunning. Interesting. Even captivating. Everything that you are, Lydia, whether you wish to acknowledge that fact or not. Now, turn around and bend your knees, so I can clasp this piece around your neck. You won't feel half so naked once it's on."

Lydia did as she was bid, albeit reluctantly. She was just so *used* to doing what other people said. But then she rallied, and stood straight once more. "You said it, Charlotte. You said *naked*. And that's how I feel. And from what Sarah was grinning and mumbling about, I'm woefully certain Nicole has had all of my gowns altered this way. The mischief that lives in that girl's head!"

'I'm sure she had all the best of intentions."

Lydia very nearly snorted. "Yes, the best of intentions. That's what she said she had when we were seven, and she decided to save our shared maid the trouble of trimming my bangs. Granted, I was silly enough to believe she knew what she was doing. I had to wear caps for a *month*. What is it about my sister and scissors?"

"I wouldn't know. Just bend your knees again, sweetheart, and let us see if the necklace makes you feel less—that is, more finished."

Lydia felt the weight of the necklace and looked down to see that the largest sapphire, completely surrounded by diamonds and fashioned as a drop, now slid rather interestingly between the cleavage exposed by the neckline of the gown. As if that could make up for that same, truly outrageous neckline.

Charlotte nudged her toward the full-length mirror that stood in one corner of the room. "There," she said rather smugly, "now how do you feel? Because you look wonderful. There are earrings as well, but I think they'd be too much for such a young, unmarried woman. Besides, look at your eyes, Lydia. They're so blue they look like twin ponds on a clear, sunlight day. Dazzling. When Rafe sees you I'll have to hold him back or else he'll confine you to your room, even though you're well within the bounds of propriety. Tanner, on the other hand, will be most appreciative, I'm sure."

Lydia opened her mouth to ask if Tanner would be appreciative because men were basically lecherous, but quickly decided that neither Charlotte nor Rafe would allow her within fifty yards of a lech…or fifty inches from Grosvenor Square if either of them thought the gown too outrageous.

"I do feel…rather nice," she admitted finally. "And more…confident, if that doesn't sound silly."

"It doesn't. Now come along, Tanner is waiting. Along with his cousin, who seems a very lovely young woman, if prone to talking so much I wouldn't be surprised to see that Rafe's ears have quite fallen off his head by the time we get down to the drawing room."

"She's pretty, isn't she? Jasmine Harburton, I mean. The cousin."

"I would say beautiful, but a man sees such things differently. I'll have to ask Rafe's opinion, once his ears stop ringing," Charlotte said with a smile. "Don't forget your gloves."

Lydia wanted to take one more peek at her reflection, as she still wasn't quite sure who she had been looking at, but tamped down the urge, for it seemed indulgent, and perhaps even vain. She picked up her elbow-length gloves, pulling them on as she followed Charlotte toward the stairs, working the soft white kid over each finger, wondering idly why fashion had decreed that a female's circulation be all but cut off in the pursuit of fashion.

She was just smoothing the kid over her left thumb when they reached the bottom of the stairs and she heard a sharp intake of breath and an awe-filled "Coo…" coming from one of the footmen.

Perhaps Nicole had been more right than Lydia would have guessed.

Buoyed by the footman's involuntary flattery, she entered the drawing room, her confident step carrying her along very well, thank you, until she saw the faintly incredulous expression come and go on Tanner's face as he stood at the mantelpiece, staring at her.

She resisted the urge to cross her hands over her bosom, and turned her attention to the dark-haired beauty just then getting to her feet so that she could curtsey to the newcomers.

Tanner stepped forward to make the introductions.

"I cannot tell you, Lady Lydia, how honored I am to make your acquaintance," Jasmine said the moment the introductions were completed. "How delightful it will be to have company once we are through that depressingly long line waiting for our hostess to vet us, and we're set loose into the ballroom like so many prisoners freed from the confines of their cells, only to find that they are now only in a larger prison, which is how

I see ballrooms, and waiting to be rescued from the wallflowers by some gentleman who then assumes we are so flattered by his attention that, of course, we will want nothing more than to listen to him *brag* about himself and his prospects or even the cut of his waistcoat for the length of the dance. Don't you think?"

Lydia, her mouth falling open unbidden, looked to Charlotte, who was busily examining her fingernails, and then to Rafe, who appeared ready to rip off his cravat and stuff it in Miss Harburton's mouth.

"Um…" Lydia said at last, "yes, I agree?"

"Good, it's safer," Tanner whispered in her ear, as he'd somehow managed to be standing next to her. "Let me tell you now, Lydia, that you have never looked more beautiful. I say that because it's true, and because I doubt either of us will get another word in edgewise between here and Lady Chalfont's. Shall we go?"

Tanner's words proved prophetic, for Jasmine talked nonstop all the way to Portland Place, all the time they were stalled on the stairs leading up into the ballroom, and she continued to talk as they were at last inside the cavernous ballroom and heading for the inevitable lines of chairs stuck against the long walls.

"You must need something to drink, Jasmine," Tanner said once he had secured them seats, including one for the chaperone, Mrs. Shandy, a nearly stone deaf woman who had no idea how fortunate she was in her affliction. "Lydia?"

"Yes, please," she said, although not before wondering if she would be too obvious if she'd fallen to her knees and begged him not to leave her with this sweet but incessant chatterbox.

"Oh, good," Jasmine said with a heartfelt sigh once Tanner had gone off to find a servant with a tray of lemonade, and most probably something stronger for himself. "I'm *so* unconscionably nervous whenever Tanner is about. And then I prattle and prattle and my tongue runs on wheels, and I hear myself saying the most inane and silly things and I can't stop myself. You must think me a ninny."

"No, of course not," Lydia said, crossing her gloved fingers in her lap. "But Tanner is your cousin. Why would he make you nervous?"

Jasmine rolled her expressive emerald eyes—really, with her coal dark hair and those lovely eyes, she was quite the beauty. "It's Papa, of course. He keeps telling everyone and anyone that Tanner and I are to be married. It was his father's dying wish, you understand. Tanner's father, not mine. Oh, you'd know that, or otherwise Papa would be dead, wouldn't he? Oh, dear, I'm doing it again. Prattling. At any rate, Tanner is such an honorable man, which is really quite vexing."

"Why is that vexing?" Lydia asked, although she decided she might know the answer to that question. Wasn't Tanner in *her* life right now because he was an honorable man?

"Why, because he'll do what his father wished on his deathbed, of course. He'll marry me. Eventually. And I really wish he wouldn't."

Lydia's heart gave a distressingly revealing little

flip inside her chest. "You do? I mean, you don't? That is…"

"Good evening, beautiful ladies. May I say, you present a veritable landscape of loveliness. One so dark, the other so fair, and both the epitome of everything that pleases. I am all but overcome."

Jasmine giggled nervously, snapping open the painted fan that hung from her wrist and frantically waving it in front of her face before turning to speak to her stone deaf chaperone, as if she knew she was not going to be necessary to the conversation between the gentleman and her new friend.

Lydia merely looked up to see Baron Justin Wilde executing a most elegant leg directly in front of her, and smiled. She doubted anyone could resist returning the man's smile, even if the timing of his arrival on the scene couldn't have been worse, what with Jasmine's news about her disinclination to wed Tanner. "Well done, my lord. Any woman would think she'd been just delivered a most fulsome compliment, when, in fact, you harbor a distrust of all women. Most especially those whom you might deem *lovely.*"

He pressed his spread fingers against his immaculately white waistcoat. "Ah, I am cut to the quick. My friend Tanner has been whispering tales out of school since last we met, I presume?"

"Nothing too dire, sir. I do, however, remember your conversation of earlier today. Should I have been studying my Molière in the interim? Are you going to quiz me yet again?"

"A thousand apologies for that, Lady Lydia. You and Tanner were the first people I dared approach since my return to the scene of my disgrace. No, I fib. I did happen to be stopped by a few others in the park, one to tell me Society never forgives a murderer, and the other to confide that her husband was in the country for the week and she hoped I'd remembered her direction. All in all, not the most auspicious of homecomings, I think you'd agree? I fear my emotions were much too close to the surface for me to be fit company."

"Your apology is accepted, sir, and there was really no need to explain. But I wonder, if you are so newly returned to England, how did you manage an invitation to this ball?"

He bent toward her, his remarkably green eyes twinkling with mischief. "Very simple, my dear. I remembered the lady's direction. A sacrifice on my part, to be sure, but worth it in order to see you again this evening."

Lydia felt hot color invading her cheeks, and was grateful she hadn't given in to Sarah's suggestion of the rouge pot, for otherwise she'd look like a painted doll at the moment. "You shouldn't say such things to me."

"Ah, but I always say such things. Being outrageous is a large part of my charm. Now tell me my sacrifice will not have been in vain, and that your dance card is not yet full."

"Far from full, my lord, as you can see," she told him, holding up the card she had been handed by one of the servants as she entered the ballroom.

"Is London peopled entirely with fools?" he asked

her, snatching the card from her hand and using the small, attached bit of pencil to scribble on it before returning both to her. "I'd dare more, but convention limits me to three or else people will expect the banns to be posted tomorrow. Miss Harburton?" he then asked, bowing to Jasmine. "It would be my honor to be added to your dance card, as well."

Jasmine looked to Lydia, who didn't understand the question in the other young woman's eyes. Was she actually turning to her for permission? But then she handed over her dance card and Justin signed it as well just as Tanner approached, carrying two glasses of lemonade.

"Ah, Tanner, here you are. I didn't presume stealing Lady Lydia away for the first dance, but do see you have her returned here in time for the second. I shouldn't wish to appear desperate by having to track the pair of you down on some balcony, would I? Now if you'll excuse me, I believe manners compel me to find a certain rather rapacious lady and haul her about the dance floor for the next ten minutes as a reward for allowing me to escort her this evening."

Justin then bowed to Lydia and Jasmine once more and turned on his heel, melting into the crowd that seemed to now border on a multitude in the large ballroom as the orchestra signaled with a rather rusty flourish of violins that the first waltz was to commence momentarily.

Tanner handed over the glasses of lemonade and then snatched up Lydia's dance card, one corner of his mouth lifting as he read what Justin Wilde had written. "It would appear, Lydia, that you have acquired an admirer," he said, handing the card back to her. "You as well, Jasmine? I assume so, as Justin is always very careful with his manners."

"I don't even know who he *is*," Jasmine exclaimed, wide-eyed. "But he is pretty, isn't he? Oh, look, there's Lady Pendergast! She always wears so many feathers, doesn't she?" She poked Mrs. Shandy with her fan, directing her attention to the rather prodigiously obese woman in purple, sailing past them as if propelled by some errant wind catching at the trio of enormous white plumes in her hair.

Tanner smiled at Lydia, and spoke softly. "Lady Pendergast's feathers, a butterfly on the wing, most anything shiny—whatever takes her fancy. My cousin is easily amused, and even more easily distracted. But the baron was being attentive to you, I think."

"The baron was only being outrageous, which I admit he does rather well," Lydia said, taking the card, but not opening it. "I think he's apprehensive about the evening, and how he'll be received."

"Justin? Apprehensive? I seriously doubt that."

They both looked in the direction the baron had taken, just in time to see him bow to an older gentleman who pretended not to see the gesture before pointedly turning his back on him.

"Oh, that's not good," Tanner said, shaking his head. "What one does, others may do, until the whole room turns its collective back on him. We managed to chase

Byron out of England only a fortnight ago, and now it would seem we're about to do the same to Brummell, as well. That can't happen to Justin. I won't allow it. Excuse me, Lydia, while I follow him, make my own feelings known on the subject of his return and my friendship for him. After all, being a bloody duke has to count for something."

Lydia nodded her agreement and watched Tanner hurry off to stand by his friend. It was as Jasmine had said, as everyone who knew him said: the Duke of Malvern was an honorable man.

Jasmine was now speaking with a young woman dressed all in virginal white, her complexion as pale as her gown, and since Lydia didn't wish to interrupt, she busied herself by at last opening her dance card, to see what the baron had written that had brought such a strange smile to Tanner's face.

The baron had scribbled his name on the second line, the fifth, and the eighth. The three dances he had mentioned. But it was the way he had signed the card that now brought a smile to her face.

Wilde. Wilder. Wildest.

What a wicked, wickedly interesting man.

The captain had been gentle, almost respectful, their attraction to each other expressed only in longing looks, but never in word or action. He had been, she was realizing more and more, not only her first love, but also her beginning. Not her end.

Tanner was an honorable man and a good friend (who had a spring in his step, according to Sarah), and a rather bemused but interested look in his eyes when she'd come into the drawing room this evening. She'd known, even at first feared, that Tanner could mean more to her than to simply be her friend. But she hadn't considered that *he* might know that. Besides, Captain Fitzgerald stood between them, a bond and yet also a division.

Baron Justin Wilde, however, was a man totally outside her limited realm of experience, a man who well could be teasing her, or he could be using his teasing to cover something that was perhaps more than a casual interest.

Why, she was beginning to feel like the heroine in a Pennypress novel. All she needed now was a menacing stepfather, or a dark castle complete with a ghost.

It was good that Rafe was a duke, and could frank her correspondence for her, as Lydia already felt certain her letter to Nicole was going to run to two sheets, if not more. Which, for a quiet person who was accustomed to little excitement in her life, was rather extraordinary, indeed.

CHAPTER FOUR

TANNER AND JUSTIN stood on the dark balcony outside the ballroom, companionably sipping from their glasses as they leaned against the railing, looking out over the gardens and the inviting paths lit periodically by flambeaux.

It was good to have Justin Wilde back in his life, Tanner thought. They'd had grand times together in the past, young men fresh from school and the country, eager to explore the world and maybe make their own mark on it. They'd laughed together, traveled to the races and boxing mills together. Raced their curricles neck-or-nothing, drunk deep in disreputable taverns, even shared an opera dancer or two. They'd been young, so young, all of them, with their whole lives ahead of them.

Now those memories seemed to be of another world, another time, one before Justin's marriage, his flight to the continent after the duel, and then many long years of war.

So many friends had been lost to that war, good men all. Jonathan, Richard, Harry…Fitz. A man needed to hang on to those friends he still had, stand with them, stand by them.

"I'm not hiding out here, you understand," the baron said after a bit.

Tanner carefully kept his gaze on a married couple—but not married to each other—seemingly intent on finding a less well-lit area of the gardens. "Absolutely not. I would never think that of you."

"It's a mob of bodies in there. The woman must have invited all of London, and all of London came."

"Perhaps even some who were not invited," Tanner said, a small smile playing about his lips.

"I'll ignore that remark. Balls can be exceedingly boring, don't you think, when there's no card room?"

"Yes, without doubt. Boring. And the wine is warm. All in all, a distinctly disappointing entertainment. I can't imagine why any of us is here. Why *are* we here, Justin? And by here, I mean on this balcony."

Justin drained his glass, and then stared into it for a while. "All right, since you're being so insistent, I'll admit it. I am hiding, perhaps just a bit. I didn't expect Molton's response. Some of the others, yes, I did expect idiots to be idiots. But not Molton. He was friendly enough when we were in Vienna. We worked together with the Austrians, securing Marie Louise's condemnation of her husband so that the Allies could brand him an outlaw."

"But now you're both in Mayfair. Molton will follow the pack, perhaps even more so if he fears that someone will remember he'd been seen with you in Vienna."

"At least Chalfont hasn't asked me to remove my unacceptable self from the premises. There is that."

Tanner turned his back to the rail, looking in at the bright, overheated ballroom. "Are you serious?" he teased his friend. "His wife is in alt, confident she has scored the coup of the Season, having you here. Her ball will be on everyone's lips tomorrow. She was mortified, she was horrified, she feared her dear husband might at any moment draw his sword and order you out at the point of it. But as you'd already killed the once…"

Justin also turned about, to lean back against the railing. "So you're saying I'm too outrageous to be in polite company, but too dangerous to exclude? How interesting. I might even like that. Shall I take to dressing all in black, do you think? Apply myself to developing a scowl?"

"You mean to combine a bit of Brummell's severe attire with a hint of Byron's pout? The ladies might enjoy that."

Justin did a fairly good imitation of a dark scowl. "Ladies always enjoy the thought that they might be part of some titillating drama or the other. It's their bread and butter. How else did George collect an entire treasure box filled with locks of pubic hair, for God's sake. Women are fools. And then we have to defend their idiocy."

"Sheila was one of Byron's conquests?"

Justin shrugged. "I never inquired. Couldn't bring myself to really much care either way, frankly, as long as she didn't do anything so publicly stupid as Caro Lamb. I've had eight long years to refine on my mistake. I failed my wife, Tanner. I wed Sheila's beauty, not concerned with more than scoring such a coup, having her on my arm. It was only once we'd gotten to know each other that we both realized we'd each married a stranger and, at heart, really didn't even like one another. Let that be a lesson to you, my friend. Admire beauty, take it to bed if you must. But marry it? No, don't do that."

Tanner knew he had to ask this next question. "You've danced twice with Lady Lydia, Justin. You admire her beauty?"

The baron pushed himself away from the railing, to look carefully at Tanner. "Am I poaching on already-fenced property, my friend? If so, you've only to tell me. My friends do not appear to be so thick on the ground at the moment that I would risk alienating one of them."

Tanner didn't know how to answer that question. Was it only a few hours ago that he'd blithely told Rafe he would gladly welcome competition from somewhere other than the grave?

He'd watched Lydia and Justin as they'd moved around the dance floor in a waltz, and she'd seemed animated, quite happy, the two of them chattering the entire time…unaware of the sidelong looks, the furious whispers.

His friend Justin was handsome, rich, affable, and intelligent. Tanner didn't mind that sort of competition. But how does a man compete with someone whose past made him also appear dangerous, even deliciously intriguing? Worse, how did one compete with a friend, dead or alive?

It was rather as if Lydia had bloomed today. First in the Park, then again once Justin had come on the scene. Tanner didn't know what had happened, was happening. Perhaps Lydia had felt herself under her more gregarious sister's thumb, and now felt free?

No, that couldn't be it. Lydia and Nicole were more than sisters, even more than simply twins. They were very good friends. Still, he could understand how comfortable it might be for a basically shy person like Lydia to allow her sister to take the center of the stage, while she watched from the wings.

He'd thought—yes, he would admit it to himself— that, once Nicole was gone from the stage, as it were, Lydia would turn to him for companionship, and that their friendship, founded in tragedy, might grow into something more.

He'd even watch as she was pursued by other suitors, confident enough in his own ability to capture her heart when the time was right, when she could be sure of her decision. Especially now, today, as Lydia seemed to be ready to face life on her own, finally out from behind her sister's shadow.

What a hell of a moment for Justin and his wicked smile, his even more wicked wit, and his romantic tragic past to show up on the scene...

"Tanner? Was the question that difficult?"

"What? Oh," Tanner said, realizing he'd become lost, perhaps even tangled, in his private thoughts. "Forgive me. I was debating whether I should discuss Lydia with anyone. But you're not just anyone, are you?"

"No. I'm an extraordinarily singular person," Justin said, smiling that winning smile of his. "Are you about to make some confession to me?"

"Hardly." Tanner came to a decision, not that he was particularly pleased with it. "No, Justin, Lady Lydia and I are friends, nothing more."

"And now you've disappointed me, and after I've been so forthright and truthful with you."

Tanner looked into the ballroom, to see Lydia dancing with a fairly well set-up young man he didn't recognize. She was talking to him, smiling up at him, just as she had done with Justin. Definitely a blooming flower, a butterfly suddenly shed of her cocoon, taking flight for the very first time, her new wings glittering in the sunlight.

"She looks very happy, doesn't she?"

Justin turned to look into the ballroom. "And that's unusual? Tanner, have I ever informed you that I loathe a mystery? And even worse, that I will now feel it my duty to pick at you and pick at you until you've told me what I want to know?"

"I'm sensing that, yes. And I admit it, I'm a poor liar. Very well. Lydia was all but betrothed to a good friend of mine," Tanner explained, once more turning his back to the ballroom. "Captain Swain Fitzgerald. He was killed at Quatre Bras."

"Damn," Justin said, also turning to lean his forearms on the railing. "A deuced tricky thing, stepping into a dead man's boots."

Tanner's smile was rueful. "I wouldn't have put it

quite that way, but yes, it is. I was the one who was with him when he died, promising him I'd take care of Lydia for him. I was the one who brought her the news of Fitz's death, delivered his personal belongings, what turned out to be his final letter to her." He drank the last of his wine and carefully placed the glass on the railing. "Oh, how she hated me for that."

"A natural reaction, I'm afraid."

"I've never seen such grief, Justin. Lydia is a young woman of strong emotions, although she keeps them well tamped down beneath her quiet, rather shy demeanor. I've often wondered since then, would I ever inspire any woman to grieve so over me?"

"Planning on sticking your spoon in the wall, are you? No, don't bother to explain. I understand what you mean. You wondered—wonder—if anyone would ever love you quite so much. We all do, my friend, and we are all, for the most part, doomed to disappointment. But we have begun to digress, so let us return to my original question. Clearly you envision a time when you and the lady are more than friends. Tell me to back away and I will."

Tanner shook his head. "No, I won't do that. I have no claim on Lydia."

"And I'm selfish enough to take you at your word, even as I believe you're still lying to at least one of the two of us. Now please tell me about Miss Harburton. Another very beautiful young woman."

"Jasmine? She's my third cousin."

"Yes, she told me that during our dance. She told me

about your father's dying wish, as well. A very... *sharing* young woman, your cousin. She certainly kept me from the burden of cudgeling my brain to make scintillating conversation with a near stranger."

"Jasmine talks when she's nervous."

"Really? Then shame on me, for I must then have truly terrified the poor child."

Tanner laughed. "Oh, it's good to have you back, old friend. I fear I've been much too sober and serious this past year, living a more quiet life."

"And yet here you are this evening, with both Lady Lydia, who you say you lay no claim to, and Miss Harburton, whom you have likewise not claimed. That's your idea of a quiet life, juggling two beauties in the same evening? And, then, as if you didn't have problems enough, a handsome reprobate with an appreciation of if not a genuine affection for beautiful women stumbles into the Second Act. Yes, Richard Sheridan wouldn't have been amiss if he'd said he saw the foundation for a rather marvelous comedy of manners, even a true farce to outdo *The Rivals*. It might have been the remaking of his career, as a matter of fact, poor dead fellow that he is."

Tanner shot him a dark look, but then smiled. "Remind me why I'm your friend."

"You don't see me in the role? I could be the black sheep with a tarnished past but a heart of gold."

"You have a heart? That's good to know."

"Ouch! Now I'm wounded to the quick. But, as I seem to be a glutton for punishment, I think we have hidden my shameful self out here long enough. And if I haven't thanked you for standing my friend in there, I do now."

"What you need, Justin, is a new scandal, to take everyone's attention away from you. That shouldn't take too long, I imagine. In the meantime, you might want to consider not, well, forcing yourself on Society."

"After this evening, I have no invitations at all, so that's not a worry. But you're correct. I shouldn't be jumping back in with both feet quite so dramatically, should I?"

"I'm sorry, Justin…"

"Don't be. I could have been hanged, you know. Having Molton and a few others dealing me the cut direct is at least not fatal. Ah, and as if I just conjured him up. Tanner, go away. You don't need to be involved in this."

Tanner saw Lord Molton advancing toward them, his cheeks flushed with drink and false courage. He stepped forward, putting himself between Justin and the viscount, placing his palm against his lordship's chest. "Not the time nor the place, sir," he warned quietly.

"Robbie Farber was m'friend." Molton leaned around Tanner to point an accusing finger at Justin. "And *he* killed him, shot him down like a dog while poor Robbie stood there with an empty pistol."

Tanner took one step to the side, once more blocking Molton's path, staring pointedly into the man's wild eyes. "Because he'd turned and fired on *two*. Do you remember that part? I do, because I was there. Farber bears at least as much blame as Justin here. Let it go.

It's over. Let the dead lie, and leave the rest of us to get on with our lives. Robbie's death was unfortunate, but it was eight long years ago. The baron is sorry. Of course he is. We're all sorry your friend is dead."

Molton once more shifted his fevered gaze to the baron, who was standing with his arms at his sides, his relaxed posture and amused smile not really aiding the tense situation, and then back at Tanner. "He doesn't care. Do you see that? He doesn't *care.*"

Molton turned on his heel and stomped back inside the ballroom.

"You could have said something, offered him something," Tanner pointed out to Justin.

"I suppose I could have, yes. We could then have asked everyone to form a line and I could apologize in turn to each and every person who thinks that firing in self-defense is a crime for which I should beg forgiveness. I apologize once, Tanner, and it would never end."

"You challenged the man to a duel, Justin. You do remember that part, don't you?"

"Did I have a choice? Answer me that, my friend."

Tanner had been present to hear what Robert Farber had said about Justin's wife. About how she had the beauty of a Venus and the sexual prowess of a block of stone, about how he could have serviced himself with more satisfaction, and saved the effort of having to talk her into bed. Robbie Farber had been an idiot, and to make such a statement in Justin's presence could by some be considered suicide, and not murder.

"No, you had no choice. You had to defend Sheila's honor. But you do have a choice now."

Justin raised one well-defined eyebrow. "Meaning?"

"I don't know what I mean. You've served notice that you're back, that's most definite. But will you continue to butt your head so forcibly up against the *ton,* or perhaps pull back for a space, let the *ton* become accustomed to seeing you in the park, on Bond Street, wherever. You seem to be trying to do it all in one go— rather pushing everyone's faces in the fact that the Crown has pardoned you."

"You keep saying that. And I'm beginning to understand the merit in your words. Very well, one more dance with the fair Lady Lydia, and I will take my leave."

"Justin?"

The baron smiled and shook his head. "You're right again. She should not be involved. Please extend my apologies to her, and excuse me as I tuck my tail between my legs and depart the scene of my latest crime."

"Justin, for the love of God—"

"No, I'm being serious, Tanner. I should have gone directly to my estate in Hampshire, remained there as word slowly filtered back to London that I have returned, and only shown my face after a goodly amount of time had passed. Which is what I will do now."

"You'll leave London? When? I'm sure Lydia would wish to say goodbye."

"I won't be stealing out of town before dawn, Tanner. I'm sure we'll meet again before I continue my penance in the country."

"While wearing a specially made hair shirt from

your favorite tailor, no doubt," Tanner said, which put a smile on his friend's face.

"We'll meet again before I go. Oh, but before I forget. I feel the need to ask a most personal question. Are you experiencing some sort of financial pinch I might be able to help you with, my friend? And feel free to tell me to mind my own business."

Tanner looked at him curiously. "Why would you ask that? No, I'm more than well-to-go, thanks to my father's prudent stewardship. He wasn't much of a father, but he did hold every penny most dear."

"Interesting," Justin said, glancing toward the ballroom. "So the necklace gracing your cousin's beautiful neck is not then a part of the famous Malvern jewels?"

"The emeralds? No, they're part of the collection. It seemed sensible to provide Jasmine with the loan of a few minor pieces for the Season. Why?"

"Why? Because they're—no, I couldn't be sure without my glass. Does the jewelry reside with her, or with you?"

Once again, Tanner glanced toward the ballroom. "With me. Justin, are you saying—"

"The emeralds are paste, yes, that's what I'm saying, or trying very hard not to say. Very good paste, but paste just the same. Tomorrow at ten, Tanner? I don't believe I have any other engagements. Most especially after I desert the dear lady whose invitation eased my way in here tonight. Perhaps I'm not a nice man, after all. I'll bring my glass, just to be certain. But I doubt I am wrong."

Tanner nodded mutely, and then watched as the baron made his way down the flagstone, only entering the ballroom at the end of the balcony, close to the stairs, to collect his hat and gloves and be on his way.

The duke remained where he was for several moments, mentally counting up the pieces of the Malvern jewelry he'd brought with him to town, and wondering if he should contact his solicitor for a more complete accounting of his funds.

Thomas Harburton had been keeping the journals at Malvern for nearly a decade, even while Tanner's father was alive. He'd know if the estate was solvent, wouldn't he? No, best not to ask him, not until he knew what questions to ask.

"Damn," he muttered under his breath, the sound of violins intruding on his uncomfortable thoughts. Another set was forming, and Lydia was expecting Justin to come claim her.

He set off across the ballroom.

CHAPTER FIVE

JASMINE HARBURTON WAS fanning herself so violently that the crimped ruffling around Lydia's neckline was actually moving in the resultant breeze.

"We have become part and parcel to a scandal, Lady Lydia," the girl said, her eyes wide with what could be horror, or delight. It was difficult to know with Jasmine. "I understand Tanner's feelings of obligation—Lord knows nobody should know that more than I—but how outrageous of him to *foist* the baron on us both, causing the pair of us to become the center of so much attention."

Then she turned to Lydia and smiled, and it became clear that delight had won out over horror. "Not only is my dance card full, but I've had to turn away two applicants. One of them a viscount, the other an earl. I'd say that Papa will be furious when I tell him, but then he may just as easily decide that there is nothing more apt to bring a man up to snuff than to believe he may be replaced. Oh, dear, I'm prattling again. I do that whenever I'm nervous. Oh, I already told you that, didn't I? I'm so sorry. It takes just the *thought* of marrying Tanner to set my tongue on wheels."

The subject of Tanner, and this assumed betrothal, had been touched on earlier, before the baron's arrival, before both Lydia and Jasmine had taken to the dance floor with him, before they both had seemed to become objects of considerable attention.

Lydia hadn't wished to appear eager to enter into any such conversation then, and she was even more loath to do so now.

She was, however, curious. Much more curious than she ought to be, she was certain. So where else to begin, but with the obvious?

"Tanner's father has been dead these two years and more, I think. Is that correct?"

Jasmine nodded furiously. "And Tanner has been back from the war for one of them, yes. Well, he was back for a minute, but then someone let Boney off his leash, as Papa says it, and he was gone again. In any event, his mourning period is most decidedly over. Papa said that's why he didn't ask for my hand that first year, which is understandable, what with his father only barely tucked into the mausoleum. And then Bonaparte did his flit and had to be dealt with—oh, I keep saying that, don't I! I'm so sorry," she said, snapping her fan shut and putting her hand on Lydia's arm. "Tanner told me about your fiancé perishing at Quatre Bras. A Captain Swain Fitzgerald, I believe he said. Such a lovely Irish name. How terrible it all must have been for you."

Lydia didn't bother correcting the young woman. After all, in her mind, the captain had been her betrothed. "Thank you."

"Oh, Lady Lydia, you're so gracious. And I'm such a muddlehead."

"Lydia, please, Jasmine. We needn't be quite so formal."

Jasmine clapped her hands to her bosom. "We're crying friends? Oh, how wonderful. I have so few friends here in town that I must declare I've been woefully lonely. Thank you, thank you."

Really, the girl was sweet, and faintly silly, and perhaps even tiring. But Lydia believed her heart was pure. Besides, she had to admit to herself at least, the subject of Tanner and his dragging feet when it came to the matter of a proposal to his third cousin interested her. Quite a bit.

"You're welcome. And, now that we're getting to know each other better, perhaps you'll explain why you've taken your cousin in such dislike."

"Dislike? Oh, no, no. Tanner is the best of good fellows, really he is. I should be very honored, flattered—all of that—if he was to ask for my hand, make me his duchess."

"Oh," Lydia said softly.

"If I wanted to be his duchess, that is. But I don't." Jasmine looked out over the ballroom and then leaned close to whisper in Lydia's ear. "My heart lies elsewhere."

Lydia's own heart performed another of those disconcerting small flips in her chest. "It does?"

Jasmine nodded furiously, her dark curls bouncing. "Papa doesn't know, and he'd be furious if he did. And Tanner is so honorable, and, Papa says, duty bound to honor his father's last wish."

"Yes," Lydia said, sighing. "Duty bound. Tanner takes such promises quite seriously."

"But that's just it, Lady—I mean, Lydia. Tanner promised his father nothing. It was Papa who promised to tell Tanner of the promise. Oh, it's all too complicated. All I know is that sooner or later Tanner will bow to the inevitable, as will I. He fights it, I fight it, but we are doomed to marriage. I'm already wearing his emeralds, which, Papa says, is as good as a declaration."

"Yes, I suppose they might be considered as such," Lydia said, looking at the beautiful, glittering stones that so flattered Jasmine's green eyes. "But if your heart is not engaged…"

"Then you understand. Oh," Jasmine sighed almost theatrically. "It is *so* good to finally be able to speak freely to someone. I could never say such things to Papa, or Tanner, or to any man. Only another woman would understand that love is so much more important than honor."

"And you truly feel you cannot broach the subject with your father?"

Jasmine shook her head furiously. "Papa has most clearly and emphatically explained my duty to me, and I certainly can't refuse Tanner's suit once he screws himself up to the sticking point, as Papa calls it. It's the land, you know. It hadn't been part of the entail, which is how Papa's ancestors ended up with it, and the late duke and his father, even his father's father, had wanted it back for ever so long. Pride, you understand. And some lovely waterways that seem to mean so much to everyone. In truth, the land isn't much at all. Most of it is very soggy, in fact. It's the water. There was once an argument, many decades ago, and my ancestor cut off the water flowing from a spring on our property, which dried up a stream that ran through the pastures on Tanner's ancestor's property and—well, the history hasn't always been pretty, I suppose you'd say."

"Couldn't Tanner simply purchase the land from your father?" Did that sound selfish on Lydia's part? And did it matter? Was the girl even listening to her?

"And wouldn't that be so simple? But, just between the two of us, I will tell you that Papa's soggy estate is *massively* encumbered. My marriage to Tanner is Papa's sure and only way out from beneath a *crushing* mound of debt, not that Tanner can ever, *ever* know about that until the marriage is a fact, oh no, definitely. Even then, how would he trust Papa to continue as his estate manager once he knew about the gambling? Without the marriage, without a lovely pension for Papa once Tanner turns him off, it would be the ruination of everything, and Papa has assured me I would not enjoy sleeping beneath a hedgerow, and the man I love is… well, he cannot marry at the moment, although he has vowed to find a way. But I don't think he will find that way in time to save me."

Curiosity turned to concern. "This man, Jasmine. Are you trying to tell me he's already married?"

The girl sighed again, this time definitely theatrically. "No. He is just poor, at least for now, although he has promised me this will soon change. But will his circumstances change in time? I think Papa is right, that I would not enjoy sleeping beneath a hedgerow, not even for love. So unless something wonderful happens, it must be marriage between Tanner and myself, before Papa's gambling ways have been discovered and he is turned off without a recommendation. You see? No marriage means no employment, no fine pension, and a really rather worthless estate gone for debt. So you must understand my dilemma. No matter my feelings, I cannot disappoint Papa."

Lydia knew she should be warning this sweet but silly girl that she should not be saying such things to what was, at heart, a brand new acquaintance. But it was all so interesting, if terribly convoluted. Certainly there must exist another way to work things out without sacrificing two people to a marriage neither of them seemed in any rush to make a fact.

Except that Tanner was an honorable man. How Jasmine's father must be counting on that fact.

Jasmine's words were tolling a death knell to any of Lydia's barely admitted dreams of a time when she and Tanner might put the past behind them and look toward a future as more than good friends.

Indeed, even Baron Justin Wilde had spent the entirety of his second dance with her extolling Tanner's virtues, telling her how humbled and honored he was to have such a friend in his time of need. She had agreed with him without offering further explanation.

Ever since that dance, while she was being part-nered by a seemingly endless succession of gentlemen

who had seemed able to have managed to avoid noticing her during previous social events and balls, Lydia
had been convincing herself that Sarah and Maisie had
been wrong, that she herself had been wrong, wishing
for something that wasn't there.

Tanner was a good friend, and nothing more; he had
other obligations. Honorable, loyal. Rather like a good
hunting hound, Nicole would probably have said in
some disgust.

But she, Lydia, had been seeing more. Not at first,
no, but ever since her return to London she had been
looking at the Duke of Malvern in a new light. One in
which he was not obscured by the ghost of Captain
Swain Fitzgerald standing between them.

And she'd begun weaving fanciful dreams. She'd deliberately refused to think about Jasmine Harburton, especially when Nicole had pointed out that a man about
to be betrothed did not spend so much time squiring
another young woman about London, poking into
museums, dancing with her at balls.

Now she understood Tanner's dilemma. His reluctant feet were being slowly bound up by his damnable
sense of honor. It was a marvel the man could even take
two steps without falling down.

"Oh, look, the musicians have returned," Jasmine said,
pointing toward the small stage with her fan. "I am promised to a Mister Rupert Carstairs for this next set, whoever
he is. I think he's fairly ugly, but I was so amazed to have
so many asking to partner me that I could hardly refuse
him, could I? Who has written on your card?"

Lydia snapped herself back to attention and opened her dance card. *Wildest.* "The Baron. Oh, dear, and I think it's going to be a Scottish reel. I loathe the Scottish reel, but only because I seem to constantly forget the steps."

Jasmine looked out over the floor as couples began assembling for the dance. "I don't see the baron, do you? Oh, here comes Mr. Carstairs. Such a pity he has no chin, don't you think? Shame on me. Nobody dances with me save Tanner, since everyone seems to think I'm out of the marriage mart. Without a title or a huge dowry, I'm good only for filling one of these chairs. And there's Tanner. But the baron isn't with him."

Lydia looked up and saw the duke at once. He was alone, and looking quite serious. And, ah, so very handsome. She'd have to stop thinking of him as handsome.

"Ladies," he said, bowing to them both, his gaze seeming to linger on Jasmine in a…well, in an *appraising* sort of way. "Lady Lydia, I'm here to tender the baron's deepest apologies, as he's found it necessary to leave without honoring your dance, and to offer myself in his place. Jasmine, where's Mrs. Shandy? We can't leave you here alone."

"Oh," Jasmine said, looking to her left as if only now noticing that her chaperone had gone missing. "She said something about seeing if there were any Gunther Ices still in the supper room downstairs. But no matter, Tanner. My partner is standing just behind you." She leaned to her right and waggled her fingers at the tall, rather thin and, yes, chinless gentleman. "Hullo again, Mr. Carstairs."

"She's such a child," Tanner said as he held out his hand to Lydia, drawing her to her feet. "How are you two getting along? She hasn't yet talked off your ear?"

"She's delightful company, Tanner. I don't think I've had time to miss Nicole at all tonight, although I would give much to hear my sister's opinion of your cousin. And we've both danced every dance."

"Would you then care to take the air on the balcony, rather than face the floor again? As I recall, you don't much favor the Scottish reel."

He tucked her hand into the crook of his elbow. "Yet I don't recall ever mentioning that I don't care for the Scottish reel."

"You never have," he told her as he steered them along the edge of the dance floor. She already believed she could feel a pleasant drop in the temperature as they neared the opened French doors.

"But you noticed." Lydia realized that, only a few hours ago, she might have attempted to see more in his notice than was actually there. "Did the baron take ill?"

Tanner stepped over the low threshold that led onto the balcony, and then assisted her so that she wouldn't stumble. "In some ways, yes, I suppose he did. An unexpected bout of conscience I believe. The evening hasn't been what he expected, although I can't say I know what he did expect."

"He has very sad eyes," Lydia said as they turned to walk down the length of the balcony. It was a beautiful night, filled with stars. There were so few nights like this in London. Having Tanner beside her made this one even more special.

"I should tell him you said so. They'd go well with his funereal black clothes and planned scowl."

"Excuse me?"

"Nothing," Tanner said, stopping as they neared a shallow set of stone steps leading down into the darkened gardens. "Shall we?"

There were other couples strolling the balcony, and a few had ventured down into the gardens. But as Tanner turned them to the right, along a side path lined with high hedges, they could have suddenly been alone in the center of the huge metropolis.

It was, she realized, the first time they'd ever been alone. Really alone.

Her heart pounded in her chest and she willed it to slow its furious beat.

He wasn't hers, he couldn't be hers. He was as unattainable as Fitz, and her memories of that good man which seemed to soften and fade with each passing day. How she hated that. How she'd hate seeing Tanner fade that same way.

They strolled slowly, her arm still in his.

"He was uncomfortable, wasn't he?" she asked at last, feeling the need to fill the silence. Dear Lord, was she becoming Jasmine?

"Justin? Yes, he was. His welcome back to Society wasn't all he'd perhaps imagined it might be, considering that many of the supposed gentlemen here tonight didn't cavil at being friendly with him during the years he was in exile. I think it came as a shock to him. No one was more popular than Justin our first Seasons in town, more sought after."

"And now he is a pariah. Two of my dance partners warned me away from him. The third felt the need to go into rather descriptive detail on the matter of the baron's crime. And all three of them told me that you should be ashamed for having foisted such an unwelcome creature on the *ton* in general and on two innocent young women in particular. Actually, I think that's why they danced with me, so that I could deliver their messages to you."

"Bloody cowards." Tanner led her to a wrought-iron bench at the side of the path and they sat down, facing each other in the moonlight. "I'm sorry, Lydia."

She smiled slightly, and forced some gaiety into her voice. "Oh, no, don't be. At first I thought this sudden popularity among the gentlemen might be traced to the gown, or to the fact that Nicole isn't here. I was rather relieved to learn that neither of those things was true. So you think I'm right, that our dance partners were using Jasmine and me to convey a message to you, and through you, to the baron?"

"Probably, yes. Give me their names. Was one of them Lord Molton?"

She shook her head. "I wouldn't be so foolhardy as to tell you any of their names. Nicole would have left each one of them standing alone on the dance floor, not caring a whit that she was causing quite the scene. But I'm not that courageous, I'm afraid. I merely informed them all in turn that I was not your guardian. I thought it a rather clever riposte at the time, but perhaps not."

Tanner took her hands in his. "I shouldn't have involved you, which I did by not warning Justin away from you and my cousin both."

She did her best to ignore the tingle of awareness that had run through her at his touch. "It's all right. This evening was quite the education. Nicole spent years anticipating her first Season, and then found it petty and insipid, so that she almost immediately sought adventure and excitement elsewhere. I, in my turn, dreaded the day we'd come to London, yet I find myself enjoying the experience for the most part. The museums, the Tower, the theaters, the book repositories, the sheer masses of people and bustle. It's silly of me, but I didn't see the meanness anywhere, until tonight."

"Justin has decided to leave London for a space, probably until next year's Season. That will give Society time to become resigned to the idea that he's back. But now I wonder if that's wise. He might only be prolonging what is bound to end with some sort of confrontation with somebody. Still, he knows I'll stand by him."

Lydia wondered if she should withdraw her hands, but it was as if Tanner didn't even realize he was still holding on to them. "I'm sure he does. That might be one reason he's leaving London. To protect you."

Tanner's fingers tightened on hers briefly. "My God, I never thought of that. I'll be seeing him tomorrow morning, and will quickly disabuse him of any idea of sacrificing himself to protect me."

"As he would disabuse you of any idea of sacrificing yourself to protect him, I would imagine. Do you know something, Tanner? I think men might really be rather silly, at the heart of things."

That brought a smile to his face, and another quick flush to her cheeks. "Spoken like a highly intelligent woman. Yes, men are idiots. Idiocy is beaten into us from the nursery cot on. And the more civilized we become, the more rules we make, the more we toss around words like honor and law, the more savage we really are. We merely dress up our baser selves in fine linen. And I'm as guilty of that as any of us."

It wasn't the most romantic of conversations. It certainly wasn't a usual conversation between a man and woman. But what it was, Lydia realized, was a conversation between equals, between friends. With no artifice, no polite skirting of unpleasant subjects, no thought to impressing each other.

"I disagree. If anything, Tanner, I believe you may be *too* good. Too honorable."

The moment she'd said the words, Lydia was appalled at her forthrightness. She withdrew her hands, faced forward on the bench, and folded those hands in her lap. "I'm sorry. I shouldn't have said that."

She felt his hand at the small of her back, and closed her eyes, focusing on her breathing, which had seemingly decided to stop occurring on its own and needed her full concentration.

"We're not speaking of men as a whole or my involvement with Justin now, are we? It's Fitz, back again, front and center."

"No, I...yes, I suppose so. You've more than satisfied any favor he asked from you where I am concerned."

"Are you telling me to go away, Lydia? Take myself off?"

She turned to him in surprise. "No! I...I don't wish to be an obligation, Tanner. That's all."

He leaned in and kissed her on the cheek, pulling back only slightly as he said, "You've never been an obligation to me, Lydia. Never."

She wanted to avoid his eyes, his closeness, but it was no good. She couldn't look away. He'd kissed her! Had it been a brotherly sort of kiss? The kiss one might deliver to a friend? What if she had known he was going to do what he did? Would she have turned her head so that he could kiss her on the mouth? What would he have done then? What was she *thinking!*

But she only said, "I was horrible to you that day, and for a long time after that. I did my best to avoid you."

"Really?" He smiled. "I didn't notice."

"Oh." She twisted her hands in her lap, a part of her longing only to raise her hand, touch her fingers to his cheek. "Everyone else did."

"Everyone else should mind their own business," Tanner said softly, moving closer to her, his mouth suddenly the center of her attention. His full, smiling mouth...

"Malvern! Ran you to ground at last!"

Lydia nearly jumped at the sudden shout, and instantly Tanner was gone, standing beside the bench, his body placed protectively in front of hers.

"Molton," he said dully. "Brittingham—Featherstone. I wasn't aware either of you were out of short pants eight years ago, let alone a friend of Farber's. And you're drunk, all of you."

"So?" the man named Molton answered. "Where's Wilde? Someone told me he'd seen him slinking away like the coward he is. Or is that him now, hiding behind you? Bring him out, Malvern. I've got something for him."

With that, Lydia heard the sharp snap of braided leather against the brick path. She knew the sound. A horse whip, probably procured from one of the coaches.

"Oh, for the love of heaven. You ass, put that away."

"Why? It's what he deserves. Wouldn't touch him, wouldn't dirty my hands on him. Wouldn't challenge him to a duel, either, wouldn't be that stupid, when the man has no honor, fires early."

"Molton, we've had this discussion. While I admire your friendship with Robbie Farber, sentiment doesn't alter facts. He turned early, and fired."

"Who cares a damn? Are we going to talk, or have us some fun?" one of the others said, slurring his words badly. "You promised Oliver and me some fun."

Lydia sat quietly, not daring to move, knowing she was hidden in both the shadows and by Tanner's body. Fear froze her body, even as her mind raced to unlovely conclusions. There were three of them, and only Tanner to face them. They were drunk, and clearly eager for an unfair fight. Did the target matter all that much, or would any target do? Had it yet occurred to Tanner that being in the right did not necessarily lend him any sort of protection?

Clearly not.

"Is that true, Molton? You talked these two young fools into stretching Justin's arms around a tree out here, while you whip him raw? Yes, that sounds like a notion that would appeal to you. I can see why you and Farber were bosom chums. Your shared sense of honor is evident. Well, so sorry to disappoint you all, but Wilde is gone, he isn't here. Which, whether you choose to believe it or not, is damn lucky for the three of you. Now, if you'll excuse me, there is a lady present, not that any of you noticed. I wish to escort her back to the ballroom. Let us pass, and if you wish it, I'll be more than happy to stand in for my good friend and then return to speak with you and your false courage some more."

He turned his back on the three men, extending his hand to her. "My apologies, Lydia. You should not have had to endure any of this. Let me take you back inside."

She heard the slither of the whip as its length was uncoiled onto the ground. "Tanner!" she called out in warning, leaping to her feet just to have him rather roughly push her toward the far side of the path, out of danger.

But his need to protect her had cost him valuable moments.

By the time he could turn, Molton had raised his hand, the whip already snaking out, meant to strike him across the back, its tip instead snapping against his cheek.

Molton's companions cheered at the quick eruption of blood, further emboldening him, so that he laughed and drew back the whip once more.

But this time it was Tanner who moved first, as if he'd never even been touched. His left arm shot out so that the whip wound harmlessly around his covered forearm and he could grab the fat braiding. A quick pull on the whip threw Molton off-balance, for the fool's wits were dulled with drink, and he hadn't let go of the handle.

With her hands pressed to her mouth so that she wouldn't scream and distract him, Lydia watched as Tanner then made short work of the man, who now lay moaning rather piteously on the brick path thanks to several short, hard punches from Tanner's right fist.

He then picked up the whip and flourished it, its length snapping in the air like a thunderbolt, proclaiming his expertise with the thing.

When he spoke, his voice was low, calm, cold as ice. "Anyone else? Come, come, gentlemen. You were looking for a good time. Don't let me disappoint you."

The younger men, big and brawny, and perhaps brighter than their first acquaintance might have led anyone to believe, turned and ran back up the path, deserting Molton, who was now sitting up with both hands raised to his face. "M'nose…you bloody broke m'nose…"

"And you deserved that, you cowardly beast," Lydia

said with feeling, and then quickly bit her bottom lip, horror-struck at her outburst.

"Nasty fall you just took, Molton," Tanner said, leaning down and lifting the man's head by the simple expedient of grabbing at his lordship's full head of hair. "Do you understand me? You came out into the gardens for a bit of fresh air, and you fell in the dark. That, or name your seconds. It's your choice. Who knows, Robbie might be lonely in the graveyard, and crave your company. God knows nobody else does."

"Let go of me!" Molton exclaimed, wiping at his streaming nose with his neck cloth. "I know what to say."

"Then it would be the first time," Tanner bit out, giving the man's head a sharp shake before pushing him back onto the ground.

He turned to Lydia. "Are you all right?"

"I'm fine." She searched in her small reticule for her handkerchief and handed it to Tanner. "You're bleeding. Does it hurt?"

He waved off the small affectation of thin, lace-edged muslin in favor of a large square of white linen he extracted from his own waistcoat pocket. He then pressed it against the slice on his cheek. "It's only a scratch, Lydia. I'm only sorry you had to witness anything so…"

"Something so very much not of your making? Please, Tanner, don't be stupid."

He took her hand and led her back up the path, the square of linen held to his cheek. When he removed the handkerchief to turn it over, she could see that the gash was nearly three inches long, curving around his cheek-bone, only nearly missing his left eye. But he was right, the wound appeared to be fairly superficial. Well, she didn't see bone, at any rate, and that had to be considered fortunate.

"I don't think I was going to say I was *stupid*. Although you're correct. I shouldn't have turned my back on the man. That was arrogance, plain and simple. I probably deserved this little scratch."

"Don't talk, you'll only make it bleed more." She shouldn't have said he was stupid, of course. She was upset, and the word had somehow simply slipped out. But, truly, men were such…idiots. Women didn't come to blows; women settled their differences without resorting to physical violence. Why, she would never even think to raise her hand to another human being.

They reached the bottom of the steps and she took hold of his forearm. "I'll go round up Jasmine and Mrs. Shandy, shall I? It would perhaps be best if you were to meet us outside with the coach. There's more than enough talk in the ballroom as it is, without anyone seeing you."

"Yes, I suppose you're right. And I'll find a servant somewhere who can go scoop up old Molton out there. Lydia?"

She was already halfway up the stairs, holding her gown up slightly so that she wouldn't trip. She half-turned on the stairs to look back at him. "Hmm?" she said, her mind filled with things that had to be done, things that could not be said, the moment when she'd be alone so that she could sit herself down and have a good, cleansing cry.

"You're very brave."

"No, Tanner, I'm not," she told him quite sincerely. "And truth to tell, I don't care for adventure, not even a little bit."

He laughed, and then winced as his wound finally seemed to give him pain. "I'll try to remember that next time I'm with you and someone comes at me with a horsewhip. Sometimes, Lydia, a man is left with no choice."

"No, I suppose not. But now that I've had a moment to consider the thing, I rather believe you enjoyed pummeling the man. Perhaps you only turned your back on him in order to encourage him to violence."

Tanner shrugged his shoulders. "Perhaps you're right."

She directed a long, level look at him, seeing a side of the man she'd never realized existed. A man who had gone to war, had learned the lesson of kill or be killed. An honorable man, yes, but very much a man. And was there anything more dangerous than an honorable man?

She turned and quickly headed up the stairs.

CHAPTER SIX

TANNER SAT IN HIS STUDY, several velvet-clad boxes of varying sizes spread out on the desktop in front of him. They were all there, all of the pieces he'd brought to town with him, including the emeralds Jasmine had worn last evening, and which she'd returned, as always, the moment they were in his coach.

She'd said the Malvern jewels made her nervous, and she always seemed happy to be shed of each piece, even as she thanked him for allowing her to wear them.

She had told him her only jewelry was a single strand of pearls that had been her mother's, and they were badly discolored because her father didn't trust any of their servants enough to allow them to wear them while they went about their duties, so that the contact of their skin and the oils on that same skin would keep the luster of the pearls bright.

He rubbed at his head after playing Jasmine's words through his mind. Good Lord, the woman could talk the ears off a donkey. But at least he knew that she owned only a single strand of discolored pearls, and that her father mistrusted his servants. For whatever that information was worth.

Had Jasmine told him all of this before they'd left Malvern hall in hopes that he would do just what he'd done…give her the loan of some of a few minor pieces of the Malvern jewels? Or did she just talk because she delighted in the sound of her own voice?

Either way, the pieces were now here, in London, and Justin had seen the emeralds, all but declared them paste.

Tanner looked down at the signet ring he wore on his right hand, the one his father had worn before him, and his father's father before him. He slipped it off, holding it up in front of him, trying to catch some of the morning sunlight. Fashioned of heavy, dark silver, deeply carved, the ring sported a center stone, a moonstone that was reportedly worth a small fortune. Now he wondered if it was real.

He propped his elbows on the desktop and pressed his chin against his folded hands. The move caused the large white bandage on his cheek to pull at him, so that he sat back once more, gingerly touching his fingertips to his cheek.

The cut wasn't as deep as it had been bloody, as Molton was as inept with a horsewhip as he was incapable of holding his drink. Most of the blow had been absorbed by Tanner's shoulder, with only the very tip of the whip finding his cheek. And if he was left with a scar it would be a small price to pay for his arrogance and, as Lydia had put the thing so succinctly, his stupidity.

Tanner smiled at the memory of Lydia's civilized outrage, that had almost immediately turned to a cool efficiency that had gotten them all out of the ballroom and into the coach with no one the wiser. What had happened after that, with Molton, he had no idea, nor did he find himself able to care. If the man had any sense at all he would have taken Tanner's advice.

After all, it was either lie, or tell the truth. And as the truth would make the man look an utter ass, Tanner felt fairly confident Justin would never hear what had actually happened out there in the gardens. But, being Justin, and far from a stupid man, he'd put the pieces together soon enough once he saw Tanner's bandage.

Which was why Tanner had spent the majority of the night cudgeling his brain for a way to keep Justin from the shops, the clubs, and any chance he might hear about Molton's injury. He'd sent a note round to Grosvenor Square at first light. Rafe's answer, and agreement, had arrived an hour ago, giving his permission to take Lydia to Malvern Hall for a welcome week's respite from the Season.

"Come," Tanner said, hearing the sharp, distinctive triple knock on the door that signaled the arrival of Thomas Harburton. He left the velvet boxes where they lay.

He watched as his cousin and estate manager entered the study, his gait hampered by the limp that had resulted from a tumble from a horse three decades earlier. The fall, and the limp, had come to Thomas courtesy of the late duke, who had recklessly crossed his path in pursuit of a fox during one of the famous Malvern hunting parties. That's when the late duke had taken him on as estate manager, to assuage his guilt.

But even guilt would not have held Thomas in the position. Tanner's father must have trusted the man.

Now Tanner looked at him. And wondered.

"I received your note, Your Grace," Thomas said, wincing slightly as he lowered his considerable bulk into one of the pair of chairs facing the desk, the ring of keys he always wore at his waist jingling almost merrily. "I've set Jasmine's woman to packing, and we'll be ready to leave tomorrow. I'll be on my way yet today, to prepare Malvern for your welcome. I'm sorry to hear of your accident. I can see why you wouldn't wish to be seen in public with that bandage." He narrowed his watery blue eyes and tipped his head as he looked at the large white square stuck to Tanner's face. "I thought people wore those cages on their faces when they fenced. And little balls stuck to the tips of the swords?"

"It was an impromptu match, and I may have been a little deeper in my cups than I'd imagined," Tanner lied easily, and then turned to another subject. "I don't wish to leave the Malvern jewelry in town while I'm gone. Is this the lot of it, Thomas?"

The estate manager leaned forward on the chair and began picking up the cases, opening them one after the other, before sitting back with another grunt. "Six pieces, yes. Jasmine won't hear of keeping any of them with us. Makes her nervous, you know. Pity to uproot the child from all the gaiety, don't you think? But not a problem, not at all. I mean, you'll only be gone the week. Unless you're planning on a more intimate atmosphere?"

Tanner ignored the man's not-well-veiled suggestion. "You know, on second thought, perhaps I should take this opportunity to have these pieces at least taken to my jeweler's. For cleaning, you understand, and to be sure none of the stones are loose."

"I can arrange that for you, Your Grace," Harburton said, not so much as a blink betraying any nervousness in the man.

So Tanner pushed a little harder.

"Thank you, Thomas. But I'd much prefer to do it myself. And, as I recall, Jasmine's birthday is next month. Perhaps I'll see some little bauble that might serve as a present."

Harburton merely shrugged, as if he didn't much care either way who delivered the jewelry to Bond Street. "One and twenty she'll be," he said, a whiff of righteous indignation entering his tone. "Could have given you a pair of heirs by now. Your father made it very clear, Your Grace, what his wishes were in the matter."

"Thomas—"

"Such a pretty girl, if a little silly, but getting long in the tooth, you know. And nobody else daring to come near her, thanks to everyone thinking you'll be declaring yourself any day now. Putting those jewels around her neck is as good as a notice in the *Times,* that's what I say."

"Yes, Thomas, I know what you say, have said quite repeatedly," Tanner said. "Now, if you'll excuse me…"

The estate manager got to his feet, pressing his hands hard against the arms of the chair and wincing as he stood. "Dog in the manger, that's what they call it, you know. Won't have her, won't let anyone else have her. Your can turn me off, Your Grace, your own cousin who stood at your father's side, Lord rest his soul, for more years than I can count. Stood as well as I could, that is, with this messed-up hip I got no thanks to him. He wanted you with my Jasmine, to atone for his guilt, as I see it. Damn near his last words. He owed me, Your Grace, and he knew it. And so do you."

Tanner looked up at the man, his expression blank. "Are you quite through, Thomas?"

Harburton's face split in a wide smile. "Now, now, you know how I can be when my hip is paining me. Damned weather, more often raining than not. Don't you pay me any mind, Your Grace. Just a loving papa, worrying over his one lone chick. You want to take my Jasmine home, then that's where we'll be going. Do you both good, spending time together."

Tanner rubbed at his forehead. "We'll be accompanied by Lady Lydia Daughtry, the Duke of Ashurst's sister as well as Baron Justin Wilde, if he agrees. A small party, but we'll try to make it a merry one." He looked up at Harburton once more. "Nothing more. Understood, Thomas?"

"Understood, Your Grace. And Jasmine will be that pleased. Said she and Lady Lydia hit it off a treat last night. But, then, my Jasmine is so easy to love, isn't she? I heard the Bad Baron was back. You were friends with him once, yes?"

"I am honored to consider the baron my friend, yes."

Tanner looked at the velvet cases one last time. "There will be no mention of the past, Thomas, is that clear?"

"Wouldn't be so crass, Your Grace. Besides, wouldn't want him shooting me in the back like he did that poor fellow he killed."

Tanner raised a hand to call back the estate manager and correct him, but then realized he was so grateful the man was leaving that he didn't want to do anything to prolong the farewell.

"One way or another, the man has to go," he muttered to himself, stacking the velvet cases one on top of the other. "An allowance, something. Whatever it takes…"

"Talking to yourself, old sport? Not a good sign, that," Justin Wilde said from the doorway.

"Justin, come in," Tanner said, getting to his feet. "Was nobody at the door, to announce you?"

"As I know who I am, I felt I could manage to announce myself. That your cousin I passed in the foyer? The man has the look of a frightened rabbit, or he did once I announced my name."

"Yes, my second cousin and estate manager, Thomas Harburton. Jasmine's father. I had all these boxes spread out on the desktop when he was here. Said I might have my jeweler look at the pieces. Clean them, check the stones, the clasps, that sort of thing. The man didn't even blink."

Justin reached inside his waistcoat and pulled out a jewelers loupe. Leave it to Justin to own his own. "Perhaps because he's innocent. Perhaps because I was incorrect in my assessment of last evening. Or," he added, opening one of the velvet cases, "perhaps he's less the buffoon than he looks. Lined up on the desktop, you say? I don't think I can award you any points for subtlety, old friend."

"It was a bit cow handed, wasn't it?"

"Far be it from me to comment on the obvious. Although I believe I'll make an exception concerning that plaster stuck to your handsome face. You should have feinted to your right before you turned. But perhaps your fears for the lady clouded your instincts."

Tanner sat down, his eyes hard on his friend. "How?"

"How? Oh, *how*. I was there, of course." He opened the case and put the loupe to his eye, screwing up his handsome features in order to hold the thing tight. "Garnets." He put down the case. "Hardly worth the effort to steal them. But pretty enough."

"The bloody hell with the garnets. You were there, in the gardens?"

"It seemed the most logical place. After all, Molton was obviously looking for some sort of confrontation. If I was gone, had deserted the field as it were, who did that leave?"

"Me." Tanner got to his feet. "I think I could do with a glass of wine. Would you care for one?"

"At this early hour? Of course, I would. I would have made myself known to you, Tanner, but you seemed to be deep in conversation with the Lady Lydia, so that I was loath to interrupt. For a man who says he lays no claim to the lady, you seemed rather…intent. At any rate, Molton and his trained monkeys showed up just as I had decided I should be no friend at all if I did not give you and the lovely lady some privacy. Happily, I hadn't gone yet, and was about to announce myself when Molton went on the attack. That was a wisty castor you placed on his phizz, as my coachman would say."

Tanner handed him a glass of wine, and took a sip from his own glass. "I left him there with his nose pouring blood. Molton. And left the the whip as well, now that I think of it. You, ah, you didn't *do* anything, did you?"

"Did I confront the man who would have horse-whipped my friend, you mean? The bumbling, stumbling, yet dangerous creature who would bring two well-born thugs with him to face one defenseless man? A pig of a fool who would frighten a woman such as the lovely Lady Lydia, with his only wound a slight rearranging of his nose? Tanner. Do you really want me to answer that?"

Tanner shook his head, then chuckled under his breath. "No, I don't think I do."

"Good choice," Justin said, raising his wine glass in a mocking toast. "So, when are we leaving for Malvern Hall?"

"You listen at keyholes now, as well?"

Justin smiled. "I confess it. I may have been on the other side of that door longer than politeness dictates, only hastening back down the hallway to the foyer once I was convinced you weren't going to wring that idiot's neck. Although I rather like that appellation he gifted me with. The bad baron. But I'm hardly that. Encroaching mushroom, isn't he?"

"My father did cause his injury all those years ago," Tanner said. "And, according to Thomas, he and my father grew very close over the course of my father's final illness."

"You weren't there?"

"I was on the peninsula. My father left no last letters to me. Not that I expected any. We weren't very compatible, and when I took myself and my seed off to be killed by some Froggie—my father's words, not mine—we became permanently estranged. I can believe he might have seen a marriage between Jasmine and myself as a way to roll the Harburton estate in with ours. But I highly doubt the marriage was his last wish. Those the emeralds?"

He stepped closer to Justin as the baron lifted the necklace and used the loupe to inspect the center stone, then moved his inspection to the smaller stones.

"Well?"

"Let me just say that I wouldn't hope to use this piece to secure a loan, were I you."

"Glass," Tanner said, looking at the necklace Justin held up in front of them both. The thing glittered wildly in the sun. A beautiful piece. He could vaguely remember seeing it around his late mother's neck. "And you're sure?"

Justin let the necklace slide over his palm and back onto the desktop. "Once, in my salad days, I gifted a woman with what I believed to be a rather stunning diamond necklace. A farewell present, as it were."

He held up the jewelers loupe. "The woman, who I

agree had to live by her wits—her beauty had begun to fade, you understand—immediately pulled one of these from her bosom, examined the stones, and then tossed the necklace back in my face. You can imagine my embarrassment. I was so dreadfully naive."

"You'd been duped?"

"Oh, most definitely and decidedly duped. And, as I hoped my future might be fairly well littered with lovely women and parting gifts, I decided there and then to be educated on the matter of jewels. But back to the stones. I would suggest you have someone else verify my conclusion, but yes, glass. Quite good glass, but glass just the same."

"Damn. I imagine the rest are equally fake." He slipped off his ring and laid it on the desktop.

Justin opened another case, extracted a set of dainty diamond earrings. Then the pearls, which he, after excusing his rather primitive but, he assured Tanner, infallible method, rubbed against his teeth. The sapphire brooch. The light blue stones, the name of which Tanner couldn't remember, had never cared enough to learn. More fool him, as it turned out.

"The garnets are real. As I said, barely worth the effort of copying them," Justin said at last, picking up the signet ring. "I'm sorry, Tanner."

"And the ring?"

"Difficult to duplicate a moonstone, especially one of this size. I'd say it's genuine. Tanner, these stones could have been replaced at any time. Last week, last year. A dozen or more years ago. Yours wouldn't be the first family to have resorted to switching out stones and replacing them with glass. We all have to live in these perilous times. And you said Harburton didn't object when you said you might take them to Bond Street?"

"Didn't turn a hair," Tanner said, slipping the signet ring back on his finger. "You were in London the last year of my mother's life. Do you remember the Malvern diamonds? An impressive mass of stones she loved with all her heart? Necklace, bracelet, those long, dangling earbobs. A brooch as well, as I recall, and some pins for the hair. Prinney was so struck by it he offered to purchase the entire set, but we knew he'd never be good for the payment. Besides, my father said the center stone in the necklace is our legacy, our pride. That's what he called it. The Malvern Pride."

"I remember. A collar, that's what such heavy, old-fashioned pieces are called. With a center stone the size of a goose egg. A stone that large and distinctive would be difficult to sell, Tanner. Not without someone taking notice. Your father wouldn't have wanted that sort of talk making its way around Mayfair, for one thing, yet no country jeweler could possibly afford to buy it."

"Unless the stones were replaced a long time ago, which you said is also possible. One or two pawned and replaced at a time, over the course of years, even decades. There's really no way to know, is there?"

"Do you still want my company at Malvern Hall? You might be happier not knowing if the Pride is real or not."

Tanner shook himself out of his unhappy thoughts. "I'm not inviting you just so you can screw that damn fool thing to your eye."

"No, of course not. You're also inviting me to assure yourself that, until you're healed at least, I won't tumble into trouble here in town when you're not here to haul me out of it by offering up yourself instead."

Tanner smiled, and then pressed a hand to his face, because the smile had set his cheek to throbbing. "Believe me when I say that it was never my intention to be horsewhipped in your place. Had I known you were there, hanging about in the shadows, I would have pointed Molton straight at you."

"No, you wouldn't have done that. You would have done just what you did, sacrificed yourself. You should really strive to stop doing that, my friend. That's why good men die, Tanner, when the bad among us seem to lead charmed lives. Somehow, it would seem the Lady Lydia knows that."

Now Tanner did laugh, and the hell with his wound. "She called me stupid."

"Clearly a young woman of superior intellect. You'll also notice that she did not scream, didn't fall into a faint. A very admirable woman, as well one with a singular beauty to rival that of the angels—a sure attraction to a bad man like me. I'll give you one last chance. Are you quite positive you don't want to warn me off?"

"If I said that I'd rather you made a dead set at her, would you believe me?"

Justin frowned, looked at Tanner intensely. "You invite competition? Why? Does this have something to do with her dead captain? You were serious about that?"

"I keep attempting to tell myself that, yes."

"Then, if I'm understanding this correctly—as far as our small farce goes, that is—the loquacious Miss Harburton is not cast in the role of future Duchess of Malvern?"

Tanner shook his head. "Definitely not."

"Admitting again that I was listening at the door, that's not what your cousin seems to believe. I think, and I'm rarely wrong, that he's already harboring thoughts that you'll be declaring yourself at some time during our brief sojourn in the country."

"He thought I brought her to London to declare myself. If I say *bless you* to Jasmine when she sneezes, Thomas is certain I'm about to declare myself. It doesn't matter where we are."

"In that case, bear with me for a moment more. I think I understand now," Justin said, holding up one finger as if just struck with an idea. "Is my presence on the scene to have more than one purpose? To be compared to you and found wanting by Lady Lydia—more fool you, if you're hoping for that—and also to romance the little chatterbox, thus keeping her occupied and out of the way? Quite the sacrifice on behalf of my poor ears, I might point out, although she's a pretty piece. It was only a horsewhip, Tanner, wielded by a fool more than half in his cups. Only one small blow you could have easily avoided if you'd only—"

"Feinted to the right. Yes, I remember."

"Or perhaps to the left. It all happened so quickly, I could manage scarce more than to stand there and admire your prowess." Justin pocketed his loupe. "I could win her, you know. The fair Lady Lydia, that is."

"Then I wouldn't have lost her, would I, because she would never have been mine to lose."

Justin's smile was wry, and almost sad. "There's that pesky honor again—don't you ever find it tiresome? But I do see your logic. At least you won't have lost to a dead man."

Tanner employed the decanter to refill their glasses. "Said that way, it sounds callous, doesn't it? But, yes. I can't compete with Fitz. In her eyes, he was perfect. I'm not perfect."

"None of us are. Even saints, I believe, are never canonized until years after they've been carried to bed on six men's shoulders. Stacked up against the bad baron, however, you're fairly close. But I warn you, I do have my charms. And ladies, even the best of them, tend to like their mischief, their excitement."

"I'm fairly certain you would have more than met your match in her twin, Nicole. Much as I like Lucas Paine, I think I might have enjoyed seeing that." Tanner shook his head. "But not Lydia. You don't know her, Justin. She enjoys a quiet life."

"Ah, I see a wager in our future. I'll tell you what, Tanner. You read the fair lady poetry on a blanket spread beneath some shady tree, like the honorable gentleman you are. And I'll—well, I'm sure I'll think of something. You may want her, my friend. But first someone needs to wake her up from whatever dream from the past you both seem to believe she's living in. Or at least one of you believe she's living in, hmm?"

Tanner opened his mouth to protest, but then shut it again. Was that what was wrong? Had he been treating Lydia as if she was fragile? Not as a woman, but still as the heartbreaking, tragic figure she had been a year earlier?

The way she'd behaved with him yesterday—in the park, at the ball, in the gardens. Her bright smile. Her almost saucy tongue. And that gown!

Had he been the unobservant witness to her first tentative steps toward breaking free from the past? With her sister gone from the scene, had Lydia decided that it was time to spread her own wings?

One might say that she had been flirting with him a bit, been less shy, more outgoing in her manner. Receptive. One could definitely say that she had been flirting with Justin, with all that business about Molière. Huh!

And more! Was it he, and not the memory of Fitz, who was the one holding her back from making that break with the past? Had she begun to chafe at his, well, his *kindness,* so that now she saw him rather as a roadblock to her future? How could he hope to inspire more than friendship, if he offered no more than friendship?

Well, damn him for a fool.

"Tanner? You're smiling. Did I say something amusing?"

"On the contrary, Justin. I think you said something

brilliant. Thank you. Thank you very much. Oh, and yes. The wager is on."

Justin raised his glass. "Hear, hear! And may the best—or even the worst—man win."

CHAPTER SEVEN

LYDIA SAT AT HER WRITING TABLE and nibbled at the end of the pen she held in her hand, staring down at the last words she'd written to Nicole.

She'd promised her more news. But to tell her one thing would not be enough, and to write to her of everything that had happened since she'd left for the ball would take volumes.

Sighing, and then realizing that she *never* sighed, Lydia dipped the pen into the inkpot and prepared to be vague.

I'm afraid I won't make the morning post now, which is a shame, since I have so little more to tell you since I gave off writing yesterday. Tanner's cousin is delightful, and rather astonishingly pretty, but what the good Lord so graciously blessed her with in looks He seems to have held back in other ways, so that she is also incredibly shallow and silly. Still, I think I like her very much.

Lydia put down the pen and looked at what she'd written.

Yes, she liked Jasmine Harburton. But *why* did she like Jasmine Harburton? Because the girl was a little silly, a little sad? Or because she didn't wish to marry Tanner?

No, she wouldn't think about that.

What else was there to tell Nicole about last night?

"Nothing," Lydia said aloud, surprising herself.

Her sister, her best friend. They'd begun life together in their mother's womb. For all the years, for all the whispered girlhood secrets and confidences, the last thing she wished to do now was to share anything that had occurred last night with Nicole, or with anyone, for that matter.

And wasn't that odd.

She dipped her pen once more, knowing she was about to lie to her sister, if only by omission.

The ball itself was uneventful, as such things usually are, aren't they? I danced several times, so that you may put away your fear that I spent the evening hiding myself behind some potted palm after you'd so vandalized the bodices of all my gowns.

There. Let her think her little prank had been the reason for her sister's social success. Nicole loved being right.

Lydia dipped her pen once more and wrote:

Oh, and the Gunther Ices were quite lovely.

She smiled, suddenly remembering how Mrs. Shandy had been loath to put down her dish and quit the ballroom so that they could join Tanner outside. In the end, she had plucked one of the confections from a passing servant and literally *lured* the woman toward the door, waving it in front of her.

What a strange evening! And yet, if it hadn't been for the drunken fools and the horsewhip, and that cut on Tanner's cheek, she'd have to say that she'd enjoyed last night's ball more than any other entertainment she'd attended since their arrival in town. She'd met a new friend. She'd danced, several times. The Baron had been silly and flattering.

And Tanner had kissed her on the cheek.

Yes, and there was the crux of the thing. Tanner's kiss. Whatever had it meant?

She hadn't expected him to kiss her; that much was for certain. Again, what if she'd taken that precise moment to turn her head, and he had collided with her mouth rather than her cheek? Would he have apologized? Or would he have taken advantage of the situation?

It all could have been most embarrassing, for both of them, so it was fortunate that the kiss on her cheek had been just that. A friendly kiss. An apologetic kiss? An impulsive kiss? A kiss is a kiss is a kiss, just as a rose is a rose is a rose?

"Stop it," she scolded herself, feeling her pleasure in Tanner's action being replaced by the uncertainties of a postmortem.

Dipping her pen point once more, she finished with a wish that Nicole would write to her soon, and then signed her name with a bit of a flourish. She had just sanded the page, placed it with the others, and was folding the pages when Charlotte knocked and entered the bedchamber.

"Good, then you're awake. Even fed and dressed," her sister-in-law said, aiming herself toward a straight

backed chair, as those of the softer and more comfortable variety lately were, according to Charlotte, *out to
trap me forever in their clutches*. "I'm told you were
home rather early last night. The ball was a disappointment?"

Lydia got to her feet, clutching the folded sheets in
front of her, holding on to a lie while she told a lie, she
supposed. "Not at all. Tanner's cousin is a lovely young
woman"—she tried not to smile as Charlotte raised one
eyebrow at that—"and we both had several partners
during the evening. And…um…and the Gunther Ices
were quite welcome in the heat."

"Yes, balls can be quite the crush. But then you can
always escape to the gardens in search of cooler air."

Lydia turned back to the desk and laid the letter on
the blotter. "I suppose that's true," she said weakly. She
was such a terrible liar, and most probably as transparent as glass. She should have practiced, the way Nicole
had.

"Of course," Charlotte went on breezily, "even while
attending anything as civilized as a ball in the center of
Mayfair, something untoward can occur."

Lydia spun about, pressing her back against the edge
of the desk, using her hands to keep herself balanced.
"You *know*. How could—"

"A passing Gypsy taught me how to read tea leaves?
But, no. Tanner told Rafe in a note he sent round early
this morning. And Rafe immediately told me, because
my husband knows how fruitless an exercise it is to try
to keep anything from his loving wife. It was an unfor-

tunate incident, and I'm so sorry you had to witness any such unpleasantness. But it's over now. And Rafe and I entirely agree that it would be best to remove the baron from London for a space. You'll all have a wonderful time at Malvern, I'm sure."

"Pardon me? When did that happen? I'm going to Malvern?"

Charlotte nodded, her eyes twinkling with mischief. "Rafe's already given his permission, yes. Just a small house party. You and the baron, Miss Harburton and Tanner."

"Me and the—that is to say, the baron and I?"

"Rafe says he can be quite amusing, not to mention marvelously wealthy and sinfully handsome. And he's technically eligible, as well, if a bit of a social outcast, although that will pass. Impeccable lineage and a deep gravy boat always see to that, eventually, or so history tells us. Oh, dear, what a puss on you! Don't tell me you've taken him in dislike?"

Had Charlotte been drinking this morning? No, of course not. But she was next door to giddy, and Charlotte was rarely giddy. Lydia pulled out her desk chair and sat down. It was either that or fall down, she supposed. "No, I most certainly haven't taken the baron in dislike. He's really rather sad, beneath all his quips and a tendency for outrageous silliness. But what has that to say about—"

"How clever of Tanner to find you such an eminently suitable…well, suitor. Yes, there was that rather nasty business several years ago—Rafe told me all about it—but he has received the king's pardon, so that's all there is to be said on that head. Still, it would be best to remove the man from the gossipmongers for a space, and what better way than to give an outward show of a house party serving as some welcome respite from a hectic Season? And if anything more were to come out of it," Charlotte said, lifting her slim shoulders in an elegant shrug, "something like, oh, a betrothal? Well, then, we'll just leave that up to the Fates."

"The fates, is it?" Lydia narrowed her eyelids. "You know, Charlotte, for a moment there you sounded just like Mama, almost as if you're planning my future for me. And as you well know, *that* is not a compliment."

Charlotte lightly slapped her palms against her knees and stood up with more alacrity than she'd been showing for several weeks. "It's settled then? You leave for Malvern tomorrow. A single night on the road should do it, Rafe says, what with the quality of Tanner's horseflesh. A week in the country, breathing fresh air, and then a leisurely return to Ashurst Hall."

Lydia's mouth had already dropped open, ready with her reply—her refusal, although why she felt the need to turn down the invitation she had not yet sorted out in her head. But mention of Ashurst Hall had her rethinking her answer. "Ashurst Hall? I'll be going *home?* But…but what about the remainder of the Season?"

"Rafe has decided that his wife is more important than whatever arguments are taking place in Parliament for the moment. Especially since I told him that it's possible I miscounted, and his son is due to make his appearance earlier than we'd first expected."

"Really?"

"No, not really. I'm more than certain of the date. But my announcement did serve to get him up and moving, I'll say that. And if you can't tell, I'm nearly giddy with the thought of returning to Ashurst Hall."

"I had noticed, yes." Lydia looked askance at her. "I never knew you were a conniver."

Charlotte grinned. "Neither did I, actually. It's rather fun. At any rate, Rafe has set preparations in motion for us to depart for home tomorrow morning. And with you on your way to Malvern at much the same time, the household will be busy today, putting everything in Holland covers. We shall make quite the grand parade of traveling coaches, won't we, heading out of Grosvenor Square. You, heading to the north, Rafe and I traveling to the south, and with Nicole causing her usual mischief somewhere in between."

"But…but…" Lydia's head was spinning.

"Rafe's already penned a note to her at Basingstoke, asking that she and Lucas come to Ashurst Hall when her visit is over. So we may all be going our separate ways at the moment, but we'll all be together again soon. There's an heir to be born, after all, and weddings to plan."

Lydia sprung to her feet once more, feeling helpless in the midst of a veritable storm of events in which she had no say, could find no way to refuse. "Weddings? Charlotte, will you stop! Please? Your baby, yes. And

Nicole's wedding to Lucas. I've been saying for weeks that we should all be returning to the country. But *weddings?* In the *plural?* I am most certainly not going to marry the baron. How could you even think that, on a single day's acquaintance?"

Charlotte's smile was breathtaking, and more than mildly mischievous. "Sweetheart, whoever said anything about the baron? Certainly not I. You really do need some time away from the hustle and bustle of the Season, don't you? The country air should clear your head."

But if Charlotte wasn't throwing her at the baron's head, then she must be tossing her at—Lydia sat down so quickly this time that her teeth jarred against each other. Nicole having the seamstress clip away at all of her gowns. Rafe pushing her toward Tanner's estate without so much as inquiring as to her opinion of such a trip? Charlotte grinning like some cat who'd gotten into the cream?

Was the whole world thinking what she had been so careful not to ever utter out loud?

Before Lydia could think of anything else to say, her sister-in-law, surprisingly light on her feet suddenly, snatched up the letter to Nicole and was gone from the bedchamber, saying she thought there might still be time to catch the morning post.

For a woman who had lately complained that she waddled worse than the ducks in the pond at Ashurst Hall, she'd certainly moved with a spring in her step.

Oh, God, a spring in her step. Would that phrase never leave her mind?

So Charlotte saw Tanner as a prospective bridegroom.

Rafe probably thought the same, and the two of them must be just tickled down to their toes that they could push her off to Malvern with Tanner on the pretense of Justin's disgrace being somehow miraculously cured by dint of a small house party in the home of a duke.

It was all so transparent. But they meant well. Nicole and Charlotte and Rafe—they all meant well.

She did like Tanner very much. Very much. And he had kissed her, if only on the cheek. And he wasn't going to marry Jasmine; at least Jasmine said so. There was no more reason to try to hide her growing affection for Tanner because he was all but betrothed to another woman, not when that woman didn't want him.

Except there was still that business of Tanner's obligation to the captain, his promise to always take care of her. If he wasn't going to marry his cousin on the strength of a deathbed wish, should she not even entertain the lowering thought that he might marry *her* on the strength of another deathbed wish?

Suddenly the memory of Tanner's brief, chaste kiss on her cheek didn't seem quite so romantic. Coupling that kiss with this sudden invitation to his estate—and everyone's ill-concealed joy over the thing…?

"Oh, dear…"

Was she imagining things, or had Tanner already approached Rafe and gained his permission? Was there an offer of marriage waiting for her once they were at Malvern, away from the wagging tongues that would be questioning: "But what about the cousin?"

It all seemed so cold, so calculated. *And here's my*

lovely estate, and there's the barns, and the horses, and the fields. Please, help me salve my conscience and marry them. Fitz would be so happy to see you well-settled.

Lydia's shoulders slumped. Oh, how dreadful!

There was something else, something horribly unnerving about the idea of everyone else so blithely deciding her life for her, as if they all knew best. After all, she wasn't a child anymore. Why did they all persist in seeing her as fragile? And quiet. And…biddable. Of the three, *biddable* seemed to be the worst.

She wasn't biddable. Nicole was flamboyant, impossible to rein in, which only made Lydia appear quiet and biddable in contrast. That's all. She had a *mind.* She could make her own decisions, thank you very much.

What would they all do if she pretended an attraction to the baron, if only for a little while. The man was already flirting with her, clearly playing some game for his own amusement. Perhaps she should flirt *back* at him, Wouldn't *that* put a spoke in all of their wheels! The thought made her feel…my goodness! She felt actually *stubborn.* Or, considering that she was very probably in love with Tanner anyway (not that anyone had *asked*), was that *petty*…?

"She's gone then?" Sarah poked her mobcapped head around the edge of the door to the dressing room, and then skipped lightly across the room, her smile wide. "Oh, milady, ain't it just grand? I heard all about it below stairs. We leave in the morning for the country. And to Great Malvern, no less. I've family there, milady. M'cousin Martha got herself bracketed to the baker what has his shop straight on High Street. Martha's a wee bit high in the instep now, but we've been chums forever, and no sayin' a person can't take on some airs when they've wed so well, I say."

"I don't…" Lydia realized she was about to be mean and petty and say something much like *I don't care a fig about your cousin Martha*. But she stopped herself in time. If she was going to shock someone by not behaving as she always did, then let it be Tanner, not poor unsuspecting Sarah. "Great Malvern, you said, Sarah? How intriguing. Is there then by chance a Lesser Malvern?"

The maid shook her head, sending one of the pins holding her mobcap to skittering across the floor. "I don't think so, milady," she said, screwing up her features, which already had an unfortunate resemblance to a maturing prune. "There's a Little Malvern, I'm thinkin', and another one. Malvern Wells? But they're all much of a piece, I think Martha said, all close together and such. But *Great* Malvern is the most important, just like m'cousin was clear to point out when she told us about her husband's new shop last Boxing Day, when she came to visit. Oh, cooee," she went on, slapping a hand against her forehead. "And it's the Duke of *Malvern* you've been walkin' out with these past weeks. Well, mark me for a looby. I didn't think of that, not even the once!"

"The duke is a friend to all of us, Sarah, most especially my brother. That's all. I am not walking—that is to say…no, never mind. Tell me more about the greater and lesser Malverns. "

Lydia smiled weakly as Sarah went on and on,

giving her time to collect her scattered thoughts. She'd have to make use of the large book of maps Rafe kept in his library. She rather liked the sound of Little Malvern; it didn't seem quite so overpowering as Great Malvern...

"And the hills, milady? Hills all over, Martha says. She called them the Malvern Hills, like they're so important that they have a name and everything. Why to hear Martha prattlin' on so, you'd think the place to be part of Adam and Eve's own Garden of Eden."

"Then there are snakes?" Lydia asked at last, hoping to stem the tide of praises for Tanner's ducal home.

"Martha never said." Sarah bobbed a curtsy and apologized for nattering on so when there was work to be done. "You'll be takin' everything, milady, seein' as how we'll be on our way back to Ashurst Hall once we've quit the mighty Malvern."

"The mighty Malvern. I like that, Sarah. Suddenly Greater Malvern doesn't seem quite so intimidating. Here, let me help you gather up my things. Is someone bringing my portmanteaus down from the attics?"

Sarah was already heading for the clothespress, clearly intent on cleaning it out with the least possible hesitation. "On their way, milady. You'll be hearing the racket soon enough, as William was sent to do the job, and he's sure to lose his grip on at least one, and send it bumping down the stairs. All thumbs, our William. When will you be wantin' to leave for the shops, milady?"

Lydia looked up at the ceiling as she heard the sound of something being dragged across the floor above her head. She felt like the lone useless bee in a busy hive. "I'm not planning a trip to Bond Street, Sarah."

Sarah paused on her way toward the bed, holding an armful of day dresses. "But Maisie, when she told me I was to pack you up, said I should be quick about it, seeing as how you needed to be ready for when His Grace fetched you off to the shops. She was uncommon clear about that, milady."

"Oh, she was, was she? Was she clear enough as to say *which* His Grace would be accompanying me to these shops?"

Sarah frowned, and then grinned. "Yes, milady, she was. Not your brother. The one with the spring in his step. That's just what she said. And then she winked. Naughty puss, she is, that Maisie."

Lydia didn't bother to agree or disagree with her maid's assessment. She was too busy wondering why Tanner would think she needed to visit Bond Street. "Thank you, Sarah. I suppose you could set out the bonnet with the blue ribbon, and my gloves. I'll be in His Grace's study if anyone should need me."

Sarah curtsied, not an easy thing to do with an armful of dresses. "You might be wantin' to wear the bonnet with the cherries on it, milady. That blue ribbon is gettin' all frayed and such, seein' as how you wear it so much. You could mayhap find another blue ribbon whilst you're at the shops, and I can sew it on for you?"

Lydia wrapped her arms around her waist, reacting to what had almost felt like a physical punch to her midsection. Replace the blue ribbon? Discard the ribbon the captain had said went so well with her eyes? *Fitz's ribbon?*

"Or you could think to maybe change the ribbon? Yellow would look very nice, what with matchin' the posies on the brim?"

"No!" Lydia quickly put out her hands, as if to scrub away her near-violent protest. "That is…I think I would rather simply change the ribbon, and not the color. Perhaps if you'd snip off a small length of it, Sarah, I could take it with me to the shops so that I can match it?"

Sarah, looking more than slightly startled—for never did her mistress ever raise her voice—nodded furiously. "I'll do just that, milady. Yes, indeed. Just that. And I'll stick it in your reticule and put it on the table downstairs with your bonnet and gloves."

"Thank you, Sarah," Lydia said, more than a little ashamed of her behavior. "I'll…I'll be in His Grace's study."

She closed the door to her bedchamber and then leaned against it in an attempt to collect her shattered nerves. What was the matter with her? One moment she was thinking about Tanner's kiss, and the next she was ready to indulge in a fit of the vapors because her blue ribbon needed to be replaced.

But she knew the answer to her own question. With or without her permission, Fitz was leaving her, finding a comfortable and permanent spot in her memory, but no longer a part of her life in the way he had been since the day she'd first seen his unique smile, heard the lovely Irish lilt in his deep voice.

A voice she could barely recall. A smile she'd last seen as he waved to her from his horse and rode off toward glory and his eventual death.

She closed her eyes. She'd been angry with him for a long time. For leaving her. For placing his damnable duty to Crown and country before their own happiness. He'd fought beside Rafe on the Peninsula for six long years. Hadn't that been enough? Even as she'd missed him, longed for him, loved him, deep inside she'd been so *angry* with him for his absence.

The day Tanner had come to Grosvenor Square, ignoring his own injuries and delaying his own homecoming until he had delivered his sad news, Lydia had screamed *No! No!* as she'd beaten her fists against his chest. In denial? Or in fury? Had she been berating Tanner, or lashing out at Fitz for being so heartless as to die on her rather than stay with her?

These were the questions she'd asked herself, over and over again. Questions she'd never shared with Nicole or anyone else. And most especially not with Tanner. She'd never asked him about Fitz's wounds, or how Tanner had found him in the midst of a raging battle, or what the captain's last words had been. Because she'd needed Fitz alive, if only in her memory.

And now she could barely remember the sound of his voice, or conjure up the smile on his face.

And the blue ribbon had frayed…

Lydia used the back of her hands to wipe at the tears on her cheeks. It was so hard to say goodbye.

And more difficult yet to face the future…

Bam-bam-bam—"William, you ham-fisted buffoon! Who said to let go?"

The sound of what had to be a heavy trunk crashing down the attic stairs, followed by the angry shouts of the head footman, had Lydia lifting her skirts to quickly make her way along the hallway and down to the foyer. Poor William, he of the bandy legs and the grace of a cross-eyed loon.

She could still hear the head footman berating him as she reached the bottom of the stairs, her smile only fading as she realized that the front door had just opened and Baron Justin Wilde was at that very moment stepping inside the mansion.

"Sir Justin," she said almost breathlessly, dropping into a curtsy.

"Lady Lydia. At last, a reason to draw breath on this dull grey morning," he responded with a bow, his left hand sweeping outward in order to flourish his hat and at the same time deftly thrust it into the belly of a clearly awed footman.

"It's the volcano, you know," Lydia heard herself saying. "Somewhere in Tambora? Rafe says we're suffering the effects of smoke and ash sent high into the sky a year ago and half a world away." She closed her eyes for a moment, thinking she probably sounded as inane, even if at least more widely informed, than Jasmine Harburton.

"So I understand, yes. And, speaking of His Grace, do you know if he is receiving callers this morning?"

"You wish to speak with Rafe?" Honestly, could she be any more silly? Now she was turning into a parrot. But, my, the baron was such a pretty man, and his smile was more than slightly disconcerting, as if he had some secret that delighted him, but that he wouldn't share. Or perhaps he would share…but he'd exact payment first.

Thinking it best not to say anything else, especially with two of the footmen showing themselves to be such an eager audience, she motioned toward the drawing room, inviting the baron to accompany her.

"I've only just come from Portland Square," Justin said as he waited for Lydia to seat herself on one of the couches at the very center of the room. He neatly spread his coattails and took up his own seat on the facing couch. "It is my layman's opinion that our patient will live."

Lydia took in a quick, short breath. "You saw his face?"

"The parts not hidden behind a plaster, yes. Nasty hit he must have taken against the edge of that door."

She nodded her agreement. They had concocted a reasonable explanation for Tanner's injury before he'd seen her back to Grosvenor Square last night. "It was. An errant gust of wind blew along on the balcony just as we were stepping outside. The edge of the door caught him on his cheek before he could protect himself." There. That sounded all right, didn't it? Maybe fibbing got easier the more you did it?

"Snapped against him like the tip of a whip, Tanner told me," the baron said, his green eyes steady on her, and not betraying a single thing he might be thinking.

Well, he might know the truth, or he might not. No, he knew the truth; his use of the word *whip* made that obvious. But he wasn't going to get any satisfaction from her! "Um…yes, I suppose it might have felt like that. You say you're here to see Rafe?"

Justin crossed one elegantly clad leg over the other. "To speak to him, yes. It only seems polite to present myself for inspection, seeing as how I will be so much in your delightful company over the next week and more. After all, one never knows when one might have need of prior permission."

"That's not at all amusing, you know," Lydia heard herself say a heartbeat after Justin smiled, a bit of the devil perhaps now peeking out of those green eyes. "You only said that to set me off-balance. You'd have more success with Miss Harburton."

"Ah, but that, with apologies to the lady, presents no challenge. I'd much rather tease you. Now, guilty as it makes me of repetition, is your brother at home to visitors?"

"I'm sure one of the servants has already apprised him of your request to meet with him," Lydia said formally. And then she ruined it by being unable to resist leaning forward to ask: "You *were* teasing, weren't you? You said you were teasing."

"Am I a man of my word, you mean, Lady Lydia?"

"You may address me as Lydia, please, as we're

going to be, as you said, so much in each other's company. But if we are to cry friends, you really must answer my question."

"And you may honor me by addressing me as Justin, please, even if you'd rather I fly to the ends of the earth on a dragon's back rather than be much in your company. And, yes, I was teasing. I very often say things only to elicit a response that may amuse me. It's a failing. But I do not always tease. The problem, if you were to see it as such, is deciding when I am teasing and when I am…deadly serious."

"Is that a problem for you, as well? Knowing when you are being flippant, and when you actually mean what you say?" Lydia asked, her blood flowing rather quickly through her veins. He did make her feel alive, that was certain. But being alive, at the level or even many levels upon which the baron seemed to operate, would probably be quite fatiguing. She had the feeling she could never quite relax her guard in his company.

He looked at her with such intensity that she had to fight the urge to rub at her nose, as if she had smeared ink on it or something when she was finishing her letter to Nicole.

Ah, Nicole. *She* would know how to handle the baron. She would return his stare, unblinking, that's what she'd do. And she'd outlast him, too.

But she wasn't her twin. Lydia looked down at her clasped hands, unsurprised to see that the knuckles were rather white.

"You and I have only barely met, Lydia," Justin said

at last, "and yet you may know me better than does the majority of my acquaintance. That's rather unnerving. Ah, and here he is, the Duke of Ashurst." He stood up, turning to greet Rafe, his bow once more elegant, and only slightly overdone. "May I take it, Your Grace, that you have condescended to meet with me even as I dared arrive without an appointment?"

Rafe looked to Lydia, and smiled. "What say you, sister? Shall I meet with the man, or simply toss him out on his ear for being an ass?" He put out his hand to the baron. "It's been a long time, Justin. You look none the worse for wear."

"It's my tailor," Justin drawled as the two shook hands. "He's the making of me. How have you been, Rafe?"

Lydia looked back and forth between the two men. "You know each other? Well, of course you do, don't you. That was a silly question."

"London is large, but society as a whole is small, Lydia. Justin here and I traveled much in the same company the single Season I was in town before my uncle purchased my commission."

"We met in a gaming hell in Piccadilly, as I recall the thing," Justin told her. "You were about to call out the dealer as a cheat, and I stopped you."

"Which probably saved me several broken bones. I hadn't noticed the two hulks waiting in the shadows to take care of any troublemakers. I haven't gambled since, you know, except for playing at tame stakes with my wife. Who beats me nearly every time, I must say."

"Ah, yes, your wife. Tanner tells me she's soon to present you with an heir. My congratulations."

"Thank you. And *soon* may be the operative word, I found out this morning. We'll be heading for Ashurst Hall tomorrow, even as Lydia is on her way to Malvern."

Justin slid his eyes toward Lydia, and smiled. "Yes. I've heard that, as well. In fact, I shall be a part of the party, which is what brings me here, not that I'm not delighted to see your ugly puss again. If you have a moment, Rafe, and a place where we two can be private…?"

Lydia rolled her eyes and looked away, now confident that the baron was doing his best to make a May game out of her, and then turned her head as the butler announced the Duke of Malvern.

Tanner walked into the drawing room with a smile of greeting on his face and the easy manner of a frequent guest, but then stopped where he was, to look at the baron. "Justin?"

"Tanner?" the baron replied in the same questioning tone, with only a hint of mockery to be found in it.

"Rafe…Lydia," Tanner said, joining them all in the center of the large room. "I'm here to escort Lydia to a shop I wish her to see."

"A shop? You're here to take her to a *shop?* Such a man of adventure, Tanner. Bordering on the hey-go-mad, one might say. How exciting for her," Justin said, and then raised a hand to his mouth. And yawned.

Lydia bit the insides of her cheeks, to keep from

giggling, but Rafe seemed to know she was struggling, and winked at her.

Tanner ignored the sarcasm. "I saw you not an hour ago, and you made no mention of coming to Grosvenor Square."

"Oh, I *wager* I did, old friend. You must have forgotten. That fresh bandage looks quite rakish, however. Lydia," the baron said, pivoting to face her, "wouldn't you say that our friend Tanner looks rakish?"

"I'd say he looks ready to knock you down," Rafe interjected, putting his arm around Justin's shoulders. "You said you wanted to speak to me privately? My study is at the end of the hall. Tanner—good to see you."

"What was that all about?" Lydia asked as she gathered up her reticule and the rest while Sarah stood by the door, ready to accompany them. "Why would Rafe say you want to knock Justin down?"

"He's invited you to call him Justin?"

"Yes, right after I suggested he call me Lydia. It seemed simpler, as we're all going to be together for more than a week, in an informal setting. Tanner? What's wrong?"

He shook his head. "Nothing." He took his hat and gloves from the footman and slipped a small coin in the boy's hand. He always did that, and the footmen vied to be of assistance to him each time he visited. "No, that's not true. Lydia, Justin is a good man. I'm glad you two have cried friends. Really."

"But?" Lydia nudged as they passed through the doorway and down onto the flagway.

"But it might be unwise to take anything he says with more than a grain of salt."

"Oh, *that,*" she said, still pulling on her gloves. "I already knew *that.*" She looked toward the Square and saw that Tanner had driven his curricle this morning. She turned to her maid. "Unless you wish to hang on the back like a tiger, I think we can safely dispense with your company this morning, Sarah."

"Yes, mi'lady," Sarah said, bobbing a curtsy. "I'll get back to packin' up your duds, then."

"Do you have many *duds?*" Tanner asked as he helped her up onto the plank seat. "I'd planned on only the one extra coach for luggage and servants."

Lydia waited until he'd walked around the back of the curricle—surreptitiously watching from beneath the brim of her bonnet, to see if she could ascertain any *spring* in his step. Alas, she didn't. Or perhaps this was a good thing. Justin had clearly upset him in some way, and she was fairly certain that she figured into that discomfort somehow. It was really rather delicious, all this attention from two handsome, likeable men. She must be careful, or it all would go to her head, make her silly.

Although she was rarely silly, so that the idea of simply allowing the Fates to carry her along held more appeal than she would have thought a week ago, even a year go. Ever.

"You won't have to go to the bother of another coach. I'll be sending most of my things straight to Ashurst Hall with Rafe and Charlotte. Unless you travel with all of your belongings?"

"Not me, but I have a feeling Justin will bring more than his share. As I remember it, he includes his own linens, much of his own food, and at least three changes of clothes per day. Very impressive, if you're not the one responsible for toting his trunks."

"So you're saying he's a fop?"

"Hardly. If he meant any of it, then he'd be a fop. But as Justin himself says, he dresses only for effect. He does, says, very many things in order to see how others will react. It amuses him."

"I've noticed that, too. But he's your friend. You like him."

"I like him very much. And I shouldn't have said anything. It was unfair of me. You're perfectly capable of making your own decisions."

"I agree," Lydia said, nodding her head, while inwardly wishing Tanner would just say what was on his mind, because she was hoping what was on his mind was what was on her mind, and if he said what was on his mind, and she said what was on her mind—no, that wouldn't work; clearly *her* mind was currently too muddled. "But thank you. You're a good friend, to warn me about your own good friend."

"Yes. A good friend," he said running his gaze over her face, his eyes rather bleak suddenly, although he quickly smiled. "Something to aspire to, I suppose." He then unwrapped the reins from the brake and looked at her once more. "The horses are still fresh, so I'd like to take them around the Square a time or two, until they've settled. Ready?"

She held onto the metal ring at the side of the plank seat, that fleeting look in Tanner's eyes enough to tell her she was in danger of losing her balance, although not because of the horses. "Ready," she said, and they were off.

CHAPTER EIGHT

TANNER KNEW HE'D MADE an ass of himself, but he was still uncertain as to just why he'd been so eager to throw his friend Justin to the wolves, as it were.

He could tell himself that he was only protecting Lydia, console himself knowing that Justin was a tease and a flirt, and breaking feminine hearts was a bit of an avocation for the man.

He could tell himself that, but he didn't believe it. Justin wouldn't amuse himself with the sister of a friend, the friend of a friend.

So why the warning?

Was he that unsure of himself where Lydia was concerned?

Well, of course he was. Only any idiot would think he could crook his finger at a woman and have her come running. although, now that he was a duke, he had been fairly well besieged with invitations from hopeful mamas and avaricious papas. That had been the only good thing about Society believing he would wed Jasmine. It gave him time to be with Lydia without her name being bandied about Mayfair, which he instinctively knew Lydia would have loathed.

But now there was Justin. He'd been happily chased by females since he was in short coats, none of them caring that he was wild, and fickle, and certain to break their hearts.

In fact, that may have been his main attraction for them. At least the sorts of females Justin seemed to favor. Tanner couldn't remember the man ever making a serious push at a woman like Lydia. He shied away from intelligent females the way a long-tailed cat stays clear of a rocking chair.

Maybe the man *was* smitten. Perhaps one melting smile, one quick, smart riposte about Molière—Molière, for God's sake!—had been enough to turn Justin away from his long-held disdain for anyone in petticoats... unless, of course, they were beautiful, dim-witted, and...and, well, *pliable*.

Tanner felt the muscles in his jaw tightening. Lydia wasn't pliable. Lydia was a lady. And if Justin didn't remember that on his own during their time at Malvern, Tanner would be more than happy to remind him, even if that meant knocking his good friend down. Repeatedly.

"How is your cheek today?"

Tanner turned to Lydia, only then realizing that he'd been quiet since they'd driven out of Grosvenor Square, perhaps even sulking, and wasn't that a marvelous way to impress her? She was sitting very primly beside him, her gloved hands folded in her lap, as if she had been content to wait until he was ready to speak with her. And how did she know he had needed a few minutes of quiet thought and reflection? But that was Lydia. She seemed to sense things. Did she know him that well, or was he simply that easy to read?

No, he couldn't be, or else she'd know how much he longed to take her to his bed, wake her from her dreaming, release the fire he felt sure burned deep inside her.

He hastened into speech.

"Much better, thank you. I only consented to the bandages so that I wouldn't frightened small children we might pass along the way."

"Then it is not merely a scratch, as you tried to tell me."

"No, it's not. However, the surgeon my butler summoned against my wishes has assured me that there should be no permanent damage beyond a scar that will fade with time. I should probably be grateful for it, as it will serve as a constant reminder to never believe myself superior to anyone, even a drunken fool who could barely remain upright on his own. It was an act of arrogance to turn my back on any angry man, no matter how incapacitated he might be, and a mistake I won't make again."

"That would probably be wise. You've been injured before. I remember the condition of your uniform when you came directly from the battlefield to tell us about the captain. There was dried blood on your torn pants leg, and you were limping."

She was bringing up that day, the events of that day, on her own? She was right, though. He'd left the battlefield as soon as he'd gained permission from Wellington himself, and ridden back to Brussels, then to the coast, to be one of the first to arrive back in England. He'd looked like seven kinds of hell by the time he arrived, but he had to be certain Fitz's name wouldn't appear listed among the casualties before he could tell Rafe and Lydia the news. That had been a part of the promises he made to Fitz.

Now he hid his surprise at Lydia's words by launching into a quick story about his wound.

"A near thing with a French infantryman's bayonet, yes, as we broke their forces and rode through the ranks. But only a slice. My mount took the worst of the thrust, unfortunately, and went down. That put me in the thick of things. I was lucky that Boney took that moment to leave the field, make good his escape back to Paris. Once that word got shouted about, his men laid down their swords and the day was ours. It had already been ours, we all knew that, but soldiers fight until they're told to stop. Or until their generals turn their backs."

"You don't see Bonaparte as a good general?"

Ah, now they were on to a broader conversation. Good. He wasn't sure he was up to another competition with Fitz at the moment. Once they were at Malvern, certainly. But he'd rather they were someplace quiet when she finally asked him how Fitz had died.

"On the contrary. He was, is, a brilliant tactician. But he truly believed he could come back from exile, return to France and rule the country in peace, rebuild it, preserve it for his son. That was his argument, at least, that as the emperor he no longer harbored any ambitions to conquer, but only a desire to serve the French people."

"Then why didn't he do that? Why did he fight?"

"Because *we* didn't believe him. What else could he do once we'd made our own intentions clear? I'm convinced the heart went out of him when his wife agreed to allow the Alliance to brand him an outlaw, an enemy of nations. It was the final betrayal, taking their son, his heir, and returning to her father's protection. As for the rest? The bravado, the march to Brussels? I'll always believe that he was a man going through the motions, Lydia, doing what was expected of him. All of Europe, along with us, had turned against him. He couldn't prevail, and he had to know that. But he was at heart a soldier, so he fought. One last decisive battle, perhaps even a miraculous victory, or at least a glorious death."

Twin flags of color burned in Lydia's cheeks. Clearly, what he'd said had angered her. "And all for nothing. There's nothing glorious about death, not his, not any of the soldiers on both sides of the battle who died for his supposed *glory*."

Tanner wove the curricle through the traffic and turned onto Regent Street, now completely convinced he knew what was happening. Once again, Fitz's ghost was sitting between them on the plank seat. Even when he and Lydia were alone, they were never alone.

He pulled up the horses as he noticed that traffic ahead of him had come to a stop. "Bonaparte had to be defeated, Lydia. We have to believe that those who died sacrificed their lives for a reason. For a greater good. To put an end to war."

She worked the fingers of her gloves more closely over her hands. "Do you think Caesar's legions thought that as they marched out to die? And what about those of Genghis Khan, Alexander, Hannibal? Aren't all wars touted as being the *last* war, the one that will ensure everlasting peace? Didn't all of these *great* leaders believe they were the one with all the solutions?"

"I'm sure they did, yes. Lydia? Has something happened? Are you all right?"

"Oh, I'm sorry. I'm fine." Then she sighed. "No, actually I'm not. I've been thinking quite a lot lately about the battle last June. Nearly a year, Tanner. Nearly a year, and I'm still trying to make some sense of all of it in my mind. Find some reason for everything that happened. Not just to the captain, but to everyone. To everyone involved in the war."

"Everyone?" Was this conversation about Fitz, or about herself? Suddenly Tanner wasn't sure.

"Yes. The soldiers, that's for certain. But also those who were left behind to try to somehow comprehend why all those deaths were so…so bloody necessary."

Bloody necessary? Well, he'd wanted to see her fire, hadn't he?

An overturned cart up ahead kept them where they were, and he put on the foot brake, took advantage of not having to watch the roadway. Ignoring the loud apologies from the drayman and the curses emanating from the various carriages and a few passersby who were shouting just for the tickle of the thing—none of which Lydia seemed to have noticed—Tanner put a hand on hers, squeezed it, and pointed out the obvious. "You're angry, aren't you?"

"Is that so wrong? Oh, I don't know what I'm saying, or even why I'm saying it. I only opened my mouth just now and heard myself blurting out the words. I'm so sorry."

Tears dampened her lashes and she tried to blink them away. Those unshed tears were a figurative punch to Tanner's gut. She was suffering, struggling with some deep dilemma, and clearly had been doing so for a long time. Worse, unless she told him more, he didn't know how to help her.

"Don't apologize, Lydia. You lost Fitz in that battle. You have every right to question the reason." Tanner sensed that she was finally going to confide in him, and he'd be damned if he'd miss this moment, no matter that they were far from private and he couldn't take her in his arms, comfort her. He didn't know what he'd said that had seemed to have inspired these sudden confidences from her. If she stopped now, how long before she'd dare to broach the subject again? He couldn't risk it. If she was suffering, then he was suffering, too. Did she understand that? Couldn't she see that? God, probably not. And why should she? He was just Tanner, the comfortable family friend.

He framed his question carefully: "Perhaps, if you're willing, I can help?"

She looked up from her meticulous smoothing of her

gloves, her eyes still shining with unshed tears that threatened to spill down her cheeks. "Yes, perhaps you can, for I've had precious little success on my own. You see, I can understand one man believing himself specially chosen for great things. I cannot understand so many others willingly putting their lives in his hands, dying for his dreams. Women don't do that Tanner. Women take care of their own, defend their own. It's only men who will leave their wives, their children, to ride out and die for somebody else's vision of what is right. Why is that? Why do you men do it, again and again and again?"

What a strange and intense conversation. Had Lydia been trying to reconcile Fitz's death with what she saw as a foolish sacrifice? He said what he assumed to be obvious. "We had no choice, Lydia. Bonaparte had—"

"Yes, I know that," she said quickly, and with some heat, at last giving up all pretense and openly wiping at her damp cheeks. "And if it hadn't been him it would have been somebody else. Just like Caesar, Alexander, and all the rest. I just don't understand *why*. What if nobody answered the call to battle? What if Caesar had called out for soldiers, and no one had taken up a sword? What if Bonaparte had declared he wanted to capture the world for France, and no man had said, yes, that sounds like a grand idea, let us help you?"

She took in a breath, sighed. "I think I've decided it's because you like it," she said, searching his face with her lovely blue eyes. "All the trappings, all the pageantry and boasting. The fine uniforms, the swords and the cannon and…and maybe even the killing. I think you all *like* it."

And you'd probably be right, Lydia. We just don't expect to die.

Tanner didn't say the words, knowing she wouldn't understand such insane reasoning. Men did like war. Some even lived for war. For victory, for power, while always hungry for another victory, more power. Men like Bonaparte, Caesar, the others she'd mentioned—they all had one thing in common. They were insatiable. And that would probably never change. Bonaparte was caged now, but somewhere out there was another man just like him, with the same ambitions. And if there weren't now, there would be. Even if mankind had to invent him, and then eventually raise up an army to defeat him.

"We fight for our country, Lydia. For our women, our children, our futures. That's why Fitz fought. England, and that means every man, woman and child in the country, was threatened by Bonaparte's ambitions. I can't speak for why so many Frenchmen took up his cause, but I know why England couldn't allow the man to invade these islands. Fitz died believing he was protecting *you*. Don't take that away from him. He was a good soldier, fighting for a good cause, in a war not of his making. Don't let him have died for nothing."

Lydia put a hand to her mouth, stifled a small sob. "Please, forgive me. I've been so…so *obtuse*. I saw only my own pain. Of course the captain didn't sacrifice his life for nothing. I…I was so angry with him when he left for Brussels, and perhaps ever since. That wasn't fair of me, was it?"

"It was reasonable," Tanner told her. "Did he know you were angry with him?"

She shook her head. "Nobody did, until now. I should have spoken with you sooner. Instead, I've been so ashamed of how I felt. I think…I think that's why it's been so hard to…to let him go. I've been too appalled with myself at having been angry with him. Thank you, Tanner."

He didn't respond with "You're welcome," because that would be ridiculous. Instead, he asked a question he'd wondered about for a long time. "You don't call him Fitz. Why?"

Lydia frowned for a moment. "I sometimes think of him as Fitz. But…but he's always been the captain. I was always Lady Lydia. When I look back on those few months now, I realize we were…dancing around each other. Neither of us daring to say what was in our hearts. But there was time for all of that. There was supposed to have been time for all of that. I believe he felt I needed some time to…to grow up. But I think we both knew what would happen when he returned home."

A small smile played around her lips. "Once, in a letter, his very last letter, he called me his dearest Lyddie. You brought that letter to me, remember?"

Tanner remembered. He'd never forget.

Take care of her for me, Tanner. She's so young, so gentle and pure. She won't understand. Promise me! On your mother's eyes, damn it. You'll take care of my

Lyddie. Make her forget me. She needs a good man, a gentleman and a gentle man. You've a good heart, and she needs someone with a good heart. Promise me, Tanner. Don't let me die without your promise.

You're not going to die, you Irish bastard. You'll go home to your Lyddie yourself. Let me talk to the surgeon. I'll find a litter and some men and we'll carry you back to town and—

Don't try to lie to me. I don't have time for lies. I'm sorry, boyo, more sorry than you can know, but my journey ends here. Mine, not hers. Listen to me. She's easy to love, I promise you that. Give her smiles, Tanner, give her little ones to cuddle. Take my hand, Tanner, and look me in the eye. Yes, like that. I have your hand on it now. I'm giving her to you. I'm placing her in your keeping. My Lyddie…

Tanner wanted to tell her everything. He wanted to tell her all that he'd promised the dying, increasingly frantic Fitz in order to help ease his passing. Mostly, he wanted to tell her that he'd never considered that promise a burden. Never. From the instant he'd seen her that terrible day, from the moment he'd held her in his arms, uselessly trying to comfort her in her bone deep anguish, he'd known. He hadn't wanted to let her go that day…he didn't want to let go of her now.

But now wasn't the time. Regent Street certainly wasn't the place. And Malvern would be cluttered with Jasmine and her father and…his competition. The competition he'd talked about so casually with Rafe. If he'd known that competition would have come in the form of Justin Wilde, would he have been so sanguine, so sure of himself? No, definitely not.

But only by letting her go, letting her move forward at her own pace, experience more of the world, could he hope to win her love. Him. Not Fitz's friend. Not Rafe's friend. *Him*.

"Tanner? I've disappointed you, haven't I?

He looked at her in some shock, realizing that once again he'd been silent too long. The cart was finally pushed back up on its wheels, and he released the brake, made ready to move on down Regent Street. "You could never disappoint me, Lydia," he said with all sincerity.

"Yes, that's very nice, and exactly what you would say. But I've just revealed myself to be shallow and selfish."

"It's selfish to wish Fitz hadn't died? It's shallow to wish there was no such thing as war?"

At last, she smiled, if that smile only appeared for a moment. "You make it all sound so reasonable. Perhaps I've been thinking too much. Nicole always says I think too much."

"No, your sister's wrong. The problem, as I see it, lies in that you were searching for logic where none exists. The only answer to the question of why there are wars, Lydia, is that there have always been wars. It's not a logical answer. It isn't even a good answer. But, sadly, until and unless someone finally finds a way to settle matters of ambition and greed without sending vast armies into the field, it's the only one we have. Fitz understood that. He knew what he was doing, and why, when he left you and went to Brussels."

"Forgive him, and also forgive myself. That's what you're saying, isn't it?"

"I don't see any other answer, do you?"

She was silent for some moments, while Tanner held his breath. A lot was riding on her answer, and he felt they both knew it. Their future, for one thing, if they were to have one, together.

Finally, she shook her head. "He's gone, and I can't change that. But I can do much better now in honoring his memory, without also being angry with him for having died. He was right, Tanner, I was still very much a child when he left me. Now, at last, I think I can forgive myself." She laid her hand on his forearm. "Thank you, Tanner. Thank you so much."

There really was nothing more to say, not without beginning the uncomfortable conversation all over again, a rehashing neither of them could possibly want. Tanner lifted her hand to his mouth and kissed the tips of her gloved fingers. "And now you're ready to see this shop with me?"

"Of course," she said, closing her hand when he released it, almost as if she wanted to capture his kiss, hold it. Or at least he'd like to think so, which probably made him fanciful.

Then she frowned as she looked where he had indicated with a sweep of his arm, and then continued her gaze until she'd visually inspected the area from curb to curb. "Where are we? I've been to Bond Street enough to know we're not there. I haven't been paying attention, have I?"

Tanner set the brake and lightly hopped down onto the flagway, a young lad of no more than ten already running toward him with his hand outstretched, eager to trade a coin for watching the horses.

He then helped Lydia down from the seat, perhaps holding on to her waist a heartbeat too long as he looked into her eyes, hoping the shadows were at last gone. His fancifulness continued, because he thought perhaps their lovely blue was a little brighter now than it had been. Justin could probably put the light of amusement in her eyes, with his wit and shameless flirting. But could he give her what she really needed? Gentleness. Understanding.

God, but he was like a comfortable old pair of hacking trousers, a warm pair of slippers. Could he be more pitiful, more pathetic? Less romantic…

"We're on Regent Street," he told her rather flatly as he tucked her arm through his and led her a few paces down the flagway. "Number 187, on the block between Conduit and Burlington, to be more precise about the thing."

"I don't think you need be that specific, no. It's enough that you know the way back to Grosvenor Square. Why are we here?"

Tanner stopped in front of a narrow shop bearing a hanging sign sporting a woodcut of a lady's boot. Also on the sign were the words *JAMs. SLY. Laydies Boot & Shoe Maker. Est. 1808.*

It had seemed such a good idea when he'd first thought of it, but now he wasn't as certain. Justin would have taken her to some fancy milliner's, coaxed her into a ridiculously flattering bonnet with bunches of flowers on it.

He was going to buy her a good, sturdy pair of boots.

Pitiful. Just pitiful…

"Not quite bootmaker to the Queen, but he does come highly recommended for his particular talents."

"But…but we'll be leaving London tomorrow," Lydia protested. "Why would I order new shoes today? They couldn't possibly be ready in less than a week."

He steered her inside the shop, a bell hanging just over the door merrily ringing as they entered. "Ah, but Mr. Sly considers himself a merchant of innovation. I'm told he maintains a rather extensive inventory in addition to fashioning footwear to order. I'm hoping we might be able to find you a suitable pair of boots."

"Boots?"

He smiled down at her as a gangly youth straightened from behind a stack of boxes and hastened toward them. The entire shop smelled of fine leather and polish. "Yes. Boots. And they're to be my gift to you. Now, aren't you going to ask me why I wish to make you a present of a pair of boots?"

Lydia was looking avidly about the strange shop. A workman's shop, really, with shelves reaching to the ceiling, each of them lined with row upon row of ladies shoes and boots. "I thought I already had. When I said *boots?* And is it proper for a gentleman to gift a lady with a pair of boots? I'm afraid I am not familiar with the boundaries set up by polite society."

He took hold of her hands. "Polite society never went tramping over the Malvern Hills. I want to show you my home, Lydia, all of it. When I was young, I believed I could see the entire world from the hilltops I hiked, my dogs at my side. Cook would pack me a lunch and I'd be gone for hours. I don't expect you to want to climb all the way to the top of any of the hills, but there are some interesting paths and ancient ruins here and there."

"It all sounds lovely. And who is to say I wouldn't decide to climb all the way to the top of one of the hills? I might like to see the entire world."

And he'd like to give her the world. But he didn't say that. He didn't say a lot of things he wanted to say. But he would. Soon.

"Mister Sly will be with you directly, milord," the young lad said after patiently waiting for an opening. "He's just now finishing up the last stitches on a pair of wedding boots for a young lady. Tapping on the heels, he is, red ones. They're a sight, they are. Would you be her, miss?"

"No, I wouldn't be her," Lydia said quietly, and then pointed to a pair of tan boots displayed on the counter-top. "But I would very much like to look at those, if I might? I may be climbing mountains, you understand."

A deep, booming voice came to them from the back of the shop. "A fine choice. Turnshoe construction, every bit of it, except for the heels. Three-four lifts in those," came a voice from the back of the shop. "Best heavy French silk, stiffened, and all lined with softest linen for milady. But the soles are sturdy, which is the point of the thing, what?"

Tanner watched as a rotund man with bright red cheeks and puffs of white hair perched on top of his ears but nowhere else on his shiny dome of a head pushed his way through parted curtains and into the crowded shop. "Yes, yes, finest leather soles and heels, and with thirteen pairs of lace-edged holes, for fashion, you know. And all done up with a single cord laced up from the bottom and then back down again so the bow can be seen peeking out from under the hem of milady's skirt. Practical doesn't mean there's no need for pretty, what? Some of my best work, if I do say so m'self. Made up two dozen pair, knowing they'd fly out the door. All the world will soon be doing what I do. But I'm doing it first, and better than anyone else. Robert, don't just stand there, boy. Fetch me my forms."

In short order, Lydia was seated in a chair elevated from the floor on a box of sorts, and James Sly was looking down at her feet and urging her to lift her hem, "Just enough to stay decent, if you take m'meaning," and Tanner was deciding whether the glint in the jolly man's eyes belonged to his love of his boots or a taste for ladies' ankles.

He decided it was the ankles.

The boot maker sat himself down on the low stool his apprentice had placed in front of Lydia, his knees spread as he shifted the stool closer to her, and grinned at her. "If you'd just slip off your right—ah, yes, that's the ticket. Robert, come here. Now, look at that foot, will you? Long, slender. See the height in the arch? There's beauty for you, shows the lady here is no slouch. Like to walk, do you, miss?"

"Yes, um, I enjoy walking. I've been walking nearly all of my life." She looked up at Tanner, and shrugged as if to say, "What else would I do—flap my arms and fly?"

Mr. Sly—and Tanner was beginning to think the man's name fit him very well—cupped his hand beneath Lydia's stockinged foot and lifted—lifted!—her leg a good two feet off the platform. She quickly put her hands on her gown, trying to keep her leg covered.

"Here, now—" Tanner protested, but Mr. Sly paid him no mind as he turned Lydia's foot this way and that as if examining it for flaws.

"Now, Robert, I'm going to have your opinion, if you please. Which form would you first think a match? Come on, quickly, lad. The six? Or the seven?"

"Um…er…" the apprentice glanced at Lydia's foot and quickly looked away. "The seven?"

"Ha! Thought you had half a chance of being right, did you? As if I'd make it that easy for you. The five, Robert. I'd wager your supper on that." He shifted his hand so that now he was cupping Lydia's heel and she had managed to all but wrap her hands around her leg, pulling her skirts close in an attempt at modesty.

"The Number Five, sir," Robert said, handing the man a wooden form of a foot—rather well carved, actually. Dear God, the man had actually carved a set of toes onto the form. Was that dedication, or a fetish?

The boot maker positioned the form alongside Lydia's foot. The two matched in length. "Do I have an eye, Robert? Yes, I do. You've a pretty foot, miss, I'll say it again. Classic."

Tanner restrained himself from kicking the fellow off his stool, but it was a near-run thing.

Fortunately, Mr. Sly didn't seem to trust his apprentice enough to have him bring the correct boots from the shelves. "You may put your foot down now, miss," he told Lydia, and then hauled himself to his feet and hustled to the shelves lining the right wall.

"Enthusiastic, isn't he?" she said, smoothing her skirts as she neatly hid her stockinged foot beneath the hem.

"This may have been a bad idea on my part," Tanner said quietly. "Would you rather we left?"

"I'd say yes, except that I do want to go tramping your Malvern Hills…and the boots really are quite lovely. Imagine, Tanner, the man has found a way to measure feet beforehand and make shoes to fit them. How many sizes are there to feet, do you think?"

"An even dozen, miss," Robert whispered, one eye on his master. "Mr. Sly, he worked it all out. Five is not all so common. Most of the ladies fall in the higher numbers. We tell them the higher numbers are better, but they're really just bigger. When I open m'own shop, I think I'll use names of flowers or some such, and no numbers."

"Yes, I can see the point of that," Lydia said, winking up at Tanner. "Dear lady, you are a day lily, how exemplary." Then her smile faded as Mr. Sly returned carrying a pair of boots, ready to take up his seat in front of her once more. She all but slammed her hands down on her skirts.

But Mr. Sly wasn't going to get the chance to touch her again. "I'll assist the lady," Tanner said, neatly snatching the boots from the man's hands and sitting himself down on the low stool. Interestingly, that put his head at knee-height with Lydia. In this position, unless he was careful in lifting her leg, there was a high likelihood of seeing parts of her he shouldn't see. No wonder Mr. Sly seemed such a jolly sort.

"Tanner, you don't have to—"

"If milady would kindly raise her foot?" Tanner said, wondering what fool would think stringing laces top to bottom rather than bottom to top would be anything but a bloody nuisance. No wonder if took females so long to dress.

She slowly lifted her leg and Tanner moved the stool forward, gently taking hold of her ankle and resting her heel on his thigh as he continued to labor over loosening the laces.

"Here, now, you're doing it all wrong," Mr. Sly said, reaching for the boot, but Tanner neatly avoided his hand.

"We know you're busy with your bride boots, Sly. Robert here will assist us. You may go."

"I may go, is it? And who do you'd think you'd be, telling me what to do in m'own shop?"

"He's the Duke of Malvern, Mr. Sly," Lydia told him sweetly. "I'm certain that when His Grace tells all of his acquaintance of your magnificent shop you will need hire several more able apprentices like Robert."

"That took him off," Robert all but crowed when the bootmaker bowed several times before hurrying back behind his curtain. "A real slyboots he is, if you take my meaning, Your Grace. He would have dropped the boot and bent down low to fetch it, all the while trying to see where he shouldn't ought see, my apologies to your lady. Does it all the time, with the pretty ones. A good Quaker, I am, only apprenticed here because m'father got himself lost in debt. I hold no truck with Mr. Sly's slyboots ways."

"Yes, thank you, Robert," Tanner said, watching as Lydia blushed. "You can get back to your duties. I have all in hand here."

And, to prove his words, he slid his hand further beneath Lydia's skirts and cupped her calf in order to hold her steady as he prepared to slide the boot over her toes.

"Tanner?"

"Forgive me," he said, his fingers feeling on fire as he felt the silk of her stocking, the sleek firmness of her calf. His imagination was beginning to run rampant. "But it's me or Mr. Slyboots."

"Nicole would say that I should be happy to have men at my feet," Lydia said, her voice rather breathless. "But I don't think she ever envisioned anything like this. Shall I push?"

It took Tanner a moment to understand what she meant. "Uh, no, I can manage it. It's these damned upside-down laces."

"Oh, but only think, Tanner. How could I bear to not have Mr. Sly's cunning little bows visible beneath the hem of my gown? Here, let me help."

She pointed her toes—she did have a wonderfully high arch; an eminently kissable arch. Nearly as kissable as her slim ankle, the curve of her calf that he could feel, longed to see.

He should let Robert take over. The boy could be no more than fifteen, and a Quaker into the bargain. Quakers probably didn't harbor licentious thoughts. Or if they did, they didn't act on them.

Tightening his grip on Lydia's calf, Tanner managed to slide the boot up and over her foot, and then rested her heel on his thigh once more, her knee bent as he used both hands to pull the boot fully up and on.

He controlled his breathing with some effort, or else Lydia might think he was breathless from exertion, rather than the truth, which was that he was manfully struggling to divorce himself from the knowledge that one feigned slip of a hand would have that hand at knee-height. Inches above that would be Lydia's garter, and then beyond that…beyond that lay madness.

With the boot fully on, Lydia leaned forward to see how it looked on her foot. Which put her head a scant foot from Tanner's. Tanner, who still had both hands a good five inches beneath her skirts, and with his gaze now exactly at bosom level.

He'd never been in danger of forgetting that Lydia had breasts. Then again, he'd never remembered her gowns revealing so much of them. When they were married, he'd insist on serving as her ladies' maid whenever she wished to wear boots. He wouldn't mind having her wear these particular boots, as a matter of fact, and the devil with her clothing entirely.

The thought of those fine leather heels digging into his bare back had him shifting rather uncomfortably on the stool. Her heel slipped as he moved and he instinctively grabbed at her leg, his hands sliding upward on the sleek silk stockings. The sole of her boot was now mere inches from his crotch, his betraying bulge.

"Oh…" Lydia said, looking down at her skirts as if she could see his hands beneath the sprigged muslin and petticoats. And then she looked at him, and he couldn't glance away, pretend what had just happened hadn't happened.

She was looking at him strangely. But not in panic. Not in loathing. He saw an unspoken question in her eyes. And he didn't know the answer.

But he hoped he did.

"You feel like nothing else in the world," Tanner heard himself saying quietly. He shifted his right hand higher, until his fingertips encountered her lace-edged garter. With her knee bent, he knew that her thighs had to be slightly parted. Her soft inner thigh was only a whisper away. He thought he might explode.

Lydia wet her lips with the tip of her tongue, an act born of nervousness, he was sure, but no less powerful for all of that.

They were only a few steps off Regent Street, with a slyboots no more than twenty feet away and a young

Quaker soon to be corrupted unless Tanner got a grip on himself.

"Forgive me," he said, withdrawing his hands and allowing her to lower her leg. "I shouldn't have…"

"No, no, it was my fault. My foot slipped. I…I think the boot fits very well," she told him as he floundered to apologize without saying *what* he was apologizing for, which would have only made things worse.

They were both very quiet on the way back to Grosvenor Square. Two people with so much on their minds, and so little that could be said. But a step had been taken. They both knew it.

Only, where would that step lead?

CHAPTER NINE

"TANNER BOUGHT YOU a pair of *boots?* What an odd gift," Charlotte said as she settled herself into a chair in Lydia's bedchamber. "And they were already made, and fit your foot? Let me see."

Lydia reluctantly cut the string on the package with her embroidery scissors and pulled out the boots. It was silly, but she had wanted to…to be alone with the boots. Relive those moments in Regent Street. Read less into what had happened. Or more. "They're for tramping the Malvern Hills. He's going to show me the entire world from the top of one of them."

"Oh, he is, is he?" Charlotte said, very nearly crooned. "Imagine that." She took hold of one of the boots and turned it about in her hand. "How strange. The laces are threaded upside-down."

And that's how Lydia felt. Upside-down. But she didn't say that, not even to Charlotte, who would probably understand. Instead, she told her all about Mr. Sly and his shop, prattling on nervously until she decided she sounded like Jasmine Harburton yet again, upon which she snapped her mouth shut.

Charlotte handed back the boot. "No, Sarah, not that one," she said as the maid began folding Lydia's grey morning gown, one she had worn these past three years, not for its style, but for its comfort. "I think we've seen enough of that gown."

"But it's one of my favorites," Lydia protested.

"Yes, I'm sure it is, and it will be fine for the country. If you wish to do some gardening, or decide on a visit to the hen house."

Sarah had placed the gown in the large trunk heading straight to Ashurst Hall and now Lydia plucked it out again, replacing it in her traveling trunk. "It will be perfect, then, for tramping across hilltops."

Charlotte motioned for Sarah to take it out once more. "Not even for that. Is there no romance in your soul, my dear? The man wishes to take you up in the hills near his home, show you his world. Alone, just the two of you. He's even surprised me by attempting to dress you for the part, which I find, if not exactly romantic, at least very thoughtful of him. Do you honestly suppose he's simply dying to show you all the flora and fauna? I know you've rarely been out of the country, Lydia, but nobody is *that* sheltered."

Sarah giggled.

"No," Charlotte went on, casting the maid a quelling look, "that gown will not do for Malvern, not for any moment of your time there. After all, it would appear that Tanner is not your only suitor. What if one of the gentlemen were to propose marriage to you and you were wearing that tired old gown? Think how embarrassed you'd be."

Lydia, who was once again in the process of stubbornly removing the gown from the larger trunk, whirled on her sister-in-law. "Nobody is going to propose marriage to me. It's a simple country house party until Tanner's cheek heals and the baron is less of a sensation."

"Are you certain of that?"

"Of course I'm certain of that," Lydia said, ignoring the rather disconcerting acceleration of her heartbeat. "If anything, Tanner will be proposing to Jasmine."

"Really?" Charlotte said, raising one eyebrow. "Then what do you think would explain Tanner's request to speak privately with Rafe in his study once you had returned from your excursion to the shops?"

"He did *what?*" The gown dropped from Lydia's suddenly nerveless fingertips. Sarah quickly snatched it up, rolled it into a ball, and kicked it out of sight beneath the bed skirts.

"Why, sweetheart, you've gone rather pale," Charlotte commented, showing a side of herself Lydia had never seen before, and wasn't sure she liked very much, thank you. "You didn't know Tanner asked to speak with Rafe? Very much the way, as it happens, the baron asked to speak privately with him a few hours ago. Rafe has been very busy today. You, I believe, will have the same problem at some point in the next week. Being very busy, I mean."

Sarah giggled, belatedly slapped a hand to her mouth, and scurried out of the bedchamber.

Lydia walked over to her dressing table and sat down, which was better than the alternative: falling down. "Justin is only teasing. He as good as said so. Speaking to Rafe was only a part of the joke. Not a very funny one, I admit."

Charlotte shook her head, sighing. "Is it so impossible, sweetheart, for you to think of yourself as attractive, in both your mind and your appearance? The sort of woman a man would see, be instantly captivated by, so much so that he feels the need to pave the way through Rafe's blessing before very seriously courting you while you're at Malvern?"

"Justin doesn't like women."

"Really? And yet I have it on rather high authority that he likes women very much. And very often, too, at least from the way Rafe explained the thing to me. Are you saying he prefers—"

"I am not!" Lydia exclaimed, feeling her cheeks go hot. "I meant he likes women…but he doesn't *like* women. Oh, I don't know what I'm saying. No, that's not true. I'm saying that Justin was only teasing me. He thinks he's amusing."

"And he isn't?"

Lydia wanted this conversation over. At least the part about the baron; she might wish to hear more about Tanner's visit with Rafe. "He's very amusing. The problem is…" she hesitated, thought for a moment, and then said, "the problem is that he knows it. I think he enjoys himself very much, sometimes at the expense of others. So perhaps I was wrong. He doesn't just not like women. He doesn't like many men, either. Most of all himself."

Charlotte looked at her with curiosity evident in her eyes. "I can see you've given the baron a lot of thought. Are you planning to rescue him from himself by any chance? It would be so like you, unfortunately."

Lydia was surprised by this statement. "Are you calling me meddlesome?"

"Good Lord, no. I'm saying that you enjoy rescuing people from their own folly. You've spent a majority of your life rescuing Nicole from her mad starts and follies. There are times I have pictured you as a sort of broom, chasing behind people and sweeping up after them. Your sister is grown now, wiser now. And besides, she's no longer your concern. Lucas is delighted with her, mad starts and all. Don't you think it's time you put down that broom and thought more about your own life? Perhaps even consider a few mad starts and adventures of your own?"

Lydia glanced toward the boots. "I wouldn't know how."

Charlotte got to her feet and walked over to kiss Lydia's cheek. "We all know how, sweetheart. We were born knowing. It's only necessary to take off the locks and bars of what we *think* we're supposed to be and let it all out. After all, we're women, and eminently smarter than men—although we're also smart enough to keep that our little secret. Sometimes, *honorable* as gentlemen feel themselves required to be, it takes a…a bit of a *nudge* from the woman who knows what's best for him. And for her, of course."

"Are you saying—?"

"Me? A woman soon to be a mother?" Charlotte put up her hands in mock horror, and then smiled with all the mischief of a young girl. "I'm not saying anything at all. But think about what I didn't say, Lydia. Think about *letting go,* just a little." She patted her sister-in-law's cheek. "It may be time for the real Lydia, the Lydia who has been so safe and circumspect enough for her twin and herself combined to come out and play."

Once Charlotte had gone, Lydia took up the boots and walked over to the window with them clutched to her bosom. She looked out over Grosvenor Square, and could almost see Lucas Paine's traveling coach driving out of the Square, Nicole waving to her from the window, blowing kisses; full of life, eager for another adventure, this time with the man she loved.

"How does it feel?" she asked the empty Square below her. "What is it like to just *feel*? To simply let go and allow events to take you where you have never been, to a place where it doesn't matter what anyone else thinks or says, but only how you *feel*?"

You feel like nothing else in the world.

Tanner's touch, and her reaction to it, had felt like nothing else in the world. The shop had faded, all of the world had disappeared in those moments as she looked into his eyes, as his fingers seared her skin through the silk of her stocking. She'd gone warm all over, a melting sensation coursing through her entire body, so that she'd wanted nothing more than to close her eyes and simply *feel*.

Was that it? Was that what she was missing in her so-circumspect life? A man's touch? Not the dream, as her brief time with the captain had been, all longing looks and silent sighs. The captain had been her childhood love, her comfortable harbor so that she could continue to believe herself safe, secure.

She felt much less than secure when she looked at Tanner, when he looked at her. She felt off-balance, unsure, and yet terribly excited. She couldn't envision their future, if it would be happy or sad. There were no guarantees; she'd learned that much when Fitz had died.

For nearly a year she'd hidden in her cocoon, berating herself for not confessing her love for the captain while he was still with her, while at the same time half blaming him for her devastating grief. To love again could mean pain, heartbreak, loss. But to simply not *try?* Was that living?

You feel like nothing else in the world.

Her carefully constructed cocoon was no longer comfortable; it had become not her refuge, but her prison. And Tanner was not the captain. He wasn't safe. He affected her as the captain had never done.

Was that so wrong? It didn't *feel* wrong…

CHAPTER TEN

"HEIGH-HO, AND AWAY, old friend," Baron Wilde crowed as he guided his mount beside Tanner's as the traveling coach with the Malvern crest picked out in gold gilt on the side doors moved through the morning fog and out of Grosvenor Square. "Oh, and look at that scowl, would you? Did you think to take up the two fair ladies and sneak out of town without me?"

"I knew you'd be along at some point, rather like a bad penny that keeps showing up again and again," Tanner told him facetiously. "Or did you expect me to send someone to fetch you from the arms of whatever opera dancer took your fancy last evening? You're still in your evening clothes, and looking somewhat the worse for wear for a man who prides himself on his appearance as you do. Long night?"

"Interesting night," Justin said, rubbing at the morning stubble that darkened his cheeks. "Brummell's finally managed to do his flit, by the way, flown to Calais, the sanctuary of all the best English debtors. Nobody knows yet, but since you and I are leaving town, it's safe to tell you."

"Safe? Did you think I'd run to alert his creditors?"

Justin flashed his wide smile. "Possibly. You are a very upstanding fellow. A veritable repository of morality and such like. I vow, I don't know how I stand you sometimes. Or how you abide me."

"I'm also very forbearing," Tanner told him, tongue-in-cheek.

"Patient as a saint, I agree."

"In addition, in case you might be wondering, I am devoid of any inclination toward begging for snippets of scandal."

"Ah. And your point?"

Tanner urged his horse forward as the traveling coach broke free of the early-morning traffic and the fresh team broke into a canter. The second coach, bearing luggage and servants, followed some space behind. Justin, on the other hand, seemed to be traveling light, although that probably meant his coach had been on the road for hours and was already well ahead of them.

"My point? Must I have one? I thought you simply wanted me to recite my assigned line, that being to look at you all goggle-eyed and exclaim in horror-struck tones: my God, man, don't tell me you helped Brummell escape!"

"I would have appreciated that sort of enthusiasm, yes. Do you think, if I were to tell you, you'd deign to at least pretend to be hanging on my every word?"

"I suppose I could try, if it means that much to you. Now, are you going to tell me how he—or should I say, you—outwitted the duns? I heard they sit in his drawing room and watch him eat his breakfast—which he probably hadn't paid for if accounts of how destitute he is are true."

"Oh, truer than true. The man had not two shillings to rub together, although he's fairly well-to-go now for a while, if he's prudent. A few of us fellow reprobates took up a collection of sorts, as a farewell gift, you understand. We owe the man something. After all, were it not for Beau, we'd still be prancing about like trick ponies in embroidered satins and dripping lace."

"Not to mention the periwigs and powder."

"Please, don't even whisper of those horrid things. And then there's daily bathing. You have to admit that the air in the ballrooms has been fresher since Brummell declared proper hygiene as the mark of a real gentleman. But I digress."

"You nearly always do. But that gives me time to ask a question, if you don't mind?"

"You nearly always do," Justin quipped. "You wish to ask me how I managed to be one of the conspirators in our small adventure. Since I've only returned to England two short days ago."

"So you said."

"Ah, you're learning. I may have only officially arrived two short days ago, but I did not say this is my first visit to my ancestral home. In truth, I've managed to be in and out of the country—incognito you understand—several times in the past few months. Securing a royal pardon is not only costly, but time-consuming. At any rate, between my growing loathing for our own

Prinney, whose pockets are now clogged with my blunt, and a hard-won affinity for outcasts, such as our prince has made Brummell, it was only logical that I should offer the man my assistance."

"And yet still I don't know what you did. We'll be at the first posting inn before you tell me, at this rate."

"It's a curse, this delicious enjoyment of the dramatic, I do try to fight it. Please forgive me. I'll be quick about the thing, then, so as not to have to leave you hanging as I go off to rid myself of my dirt and change into fresh clothing, all courtesy of the estimable Wigglesworth. My coach is already waiting for me at the Hoof And Claw. That is our first stop, yes? I seem to remember your passion for their dumplings."

"Your memory is long, if not entirely accurate. Her *name* was Dumpling, and that was a long time ago," Tanner said, stifling a grin. "I'd like to get to Malvern before Christmas, you know, so if you're above an hour primping in your bath, we'll leave you there."

"You're to be mine host, not my taskmaster," Justin pointed out, and then shrugged his broad shoulders. "Very well. As my reputation couldn't be more tarnished, I volunteered to be the one who escorted Beau to the opera in my coach. One of the more déclassé duns attempted to share said vehicle, but I disabused him of that notion. It was a rare treat, watching him and a half-dozen others of his ilk running alongside the coach in an attempt to keep our dashing debtor in their sights."

Tanner could readily imagine the scene, and easily saw the humor in it. "And after the opera?"

"Yes, that was an interesting discovery. Duns, as a species, would seem to have very short legs, and rather limited stamina," Justin remarked, clamping an unlit cheroot between his teeth. "I'm afraid they couldn't keep pace with my team, which made quick work of eating up the road between London and the estate of a fellow conspirator who had hidden Brummell's carriage. We said our farewells—a vastly touching scene, really—and the man was off on Dover Road, heading toward the tide and the small vessel waiting for both he and his carriage at the docks. I imagine he was sipping wine at some café in Calais before I managed my return to London."

Tanner shook his head. "All of that, Justin, and you barely knew the man."

"Or he, me. Still, he left me his seat at the table in the bow window at White's."

"He *left* it to you? He isn't dead, just gone."

"You were always such a stickler for accuracy. All right, I'll admit it. I bought the thing. For some reason, and rather belatedly, the man didn't wish to be indebted to yet someone else—me."

"You bought his seat? The actual chair?" Tanner laughed so hard his mount snorted and began sidestepping until his master returned his attention to the reins. "Have you decided to become an arbiter of fashion? Are you going to sit in the window and critique the rigouts of every hapless man and woman to trip down the flagway?"

"Yes, that about says it. Ought I get myself a

quizzing glass, do you think? To go with my funereal black and melancholy scowl."

"I think you should get yourself to the posting inn. Either that, or find your own way to Malvern."

"And give you a clear path to the affections of our fair and—thanks to your honorable idiocy—fair game Lady Lydia? I think not." And with a flash of his devilish grin and a tip of his hat, Justin dug his heels into the flanks of his mount and was off, down the road…leaving Tanner to mutter curses only his horse heard, which did him no good at all.

He urged his mount forward, alongside the coach, and dipped his head so that he could look in through the window, to where Lydia and Jasmine were seated.

Jasmine saw him first, and quickly lowered the window. "Was that the baron who just sped past us? He looked marvelously dashing, with his neck cloth loose and flying out behind him. Oh! I shouldn't have said that. Are you going to join us, Tanner? The coach is very well sprung, and the seats much more comfortable than those in Papa's carriage. We'd be happy to have you join us, although you'd have to ride backwards. Lydia and I have discussed this, and we both agree that we'd probably take very ill in our stomachs if we were to ride backwards. Well, I agreed. Did you say anything about that, Lydia?"

"I don't recall," he thought he heard Lydia answer quietly.

"Perhaps later," he told his cousin, and then looked past her, to where Lydia was doggedly attempting to work her embroidery hoop, even along this rather bumpy stretch of roadway. Her lips were compressed, and there was a white line ringing her mouth. "I thought perhaps you'd care to ride with me to the posting inn, Lydia? I noticed that you were wearing your habit."

She looked at him with such relief in her marvelous blue eyes that he instantly decided that Jasmine had probably been chewing off her ears for the last hour. Did she really think pretending an interest in her embroidery was enough to discourage Jasmine's prattlings? "I would like that, yes, thank you."

Tanner signaled to the coachman to pull to the side of the roadway and stop, and five minutes later Julia was mounted and riding beside him, far enough back from the coach to not have the two of them covered in dust within moments.

"Jasmine was proving to be her normal nattering self?" he asked her as they moved ahead at a slow canter.

"She says she natters when she's nervous. I didn't suppose that *I* made her nervous, but it appears I must. Or else it is simply returning to Malvern that has her feeling overset."

"Anxious to be going home, or unhappy to be leaving London, do you think?"

Lydia seemed to consider this for a moment. "I think she's anxious to be home. She has…friends in the vicinity."

"Are they all deaf, do you suppose, like Mrs. Shandy? No, don't answer that, it was mean of me."

"She's aware of what she's doing. She simply can't seem to stop talking. I would hate to be so nervous."

"Now I'm doubly ashamed of what I said. It's her father, you know. He pushes her and pushes her—toward me, mostly. Her ambitions for herself don't match his."

"She'll have to stand up to him at some point," Lydia said firmly, surprising him. "Nobody else should be allowed to arrange someone else's future."

Tanner immediately was tossed back to his promise to Fitz. The man had been arranging Lydia's future, even as he lay dying. And, if Thomas Harburton was to be believed, the late duke had arranged his son's future from his deathbed. Was Lydia trying to tell him something without actually saying it? But if so, was she speaking of his father, or of Fitz? Could she somehow know what her captain had planned for her if he were to die in battle? If she did, clearly she didn't approve.

Just what he needed, another hurdle.

"I've never seen you ride," he said, steering the suddenly uncomfortable conversation elsewhere. "I knew Nicole did, but not you."

"Nicole doesn't merely ride," Lydia said, smiling. "She and her Juliet terrorize the countryside. Daisy and I are content to amble along, admiring the view."

"Sometimes, the slower you go, the more you can savor the route and anticipate the arrival." Was he speaking of horses now, or his slow pursuit of Lydia herself? He knew the answer to that question—but did she? They both talked, but how much did either of them really say, and how much of their conversations, the important parts, lay in what was not said?

Her cheeks colored slightly, and Tanner knew he couldn't credit that color to the few minutes she'd been in the warm fresh air. His hopes soared. He was really quite the pathetic fellow, and he knew it.

He hastened into speech: "What were you and Jasmine—Jasmine, mostly, I'm sure—talking about? Were you listening at all?"

Lydia smiled at him. "There was little else to listen *to*. She was only telling me about Malvern. So far, I know that the house is big. And huge. And enormous. She's quite intimidated by its size, probably because, as a young child, she once got herself lost in the West Wing. But you know that because you are the brave hero who found her, rescued her, and carried her safely back to civilization when she was convinced she would be lost forever and succumb to cold and hunger."

"Good God, she said that? Did she also tell you that she'd closed herself up in a linen cupboard and fallen asleep? How did she expect to be found? And she wasn't that young, Lydia. I believe she was twelve or thirteen at the time, at least. She hasn't gone a step farther than the drawing room since then whenever she and her father visit. She's a…she's rather timid about some things."

"And with a tendency to overstate matters, it would seem. But now you're no longer a brave hero, are you?" she asked, humor in her voice. "That's too bad, as I was quite impressed when I believed you to be one. Perhaps you've done something else worthy of my maidenly awe and admiration?"

She wanted to bandy words with him, did she? Well, he was more than amenable. Words could be quite… evocative.

"Not lately, no. But I shall endeavor to do so at the earliest possible moment. Did you have any special feat of derring-do in mind?"

She pretended to consider his question, and he felt his heart swelling, because she obviously felt comfortable enough with him to tease him.

"Are there dangerous dragons at Malvern?"

"The fire-breathing sort, you mean?" He refrained from saying Justin's name.

"Are there other sorts?"

"Oh, yes," he said with all the solemnity he could muster. "Several, in fact. The horny-toad sort, for one. All bumpy, you understand, and his breath gives you warts. The double-tailed sort—they make a real havoc when they're happy and begin wagging those tails. Many a village cottage has had to be re-thatched over the years thanks to those considerable appendages. Lastly, there's the red-eyed five-legged nut-hatcher. Although, sadly, we haven't seen any of them ever since the walnut trees were felled by a blight some years ago and the lack of their favorite food forced them to relocate. I heard a few have been spotted feeding somewhere in the vicinity of Bagshot Heath, but that may only be rumor."

"A pity, as I would have liked to see the red-eyed nut-hatcher."

"Red-eyed, *five-legged* nut-hatcher," Tanner said. "The four-legged sort is still flourishing quite well with the hazelnuts."

"I stand corrected, thank you. I suppose I'll simply have to make do with having you slay one of the double-tailed sort. You'll not want to risk warts, after all. Brave heroes, I'm convinced, should not be plagued by warts."

"They would vastly take away from my conse-quence, I agree. And if the dragons have all gone in search of greener pastures? How then am I to impress you, fair maiden?"

"Oh, I'm sure you'll think of something," she said, and then her eyes got rather wide and she looked away from him.

"Lydia?" he asked after giving her a few moments to compose herself. Clearly she was as unused to verbal sparring with a man as he was with a woman. They were two rather reserved people, actually, except for the fact that they were trying, perhaps too hard, to not be so very circumspect anymore. Staid. Safe. Careful.

"Yes?" she asked him, sitting very erect and proper on the sidesaddle.

"Have you brought along the boots?"

Did she know what he was asking her?

Slowly, she turned her head toward him and looked him full in the face. As if she'd come to some sort of decision. "You said I would be able to see the world from the top of one of the hills. How could I not bring the boots? I'm…I'm very much looking forward to ev-erything you can show me."

Tanner's mount danced a bit as he accidentally tugged on the reins. Either she knew what he'd been saying, or she was so innocent he should pack her up the moment they got to the posting inn and send her home to her brother.

"There are so many things I want to show you, Lydia," he said, watching her closely.

"And so much I want to learn," she replied softly, her long lashes coming down to hide the expression in her eyes.

So beautiful. So chaste and demure.

Was she telling him without telling him that she was ready for more? He believed she was. Hoped she was.

He had Rafe's blessing, along with his advice that a woman can weary of being treated like a fragile flower. If that hadn't been enough, there had also been the whispered words from Charlotte as he quit the study: "Tell her, Tanner. Show her. She's ready to wake from whatever dreams she's hidden in for so long. She longs to be a woman. Don't let anyone else be the one who wakes her. Not if you love her."

Ahead of them, the coach began to slow as they approached a small hamlet and the Hoof and Claw. A fresh team and food and drink would greet them on their arrival. Along with the Baron Justin Wilde, currently prettying himself up in one of the bedchambers, cheerfully determined to make his friend's life as complicated as possible.

"At my invitation, no less," Tanner muttered under his breath.

"Pardon me? Did you say something?" Lydia asked him as they turned their horses into the inn yard.

"I asked if you're hungry. Justin promised to order us a meal."

"I was so busy saying goodbye to everyone that I completely forgot breakfast. Is that why he rode ahead? That was very thoughtful of him."

"That's Justin, thoughtful. The man is positively brimming with thoughts all the time. Let me help you down."

Tanner dismounted, handing the reins to the young ostler who'd run up to grab them, and walked around his horse to raise his arms to Lydia. She kicked her foot free of the stirrup as she lifted her other leg up and over the pommel before resting her hands on his shoulders.

Gripping her slim waist, he allowed her body to slowly slide down his, holding her still until the ostler had led their mounts away. He searched her eyes with his gaze, longing to tell her how beautiful she was, how just the sight of her smile could steal his breath from him, make him want to promise her not just the world but the sun and the stars. Instead he said quietly, solemnly, "I don't say things as well as Justin does, Lydia. But when I say something, I mean it."

She lifted a hand to his bandaged cheek, cupping it gently for the space of a heartbeat. "I know. I'll remember."

He felt foolish, even disloyal to one of his best friends. "I'd never hurt you."

"I know that, too." Her hand drifted back down to

her side. "They're probably wondering where we are. Shall we go inside?"

He nodded, then stepped back and offered her his arm.

CHAPTER ELEVEN

JASMINE AND LYDIA were given over into the capable hands of the innkeeper's wife and escorted to a room set aside for them, to refresh themselves, while Tanner was also shown to a chamber, perhaps the same one occupied by the baron.

"Oh, isn't this a lovely room?" Jasmine said as she headed straight for the pitcher of fresh water and the white earthenware washbasin. "Do you mind if I clean my hands first? You've been riding, and even with gloves, you're probably very dusty and smell of horse, and I wouldn't want to wash in dirty water."

Since the girl was already pouring water into the basin, Lydia didn't bother to answer what would have seemed an insult from anyone even an inch more cunning than Jasmine Harburton. She only walked to the small mirror hanging above a dresser to check on the position of her hat, the rather small, silly one that mimicked a man's curly brimmed beaver, but was worn at a rather rakish angle atop her blond curls, angled down over her left eye. Perhaps it was the color she liked best, a perfect match to her emerald green riding habit. Or, more probably, what made the hat so special was the fetching array of peacock plumes stuck to the back of it and standing in the air a good eight inches or more, and the half-veil that she'd pulled down once she was aboard Daisy, so that when she'd looked at Tanner, it was through the clever wisp of veil. She felt jaunty in this hat. Even sophisticated.

Full of false courage? Goodness, if a hat could make her feel this way, imagine how courageous men felt when they'd strapped on a sword. Were both women's hats and men's swords to be considered weapons? And what battle did men and women fight?

"Now there's a question I would *never* ask Charlotte, because she'd probably answer me," she told her reflection quietly.

Still, she'd certainly have to blame something for her outlandish behavior out there on the road with Tanner, so it might as well be an inanimate object like a hat. Every time she'd opened her mouth a part of her had been astounded at the words she heard herself saying. And then she'd touched his cheek. Simply reached up and touched him. The gesture had seemed so right, so natural. He was so earnest, so sincere, telling her he would never hurt her.

And all when she was wishing he would grab her, crush her against him, give life to the feelings that were bubbling so close beneath her surface these past days. In the solitude of her rooms, lying in her bed, picturing his face…she had felt the same stirrings she'd experienced when she'd touched him moments ago, heat burning through her glove, searing her. Searing him, as well?

She thought it might. No, she knew it did. He wanted her, as Nicole would term the thing. Carnally. He wanted her body. She'd be an utter fool not to know that, sense that.

She wanted his body. His mouth on hers. His hands on her body, teaching her, awakening her as she so longed to be awakened. She wanted to understand these longings, this surprising awareness of her body whenever he looked at her.

Lydia was not a fool. She knew she wasn't simply driving down to Malvern to see the sights, or to bear Jasmine and Justin company, make up the fourth in a casual game of whist after supper.

They'd be alone, she and Tanner, at some point. Even if that meant tramping the hills until he stopped being so honorable and careful and gentle with her. Even if that meant she had to *give him a nudge.*

"All right, Lydia, your turn," Jasmine trilled, already ruching up her skirts. "I'll just step behind this screen and…well, do you mind if I use it first?"

It took a moment for Lydia's mind to drag itself away from what were definitely uncommon thoughts for her and back to the mundane. "There's only the one?"

Jasmine's voice came from behind the screen. "Oh, no, look at that. There are two. How thoughtful. Now I don't feel so bad about racing ahead of you. But I had to go *so badly,* for at least the last half hour. I thought about knocking on the panel and informing the coachman, but how does one say anything so intimate to a man? Certainly I couldn't do it. There," she said, coming out from behind the screen and once more unerringly heading for the wash basin. When she was done, she picked up the second clean linen towel and used it before tossing it onto the floor, as she had the first one.

Looking at the two crumpled towels after she'd been behind the screen, and then lifting the pitcher, to learn that Jasmine has used up all the water, Lydia felt a little niggle somewhere inside her. A small but growing suspicion that possibly Jasmine wasn't entirely the sweet, silly widget she appeared. For all her prattling and confessions of nervousness, she certainly did seem able to plow forward and get exactly what she wanted.

Like the front-facing coach seat, which she hadn't offered to share until Lydia had expressly asked her to move her skirts (spread from side-to-side), so that she could ride facing the horses, as well. And then there was the matter of the small basket of sugared rolls Tanner had ordered packed and placed in the coach for the two of them. Or there had been. When Lydia had decided to try one, as the sweet smell lingered inside the closed coach, it was to find that Jasmine had already eaten them all on the way to Grosvenor Square. Yes, she'd apologized quite prettily, saying she was such a selfish pig and so ashamed—but the sugared rolls were still gone, weren't they?

Now there were the towels, and the clean water, and even the chamber pot, if there had been just one.

She mentally scolded herself for thinking badly of a young woman who could be considered rather thoughtless and even ill-mannered, but who could certainly not be termed selfish. Although she did, one way or another, always seem to get what she wanted, didn't she? Even as she protested she didn't want any of it.

Like a Season in London.

Like all her pretty gowns.

Like the Malvern jewels she wore around her neck.

Like Tanner?

Picking up one of the towels and taking up the soap, Lydia looked over her shoulder and said conversationally, "You must be so anxious to get to Malvern."

"I must?" Jasmine frowned prettily as she patted at her curls, but then smiled. "Oh, yes. I am so much more comfortable in the country. Tanner is a dear to give me this respite from all of the hustle and bustle."

"I meant you must be anxious to see…your friend."

"How did you—oh!" Jasmine lowered her eyelids, and Lydia could actually watch the progress of a flattering blush rushing into her cheeks. "Oh. You mean Br—Bruce. No, I cannot think of him," she declared at last, dramatically. "I must not."

Had the girl been holding her breath, forcing color into her cheeks? No, that was ridiculous. *She* was being ridiculous, Lydia told herself.

"That's his name? Bruce?"

Jasmine nodded empathetically, biting her bottom

lip while bright tears gathered in her eyes. "I'd really rather not say."

All right, that was more than enough! She hadn't lived with Nicole for over eighteen years without being able to tell when she was being put on. And Jasmine wasn't half so accomplished in the art of deception as was Lydia's twin.

She dried her hands on the small dry spot left on the towel, and then folded it and laid it beside the basin. "Tell me about him, please. Tell me about Bruce. For instance, does he have a last name?"

"I didn't know you could be so mean, Lydia, to force me to—very well, if I must. It's Beattie. Bruce Beattie. Oh, but it makes me so sad to speak of him."

Force yourself, Lydia thought meanly, but only said, "Is he a laborer on the Malvern estate? Is that how you met him?"

Jasmine shook her head. "He…he's the schoolmaster in Greater Malvern, which is very close by our small estate, and Tanner's, of course. We…we met at church."

"A schoolmaster? That's a very respectable occupation."

Jasmine sighed piteously. "Not when your father dreams of seeing his only child made a duchess. But I've told you all of that."

"The deathbed request, yes. I remember. You have much to be sad about, Jasmine," Lydia said, pulling out pins in preparation of taking off her hat, even though it hadn't moved a bit since Sarah had first pinned it to her curls. But she wished to be alone with her thoughts for a few minutes and was even willing to sacrifice the hat to that purpose. "And I'll wager that my insensitive questions have quite robbed you of your appetite." *The questions, and a full basket of sugared rolls.*

"I suppose so. But I can't allow myself the indulgence of turning maudlin. Tanner would notice—he always does—and would ask questions of his own. I will have to force myself to eat. Will you soon be ready to go downstairs?"

Lydia had two pins clamped between her teeth, but managed to tell Jasmine to go on without her, and inform the gentlemen that she'd be down directly.

Once alone in the room, her gaze went to the reticule Jasmine had left lying on the bed along with her gloves and bonnet.

No. She wouldn't do it. She wasn't a snoop. In addition, she was thinking unlovely things about a girl whose only sin was a bit of thoughtlessness. Along with a penchant for melodrama…and sugared rolls.

She left her hat on the dresser and slowly approached the bed, clasping and unclasping her hands, her palms itching to pick up the reticule, pull open its drawstring closing, and take a peek inside. Ladies often carried some of their most favorite keepsakes with them at all times. Didn't she still have the piece of blue ribbon pinned inside her own reticule?

Nicole would do it. In a heartbeat, Nicole would do it. If she wanted to know something, she never stopped to consider if the thing was right or wrong. It would only, to Nicole, be *necessary.*

"Oh, the devil with it," she breathed at last, tossing good manners to one side and snatching up the reticule.

The first thing she saw when she looked inside was a single sugared roll. No wonder she'd been able to smell the rolls long after they were gone. Because they hadn't all been gone, had they?

All reluctance to snoop deserted Lydia at the sight of that sugared roll. With narrowed eyelids and new determination she pushed her hand past it to see a lace-edged handkerchief, a small mirror, three silver coins, and a much-folded piece of paper.

It was the paper she withdrew and unfolded as she walked to the window and the sunlight. "What fine penmanship, just as a schoolmaster should have," she said, her voice sounding loud in her own ears. And then she began to read…

My beloved,

As I lay here in my lonely prison, the intoxicating taste and sweet musky scent of you still mocking me, our hungers only momentarily slaked, my loins grow taut with desire, already anticipating our next passionate coupling—

Lydia gasped and quickly closed her eyes, whether at the meaning of the words or the overblown ridiculous nature of them she didn't know. She should stop reading right now, right this very moment.

Really. She should.

—I wonder if, even now, you know how securely you hold my heart, as well as my body. We will be together soon, forever. No more clandestine meetings, no more

*hurried loving fraught with the danger of discovery. I
weep when I must leave you, I berate myself for a
coward and a fool each moment we are apart. Soon,
sweet angel, soon. I promise you I shall l find a way.
We will fly these damp shores forever, you and I, and
you will be my queen in Paris for all of our days.*

Your beloved, always,

The note was signed simply with a large, flower-
ing letter B.

Lydia noticed that another line followed that signature.

*P.S. Remember what you promised. The key to our
future, my darling.*

The request made no sense, and Lydia dismissed it
as unimportant when measured against the rest of the
nonsense she'd just read. She folded the letter once
more, careful to make use of the same creases, and
with shaking fingers replaced it in the reticule.

Shame on Bruce Beattie! Taking advantage of a
naïve young girl, making her promises he couldn't
keep, all while stealing her virginity from her, knowing
full well that her father would never allow the marriage.

She wished she hadn't succumbed to her curiosity,
even forgave Jasmine the sugared roll, and offered up
a quick, silent prayer that Mr. Beattie's words were not
now indelibly imprinted on her brain for all time.

There was a knock at the door that made Lydia nearly
jump out of her riding boots, followed by Tanner's voice
asking her if she and Jasmine were ready to go downstairs.

She took one last peek in the mirror, hoping she

didn't look as guilty as she felt, saw that her curls were mussed, and decided she didn't care. She took a deep, steadying breath and then quickly opened the door. "Tanner. Hello. Jasmine has already gone. I...I had some difficulty with my hat."

He reached out and touched the loose corkscrew curl that had managed to fall forward on her forehead. "Now I'm torn. Do I like the veil best, or this fetching curl?"

She was still too overset thanks to her snooping to take much notice of his flattery. "Tanner, don't tease," she said, pushing the curl back in place. "Shall we go down?"

Lydia first saw Baron Justin Wilde lounging at his ease, one shoulder propped against the doorway to the private dining room inside the small inn, appearing fresh, devilishly handsome, and every inch the epitome of fashion in his impeccable attire. And, goodness, but didn't he know it.

He pushed himself upright and made a show of pulling his watch from his waistcoat pocket. Flipping open its ornate golden lid, he then raised his eyebrows as he checked the hour. "It may be time to reconsider your horseflesh, Tanner. I've been waiting on your arrival this past half hour or more. But it was worth the wait to have the pleasure of your company again, fairest Lydia."

Suddenly Lydia was very out of charity with men who said anything, any nonsense at all, in order to beguile women. "Thank you, Justin. You're rather a marvel yourself, as if you were unaware of it, which I feel certain you are not, posing as you were a moment ago."

"Close your mouth, Justin, she got the better of you. Oh, and for all your supposed waiting on us, your hair's still damp," Tanner pointed out as Justin stood back and winked at Lydia as she was escorted past him and into the room. "You might also be slightly out of breath, probably from running down the back stairs only moments ahead of our arrival. The door to our shared chamber was still swinging back and forth when I approached it. Where's Jasmine?"

"Your cousin? I have no idea. Have you misplaced her? For shame, Tanner."

Lydia and Tanner exchanged looks. "I may have inadvertently said something to upset her while we were upstairs," Lydia told him. "But surely she wouldn't have just gone off on her own. Would she?"

"God knows," Tanner ground out, already turning for the doorway, Lydia right behind him.

"Mind if I start without you?" Justin called after them. "Never mind, I'll take that growl as a yes. Do hurry back."

"Where would she have gone?" Lydia asked Tanner as they first poked their heads into the taproom, and then headed outside, to the dusty inn yard. "Does she often take herself off to sulk?"

"How do you think she got lost in the West Wing at Malvern?" Tanner said, raking his spread fingers through his dark blond hair. "What did you say to her?"

Since the truth was not hers to tell and therefore out

of the question—as well as self-serving, something she had already considered—Lydia ignored him, and only pointed to a path that led into a stand of trees. "Could she have gone that way?"

Her question was answered by Jasmine herself, who just then appeared on the path, her arms filled with wildflowers. The sun filtered down on her through the trees, setting small fires in her dark hair, and she looked the picture of innocence, of youth, of ethereal beauty.

"Christ on a crutch…" Tanner swore under his breath, clearly not impressed.

"Yoo-hoo, Tanner, Lydia! Have you been looking for me?" she called out, hastening across the inn yard to them. "Oh, dear, you're frowning, the pair of you. Of course you have been looking for me," she said, her slim shoulders slumping, her smile fading as her bottom lip began to tremble. "I'm so, so sorry. Only I saw these pretty blooms on the table just inside, and a servant told me the flowers grow wild all along the stream just down that path, and how could I resist? I simply knew I had to see them, fill my arms with them, and make dearest Lydia a present of them." She thrust the flowers straight at Lydia. "Here. Please let them be my apology for using both of the towels earlier. Did you think I didn't notice?"

Lydia would have liked to ask her what she'd give her to make up for the pilfered sugared bun, but only took the flowers, some of them still with their roots, and dripping mud, she noticed, and held them away from her body. "Thank you, Jasmine. That is very kind of you."

"And rather foolish," Tanner said, handing Jasmine his handkerchief, for her hands were muddy. "You shouldn't have gone off on your own. This isn't Malvern."

"Yes, Tanner," she answered quietly, handing him back the handkerchief, which was now streaked with mud. He looked at it rather blankly for a moment before folding it and shoving it back in his pocket. "I won't do it again, I promise. Now, do you suppose the inn-keeper's wife will have a pretty vase for us, hmm? The flowers will make a lovely centerpiece as we have our little meal. I'll just go ask her, all right?"

"She's such a child," he said as they watched her race into the inn after snatching the flowers back from Lydia.

"In some ways," Lydia said, thinking once again of the note she'd found in the girl's reticule, suddenly feeling quite aged, and distressingly virginal. "Did your father know her well?"

A small smile tickled at one corner of Tanner's mouth. "You think he was punishing me from the grave, with that deathbed declaration of his? I've thought of that myself, more than once. Not that I can believe he made any such statement."

"You don't?" Lydia's heart skipped a beat. Really. It was most disconcerting how talk of Tanner's future affected her. "Is that why—"

"Why it has been over two years, and I still haven't declared myself to her?" He was looking at her very intensely. "No, Lydia. That is not the reason, and it hasn't been, not for a long time." He took her hands in his.

"Lydia, we really should talk. Lord only knows how much privacy we'll have at Malvern. Would you care to go see the wildflowers?"

"Yes, I...I think that would be—"

"*There* you are! What's the matter, Tanner, can't you remember the way to the dining room?"

"Go away, Justin," Tanner said, still looking at Lydia.

"Go away, Justin, is it? Oh, foul, foul! That's the reward I get for ordering us all a fine meal—dearest Jasmine is making heavy inroads on the ham, by the way, if you were planning on having any of it yourself. Now come along. There will be plenty of time for billing and cooing once we're at Malvern. If we ever manage to make it through this supposed quick stop and back on the road, that is. Lydia, my arm," he ended, extending his bent arm to her so that she had no other choice but to take it. She looked over her shoulder as she was directed into the inn, and Tanner was following them, a scowl on his handsome face.

"I've ordered up a variety of the plain fare offered here," Justin told Lydia as he guided her toward the private dining room, "but you needn't confine yourself to that, as I've also brought along several tins from my own kitchens. Have you ever tasted honeyed figs?"

"No, I can't say that I have. I don't believe I've ever even seen a fig. They sound...interesting," Lydia said as he pulled out a chair for her and then sat himself down beside her, leaving Tanner to take up his seat across the table, beside Jasmine. He was still scowling, which for reasons she didn't wish to investigate as they might brand her as silly and shallow, seemed to be cheering her no end.

"Well then, I can see that it is my current duty in life to remedy that sad lack. Did you know that, in some of our more exotic countries, the fig is known as an aphrodisiac?"

"Enjoying yourself, Justin?" Tanner gritted out, pouring himself a glass of wine.

"Oh, yes. Immensely. We both are, aren't we, Lydia?"

She refused to answer, but only watched as he opened a tin that had been wrapped in a thick towel and spooned what had to be a sweet-smelling half-fig onto his plate. He then topped it with a dollop of—"what is that?"

"Goat cheese, my dear. Nothing quite like good country goat cheese, which mine host provided, bless him." He then cut the fig in half once again and lifted a piece toward her, speared on the end of his fork. He placed his other hand beneath the fork, to catch any drips of honey. "It's still warm, the fig, that is. Here you go—ambrosia for the lady."

With no other recourse than to refuse and seem silly and unadventurous, Lydia opened her mouth and Justin fed her. Her lips closed around the fork and he smiled when her eyes widened as the sweet and yet tangy combination of fig and honey and goat cheese exploded on her tongue.

While the fork was still between her lips, he lifted the other half of the fig in his fingers and, his face close to hers, popped the thing into his own mouth.

It was all so curiously intimate.

"Oh, for the love of heaven, Justin, give over. You're making a cake of yourself."

Lydia watched as Justin smiled around his mouthful of fig, and then winked at her as if Tanner's reaction had been just what he'd wished for.

"I shouldn't think I'd like to try that at all," Jasmine offered, without being asked. "They look funny. The figs, that is, not Lydia and Justin, or at least not so much. And I don't much care for goat cheese. Spit it out if you want to, Lydia, I'm sure no one would mind."

The loverlike expression on Justin's handsome face turned to one of almost abject horror as he looked across the table at Jasmine, while Tanner began to laugh out loud in real pleasure.

Perhaps it would be fun to be courted by two men, two such very different men. Lydia hid her own smile behind her serviette.

CHAPTER TWELVE

"SHE THINKS YOU'RE amusing, you know," Tanner told Justin once they were back on their horses and on the road once more, Lydia and Jasmine inside the coach. "Rather like a trained monkey."

"Ah, but much better dressed, you'll admit," Justin said, clearly not taking offense. "Are you ready to rescind your invitation?"

"I didn't *invite* you to pursue her, damn it. I only said she is not mine to…to—oh, stop grinning. Now you look like an ape."

"You know what's wrong with you, Tanner?" Justin said amicably, pulling two cheroots from his pocket and offering one to his friend. "You're too good."

"I wouldn't count on that quite so much. I'm feeling less *good* by the minute. Now, how in hell are we going to light these things?"

Justin reached once more into his waistcoat pocket and produced a small bleached stick, the top half of which appeared to be coated with something. "Observe, Tanner, as I do magic."

So saying, he then struck the coated end of the stick against his saddle, and the stick caught fire.

"Hurry, the magic doesn't last that long," he said, and Tanner leaned half out of his saddle toward Justin, cupped his hand around the tip of his cheroot and the small flame, which did indeed die quickly. "Good, now I'll light mine from yours, if you don't mind."

Tanner passed over his cheroot. "What was that?"

"Should it have a name? Wigglesworth discovered them in a chemist's shop in a place called Stockton-on-Tees. Quaint name, don't you think? At any rate, I've only a few left and the apothecary doesn't see the sense of making more. And you couldn't be *bad* if you applied yourself, so I will continue to *count on it.*" He blew out a cloud of blue smoke as he inspected the end of his cheroot. "Do you think the apothecary was right in saying his magic flame could be poisonous? Something about the mixture of all the chemicals and such. I don't taste anything too vile. What do you say."

"Nothing that wouldn't end with me burning in Hell and its own poisonous chemicals," Tanner said, now examining the glowing tip of his own cheroot. "Have you ever considered that you might have crossed the border from engaging eccentric into the realm of the genuinely unhinged?"

"Many times, Tanner, many times, but then I console myself that I am not as yet baying at full moons. Now, back to the dear Lady Lydia and your dogged refusal to warn me away and thus clear your path to her affections this week. And please consider this to be your absolute final chance to change your mind."

"I'm not going to change my mind. Granted, I think

she enjoys you." Tanner was careful to keep his expression neutral. "Rather as she might a performing bear at a country fair. Besides, she seems fully aware that you're not on the hunt for a wife, her or anyone else."

"Been warning her away from me, have you? Shame on you."

Tanner nodded. "Yes, shame on me. But, damn it, Justin, this isn't a game."

"I agree. I spoke privately with Rafe before we left the city," Justin said, taking another long pull on his cheroot.

Tanner quickly glanced at his friend's profile, which betrayed nothing. "You're serious? You barely know her."

"And I hardly could, not without Rafe's permission, now could I? I am, after all, and for all of my vices, a gentleman."

"Don't do this, Justin. Lydia's been through enough, losing Fitz. She doesn't know about your ridiculous notion of some wager between us. She might not realize you're only amusing yourself."

"Is that what I'm doing? Can any of us be sure of that? As you already know, and have foolishly not yet acted upon, Lydia is a most singular woman, unlike any other of my extensive and varied acquaintance. She has, one might say, opened my eyes to whole new realms of possibilities I didn't know existed," Justin told him, clamping the cheroot between his even white teeth, looking every inch the unrepentant rake he was known to be. "Now, if you'll pardon me, I'll leave you to answer the question of what I am doing for yourself. I feel the need for a gallop." He dug his heels into his mount's flanks, and he was off, past the coach, leaving Tanner once more in his dust.

Which meant he couldn't remind Justin that the many women of his "extensive and varied acquaintance" hadn't really varied—he'd chosen his women for their beauty and his personal enjoyment. Of course Lydia was different. She was a lady in more than name. And she saw Justin for who he was, which had to intrigue the hell out of him.

The remainder of the afternoon passed in agonized slowness for Tanner, with one of the team of six matched bays throwing a shoe and delaying them at yet another inn, and Jasmine once more wandering off, this time not to be found for a full half hour. At which point, again, she apologized, blinked back tears, and then, after inquiring if they would be staying the night at their usual stopping point, went skipping toward the waiting coach as if all was forgiven.

Tanner had watched Lydia watching Jasmine, wondering at the rather concerned look on her face, but even though she then turned to him as if she wished to say something to him, she only shook her head and followed his cousin into the coach.

Jasmine was probably wearing at Lydia's nerves, which was certainly reasonable to assume. At least she would find some respite at the Crown and Sugarloaf, as he'd sent one of his grooms along hours earlier, to reserve three rooms for the travelers, and another three attic rooms for their servants, who would probably arrive in another few hours.

He'd left Justin to make his own arrangements, and the inestimable Wigglesworth was probably already replacing the inn's sheets with the baron's own and terrorizing the kitchen staff by commandeering it in order to personally prepare his master's evening meal.

A smile played around Tanner's mouth as he gave up trying to be angry with Justin. The man probably couldn't help himself. He'd been born to more wealth than any ten men would ever need, the pampered only child of a doting father and a mother born into a filthy rich (Justin always made that joke himself) coal merchant's family and never able to forget that fact. Her money might not have bought for her the social position she'd longed for, but that didn't mean she couldn't live as if she were Lady Jersey herself. She'd been delighted beyond words to have somehow produced such a beautiful and witty son, and she'd impressed upon him the value of showing the world that he was every inch the gentleman, with no coal dust to be found on *his* feet.

Justin may have taken her lessons too far, but that wasn't for Tanner to say. He only knew that the man might be referred to as *that fop,* or *that killer,* but never as *that blown-up cit.* He imagined that must be some sort of accomplishment for a man many of the high in the instep *ton* otherwise would have condemned dismissively as being only one generation away from the shop.

A flash of sunlight on something metal caught

Tanner's attention and he looked to his left just as a horse and rider broke from the trees and onto the roadway. He reached for the pistol mounted on his saddle before the wide smile on the well-dressed rider and a genial wave of his gloved hand had him turn the gesture into a reassuring pat to his mount's neck as the rider fell into tandem with him.

"Good day to you, sir," the man said, tipping his jaunty curly-brimmed beaver, revealing a full head of bright red hair and a black patch tied over his left eye. He held out his gloved hand. "Benjamin Flynn is the name, late of his majesty's Fourth Foot, for my sins. Would you be minding overmuch if I was to join you for a space? I've been riding cross-country, but now that it's coming on to dark, I thought I'd best get myself back on the road before old Charger here stepped in a rabbit hole and I came to an ignominious end."

Tanner reached his hand across the gap between the two horses. "Tanner Blake, and no, I wouldn't mind. Traveling far?" he asked, seeing the blanket roll tied behind Flynn's saddle. It was nice to hear that Irish lilt in the man's voice, which reminded him a bit of Fitz.

"And that I won't be knowing until I get there. I've mostly been moving about ever since coming back from Brussels. Can't seem to settle myself anywhere for very long. For now, I'm thinking I'll be seeing what this fellow Will Langland was so taken with. Let's see, how does it go? Ah, yes, 'And on a May morning on Malvern hills.'"

"*The Views of Piers Plowman,*" Tanner said, nodding.

"How I loathed reading that damn thing, and my tutor for forcing it on me. So, you're looking for truth in a 'fair field of folk,' are you?"

"Can't say as I've had much luck in finding it anywhere else," Benjamin said, his grin wide and open. "So you know the poem?"

"Only the bits I haven't been able to beat out of my memory. My home is in Malvern, so Langland's ditty was pretty much considered a requirement to residing there. My friends and I are traveling there now."

"Is that a fact? Well, then, is it possible you could be telling me of a good inn to stay the night, hmm? I'm longing for a hot bath and a bed that has at least a hope of not being damp."

"We're stopping at the Crown and Sugarloaf, which is only a few miles from here. I'd consider it an honor if a fellow veteran of our last battle with Bonaparte would join my party and myself for supper."

"Well, now, how could a man refuse an invitation like that and not be called daft? Thank you kindly, Tanner."

As they neared the inn, Tanner wondered how Lydia would react to Benjamin's Irish lilt, and the fact that he'd fought in the Fourth Foot, which had been a part of the forces that had been at Quatre Bras, where her Fitz had died.

Perhaps Justin was right, and he was "too good." Or, even more likely, simply an idiot. Yes, he'd wanted—still wanted—Lydia to choose him, and he wanted her to be sure of her choice, not just settling for him because

Fitz may have, God forbid, suggested that solution to her somehow.

But of all the "competition" he could have chosen, how had he ended up with the dashing Baron Justin Wilde, who could charm birds down from the trees, and then gone even further, all but inviting Fitz's ghost to the party?

CHAPTER THIRTEEN

THE COACH CARRYING Sarah and the other servants had yet to catch up with them, so Lydia was grateful for the services of one of the maids at the Crown and Sugar-loaf in assisting her with her bath and in buttoning up the back of her gown. She would have liked to wash her hair, but that would have made her unconscionably late for supper, so she refrained.

Mostly, she was grateful to not have to share a chamber with Jasmine. Try as she might, she could no longer be comfortable around the girl.

Not that she was *judging* her. Although she certainly disapproved of her behavior with her Bruce Beattie, she had convinced herself that Jasmine had been seduced by a cad without a shred of moral rectitude, and she could not be blamed for allowing her silly young head to be turned by Mr. Beattie's amorous attentions.

"And aren't you a prig?" Lydia said to her reflection in the mirror hung over the dressing table. "Jasmine is living a great adventure. What are *you* doing?"

Since the answer to that question was *nothing,* Lydia didn't bother saying it aloud. Instead she applied herself once more to the reason she could no longer like Jasmine Harburton.

The girl was selfish. Brainless. Reckless. Juvenile. Self-serving. Pretending to be something she wasn't, and probably hadn't been for some time.

Up to something.

Yes, that was it—that last one. Jasmine Harburton was *up to something.*

But what?

Thanks to Nicole and a lifetime of watching her do her mischief, Lydia had developed a talent for sniffing out mischief, conniving. Nicole's mischiefs had always been harmless, if at times bordering on the dangerous—like her midnight rides on her Juliet, dressed in the cast off trousers of their male cousins. But they had never been sly or mean.

Lydia didn't think she could say the same about whatever Jasmine was up to, she and her Mr. Beattie.

She didn't know why she felt that, she just did. And that left her with a dilemma she didn't want to think about: whether or not she should tell Tanner what she knew, what she thought.

First of all, she would be telling tales out of school about Jasmine and her…friend. Secondly, and nearly as important to Lydia, she would be condemning herself as a snoop.

So, no, she wouldn't tell Tanner.

That left Justin, didn't it?

He would only laugh to hear that Jasmine had been carrying on clandestinely with the local schoolmaster.

And he'd be delighted that she had snooped, because he would have done the same thing.

Yes, that's what she'd do. She'd bring Justin into her confidence. Because he was silly, he was smart, she was certain he was not easily shocked, he might even have some suggestions for her…and although she hoped he liked her, it wouldn't break her heart if he didn't.

Only Tanner could do that.

"Lydia? Are you ready to go down to supper?"

Once again she put her hands to her breast, feeling her heartbeat skip at the sound of Tanner's voice on the other side of the door. Unless she did something about that ridiculous overreaction, she might soon do her heart some injury.

How long would he insist on walking on virtual tiptoes around her? How much longer could she let him be such a gentleman?

Because Nicole was right when she'd said, oh, so many times, that always being good was horribly *fatiguing*. It hadn't used to be, but it was now.

She crossed to the door and opened it, and then stepped back, inviting Tanner inside, telling him that she would be just a moment, as she wished to check on something in her reticule. My, lying was easier than she'd imagined.

He'd also taken the time to bathe, and his dark blond hair was even darker as it curled behind his ears, one lock falling onto his forehead. Her fingers itched to touch it.

He looked relaxed in his evening clothes, which were well-tailored, but not fitted to his form in the way

Justin's were. Tanner clearly favored comfort over fashion, and she was glad, as she also would like to think that she wore her clothing, it did not wear *her*. Lovely as her gowns looked now that the necklines had been lowered—and, as she'd found out as she'd had to draw in her breath in order for the maid to fasten the last of her buttons, Nicole must also have instructed the seamstress to make them more formfitting—she missed the comfort of how they had been.

"I've invited someone to join us in our private dining room," Tanner said as she pretended to hunt for something in her reticule. "I hope you don't mind. A soldier I met along the road. He's also traveling to Malvern."

"Oh?" she said absently. "That was very nice of you. Ah, now I remember. I left that handkerchief in the pocket of my riding outfit." She put down the reticule and walked over to him. "Did he say where he had fought?"

Tanner seemed to hesitate before answering her. "Quatre Bras. He said he was Fourth Foot, and I know they were there, among other sections of the battlefield during the course of those two days."

Lydia felt a fist forming in her midsection, but ignored it. "It's all right, Tanner. But thank you for warning me."

"His name is Benjamin Flynn. He's Irish."

"Oh my goodness, Tanner, stop looking at me like that. I'm not going to dissolve into a puddle of tears any time I see an Irishman who may have fought at Quatre Bras, or anywhere else for that matter."

"I know that," he said, raking his fingers through his hair, performing an action in frustration she'd only moments earlier wished to do for quite another reason entirely. "I only thought it fair to warn you."

"And now I've been warned." She took another step in his direction, close enough to him now to be aware of the clean scent of his soap. "Have you noticed, Tanner, that we're alone here together? You and I. Nobody else is in this room with us. Please. Stop opening the door to anyone else, to any other time."

He lifted her hands in his, slowly kissing first one, then the other, as he looked down into her face. "If this room were filled to the rafters with other people, along with the shades of a thousand more, I would see only you."

What a beautiful thing to say to her. She'd never heard anything more beautiful. "Tanner..."

"I so want the two of us to spend time together at Malvern. I want...so many things. But I don't want to rush you," he said, just as she was about to—well, she didn't know what she had been about to say. Just *Tanner*.

"We've known each other for nearly a year," she pointed out, and then immediately wishing she hadn't, for all that did was bring back the memory of the day he'd told her about Fitz. The day she'd railed at him, physically beaten at him, screamed out how much she hated him. "That is to say..."

"May I kiss you, Lydia?"

She swallowed, the action almost painful. Her mouth

had gone suddenly dry, her tongue all but cleaving to the roof of her mouth. She could only look at him.

"I'm sorry. It's still too soon. I apologize—"

He didn't say anything else because she had gone up on her tiptoes and pressed her mouth to his. She wouldn't allow him to say anything else. Wouldn't let him be honorable, and polite, and so stuffed full of *goodness* that he would walk away from her, even now.

His arms went around her and she sighed in relief, sighed right into his mouth, for he had opened his over hers, an action that sent a wave a giddiness racing through her.

She slipped her arms up and around his neck, fearing that he would come to his senses before she could understand what it was his kiss was doing to her, and held on tight. Her first kiss. Her second love. Reality dueling with the dream.

Reality winning.

Tanner withdrew slightly, but only to slant his head so that he could draw her more closely against him, bite softly at her bottom lip before fully taking her mouth once more.

His hands were on her waist now, nearly spanning it, making her feel small, but not fragile. Instead, she felt real, perhaps for the first time in her life; knowing who she was. She was Lydia. She was a woman, with the desires of a woman, not the dreams of a half child. *Alive*, for the first time in her life.

The three quick, staccato knocks on the door just behind them were more than enough to have them springing apart rather like guilty children. The sound of Justin's voice as he asked, entirely too jovially, if Lydia happened to know where Tanner had taken himself off to.

Tanner kissed her one last time, quickly, and then put a finger to his lips.

Lydia nodded, took several deep breaths, and finally answered, "No, Justin, I'm sorry. I don't know where he is. But I'll be down directly."

"Shall I wait for you?"

She looked at Tanner, who shook his head, pointing to her...was he pointing to her mouth? "Uh...thank you, but no. I'll see you downstairs."

"Very well. And if you see my good friend Tanner anywhere, do tell him to behave."

"Um...yes. Certainly. I'll tell him." Lydia turned shocked eyes on Tanner, who merely rolled his as he shook his head in clear exasperation. "He knows you're in here," she whispered, and then pressed her ear against the door, listening as Justin's footsteps faded down the hallway.

When she stepped away from the door, it was to see Tanner dipping the corner of a towel into the cool water in the basin.

"He knows," she repeated unnecessarily. "And he thinks it's amusing. What a strange man."

Tanner pressed the cool wet cloth to her mouth and told her to hold it there. "That will calm the slight redness I seem to have caused. Yes, Justin's a strange man as well as quick to notice things like a just-kissed mouth. I don't think we want to amuse him any further, do you?"

Lydia pulled the cloth away from her mouth and

shook her head. "We most certainly do not. How is it now?"

"Your mouth?" Tanner smiled, and her heart melted. "Eminently kissable, as always. Frankly, I should thank Justin for knocking on the door when he did."

She felt a blush stealing into her cheeks. "Yes, I suppose we should be grateful to him." *But I'd rather box his ears.*

Tanner put a bent finger beneath her chin and raised her face to his. "We have time, Lydia. All the time in the world to be sure. And tomorrow we'll be at Malvern."

Nodding, she stepped back, away from temptation, fighting back the words *Fitz thought he had all the time in the world, too.*

Tanner leaned in and kissed her cheek, lightly squeezed her upper arms. "I'm now going to do the bravest thing I've ever done. I'm going to turn and leave you here. I'll see you again downstairs."

Once he was gone, she leaned her back against the door and closed her eyes. She'd kissed him? She'd really kissed him? He may have *talked* as if he wanted to kiss her, had even asked if he could kiss her, but it was *she* who had kissed *him*. And he'd walked away?

If he got any more *honorable* she might have to box his ears, too!

After checking her mouth in the mirror, and then resorting to a bit of rice powder from her dressing case to cover a slight redness on her chin that hadn't been there before Tanner had kissed her, Lydia stepped out into the hallway, turning left toward the stairs.

She was greeted at the bottom of those stairs by a tall, well set-up red-haired man wearing a rather flattering black patch over his left eye. "Good evening, miss," he said, bowing politely, if rather nervously. "Would you perchance be either the Lady Lydia, or Miss Harburton?"

She felt a small stab at the revealing lilt in his voice, but only smiled. "I am Lydia Daughtry, yes. And you must be Mr. Flynn?"

"That I am, my lady, standing here and feeling as helpless as the devil in a high wind that I don't recognize a duke when I'm riding next to one. Imagine, having the cheek to just go sticking out my hand to a man I should be bowing to and pulling at my forelock, I suppose. I've been pacing about out here these past five minutes or more, screwing up the courage to either sit myself down with my betters or just to take myself off."

"If His Grace invited you, he meant what he said, Mr. Flynn." Goodness, but he was big. Just like the captain, who could make her feel small and coddled, protected. There was just something comfortable and soothing about the lilt in an Irish voice, the softness in Irish eyes. "Now why don't you please escort me to the dining room, as I've just realized I have no idea where it is."

Flynn inclined his head to her and offered his arm. "It would be my distinct pleasure, Lady Lydia, and my greatest hope that you tell no one I'm hiding behind your skirts."

She laughed at that, and was still smiling when they entered the private dining room at the rear of the inn to see that everyone else was already there.

Tanner and Justin rose to their feet, shook hands with Mr. Flynn, and Tanner introduced him to Jasmine.

"It is an honor and a pleasure to make your acquaintance, Miss Harburton," Flynn said, bowing.

Jasmine quite pointedly ignored him. "Tanner? Can we please *eat* now. I've been patient ever so long. Really, Lydia, I would think you could have been down sooner. In consideration of others."

Lydia felt an unaccustomed urge to box ears this evening, it seemed, because she would like nothing more than to box Jasmine's at the moment. The girl had wandered off twice today, upsetting her cousin, delaying their journey, and now *she* was complaining about being forced to wait on somebody else?

"You're right, Jasmine," she only said, taking up the chair Mr. Flynn had pulled out for her. "I do apologize for my tardiness. Thank you, Mr. Flynn."

"Always my honor, Lady Lydia, to assist a beautiful woman," Flynn said, seating himself beside her before unfolding her serviette and handing it to her.

"Jasmine," Tanner prompted. "Lydia has apologized. As should you, frankly."

But, and probably more noticeable for how seldom silence was all that was heard when Jasmine was in a room, the girl did not accept the apology.

Lydia spread her serviette in her lap before looking across the table at the young woman, who was now glaring at her with hatred naked in her lovely green eyes.

"I'm no longer hungry. And I think you're horrid, all

of you," the girl said, and the gentlemen pushed back their chairs and hurriedly got to their feet as Jasmine, her own serviette pressed to her mouth, raced out of the room, sobbing.

"Volatile little thing, isn't she?" Justin said calmly, seating himself once more and reaching for the domed lid of one of the many silver pieces that adorned the table. "Ah, well, more for the rest of us, as they say. Mr. Flynn, do you perhaps care for some *Potage a la Monglas?* It's a particular specialty of my man, Wigglesworth."

The look on Mr. Flynn's face was so comical that Lydia had to cough to cover a laugh. "Chicken soup, Mr. Flynn. The baron is only having fun with you."

"The correct term is *fowl,* Lady Lydia, if you please. White-legged, as Wigglesworth will settle for nothing less. We don't insult such fine birds by calling them mere *chickens.*"

"I stand corrected, although I doubt the *fowl,* in its current condition, really cares overmuch," Lydia said, as always enjoying the baron's banter. "But I notice you haven't corrected me on the notion that you're having yourself some fun at Mr. Flynn's expense."

The big man visibly relaxed. "Oh, so is that what he's doing? He needn't have bothered. I'm already shocked all hollow by this lovely mass of silver everywhere. I didn't know any inn could be so fine."

Justin laughed shortly. "And now who is having fun with whom, Mr. Flynn? Tanner, pour the man a glass of wine. I do believe we're going to pass a most enjoyable evening. Why, we may all even be able to get a word or two in edgewise."

Lydia was inclined to agree, but couldn't help but worry about Jasmine. "Should I go upstairs to see if I can coax her back to the table? She really should eat something, Tanner."

"No," he said firmly. "If she wants to sulk, let her sulk. I'll have a tray sent up to her room. I don't know what set her off, and I find that I really don't care to know."

"Then perhaps I should join her, and leave you gentlemen to your meal," she said, realizing that she was now the lone woman at table with three gentlemen, and with Mrs. Shandy and Sarah still not arrived at the inn. Drat Jasmine for being so selfish!

"Do you really want to join her, Lydia?" Tanner asked her.

"No," she admitted quietly. "I'm afraid I have little patience for sulks."

"Yet such a pretty little thing," Mr. Flynn said, lifting his wine glass. "To all the pretty ladies, absent or otherwise. Where would we be without them?"

"Out hunting for them?" Justin opined merrily, clinking glasses with the man.

Lydia smiled, as she knew she should, but then thought again of the look of hatred in Jasmine's eyes. That look had been directed straight at her, certainly not at Mr. Flynn, who she didn't even know. But why? Had she somehow found out that the letter in her reticule was no longer her secret? If so, she really did have to apologize, which would be horribly embarrassing for both of them.

She was saved from making a decision with the arrival of Mrs. Shandy, who bustled into the room with many a head bob and curtsy before taking up a chair in the corner and pulling her knitting from a huge bag she'd carried with her.

"Oh, good. We're all decent now," Justin remarked before personally preparing Jasmine's empty plate for the woman and then placing it on a small table Tanner had drawn up to her chair.

"Oh, Your Grace, but I couldn't," Mrs Shandy said, actually blushing.

"Nonsense," Tanner said. "Lady Lydia is made that much more comfortable by your presence, and everyone else, I'm assured, is already being fed in the taproom. You should not have to forgo your dinner. You've been on the road all the day long. Justin, some wine for Mrs. Shandy?"

"Certainly. And shall I cut her meat for her while I'm at it, do you think? Trim away any little bits of fat?"

"This was your idea, you know," Tanner said as Lydia placed Jasmine's knife and fork on the small table, along with handing the thoroughly flustered chaperone a serviette.

"I think you're both very sweet and considerate," Lydia said, returning to her own chair.

"We're adorable, actually. Especially my good friend, Tanner. I, on the other hand, always have ulterior motives."

"Yes, I know," Lydia said quietly, not that the deaf-as-a-post chaperone would hear her at any rate. "You have amorous designs on Mrs. Shandy."

Justin laughed out loud. "Gad, but I could love you, Lady Lydia." He looked down the table at Tanner. "You're the only other person I can think of who'd dare to turn my own words back on me, to make me the butt of my own joke. It's very refreshing."

"I can't speak for the lady Lydia," Tanner said over the rim of his wine glass, "but I know I exist only to amuse you."

"Oh, foul, foul! And I'm not speaking of white-legged chickens. It's time for a change of subject before I feel skewered clear through. Mr. Flynn, if you don't mind me shamelessly using you in order to get my own neck off the chopping block—how did you manage to get that patch? And so as not to stray too far from the subject, it's dashed appealing to the ladies, I'd imagine?"

"It has gotten me more than a few appreciative glances, yes. Something about the wounded hero, I suppose. Is that what it is, Lady Lydia?"

She didn't know what to say, and looked to Tanner helplessly. "I…I would suppose most women would feel sympathy for a man who had been injured in defense of his country."

Mr. Flynn nodded his agreement. "Doesn't seem fair, does it? It's the ones who didn't come home who deserve their sympathy. Poor buggers. Oh, excuse me, Lady Lydia."

She lowered her gaze to her plate, feeling tears stinging at her eyes. It was his voice, the Irish lilt, that's all it was. Bringing the memory too close.

"You've said you've been traveling, Mr. Flynn,"

Tanner said almost abruptly. "Where all have you been?"

"Please, Your Grace, I haven't been Mr. Flynn for a dozen years. I answer much more readily to captain."

Lydia's head jerked up and she gasped involuntarily. "Captain? And His Grace told me you were in the Fourth Foot? You were at Quatre Bras."

She could feel Tanner's eyes on her, but she refused to look at him. She had to prove to him, and to herself, that she wasn't still mired in her memories of Fitz, yes. But she wouldn't be human if she didn't at least ask. "Tell me, did you happen to have had the acquaintance of Captain Fitzgerald? He...he perished at Quatre Bras."

Captain Flynn smiled. "Fitz? Oh, that I did, my lady. Many a fine time we had before Boney showed up to spoil the fun. Quite the man with the ladies, Fitz was."

"That's a lie," Tanner said in a voice as icy as a January morning, glaring at Flynn. "That's a bloody damn lie."

Lydia's heart was pounding so hard in her ears that she could barely hear. Her chest began rising and falling rapidly as she breathed quickly, trying to regain her breath, the breath Captain Flynn's words had taken from her.

The captain looked from Tanner to Lydia, and then shifted to Justin, who was sitting very much at attention now, all traces of the carefree fop gone as if peeled away by Flynn's words.

"Oh, dear me. I do believe you've managed to outlive your welcome, Captain Flynn," the baron said, his voice as soft as the caress of silk.

Captain Flynn slowly pushed back his chair and got to his feet. "I don't understand. But nobody calls Benjamin Flynn a liar. There's a lady present, or I'd already have bloodied your nose, *Your Grace.* But I must insist that you come outside with me."

"Tanner, don't disturb yourself if you please," Justin said, putting down his wine glass. "I owe you for ridding me of a piece of offal the other evening. I'll be happy to do the same for you. We don't want that cut to open again, now do we?" He got to his feet, his gaze never leaving Flynn's face. "Please allow me the honor of grinding that ugly puss of yours in the dirt."

"Not enough, Justin, damn it. He'll apologize."

Tanner was also on his feet. The room was suddenly filled to the brim with anger and men with their hands drawn into fists, ready to wreak havoc on each other. They couldn't seem to wait to have the opportunity to beat each other into pulp.

This is how wars begin, she thought in disgust. *And they like it.*

"Enough!" she heard herself say as she, too, got to her feet. "Nobody will be bloodying anyone's nose or grinding anyone's face into the dirt. Captain Flynn, you were mistaken in your recollections. Captain Swain Fitzgerald was my betrothed."

Flynn's lone visible eyebrow lifted high on his forehead. "Oh, so that's how the land lies, does it? Swain, you said? I then retract my words, my lady, as surely I was thinking of someone else. I most certainly was mistaken in my memories."

He was saying all the right words, but he didn't sound convincing, or convinced.

"Yes, you were mistaken. Tanner? Please?"

"Just get out, Flynn," Tanner said wearily. "But you'll have to understand that it would be better if you were to find yourself another inn for the night. And have yourself a pleasant trip tomorrow, to anywhere else besides Malvern. You'll have to search for truth elsewhere."

"I entirely agree. Now shoo," Justin said, sharply snapping his serviette in the air before sitting down once more, spreading the white linen on his lap, signaling his dismissal of the Irishman and any threat.

Flynn quit the room without another word, so that they were left just the three of them (Mrs. Shandy couldn't really be counted, as she'd fallen asleep in her chair), with two obviously vacant chairs making them a very odd arrangement for dinner.

"Ah, that's eminently better. Tanner, you really must stop inviting all and sundry to break bread with us. You never know the sort of riff-raff that can masquerade as gentlemen, although I will say his jacket was rather fine. Now, who's for some beautifully carved beef, hmm?"

The tension in the room somehow gone with Flynn's exit, Lydia sat down again all at once, unable to remain standing on legs suddenly too weak to support her.

"He was mistaken," she said after a moment.

"I was with Fitz from the time we got to Brussels until the end. Yes, Lydia, Flynn was mistaken. I swear it to you."

She wasn't the hysterical sort. Her outburst had shaken her, but she had to believe what she had to believe. She simply had to! Her bottom lip trembled, so that she quickly caught it between her teeth, and didn't speak again until she felt more in control of herself. "Thank you, Tanner. Justin? If I might have a slice of that beef, please. It does smell delicious."

CHAPTER FOURTEEN

TANNER SAT IN A CORNER of the taproom that was dark
save for the glow of the fire that was needed thanks to
the thickness of the inn walls and the pervading damp
of this year without a summer. He had an untouched
snifter of French brandy dangling forgotten in his right
hand, delivered courtesy of Wigglesworth, a burned-out
cheroot in his left. He sat with his weight on his lower
spine, his booted legs stuck out in front of him so that
he could watch the firelight dance on the polished toes.

"Ah, the Duke of Malvern At Leisure," Justin said,
subsiding into the facing chair that flanked the fireplace. "Or should I amend that? The Duke of Malvern
On The Sulk. Lydia doesn't like sulking. Do try to do
more of it, you'll increase my chances with the fair
lady."

"Go away, Justin."

"Go away, go away. You keep saying that. A lesser
man would be insulted. But I would then go away, if it
were in my nature. Alas, it is not. So. Tell me. Was her
sainted Fitz true to her, or was that one-eyed bastard
right?"

Tanner shook his head. Something had been bothering him all evening, and he thought he'd finally figured out what that something was. "It's more than that. I don't think our Captain Benjamin Flynn is who he says he is. Granted, that he had suffered a grievous wound in the battle may have influenced my decision to invite him to join us for supper. But, truthfully, the moment he said he was at Quatre Bras I began to wonder. I dismissed my misgivings, probably because I thought—well, never mind what I thought. My motive isn't flattering to me."

"You wanted to see how Lydia reacted to meeting an Irishman who'd been at Quatre Bras with this Fitz of yours—hers and yours. It's understandable."

"Is it?"

"For a man in love? I imagine the impulse was impossible to resist. Still feeling a dead man's hand on your shoulder, aren't you?"

"At times, yes. Less and less. What man gives his woman to another man, Justin? Even dying—who would be that unselfish?"

"A very good man, I'd say. I'm sorry I never knew him; it was my loss. But we both know that, at the end of the day, it will be Lydia who decides. Not you, for whatever solid and upstanding reasons you might put forth to try to confuse the issue, and not Fitz, for all his dying pleas. She'll either love you for you, or she won't. Like you, she's too honorable to do anything else. You're quite the pair."

Tanner lifted his chin from his chest and looked at Justin quizzically. "When did you get so smart?"

"I've always been smart. It's just that nobody expects it of me, so that I seem doubly intelligent when I deign to say something even remotely profound."

"I wouldn't go so far as to say you were being profound just now." He shifted in his chair, looked at his right hand as if surprised to see the snifter. "Wasn't she magnificent this evening? Asking you prettily for a slice of beef, acting as if Flynn's words hadn't just knocked her legs out from under her?"

"Ah, yes, we're back to Flynn. You intrigue me with this notion that the man isn't who he purported himself to be. The question is, if he is not Captain Flynn, then who is he?"

"I wish I knew. I just know his appearance was too convenient. Face it, Justin, what are the odds of us meeting up with a man who had fought at Quatre Bras? An Irishman, and a captain to boot. And one thing more. Looking back at the entire incident, I think Jasmine recognized him."

Justin lowered his cheroot. "I beg your pardon?"

"I know. Ridiculous. There was just something suspicious about her reaction when he entered the room with Lydia. My cousin has never been adept at hiding her emotions, and I think she was…angry."

"With Lydia, yes."

Tanner shook his head. "Who's to say? She was looking across the table at the two of them. At any rate, while you and Wigglesworth were conversing after dinner about whatever it is the two of you converse about—"

"We were discussing my ensemble for tomorrow. It's a nightly ritual. I could probably forgo the exercise, except that Wigglesworth would be devastated. But do go on."

"Pardon me for allowing you to interrupt me with tales of the minutiae of your life."

Justin looked at him quizzically. "Oh, dear. You begin to sound like me. That isn't good, Tanner. I rely on you to be above such remarks."

"It turns out I'm not above much of anything if I think Lydia is being hurt. But I apologize. May I continue? While you were consulting with your keeper, I visited the other two inns here in the village. Flynn was at neither of them. I returned here and asked one of the ostlers if they'd seen him ride out. I was told he'd ordered his horse saddled and rode out of the village, toward Malvern, or at least in that direction. There's no moon tonight, Justin. Where the hell would a stranger to this part of the country go on a moonless night?"

"Straight into a tree or a ditch, I'd imagine, at least eventually. Are you going to confront your cousin?"

"Not here, no. I'll wait until we reach Malvern. Although I don't think Jasmine is capable of any sort of intrigue."

"More hair than wit, I agree. Just the sort of woman who once appealed to me. Beautiful, and easily dazzled by bright shiny things, but not overstuffed in the brainbox."

"Too bad. I'd make you a gift of her, if I didn't like you so much. She really is quite wearing on the nerves, something I didn't fully realize until I brought her to town with me for the Season. But I'm thinking more of her father."

Justin deftly opened an ivory-topped snuffbox with one hand and took a pinch, raised it to his right nostril, and sniffed delicately. "Thank you, no. I don't want him, either."

Tanner smiled, which was what Justin had wanted him to do. "I think Thomas may have decided my interests lay with Lydia, and not Jasmine. Although why he'd want to hurt her…"

"Oh, don't stop now."

Tanner at last took a sip from the snifter, the brandy bitter on his tongue. "He's looking for ways to turn her away from me. Bringing up memories of Fitz could do that."

"Yes, all that business about you being the bearer of sad news and such. And why would he want to do that?"

"Why do I bother talking to you? You already know."

"Yes, I think we both do. He would have Lydia turn away from you so that you at last give in and marry his little babbling darling, make her a duchess, and thereby fill his pockets. This much we could have deduced even before Captain Flynn's appearance tonight. And? Finish it, Tanner."

"The Malvern jewels. It would be in very bad taste for me to send my father-in-law to prison. Because only an idiot would believe I'd never discover the substitutions."

"I've been out of the country for a long time, I grant

you, but I believe the punishment for theft on such a grand scale is to be hanged, or at the very least transported. Now, this is all conjecture, knowing that the jewels could have been sold years ago, but excuse me if I allow fancy to take me further into the realm of speculation."

"Don't bother. I'm already there," Tanner said, getting to his feet. "I marry her, give her a male heir, and then suffer a fatal accident. Her father serves as Jasmine's advisor and the child's guardian, and spends the remainder of his life swimming nicely in a nice deep gravy boat made up of my lands and fortune. At some point I'm certain there would be a terrible robbery at Malvern and the paste jewels would disappear."

"All the dark melodrama of a Pennypress novel," Justin said, nodding. "Unfortunately, also plausible. So, who was our Captain Flynn, this man we should probably be thanking for being so clumsy?"

Tanner shrugged. "A hireling? I'm just certain poor, transparent Jasmine recognized him, has probably seen him with her father, and knew him for a liar. I imagine her reunion with her father at Malvern isn't going to be pleasant. After all, she might not be the brightest person, but she has to know that she is being manipulated."

"And, it would appear, the thought that her father's plans are moving on to possible fruition—marriage to you—is enough to cast her into strong hysterics. I hadn't realized you were such a terrible catch."

At last, Tanner smiled. "Her reluctance is rather lowering, isn't it? Truthfully, that reluctance is her most appealing trait." He reached into his waistcoat pocket and withdrew a small, thick key. "If you don't mind, I'm hoping you'll ride ahead of us tomorrow, as I'm planning to show Lydia a bit of Malvern from horseback before we reach the house. The Malvern collection is in a locked box secreted in a cut-out behind the portrait of the first duke. In my study. Probably not the best hiding place."

"But changing it now might be rather like locking the stables after the horse thief has been," Justin agreed, pocketing the key. "I'd be happy to pass the time by examining the jewels. Then it's done, and we can move on to what seems to be more skullduggery in the making. You're such a fine host, Tanner, planning this amusement for your guest."

Tanner shot him a darkling look. "Thomas is probably already in residence, as he left for Malvern within hours of my telling him our plans. He says, to alert the staff to our arrival."

"And Lord knows what else," Justin said, nodding. "I'll be careful to avoid him."

"Thank you, Justin. At least that's off my mind. Now I need to go upstairs and speak with Lydia."

"Do you think that's wise? She said she knows Flynn was mistaken. She was hurt by his words, certainly. But how much more upsetting to think that she has unwittingly become part of a conspiracy?"

"I'm not going to tell any of that. After all, we may both be mistaken."

"Oh, now that wounds me. *You* could be mistaken. *I,* on the other hand, am almost always right. And as I concur with your conclusions, the chances are quite high that our Captain Flynn was sent here by Thomas Harburton expressly to undermine your budding romance with the fair Lydia."

"Because I was with Fitz, and never told her that he was spending the months before the battle amusing himself with half the ladies in Brussels? I watched her mourning him, suffering, and all while knowing he'd been unfaithful to her?"

"You cad," Justin said, shaking his head in mock horror. "Then again, just another example of the honorable Tanner, choosing not to besmirch her memories of the man, even as you hope to court her yourself. Although she wouldn't have believed you if you'd said any such thing, probably sent you away forever. My goodness, being honorable does open a person to re-criminations no matter what one does. I must remember to never decide to become moral."

"I don't think any of us has to worry much about that," Tanner told him. "You enjoy your reprobate status entirely too much."

"Thank you. Did I forget to point out that, if the dear Lady Lydia were to take you in distaste, I remain available to comfort her? You could mention that as she tosses you out on your ear."

"I'll try to remember," Tanner said, aiming his unlit cheroot at the fire. "Now, if you'll excuse me, I'm off to be honorable."

"I know." Justin sighed. "What a waste of a perfectly good evening."

The clock in the vestibule of the inn chimed out the hour of ten as Tanner climbed the stairs to Lydia's chamber. He'd thought to give her time to weep, for he was certain that she would have needed to release her feelings at some point, but he couldn't allow her to spend the night wondering about Fitz's loyalty to her, his love for her.

As he turned down the hallway, a maid carrying a tray of dishes was just letting herself out of the chamber assigned to Jasmine. "If I might?" he asked, lifting the cloth from the tray, and then he smiled at the sight of all the empty plates. Clearly Jasmine had gotten over her snit. "I see Miss Harburton retains her usual healthy appetite, Mildred."

"Yes, Your Grace," the maid said, bobbing a curtsy. "She's tucked up proper and all but fast asleep. I asked if she wanted me to stay with her—seeing as how she's in a strange bed—but she said she was fine."

"Thank you, Mildred. I imagine you'd like to seek your own bed now. It was a long day on the road."

"Yes, Your Grace." The maid bobbed another curtsy and hastened toward the back stairs.

Tanner rapped lightly on Lydia's door, quietly announcing himself, and then wondered if she, like Jasmine, had already retired for the night. Had he left his visit too late?

The door opened quietly on a room dark save for the light of the fire and a few small candles, and Lydia appeared in the doorway. She was dressed in a virginal white dressing gown that ruffled prettily beneath her chin, and her lovely blond hair was down, floating over her shoulders. As his body attempted to betray him, he carefully kept his gaze at eye level. "I'm sorry. I wanted to talk to you about what happened earlier, but I see I've probably left it too late."

"Please don't go," she said, opening the door wider. "I…I've been waiting for you, actually, hoping you would come. But you're not going to apologize for kissing me, are you? Because I'd really rather you didn't."

He slipped inside and quietly shut the door. "That's good, Lydia, because I'd really rather I didn't, too. I will say that's it's probably a good thing Justin came along when he did. I didn't frighten you, did I? Oh, wait," he added, feeling flustered, and he was never flustered; if Justin could see him he'd be rolling on the floor, clutching his stomach in mirth. "I should prop the door open, shouldn't I?"

Her smile was very nearly indulgent. "I can always scream for help if it becomes necessary. Leave it closed."

She stood in the middle of the room, clearly unaware of how the firelight licked at her hair, making her appear almost an apparition rather than flesh and blood. The brandy had made no impact on him, but the sight of her made him feel nearly drunk with emotions he'd never experienced in his lifetime.

Had he even been alive until she'd come into his life? He couldn't be sure. He'd gone through the motions, yes. The good son, the good friend, the good soldier. Sane, conventional, reliable. *Honorable.* He'd done what was expected of him, always.

But now he wanted something for himself. And what he wanted was to hold Lydia Daughtry close against him for the rest of his days.

"Flynn left the village," he heard himself say as Lydia sat herself in one of the two shabby leather chairs flanking the fireplace. "I went searching for him, which he must have expected, so he left."

"That was probably wise of him. You looked ready to take a horsewhip to him, the way those men had planned to punish Justin. Violence solves nothing, Tanner. I thought we already agreed on that the day we discussed war."

Tanner gestured to the vacant chair and Lydia nodded her agreement, so he sat down. "I wasn't contemplating a war. It was more of an annihilation. The man was wrong. He didn't even know Fitz."

"Yes, I know. There were so many Irish in the Fourth Foot. Fitzgerald, Fitzpatrick, Fitzsimmons, Fitzhugh. On and on. I imagine at least half of them were addressed as Fitz by their associates. Captain Flynn was mistaken."

It's more likely he was mistaken that he was Captain Flynn, Tanner thought, but did not say. "Still, it couldn't have been easy for you, hearing what he said."

Lydia fingered the long white ribbons that had been tied at her neck and fell to her lap. "For a moment, no, it wasn't. But then I was much more upset to think that you might go outside with the Captain. You…you could have been injured. And for nothing. If there is one thing I know, Tanner, it is that Fitz loved me."

Tanner tried not to smile. "You were worried about *me?* That's why you intervened?"

He could see her cheeks flushing a becoming pink. "Now you're going to tell me I was being silly. But you do still have that bandage on your cheek, and if the wound were to open it could prove very painful."

"True," Tanner pointed out, "but Justin had already volunteered to beat the man into a jelly for me, remember?"

"Yes, I heard him. The two of you were all but strutting about like roosters in a barnyard, that's what you were doing. And there was Captain Flynn with only the one eye, and only one man against two. And all because of me. There was no way for it all to end well, Tanner. I didn't want to interfere, but you left me no choice."

Tanner was trying to understand. "So you *are* angry with me?"

She shook her head, sighing. "No. I'm angry with *me,* because if Captain Flynn had taken a single step in your direction I quite fear I was prepared to conk him on the head with one of Justin's silly silver dishes."

"Really," Tanner said, doing his best not to throw back his head and laugh out loud. "Pardon me, but didn't you say that only men are foolish enough to fight wars for the glory of someone else, and that women only fight to take care of their—"

He stopped, almost physically stunned as the meaning of her near-action became clear to him, and finished silently: *take care of their own.*

"Fitz gave me to you, or you to me—sometimes I'm

not sure anymore," she said quietly, her voice so low he had to lean forward to be sure he heard her. "That letter you brought to us? The last one he'd written to me? He planned never to post it, not if he lived through the battle. He knew if he…if he died, that you would bring it to me."

She raised her head, her expressive blue eyes swimming in tears. "He imagined he might die. But not you, he seemed sure you'd survive. Don't you find that strange?"

Now this was a conversation he'd never really planned on having with her. "We all of us make arrangements with another soldier, a friend, to take our belongings home if something should happen. I'd given Fitz my own Will, just as he'd given me his. But, yes, Lydia, he did think he was going to die when the battle finally came. He said he'd had a premonition or some such thing. I teased him that he was just being Irish, and maudlin, but he'd come to believe he'd never return to England, that he could already feel a goose walking across his grave. There was no talking him out of it."

She bit her bottom lip, and a single tear ran down her cheek. "Tell me, please. Tell me all that he said."

"You don't need to hear this, Lydia."

"Oh, Tanner, but I do. Please."

Would he be exposing Fitz's darkest fears to her for no reason save curiosity? How could she understand the workings of a mind passing time, waiting, waiting for the beat of the drums, the blare of the trumpets, the inevitable call to battle? A man's mind can play terrible tricks in the weeks and days and hours before he goes off to kill or be killed. God, one of their very best generals had only left home for Brussels after lying himself down in a fresh-dug grave, telling his servant, "Why, I think this will do for me." Poor Picton, he'd survived Quatre Bras only to have his brains blown out on the fields at Waterloo.

And yet, certain he would die, he'd answered Wellington's call, just as Fitz had done. Bravery or foolishness? Dedication or insanity? Was it fair to judge such things from a distance?

"All right," Tanner agreed at last. "Fitz told me he'd never thought about dying, all those years he and Rafe served together. Not seriously, anyway. That was obvious to anyone who ever saw him in a fight. Fitz would have drawn his sword and charged the Devil himself across a battlefield. It was only when he had so much to lose that the reality of his own mortality began to terrify him. You, Lydia. You were everything to him."

He was silent for a few moments, trying to find the right words, when there were no right words. "He never thought he could be so blessed, and was convinced the Fates would find a way to deny him such happiness."

Lydia nodded her head, wiped at her damp cheeks. "So it is what I thought. It's…it's almost as if he'd still be alive if he had never met me."

"Jesus," Tanner said softly, immediately realizing the importance of her words. "How long have you lived with the idea that you caused his death?"

She turned her head toward the fireplace, as if suddenly interested in the flames. She put a hand to her mouth and sat quietly for long moments, composing herself, while Tanner held his breath.

"I don't know," she said at last, turning to face him once more. "Months, I suppose. Then I decided it would be easier to be angry with him for going off to fight Bonaparte when he thought he wouldn't come back. But…but it still hurt." She wiped at her cheeks again with trembling hands, her voice breaking, "It still hurt so much. Love…love brings so much responsibility with it. I don't know how anyone survives it…"

When she lapsed into silence once more, Tanner knew he was left with no choice but to go to her, gather her up in his arms, and take her with him into his chair. She needed to be held. He needed to hold her. She offered no protest. Her arms went up and around him, her head burrowed into his shoulder.

His desire for her was always just beneath the surface, but his concern for her, his love for her, overpowered any thoughts other than wanting to comfort her in her pain.

Her body was warm and pliant against him, showing him how she trusted him, how she relied upon him, felt secure with him. But did he have any real answers for her?

No, he didn't. No mortal could.

"I lost so many of my dearest friends at Waterloo, men I loved as brothers. We all did. Rafe, Justin, everyone. It was hell on earth to be left behind, with so many others gone, all with no rhyme, no reason. But it gets better, Lydia," he whispered against her hair. "With every day that passes, it gets better. Slowly, we learn to live again. We forget the bad and remember the good. It's the only way to truly honor the love we knew and find the courage to open our hearts again."

"I want to do that," she said, and he had to hold his breath to hear her, as her whisper was so tentative and quiet. "But then, at the ball, and again tonight…when I thought you might be hurt, all I could do was feel the chance slipping away again. I don't know, Tanner. I don't know if I can dare to risk opening my heart again. That makes me a coward, doesn't it?"

Tanner closed his eyes, feeling tears burning in them. Did she realize what she'd just admitted?

His joy at hearing that she might love him, however, was nearly overshadowed by the realization of what that love meant.

Loving was all he'd thought of; loving Lydia. Being loved in return? That held responsibilities he'd never considered.

He kissed her hair. "I would never hurt you."

"You say that. You've said it before, and I know you mean it. But people can't help hurting each other, not if that person is…important to the other person."

They were silent for some moments, a burnt log splitting and dropping into the fire the only sound in the room. He'd taken her hand in his, lightly rubbing his thumb over her soft skin, and she kept her head against his shoulder.

There was no passion. Just two people, comfortable together. Safe, together. Maybe even afraid…but together. And that was all right. He was willing to move at her pace, follow her lead. It was enough for now that he was holding her, trying to tell her, tell himself, that she was safe in his arms.

Tanner squeezed her fingers.

"You really would have conked Flynn on the head if he'd made a move toward me?"

"Now you're laughing at me."

"No. Well, not exactly. Mostly, I'm picturing the look of dismay on Justin's face if you'd dented one of his fine silver lids on Flynn's head."

Lydia's shoulders shook a time or two, and then she pushed herself slightly away, braced her hands on his shoulders, and smiled into his face. "He would have been aghast, wouldn't he?"

"Aghast and agog, certainly. Not rendered speechless, because that will never happen. But it might have been fun to see. It's almost a pity Flynn raced off, or I could go drag him here now and…well, and let you have a whack at him."

"I really would have hit him, you know. I was a bit aghast and agog at how very much I longed to hit him. I…I've never understood anyone using violence. I frightened myself with how logical violence seemed at that moment."

"Many things seem logical at the moment," he dared to say, tipping his head slightly, his gaze intent on her face. "For instance, it seems very logical for me to kiss you now."

Her smile relaxed his taut nerves. They'd taken

another step, moved further away from the past. Toward each other. Only one final step remained. "Really? Perhaps I should have let you keep the door open."

"Are you saying that, if I were to kiss you now, you'd feel the need to scream?"

She shook her head almost imperceptibly. "I don't think so, no. Should we try it and see? It would be my second kiss. And both in one day."

Tanner cupped her cheek in his hand, and heard her quick intake of breath. The firelight played in her tumbled curls, warmed her flawless skin with color. "I'm not sure two kisses would be enough."

"No? How many then?"

He put his mouth to hers. Gently, tenderly, their lips slanted against each other, Tanner holding himself back until hers softened, became accustomed to him.

And then, reluctantly, he slowly broke the kiss, his heart singing when she seemed equally reluctant to end it.

"How many, Lydia?" he said, his voice full with emotions he hadn't known existed. "I could stay here, kissing you, until the sun fades away. Until the stars fall into the sea. Until we're both—"

But she had turned aggressor, wrapping her arms around the back of his neck and pulling him toward her, banishing all coherent thought as she sought his kiss.

This time, giving himself some slight slack in the leash he was trying so hard to keep on his emotions, he opened his mouth over hers, coaxing her with teeth and tongue until she relaxed her lips and allowed him entry.

Her body seemed to melt into his as he taught her the power of a kiss, the depth and breadth and heights of the miracles of physical sensation, this prelude to an even more intimate plundering of her secrets. That final step. Total possession.

She shifted slightly on his lap and his arousal had to be noticeable to her through the thin cloth of her night-rail and dressing gown. God knew he could feel her every curve as she pressed against him.

"Lydia. Sweetheart. We need to stop now," he said against her hair as he fought what would soon be a losing battle with his desire for her.

"No," she said, tipping her head so that he took up the invitation, pressing kisses against the slim column of her neck. She reached down and found his hand, raising it with hers, pressing his against the center of her chest. "Do you feel it, Tanner? That's my heart, finally beating again. I feel alive, Tanner. I so need to feel alive again. I don't know what I'm asking. I just know that I'd die again if you left me now. Please."

It would take a man ten times, one hundred times stronger than he to leave her now. "You do know what you're asking, Lydia. We both do. And God help me, I'd rather cut off my own arm than leave you now."

He stood up, holding her high against his chest, and walked to the tester bed that hid in the flickering shadows, and set her on her feet beside it. She seemed so small to him, the top of her head barely reaching his shoulders. He felt huge, and clumsy, and more nervous than he'd been at sixteen.

Shrugging out of his jacket in front of her made him feel ridiculous. Kissing her as he unbuttoned his waistcoat seemed almost unnatural. He'd never thought about his own nakedness, how it might affect a gentle and reserved woman like Lydia, even frighten her.

But when Lydia began opening the buttons on his shirt he forgot his nervousness. This was wrong, even as it was so very right. But right or wrong, it was going to happen. Without words, she was telling him that what he wanted, she wanted.

With Nicole for a sister, and Helen Daughtry as her mother, Lydia had to know…the mechanics of the thing. But her fingers didn't falter, even as the last button slid from its moorings and she touched a hand to his bare chest.

Branding him hers forever.

She wanted him. She at least wanted something. She'd been hovering around the edges of life for all of her years. He knew it, she had said as much. Even her love for Fitz had not broken her free from whatever safe cocoon she'd felt she'd needed.

But now she was here, and he was here, and she'd chosen him to make her feel alive. The world wouldn't dare to tear them apart now…

He tugged his shirttails free of his fawn trousers, grateful that Justin's insistence on dressing for supper had forced him into evening shoes rather than high-top boots. He stepped out of them now, and then dismissed the thought as unimportant.

Because he was undoing the long thin ribbons on

Lydia's dressing gown now, kissing each bare shoulder as he gently eased the material aside until the gown lay puddled at her feet.

She was looking at him, not blinking, her breasts rising and falling as her breaths quickened, went shallow.

"I said I'd never hurt you," he told her, pulling her close, cupping her rounded buttocks as he introduced her to his arousal. "But that's not possible, Lydia. Not this one time. You know that, don't you?"

"I know that," she said, her palms against his chest, her blue eyes clear, untroubled by any notion that she was making a mistake. "Maman explained it to us. She was very explicit."

Tanner suppressed a wince. Helen Daughtry had the morals of a cat; the entire *ton* knew about her appetites. "Then you…know."

"I know what she said. But Nicole promised me it's nothing like anything Maman said."

A small smile tugged at Tanner's mouth. "Oh she did, did she. And what did your sister say?"

"Just that. It's nothing like anything our mother told us. And then she smiled, rather the way you're doing now, as a matter of fact. Tanner, must we talk? If you've changed your mind I certainly under—"

His answer was to pick her up and deposit her in the center of the turned-down bed, then follow her down. He pulled the covers up and over them, even though he longed to not just touch her, possess her, but to see her. But that might frighten her.

He was careful to kiss her without attempting

anything more intimate until he could tell by her reaction that her body was telling her it needed more, that there had to be more.

Only then did he place his hand on the curve of her hip, drawing her slightly onto her side, in closer contact with his own body. When he cupped her breast she made a small mewling sound deep in her throat. He could feel her nipple harden against his hand.

The bud, still covered by her nightrail, was irresistible to him and he closed finger and thumb around it, lightly tugging on it as he began to plunder her mouth. He ran his tongue over the roof of her mouth, lightly nipped at her bottom lip before drawing her tongue into his own mouth, his body tensing as she began her own tentative exploration.

When he could bear no more, he reached down, took a fistful of cloth, and began tugging up her nightrail, whispering nonsense words of encouragement as she lifted her hips, making it easier for him.

The feel of her silken skin, her sweet, untutored reaction to his touch, was like a benediction to him, and an impossible to ignore invitation.

Somehow he managed to rid himself of shirt and trousers and hose, all while never moving more than a whisper from Lydia, every moment not spent touching her an agony to him.

Fingers spread, he settled his hand on her flat belly, leaving it there for long moments as he kissed her mouth, her eyelids, her throat. She slid one arm up and over his shoulder, turning more toward him, her body moving restlessly. If he needed, she also needed. She was telling him so with her body.

He pressed her onto her back once more, and dared a new intimacy.

The skin between her thighs was like warm silk. She tensed at first, and again he was careful to go slow, even as his own body was crying out to cover her, possess her.

"It's all right, sweetheart," he whispered as he slid one leg over hers, wrapping his lower leg around her calf, letting her feel him, urging her legs apart. "Let me touch you. The rest will be easier if you let me touch you." He found the center of her, her sweet heat, and stroked her until he felt her hips lifting with each stroke, seeking his touch. "Yes, that's it. It's good, isn't it? So very good. Let it happen, sweetheart. Just let it happen."

"But what…I…"

Hovering over her, looking down into her face, watching her eyelids flutter closed as she tipped back her head, Tanner at last understood why he'd been born. He'd been put on this earth to love this woman. Protect her, comfort her. Laugh with her, cry with her. Love her…always love her.

Lydia's eyelids flew open and she looked up at him in sudden surprise. Her hips lifted one more time, then stilled. He covered her mouth with his as he felt the small convulsions of her body, the glory of feeling she hadn't known existed until that moment.

And then, before he could tell himself that he should hold her now, calm her, and then leave her, he levered himself over her completely and sank into her. He felt the resistance, but it was quickly gone and he was deep inside her, his heart beating so fast he wouldn't have been surprised if it burst in his chest.

"It's all right, it's all right," he told her as she raised both arms around him, digging her fingertips into his bare back. "Let me love you."

She kissed his chest, his throat, his face, as if she needed the feel of him, the taste of him. Her passion became his passion. He moved slowly at first, still worried for her, but when she began to move in rhythm with him it was impossible to resist her sweet temptation.

Bracing his hands on either side of her head, he raised himself up as he thrust into her again and again, faster and faster, until she gave a small cry that seemed to trigger his own release.

He collapsed against her, spent, his breathing ragged, his heart still racing at a gallop.

He'd thought himself experienced. As Justin would have termed it, a man of the world. But making love to—no, *with*—Lydia was something totally out of his experience. He'd never cared so much, never wanted so much, never needed to hold a woman afterwards as he did now. Just to be with her, just to feel her head resting against his shoulder, just to listen to her even breathing as she slept…wondering if her dreams were of him. Praying that they were…

CHAPTER FIFTEEN

LYDIA WAS COMFORTABLY sore when she woke, and alone. The room was still dark, the fire almost dead in the grate. She wondered what time it was, and if she'd somehow sensed Tanner leaving, and that had wakened her.

Turning on her side, she hugged the pillow that carried his scent close to her, burying her nose in its softness.

And then she giggled.

Charlotte had told her to give him a little nudge.

Sometimes, honorable as gentlemen feel themselves required to be, it takes a...a bit of a nudge from the woman who knows what's best for him. And for her, of course.

Lydia supposed she'd done more than that. She'd all but begged Tanner to kiss her, to carry her to bed.

Think about letting go, just a little.

Only a little? "Oh, Charlotte, you couldn't know what it is to soar above the clouds, if you could say something like that. Or maybe you did..."

Lydia turned onto her back and stared up at the

ceiling, feeling rather stupid. She saw it now, how they had all conspired to shake her out of her doldrums. The lowered necklines. Rafe's quick agreement to a week at Malvern. Charlotte's *little nudge*. Why, they'd all but given her permission, set the table for her, and told her to enjoy her meal.

Because they'd all known what she had been fighting against for so long; her feelings for Tanner. And, obviously, they all approved.

How could they have known of his feelings for her? How could they have been so certain?

Her eyes went wide. "He told them. It's the only way."

She could recite from Molière, quote full verses from a dozen poets or more. She knew a smattering of Greek, could conjugate verbs in nearly flawless French. She could name every capital of every country in Europe. She could recite the history of the English monarchy throughout all of its twisted pathways by rote.

But she didn't know when a man was in love with her?

With her beloved captain, it had been different. She had been different. Young, knowing nothing of what it truly meant to love a man, what it felt like to need to be always near him, constantly long to touch him. To want everything he could give her, everything she could offer him in return…with no hesitation, no hint of shame.

Her love for Fitz had been a quiet love, a simple love.

Fitz had been long winter afternoons spent before a roaring fire at Ashurst Hall, reading Shakespeare together, listening to tales of his boyhood in Dublin, feeling important to someone. She hadn't been ready for more, and Fitz had somehow known that. He'd been her first step toward womanhood.

Tanner was the smile that warmed her all over. The voice she could listen to for hours. The distinctive footfalls on the tiles in the foyer that always set her heart racing. The face that lived in her dreams.

She'd hated him so much when he'd come to tell them about Fitz. She'd feared him more when his face began taking Fitz's place in her dreams. She hadn't been ready for him last year and had avoided him on his infrequent visits to Ashurst Hall. She hadn't been ready for the way he made her feel.

But never could she forget him.

Now she knew why.

The captain was her past, a very important part of her past. He was her beginning.

Tanner was her everything. Her today, and all of her tomorrows.

Lydia used a corner of the sheeting to wipe at her damp eyes and hugged the pillow close once more. Life wasn't easy, being able to feel could be a blessing or a curse…but she was ready for it, all of it. With Tanner, she was even eager for every moment.

Time had this way of moving on, and with its sure passage, the bad faded, and a person could once more open herself, open her heart, to what was good. There was more than one chance in life, and only a fool wouldn't see that, and take that chance. As Tanner had said, they owed that to those who couldn't move forward with them.

She snuggled beneath the sheets, looking toward the window dotted with raindrops that must have fallen earlier, hoping for dawn so that she could see Tanner again. There might be some awkwardness at first, having just been so intimate with each other, but her eagerness to see him immediately banished that worry from her mind. If she could just sleep again, the time would pass more quickly…

She closed her eyes, and then opened them again nearly as quickly, alert to a noise from somewhere behind her. But only the wall was behind her, the one between her chamber and Jasmine's.

What was that sound? Is that why she'd awakened in the first place?

Pushing down the covers, Lydia climbed out of her bed and put her ear to the wall. And heard it again. The sound of weeping.

"Oh, for goodness' sake," Lydia grumbled, knowing that she couldn't ignore that sound, much as she wished she could. Using the tinderbox on the table beside her bed, she lit her single candle and quickly looked about to locate her dressing gown. There was no clock in the chamber, but she could nearly make out clouds in the sky, so it must be close to dawn.

Had Jasmine been crying all night? Was she even now sobbing in her sleep? And for what? She'd behaved irrationally at supper, childishly. Lydia, as was the case for most even-tempered people, had little sympathy for the girl's histrionics...but that didn't mean she could go back to bed and pretend she hadn't heard her.

Picking up her candle, she quietly let herself out of her chamber after peering up and down the hallway, hoping it wasn't late enough for the maids to be stirring. Assured she wouldn't be discovered, she padded on bare feet to Jasmine's door and knocked.

"Jasmine? Jasmine, it's Lydia. Please, may I come in?"

"No! No, go away!"

Lydia rolled her eyes. Really, she may not be much for intrigue and stealth herself, but Jasmine's lack outstripped hers by a good measure. "The whole inn will be standing out here with me if you don't lower your voice. Now let me in or I'll find someone to summon Tanner."

She counted to ten under her breath and was just about to knock once more when the door opened a few inches and she slipped inside. A quick glance to her left told her that Jasmine's bed was placed directly on the wall that separated the two rooms.

If she had heard Jasmine, had Jasmine heard her? And Tanner? That could prove embarrassing.

Once her eyes had become accustomed to the dimness, Lydia went about the small chamber, using her candle to light several others, before she turned to look at Jasmine.

The girl was clad in a rather fetching dressing gown embroidered with yellow rosebuds. Her dark hair hung loosely past her shoulders, framing her small, almost elfin face. She really was beautiful…until she opened her mouth and let her tongue run on wheels, that is.

"What's that on your cheek?" Lydia asked after a moment, lifting her candle and walking toward the girl. "No, don't turn away from me. Your left cheek looks… bruised."

Jasmine pressed a hand against her tear-wet cheek. "It's…it's all my own fault. I behaved so badly last night at supper. I don't know what came over me, I really don't, Lydia. I suppose I was hungry. Papa says I'm never nasty except when I need to be fed. But then I left the supper room without so much as a bite."

"I believe that's called cutting off one's nose to spite one's face," Lydia pointed out quietly. "But I thought Tanner was going to have a tray sent up to your room."

Jasmine nodded furiously. "Oh, he did, he did. But I simply couldn't eat by then, having told myself I deserved to be miserable. Papa would have been infuriated if he could have seen me. He says to be careful to always make a good impression on Tanner. I sent away the tray without taking so much as a bite."

"A nose and one ear," Lydia muttered, shaking her head. "But what does that have to do with that bruise on your cheek?"

At last Jasmine lowered her hand, and Lydia got a good look at her cheek. The skin wasn't broken in any way. Her cheek was red, swollen. And there was something else. Evidence of a slight abrasion along the right side of her chin.

Very like the one Lydia had needed to cover with rice powder before going down to supper.

A day earlier, and Lydia wouldn't have known what she was seeing. But a day earlier had been a lifetime ago in experience. Now, she knew, and her first thought went to schoolmaster Bruce Beattie. Was he here? Had he ridden from Malvern because she'd somehow sent a message to him, and he couldn't bear to wait until tomorrow to see her? Had Jasmine slipped out of the inn to see him? But, no, she couldn't ask those questions. She'd have to explain too much in order to ask those questions.

Jasmine crossed to the small dressing table set in front of the single window and sat down, inspecting her reflection in the fly-spotted mirror.

"Oh, dear, I really did it, didn't I? You don't suppose I broke anything, do you?" She touched two fingers to her cheek, wincing, before wiping away her tears with the hem of her dressing gown.

"I can't be the judge of that if you don't tell me what happened."

Jasmine turned her back on the mirror, her bottom lip trembling. "It does hurt, Lydia. That's why I was crying. I'm so sorry I disturbed you. Inn walls are so thin, aren't they? Do you know gentlemen often sleep six or more to a room in places like this? I can't imagine how anyone could—"

"Jasmine," Lydia interrupted without a trace of regret, "you can prattle on all you like, but I will continue to ask my question, and sooner or later you will answer me. Me, or Tanner. It's your choice."

"Why? Is it important in some way that everyone know how foolish I was? I didn't know you could be so cruel."

"Neither did I, but I seem to be discovering that there are limits to my patience. You are fast approaching one of those limits."

Jasmine sighed, her slim shoulders rising and falling half in petulance, half in resignation. "Oh, very well, since you're going to be that way. It's all so stupid. Mildred offered to sleep in here with me, and I should have agreed, but I didn't. So I didn't know where she was in this place, and I was *so* hungry. So…so I went searching for her."

"Like that? In your dressing gown?" That Jasmine possessed a healthy appetite did not come as any shock. There was, after all, that business with the sugared buns in the not so distant past. But she'd actually go traipsing about the inn in the dead of night to feed it? That was unsettling.

"The servant stairs are just outside my door, across the hallway. It wasn't as if anyone would *see* me, Lydia. I'm not such a dunce. The stairs lead up to the attics and straight down to the kitchens."

Lydia rubbed at the back of her neck as she perched herself on the side of the bed, suddenly feeling very much older than Tanner's cousin. "And which way did you go?"

"Well, *up*, of course," Jasmine said, her tone implying that this was a question silly in the extreme. "I know nothing of kitchens. How could I? So I held my candle high and tiptoed carefully up the stairs, calling out Mildred's name. But she never answered me, and I belatedly considered the possibility that the male servants of the inn patrons might be sleeping in the attics, as well. Tanner's man, and the baron's, and possibly even more. That gave me pause, I must admit to you, so I turned on the landing to make good my escape. But I forgot to be careful. I tripped on the hem of my gown—Mildred will hear about that, I tell you, as I've warned her that this hem is too long—and very nearly came to grief before I could catch myself. But not before I'd landed very heavily against the wall, and hit my cheek. I don't think it's broken. It can't be broken, can it?"

"How badly does it hurt?"

"Not so much anymore," Jasmine admitted. "But I was very frightened for those few moments I believed I might plunge to my death. I'll have nightmares for months and months of tumbling down dark stairs."

Lydia remained unmoved by the girl's tears, but offered, "I sincerely hope not. And what about your chin?"

"My chin?" Jasmine tentatively touched the center of her chin.

"No, not there. On the right side of your face. Far away from the bruise on your cheek where you collided with the wall, I would think. Did you perhaps *bounce?*"

When Jasmine turned on the low bench, to inspect her chin in the mirror, Lydia bent down and picked up one of the girl's slippers, abandoned on the carpet. She turned it over, touched its soft kid sole, and felt dampness. Quickly, she dropped the slipper beside its mate, her only conclusion the obvious one.

Jasmine had been outside.

She was leaning close to the mirror now, touching one finger to her chin. "Is this what you were referring to, Lydia? My goodness, I can't imagine what happened. Unless it is these terribly rough sheets. When I was crying, you understand, and trying to hide my sobs by screwing my face into the pillow. I have such tender skin, you understand. Ah, to be like the baron, and be able to afford to travel with my own linens. But that is neither here nor there, is it?"

She pushed back the bench and stood up, turning to smile at Lydia. "I'm feeling much better now, although very stupid for having wakened you. Please, go back to bed. I promise to be quiet now. Unless the hungry growling of my empty stomach can be heard through walls?"

Lydia got to her feet, barely able to look at the girl. She wanted to be on the other side of that door, as far from Jasmine as possible. But with her hand on the latch, she gave in to temptation. "Yes, you never got as far as the kitchens, did you? A pity there are none of Tanner's cook's sugared buns left anywhere. Well, good night, for whatever is left of it."

Jasmine's gaze slid quickly toward her reticule before she straightened her shoulders and looked at Lydia once more.

Had the fairly vacant eyes now narrowed with... what? Cunning? A pretty girl, her face didn't wear that particular expression very well. "Yes," she said, and then sighed. "Lydia, may I ask you something?"

Lydia wanted her bed, and to be away from Jasmine, perhaps the latter more than the former. "Can it wait until tomorrow?"

Jasmine sniffled, bottom lip trembling. "I suppose it must."

"Oh, all right. What do you want to ask me?"

The trembling lip reformed into half of a pleased smile. "People often say things and don't mean them, don't they?"

Lydia tilted her head, wondering where on earth that question had come from. "Yes, I suppose they do."

"Then if someone says they'll do something if someone else says they won't do something—then they probably won't really do it?"

Lydia considered this. "I…I imagine that would depend on the person doing the saying. Are you talking about someone issuing an ultimatum?"

Now Jasmine frowned. "An ultimatum?"

Really, the girl was exhausting. "Yes. That would be like saying that if you don't stop asking questions and let me go to bed, I shall box your ears, and you then saying you'll ask more questions anyway."

"So you'd be angry if I asked more questions?"

Lydia resisted the impulse to roll her eyes, which she really shouldn't do, because everyone else could see her disgust when she did that. Not, she supposed, that Jasmine would notice. "Yes, I'd be angry if you asked more questions. As, I feel the need to point out, you just did."

"But you won't really box my ears."

"No, I suppose not. Jasmine, what do you want to know? Really."

"Oh, nothing," the girl said, smiling brightly once more. "You answered my question. People say things, insist on things, but then don't do what they said they'd do if you refuse to do what they want you to do. Especially if you do."

Lydia was beginning to think she wasn't awake at all, but trapped in some bizarre nightmare. "Especially if you do what?"

"Do what they said you had to do so that they don't do anything else, of course. Then they won't do it— what they'd said they'd do, I mean. I feel much better now. Thank you."

"I suppose you're welcome. Goodnight, Jasmine," Lydia said. Closing the door to her own chamber, she leaned against it, happy to be away from Jasmine's ridiculous ramblings.

But she couldn't forget that Jasmine had lied to her, and that she'd been outside. She had to wonder at what she had discovered. And, if her conclusions were correct, what did it all mean?

Worse, how could she possibly tell Tanner? After all, this was his cousin. And, if she provided him with Mr. Beattie's name, she'd also have to admit that she'd been, for lack of a more comforting word, snooping. *Before* Tanner had come to her, loved her. When it could still be believed that he would eventually honor his father's last wish and wed Jasmine.

Then she remembered what she had decided earlier last evening. Justin. She would tell Justin, and he would tell Tanner. At least then her embarrassment would be from a distance.

A slight knock on the door had her nearly crying out, and when the door began to open, she jumped back out of the way, fearful that Jasmine had come to confront her about the letter in her reticule.

But it was Sarah, rubbing one eye as she yawned open-mouthed, then blinked at the sight of her mistress. "My lady," she said, dropping into a curtsy, her aging knees creaking. "I thought I could just sneak in and build up the fire before you had to put your feet on a cold floor."

Lydia was suddenly very aware of her bare feet beneath the hem of her dressing gown. "Why, thank you, Sarah, that's very considerate of you. But as you can see, I'm already awake. We're to make an early start of it, are we?"

Sarah was already kneeling in front of the fire, adding two small split logs to the grate. "Yes, my lady. We should be at His Grace's before noon, if we set off within the hour, or so says his man, Hawkins, when he roused me from my cot. It's still dark, I told him, but he said that's the rain, and we don't want too much of it laying on the roadway between here and the better roads up ahead. Mr. Wigglesworth is already in the kitchens, causing an unholy ruckus. I'm about terrified to go asking for a cup of hot chocolate for you."

"You've seen Mr. Wigglesworth, Sarah?" Lydia

asked, curious about this man who ran about making Justin's life comfortable and everyone else's a horror.

"Only the once, and that was enough." Sarah got to her feet with an *ummph* to help her up, and headed for the rumpled bed. "I shared my room with Mildred, my lady. Miss Harburton's maid? Now there's a woman could talk the buttons right off a coat. I'd never be one like her, talking about you the way Mildred does her mistress."

Lydia forgot about Wigglesworth. "Really, Sarah? What sort of things does she say? I mean, not that I should be asking you, or you should be telling me."

Sarah shot her a smile and a wink as she began plumping up the pillows. "Oh, this and that. About how Miss Harburton never gives her any of her castoff finery, or any of her candle stubs neither. Real tight-fisted she is, and her papa along with her. And the same with whatever comes out of the kitchens. Never once a *have a bun, Mildred,* or even a *you can have the rest of this lovely cheese for yourself, Mildred.* That sort of thing? Not that there's much of anything left when Miss Harburton gets through, Mildred says. Mildred was hoping for a bit of a taste of Mr. Wigglesworth's fine joint of beef last night, but Miss Harburton didn't leave so much as a crumb for a mouse on that tray His Grace sent up to her. I told Mildred, I told her you always give me a taste of anything that's sure to never make it to the servant's hall. It's just polite, I told her, and what *real* ladies do."

Lydia didn't hear the compliment as she was already mentally going over her conversation with Jasmine.

She hadn't eaten a thing off that tray Tanner had sent up, she'd said. The fib supported her reason for supposedly going in search of Mildred, but she had delivered that particular part of the lie so quickly, so easily, so glibly, that Lydia hadn't questioned it.

That ease bespoke a quick mind for mischief and extensive experience in the art of lying, the practice of deception. Why, she'd make Nicole seem a raw amateur.

I can never believe another word the girl says, Lydia decided silently. *Not another single word.*

"Oh, dear," Sarah said, her hand holding up the coverlet, clearly in the act of making the bed look less rumpled—Sarah believed a person left a room as she found it or else her carelessness would reflect badly on her mistress. "I didn't know it was coming on to your time, my lady. Weren't we just done with that? I could have—"

The maid's mouth snapped shut and her fair face turned nearly beet red. She quickly began stripping the sheets from the bed. "Never you mind, my lady. Probably just a little something left over, and riding up on Daisy stirred it up a mite. I'll just take these downstairs and give them a wash myself, if you don't mind waiting a bit on that chocolate? Save the maids here a bit of work. And I'll order up a nice tub for you, as well. Lots of hot water to soothe you where you're a little sore, love…riding on Daisy, that is."

Lydia waited until Sarah had bustled out of the room, the betraying sheets bundled under her arm, before sinking against the edge of the bed, overwhelmed with embarrassment.

And then she laid back on the mattress, trying not to giggle, thinking how lucky she was that she didn't treat Sarah as Jasmine did Mildred, or the whole inn would know within five minutes that Lady Lydia Daughty had waved farewell to her virginity last night at the Crown and Sugarloaf...

CHAPTER SIXTEEN

TANNER WAS LINGERING at the bottom of the stairs, hoping he appeared no more than a man at loose ends, yet fairly certain he more resembled a lovelorn youth waiting for a glimpse of his beloved.

Leaving Lydia had been the most difficult thing he'd ever done. Warm with sleep, her soft, even breathing invaded his soul.

They hadn't spoken. With their passion spent, it had been enough for him to draw her close, kiss her hair, feel her cheek against his chest, glorying in the knowledge that he hadn't hurt her more than necessary. She'd found his hand beneath the covers and brought it to her lips, kissing his fingertips before sliding her fingers through his and holding his hand that way as she fell asleep.

He'd never felt so powerful, never known himself to be so vulnerable. She trusted him. If anything ever happened to her, his life would be over. Love was wonderful, but also terrifying. And he wouldn't trade how he felt for all of the riches of the Orient...

"Nothing else to do save prop up that wall?" Justin

said, popping the last of a sweet roll into his mouth, clearly having just quit the private dining room. "If I'd known we had all this time to be leisurely, I wouldn't have chanced insulting Wigglesworth by all but bolting down my breakfast. The man suffers from a delicate disposition, you understand."

"My apologies to Wigglesworth's disposition. We're merely waiting on the ladies," Tanner told him, mentally shaking himself free of his thoughts. His mind had to be sharp around Justin; only a fool would think otherwise. "They've breakfasted in their chambers and should be down shortly. Last night's rain has probably made a mess of the road. If we'd ever see the blasted sun, we could wait for the mud to dry, but there's little hope of that. Now, is that explanation enough, or must I go grovel at Wigglesworth's feet for you?"

"He'll survive. Ah, and here comes your lovely cousin. Whoops, and there she goes again. She must have forgotten something. Well, in any event, when she returns, I shall escort her to the coach. Or would you rather I waited for Lydia? No, no," he said, holding up one manicured hand, "I believe I know the answer to that one."

"I don't believe I like your smile," Tanner said warily.

"Really? And here I thought you enjoyed my company. Why, I even came to your chamber last evening, on about midnight, to share some thoughts I'd had—brilliant, all of them—on how we might go on after I've inspected the remainder of the Malvern collection. But you must have been fast asleep, because you didn't answer my knock. Imagine that, a soldier who has learned how to sleep soundly in an unfamiliar place. You must tell me how you've managed that."

"You don't sleep well, Justin?"

"In unfamiliar places? Truthfully, no. And there have been too many of them over the years. Perhaps I will go home once our small investigation at Malvern is complete. I doubt there will be any reason for me to linger."

"You know you're welcome to stay as long as you wish. I didn't invite you just to have you look at the damn jewelry. To tell you the truth, I haven't thought about those stones since we spoke yesterday."

"And one can only wonder why," Justin drawled, his smile all-knowing.

"Never mind that. Please, I want you to stay with us at Malvern. You're my friend."

"Yes, I know. That friendship is one of the great gifts of my life. I wish to preserve it."

"Now what the bloody hell does that—"

Tanner sensed Lydia's presence at the top of the steep stairs even before he turned to see her slowly descending them, carefully lifting the hem of her riding habit as she held tightly to the railing. Her eyes were on the steps, but as she neared the bottom she raised them, looking directly into his.

The expression in those beautiful sky blue eyes came like a punch to his ribs, for he saw nervousness, shyness...and joy.

"Lydia," he said quietly as he approached the stairs,

his hand held out for her to take it. She slipped her fingers onto his palm and he closed his over hers before raising their joined hands. His gaze never leaving hers, he kissed the smooth skin on the back of her hand.

How long they stood there, Lydia slightly above him on the stairs, speaking volumes to each other without uttering a single word, Tanner didn't know. Because nothing else mattered; nothing and nobody.

"Tanner? Yoo-hoo, Tanner. I can't get past you and Lydia if you're going to persist on standing here like this. Is there something wrong? Did she trip, hurt her ankle or something? I vow these staircases are so steep, it's no wonder we haven't all come to grief on them—oh, not that anyone *has,* of course."

He would have missed it if he hadn't been looking at her so intently, but Tanner saw the quick roll of Lydia's eyes as Jasmine pushed past them.

"Oh, good morning, Justin," Jasmine went on, once she'd paused to take in her surroundings. "Goodness, and here we all are, all muddled together in this small hallway. Have you all been waiting for me?"

"All of our lives," the baron drawled, bowing in her direction before holding out his bent arm to her. "It would be my esteemed pleasure to escort you through the raindrops to the coach, whilst your cousin takes care of Lydia. Friend? You will take care of her for me, won't you?"

The two men faced each other across years of friendship.

"Always," Tanner said quietly.

Justin inclined his head slightly, and then smiled

that enigmatic smile of his. "Yes, I believe you will. Jasmine, shall we two be off? Wigglesworth awaits without, armed with an umbrella."

Tanner watched them go.

"Is the baron all right?" Lydia asked as Tanner helped her lift the hood of her cloak up and over her hair.

"Yes, he's fine," he assured her. "I think Justin's taking a new look at his life, possibly at life in general. There's more to both, I believe, than he's ever before taken the time to see, or even believed existed. I only hope he finds some of it for himself."

"I don't understand," Lydia said, slipping her hand into his. The gesture was so simple, yet so symbolic of their new easiness with each other, their intense awareness of each other.

"I know. But he does. I'll explain later. Much later, or else you'll feel sorry for him, and he would sense that in a moment." He tipped up her chin. "Are you all right?"

Her cheeks turned a becoming pink. "I'm fine, yes. Tanner, I—"

He touched his mouth lightly to hers, unable to resist any longer; a quick, stolen kiss, but with clinging lips and a soft sigh from Lydia when it was over. "I can't wait to show you Malvern. I want you to love it."

"I'm sure I already do," she said quietly.

And both of them knew what they were really saying.

"We, um, we need to go now. They're waiting for us."

"Yes, I—oh my goodness."

Tanner looked past the just-opened door to the hulking shadow standing outside the doorway, a large black umbrella clutched in one ham-sized fist and held above his head. The man was clad all in black, a long cape swirling about his tree-trunk legs that were spread wide apart, as if he was keeping himself steady on the deck of a ship tossing on a stormy sea.

He stood nearly as wide as he was tall—and he was inordinately tall. His massive head and considerable cheeks seemed to shine by dint of the wall mounted candlelight reflecting off enormous quantities of rain-speckled black frizzed hair. His black eyes were impervious to the candlelight, however; they were flat and so devoid of expression that a fool would know there were no cheery thoughts going on anywhere inside that colossal head.

In short, the newcomer had all the jolly air about him of an undertaker come for the body of the deceased and determined to be paid in advance for the courtesy.

No wonder Lydia was now clasping his hand so tightly.

"Ah, Wigglesworth," Tanner said, attempting to keep a straight face, for he had been witness to this reaction many times. "Thank you for coming back for us."

"You're most entirely welcome, Your Grace," Wigglesworth said, delicately stepping out from behind the giant and entering the small foyer. Clad all in impeccable light grey, down to his hose and kid shoes, not a raindrop marred the thick silk or wilted the masses of lace at his throat and wrists.

Wigglesworth was the picture of sartorial perfection, albeit one that would have been painted two decades previously. The only impediments to perfection were his size (bantam roosters might be taller, or at the least, carry more weight), and the fact that he possessed the high-pitched voice of a lady who has just discovered a mouse in her pudding.

He swept off his wide-brimmed hat—the one with the snowy white plume curling about it—displaying a finely powdered periwig, and made an elegant leg toward Lydia.

"My lady, your servant."

"We'll go with you now," Tanner said once Justin's servant had turned and made another elegant bow in his direction.

"How very gracious. Only at your convenience and in your own good time, Your Grace," Wigglesworth trilled. "Brutus and I are content to await your pleasure. Brutus, having delivered our invitation to His Grace and his lady, I am ready to make progress to my coach, if you please. He'll return directly for you, Your Grace. Tell them you'll be back directly, Brutus."

The giant grunted low in his throat and then smiled a smile that would make lesser men—perhaps even dozens at a time, and all well-armed—call out for their mothers.

"Very nicely done," Wigglesworth complimented the man. "And now—Brutus, *up!*"

Brutus flung back one side of his cloak and picked up Wigglesworth at the waist as if he weighed no more than a feather. His plumed hat now in his hand, Wigglesworth disappeared beneath the cloak and Brutus turned away from the doorway.

"No wonder his pretty slippers are so clean. *Brutus?*" Lydia said, her eyes wide as if she'd just seen something very singular. Which she had.

"Hmm, yes," Tanner said, believing he needed to explain Brutus to her. "He doesn't speak. He may be able to, but no one has ever said. Probably because no one has ever dared to inquire. Justin may know, as Brutus is his discovery, but it would be impolite to ask."

"What an odd pair the two of them are. Or should I say the *three* of them?"

"Justin would be the first to tell you he doesn't like being thought ordinary."

"Yes, that's rather obvious. I like him very much, but I will confess that I don't truly understand why he's chosen to be the way he is. I'm convinced there's so much more driving him than that unfortunate duel and having to be gone from England for so long."

"The duel and banishment weren't enough? He's got some other deep, dark secret? No, there's nothing. He's simply Justin. Someday, hopefully, he'll find someone who will force him to not just laugh at the vagaries of life, but to become a part of it," Tanner said thoughtfully. "He deserves that, and I think he's made his beginning. In the meantime, we'll just enjoy him for the good friend he is. In any event, for now you'll admit the partnership between Brutus and Wigglesworth is a good one. Would *you* listen to Wigglesworth if he strutted into your kitchen, demanding he be allowed to commandeer it for his master?"

"He hasn't a very commanding appearance, no," she said, smiling.

"Ah, but then Brutus enters behind him, and everyone in the kitchens is suddenly all smiles and how may I assist you. Justin thinks he's a genius to have thought of it, which he did after the first time Wigglesworth found his lovely suit of clothes with himself inside it deposited on the dung heap. He also told me that the only person who doesn't realize what's going on is Wigglesworth, who believes it is his own consequence that opens all doors for him. Now, quickly, as it's still raining fairly heavily, do you want Brutus to carry you to the coach?"

"Would it be terrible of me to admit that, even if the man is relatively harmless, I'd probably rather drown than to disappear inside that cloak?"

"I was hoping you'd say that." Tanner bent and scooped her up into his arms as the very large Brutus and the equally large umbrella stood once more just outside the doorway. She clung to his neck and he carried her across the innyard to the coach, Brutus trotting along beside him, the umbrella covering them.

Justin pushed the door open and Tanner deposited Lydia inside, then entered the coach himself, a rather ungainly move, as Brutus had decided to give him a helpful boost that nearly sent him headfirst into the other door.

"Lose your footing?" Justin asked, outwardly all concern.

"No, I always enter my coach on my knees," Tanner grumbled as Lydia grinned down at him.

"How odd. But, if it makes you happy, who am I to cavil?"

"We've got more than five hours to be packed in here together unless the rain stops, Justin," Tanner pointed out as he picked himself up and deposited himself on the seat beside his friend, across from the ladies, who would be allowed to ride in the forward-facing seats. "Don't make me have to shoot you before we're out of the innyard."

"Ah, touché! Lovely day for a drive," Justin went on quickly. "I must come to the country more often. It's so…bucolic."

"I can't wait to be back at Malvern," Jasmine said, oblivious to Justin's facetiousness, as she was lamentably oblivious to most anything that didn't affect her directly, Tanner had decided. He shot her a look as she launched into a tangled mass of description of his home that wouldn't have had him recognizing it if he hadn't known the subject of her ramblings, and held up a hand to interrupt her.

"Jasmine? What's wrong with your face?"

"My face?" she responded in shocked tones, raising a hand to her left cheek, which was just where he had been looking. "Nothing's *wrong* with my face. What a horrid thing for you to say to me, Tanner."

He didn't consider himself to be on a par with a Bow Street Runner, but he did have some powers of observation. Jasmine was right-handed. If she were to touch her face in response to his question, she should have raised her right hand, to her right cheek. But she'd raised her left hand, to her left cheek. "Are you wearing powder?"

"I most certainly am not wearing—" She looked at her gloved hand as she took it away from her cheek, and saw the powder that had transferred to the leather, leaving a faint outline of her fingers on her reddened skin...rather as if she'd just slapped herself. "Oh! Oh, I *hate* you!"

"Rice powder and raindrops don't do well together, do they?" Justin said, handing Jasmine a handkerchief he'd slipped from his waistcoat. "But shame on you, Tanner. I was fully prepared to sit here for the time it takes us to slog through the countryside to your ancestral home without ever once mentioning that Jasmine's face had begun to, well, *run*. That's the sign of the true gentleman, you know. There are many others. Should I write them down for you?"

Jasmine sobbed into the handkerchief, which wasn't affecting Tanner as she probably supposed it should. He looked to Lydia, whose blue eyes were twinkling in humor at the way Justin had been teasing him. Well, wasn't it lovely that they were both so amused. He'd like to be amused, too, but Jasmine was difficult to ignore, for he knew her tears could soon escalate to a full-out bout of hysterics. Lord knew he'd witnessed enough of them over the years. "Do *you* know what the devil's going on here?"

"I do, yes. Jasmine told me she tripped over the hem

of her dressing gown last night, and her cheek collided with…the doorjamb. But we concluded that she hadn't broken anything."

"The doorjamb is intact? How wonderful."

"Justin," Tanner growled, "don't help. Jasmine, are you sure you're all right? You should have told me. We could have remained at the inn another day, until you'd recovered, even brought in a doctor to check on you. Is the cheek very painful? It looks swollen, too, now that I can really see it."

"It's horribly painful," Jasmine said, sniffling. "And now you're telling me that I'm *ugly*. How could Papa think I should want to marry you?"

Once again Tanner looked to Lydia, mutely appealing for help while at the same time mulling the idea that riding atop the coach, even in this downpour, would be preferable to listening to Jasmine.

Lydia leaned close to Jasmine, cupped a hand beside her mouth, and whispered something in Jasmine's ear. His cousin's eyes went wide, then very narrow, as she jerked her head away, glared at Lydia.

Lydia crooked her finger so that Jasmine came closer, whereupon Lydia whispered in her ear again, and when Jasmine turned to her, her mouth a small O of shock, Lydia nodded her head a single time.

Jasmine nodded back, as if the two of them had come to some sort of agreement—one that suited Lydia much more than it did his cousin.

"She'll be fine now," Lydia announced placidly, sitting forward once more and folding her hands demurely in her lap, the very picture of ladylike calm. "Won't you, Jasmine?"

As if to prove Lydia's words, his cousin immediately smiled brightly, apologized very prettily to everyone for "being such a goose," and then declared that she would close her eyes now and hope to sleep for the remainder of the journey, as she had spent a restless night.

At which point Lydia once again rolled her eyes. Tanner saw the reaction because he'd been looking at her, and not at Jasmine.

And then, just as she had asked Justin to please carve her a slice of beef last evening after Flynn had been routed from the private dining room, she turned her attention back to that man to politely press him to tell her all about Wigglesworth and Brutus.

Clearly, as the subject of Flynn had been dismissed, the subject of Jasmine's bruised cheek was now being dismissed.

Which didn't mean Tanner wasn't going to open that subject again later, when they arrived at Malvern...

CHAPTER SEVENTEEN

A WATERY SUN BROKE through the low, overhanging clouds just as the coaches passed through a charming village Tanner told them was no more than five miles from Malvern. The rain had stopped two hours earlier and the roadway had been drying, but it was the advent of sunshine that brought out Tanner's invitation that he and Lydia continue to his estate on horseback.

Lydia looked toward the slumbering Jasmine, and then across the coach, to where Justin sat, his curly brimmed beaver cleverly lowered over his eyes so that it was impossible to tell if he was awake or asleep.

"Oh, but we probably shouldn't leave Jasmine without a chaperone," she whispered. "Should we?"

"On the contrary, my dear," Justin drawled, pushing back his hat. "You should not be leaving *me* without a chaperone. Compromise is a weapon that cuts both ways, as many an unwary fellow married to some totally unsuitable miss who somehow managed to get him alone just before her conniving mama sprung into the room with witnesses and triumphantly crying *aha* will doubtless tell you."

"You're really incorrigible," Lydia told him, laughing.

"Yes, I know. I also would very much like to be on horseback myself, after so many hours confined to this coach. Not that the company hasn't been delightful."

"Well, then, join us, please."

"I would, Lydia, save that I also wish for a good gallop. And I do believe I remember the way, having ridden it with you. I'll meet you all at Malvern, shall I?" Without waiting for an answer, he turned and opened the small door cut into the well of the coachman's perch.

She hadn't questioned Sarah laying out her riding habit for a second day, believing it easier for the maid, who would not then have to perhaps ask that another trunk be downloaded from the traveling coach.

Besides, she wasn't vain. Sarah had nicely brushed the riding habit and it was certainly fresh enough to be worn again. There had been three trunks in Jasmine's rooms last night, Lydia had noticed. It felt rather gratifying to think that she, Lydia, was more practical.

Within five minutes, the coach had pulled to the side of the roadway, the horses were untied from behind the close-following servant coach, and the protective blankets removed from their saddles. Mildred was moved to the crested coach to be with her slumbering mistress (and prop her up if she began to tilt as the coach rounded some curve), and all three riders were mounted and ready to move on once more.

Almost, Lydia thought, as if the whole thing had been planned.

"Well, I'm off," Justin said, tipping his hat to her. "A ride across country is just the treat this beast needs."

"Are you referring to your mount, or yourself?"

"Ah, a very good question, Tanner. I know you won't mind if I ask your butler to bring me one of your best from the wine cellars while I await your arrival. I'll consider it a magnanimous gesture, somewhat a consolation prize on your part."

"What did he mean by that?" Lydia asked as Justin's horse sprang forward into an almost immediate gallop, clearly eager to stretch its legs.

"Who knows what Justin means by anything he says. Sometimes I believe he speaks just to amuse himself with the sound of his own voice."

"No, you don't. Believe that, I mean."

Tanner urged his mount forward at a slow walk beside her Daisy as the trio of coaches disappeared over the rest of the next hill. "You're correct, I don't. I think—no, I know—that he fancied himself falling in love with you."

"Oh. That," Lydia said with her usual sangfroid, at which point she felt Tanner's head swivel sharply to look at her. "Pretending he was speaking with Rafe before we left London the way he did? I knew he was only teasing everyone. Nobody tumbles into love so quickly."

Tanner reached across the space between them, to lay his hand on hers. Shocked and thrilled by this unexpected touch, she looked into his eyes, seeing her world there.

"Yes, Lydia, sometimes they do. Sometimes, against

all reason, and at the most inconceivably disastrous moment any sane man could think possible, they do."

The day he'd come to tell them about Fitz. She felt hot color in her cheeks that had nothing to do with the now blazing sunshine. "I hated you. For what you were saying. For being alive…"

"I know."

Lydia bend her head to kiss the skin of Tanner's wrist, above his glove. "Fitz was a very smart man, wasn't he?"

"I feel like we have his blessing, yes."

She blinked back tears. But these were healing tears, and they washed away any lingering doubt she might have had that she should be allowed such happiness, born of such deep sorrow.

Tanner squeezed her hand before letting it go. "If you're up to riding across country, there's a spot on the hills I've visited often over the years. I'd like you to first see Malvern from there."

"I think I'd like that very much." She swiped quickly at her damp cheeks, and smiled at him. "But remember, I'm not the rider Nicole is. No fearlessly flying over five-bar fences for me."

He pointed to a small lane to their left, and they headed toward it, and moments later were out of sight from the broader road. Because the packed earth was still somewhat soft from the earlier rain, she could see the imprints made by Justin's mount minutes before.

"Pardon me for saying this, but thank God for that. Lucas enjoys her adventurous spirit, but if you were likewise inclined, I'd never have a quiet moment, for worrying about you, for the fear that I could lose you."

Lydia smiled, her heart warm. Had there ever been such happiness in the world? Nothing stood between them now, nothing and nobody. No shadows, no more obstacles, real or imagined, to overcome. The road ahead, the life ahead, was all theirs. "Then I should promise to always be staid and boring and…safe?"

"Safe, yes. I find you far from staid or boring." His smile was all she could hope for. "But if you wouldn't mind?"

"Not at all. I hereby solemnly promise to be just who I am. Quiet, somewhat studious, and harboring not a single desire for adventure. Oh, and safe."

"And I promise to love you for all of our days, and all of our nights, for all of our lives."

Lydia's breath caught as she turned to look at him.

He smiled sheepishly and shook his head. "I've been wanting to say that to you for so long. I've pictured the moment in my head a dozen times—the time, the place. And now I've just blurted it out. I'm sorry."

"I'm not," she said quietly.

He looked at her for long moments, and then nodded, almost as if he found it hard to speak; even humbled.

But he was the Duke of Malvern. A brave soldier. Wealthy, handsome; a friend to be treasured. A gentleman. Respected. A good man.

And she had reduced him to speechlessness? *Her?* How…why? What did this wonderful man see in her that she had never recognized in herself?

For all of her life she had stood in Nicole's shadow. Hidden there. And happily so.

But Tanner had seen her, found her, touched her in a way that no one and nothing else ever had. He was her sunlight, and she'd never seek the false safety of the shadows again.

Everyone, she realized as her heart took wing, flies in their own way. But everyone can *soar.*

"We leave the lane here, and ride across country," Tanner told her, waking her from her thoughts. "Are you ready?"

She nodded, shifting her grip on Daisy's reins. "Yes. I'm ready. I really am."

It was impossible to speak to each other as they rode, sometimes in single-file when the pathways narrowed between the increasing number of trees. They rode alongside the hedgerows between planted fields. But those were soon left behind, to be replaced with low rolling hills of the greenest of green grasses and more trees.

She could see higher hills dotted across the distance, green-topped heights that seemed to roll on and on, to the ends of the earth. The air was fresh, and fragrant, the breeze warm against her cheek. Everywhere she looked was land that seemed untouched by anything save the sun and the rain, almost sacred, so beautiful the sight brought tears to her eyes.

And then Tanner put up his hand, indicating that they should stop here, just before the crest of another low, rolling hill.

He dismounted, tied his mount's reins to a hanging branch of a nearby tree, and then approached Daisy.

"If you don't mind, I'd like us to walk from here. Malvern, my home, yours if you'll have it, can be seen from just on the other side of this hill."

Lydia leaned toward him, the move so natural now. She felt no hint of shyness as he lifted her down from the sidesaddle. As he held her, kissed her.

Hand-in-hand, they climbed the easy rise to the top of the hill, the long, sweet-smelling grass rising to her knees, dancing in the breeze.

Tanner moved confidently, at ease in his own environment, and clearly proud to be showing her his home.

Oddly, Lydia supposed, she'd never really considered her surroundings. Not that she would have wished to live in a hovel. But whether it had been the comfortably rundown Willowbrook when her mother deigned to keep her children with her or the glories that were Ashurst, as long as she had her books, a garden, and good company, she believed she could be content anywhere.

Even London wasn't so bad, because there was always a quiet window seat or cozy nook somewhere, a soft blanket to spread over her lap, and a world of books at her fingertips.

But she did much prefer the country. The quiet, the slower pace, the familiarity of family…

"Oh." Lydia stopped, tried to catch her breath that had suddenly deserted her as the hill gently sloped downward below her feet and the jewel that was

Malvern lay before her in the distance. The sunlight twinkled off the four full stories of mullioned windows, most of them set in pairs or threes and fours and edged with smooth light grey stone…with matching huge, arched sets stretching a full two stories high fronting each of the wings that jutted forward on either side of the center section.

The structure itself was of deepest gray stone, but it did not look heavy, and most certainly could not be dark, not with all those windows. Two dozen chimneys must have marched along the roof, but all in a very orderly fashion, and not at all higgledy-piggledy.

Tanner's coach sat on the gravel drive in front of the main doors, until the driver on the box took up the reins and horses and coach moved on, taking a turn some ways from the mansion, heading toward the two other coaches that were already in the stable yards. She and Tanner would be the last to arrive.

Lydia was in no hurry. She could rest here for hours, just looking at Tanner's home. Her home.

She could see the lush gardens to the rear of the structure, the artfully planted trees, the stables in the distance. Malvern hadn't been built on the land, it was part of it, nestled in its own sweet valley, snug, for all that it was so very large.

Tanner stood close behind her. He slipped his arms around her waist, rested his chin on her head. "Look hard, sweetheart. Do you see our children playing hide-and-seek in the gardens? Do you see us sitting in the shade, the baby laughing on a blanket at our feet as I read to you?"

She saw it. She could see it all. Her bottom lip trembled. "What are you reading?"

"Oh, it all depends on that, does it?" he said, laughter in his voice. But when he spoke again, his voice was low, and filled with emotion. "Very well. '*And on that cheek, and o'er that brow, so soft, so calm, yet eloquent, the smiles that win, the tints that glow, but tell of days in goodness spent, a mind at peace with all below, a heart whose love is innocent.*'"

"Byron. But I am, you know. At peace with all below, and all above, as well." She sighed in pure contentment. "It's perfect. Everything is so perfect. Like a dream."

He turned her toward him, looking down into her uplifted face, his expression one of love freely given, and if there were any shadows in his eyes, she would not see them. He removed the pins from her hat and let it drop to the ground, then took her face in his hands. "Then may we never wake up…"

His kisses were soft, gentle. Each one a promise. To love her. To always be there for her. Father to their children. Comfortable, sharing. A hand to hold. A smile like no other. And all that he gave her, she would give back a hundredfold…gladly. He held her heart, he held her soul, her body.

He was hers, and she was his. And it was right.

Slowly, they sank to their knees in the long, soft grass. Holding each other, their kisses deepening, the sweet taste of passion rooted in love shaking them, nearly overwhelming them with its power.

Slowly, he laid her back against the warm, sweet-smelling grasses.

She rose against his touch, wordlessly telling him to take what he wanted, even as she moved her hands over him, longing to touch, aching to hold. Sensations still new to her caught at her breath; the sweet ache between her thighs urged her on, all inhibitions flown.

Everything she ever wanted, an entire world she hadn't known existed. She knew she had found all of that and more in his arms.

No more shadows. Tanner had brought her into the sunlight. The past was gone; hers and his. Together, they were reborn. There was nothing now but their future, together.

He fit inside her as if fashioned especially for her, as she had been for him. Two halves made whole in each other.

Together, they climbed the heights. Together, they soared. Their passion shared, as they would share everything for all of their days and all of their nights, as long as they lived.

When it was over—No, it would never be over! Not for them!—Tanner kissed her hair, her bared breasts. He gently stroked the heated flesh between her thighs, soothing her as she slowly came down from the heights.

"I want to make love to every inch of you, kiss you everywhere, taste all of you," he said quietly. "Touch you, see you, watch your beautiful face as I slowly sink into you. I want to feel each move you make beneath me. Your heat enveloping me, pulsing all around me, taking me in. Giving you my seed, growing our life together. I had no life until you, Lydia. I was only alive. And I didn't know the difference…"

His words, his intense eyes, his intimate touch, all had their combined effect on her, and on her body. As he spoke, he had begun slipping his fingers inside her, and her passions had risen once more.

She strained against his hand, her eyes never leaving his face as he seemed to find her very center, rubbing his thumb over her, robbing her of breath, all of her feeling concentrated on the blossoming sensations that grew, and then grew again.

"Tanner…"

But she couldn't say more. The words that would tell him how she felt had not been invented. She could only whimper wordlessly, try to breathe without moving. It was impossible to keep her eyes open, and when she closed them, rainbows of light danced against her eyelids as she arched her neck backward, her entire body a bow, bending to his will. *Never stop, never stop, never stop…*

She moaned as he seemed to move away from her, but then he was back, still with his fingers deep inside her. But now there was heat, hot and wet, closing all around her. The strokes against her aching flesh became faster. Nearly unbearable in their sweetness.

She felt herself being drawn into the warmth, felt the gentle tug and release, the sensation of soft breath against her heated skin.

And then she knew. *I want to make love to every inch of you, kiss you everywhere, taste all of you.*

She hadn't known. Couldn't have imagined. She'd been too swamped with feeling, floating on a cloud of sensation. But it was right. It felt so right.

And she *needed,* so much.

The more Tanner suckled on her, the more she sensed that he was taking her somewhere she had never been, yet longed to travel to with him. She could no more be passive than she could stop breathing.

Pressing her heels against the earth, she lifted herself to him, began to move in concert with him, sealing herself against him as his tongue searched her, found the center of her yearning, a white hot center that begged for his touch and then rewarded them both by gathering up all of the sensation in the world and releasing it in rhythmic explosions.

Even before she could realize that she was flying, soaring, Tanner covered her, plunged inside her, so that her body convulsed around him, drawing the seed from him, taking it deep into her womb.

Planting the seed that would grow from their love…

CHAPTER EIGHTEEN

TANNER SMILED AS HE SET Lydia's silly, veiled hat on her head at a slightly more rakish angle than she had done, and then handed her the pins to secure it in place.

They'd had the devil of a time finding those pins—needles in the haystack of the long grasses they'd flattened beneath their bodies not that long ago.

"I'm sure that can't be right," she said as she secured the last pin.

"I like it," he told her, touching the tip of her nose with his fingertip. "I like that, and I like this…" he drew his finger across her bottom lip, swollen from his kisses. "And I like this," he pursued, running his finger down her throat, to the small hollow at the base of it, where he could watch her heart beating.

"They'll be sending out a search party soon, Tanner," she said reasonably, "sure one of us has fallen from our horse and the other is afraid to leave him."

"Him? Then I've been cast in the role of the unhorsed?"

She reached to stroke his cheek. "Oh, yes. I'm much too careful to ever fall. I hold your love, and I promise always to be careful to protect it. I only ask that you do the same."

He turned his face into her palm. "Always. I know what I want now. Your love, and Malvern, and our life together. A quiet life, filled with love."

She smiled. "And if another great man came along with another bold and glorious cause born of ambition?"

"Another Alexander? Another Bonaparte? No, Lydia, I've fought enough battles. I'll protect my own, you know that. But I've no more need to search for glory. Not when it stands in front of me."

"I love you, Tanner. No one has ever loved anyone more than I love you," she whispered, and he realized she hadn't said that before now. He knew she loved him. Of course he knew that. But hearing her say the words shook him.

He nodded, emotion tightening his chest. "Charlotte wanted us to wed at Ashurst, but that might take some of the bloom from Nicole and Lucas."

She nodded, her easy acceptance of what had been his rather abrupt proposal just like her. Lydia, the calm. Lydia, the practical. Lydia...the fire in his arms.

"That is true. Two weddings, and with a baby perhaps arriving in the middle of all that ceremony? It is quite a lot all at once. And you and Charlotte and Rafe have already planned all of this between you?"

Lydia was never flustered, so he couldn't tell if his words had pleased her or upset her. "I wouldn't say *planned*. Discussed? Still, if it's all right you, we'll marry here quietly, in the Malvern chapel, and then travel to Ashurst to watch your sister arrive at the church on horseback or whatever it is she's planning."

"On horseback, yes. With a gaggle of little girls dressed in long white dresses and streamers in their hair tossing rose petals in front of her."

God. Was he being selfish? Denying Lydia all the pomp and ceremony? "If you want—"

"No, thank you. I'm much more interested in being your wife than I am in being a bride."

Tanner relaxed. "After gaining Rafe's blessing, I managed to secure a Special License before we left London. Being a duke does have its influence. We…we could be married as early as tomorrow."

"Tomorrow?"

"I know, I'm rushing you. But I don't think I can wait a day longer."

Her sweet smile banished his fears, while the hint of mischief in her lovely blue eyes reminded him that she was not without spirit. She put a hand to his jacket and then held up a bit of grass they'd missed while brushing off their clothes. "I don't think we've *waited* all that much."

His smile grew into a wide grin. "True. And after tonight, we'll never be apart again. Why, you may even grow sick of me."

"Yes, I probably will," she agreed, the corners of her lovely mouth twitching as she suppressed another smile. "In fifty or sixty years."

"I'll hold you to that." He took her hand and led her over to Daisy, and then cupped his hands for her to use them as a sort of mounting block as he lightly tossed her up and into the saddle.

He mounted his own horse, debated for a moment asking Lydia to ride the rest of the way across country, up and over the hill they'd crested on foot, and then down toward Malvern, but in the end he thought it would be best if they kept the lane.

She hadn't complained, but he knew she must be at least slightly sore from his lovemaking. As soon as they arrived he would order a hip bath brought to her chamber.

He led the way, for the lane was really not much more than a track worn into the hillside. They descended slowly, the lane switching back on itself several times, sometimes taking them through a canopy of trees, sometimes giving them new, closer views of Malvern.

As they neared the newly scythed expanse of lawn, once again shaded beneath a canopy of trees, his mount began to sidestep nervously, snorting through its nose as if it had perhaps caught a scent. "Anxious, are you? Almost home, boy," he said, patting the horse's neck. But the stallion continued to dance, jerking against the bit in its mouth.

Instantly worried for Lydia, Tanner looked about in the underbrush, half expecting to see the tusks of a wild boar, even though there hadn't been one seen in the area for years, thanks to the careful husbandry of his foresters.

But what he saw wasn't a boar ready to charge. What he saw didn't move at all. In the space of a heartbeat he considered pretending he hadn't seen what he'd seen, urging Lydia ahead of him as he kept his mount between the trees and the path, and then discarded both ideas as she called to him.

"Is something wrong, Tanner? Your horse seems agitated."

He turned his mount and blocked the path. "I think there's been an accident," he told her, dismounting. "Someone's lying just off there, in the underbrush. Please, stay where you are."

"Is it Justin?" Lydia asked, worry evident in her voice. "He came this way, didn't he?"

Tanner had already dismounted, and tied the reins to a branch to keep his mount from bolting. "No, it's not Justin. I would have recognized his clothing even at a distance."

"Wait, let me come with you."

He shook his head. "No. Whoever it is—he's not moving."

"Oh, God." Lydia closed her eyes for a moment, and when she opened them again, she nodded. "I'll do as you say. Please hurry."

But there was no reason for hurry, Tanner realized after only taking a few steps into the undergrowth to see Thomas Harburton, his eyes wide open and staring at nothing. He was lying on his back amid weeds turned dark with his life's blood, his throat neatly sliced from ear to ear. No wonder his mount had gotten so agitated; it had been the smell of all this blood.

"Tanner? Who is it? Shall I ride for help?"

Tanner stood his ground, keeping himself in between the body and the path. "It's uh, it's one of my workers.

He's beyond our help, Lydia, but please ride and tell Justin to come up here."

"Justin? Tanner, what's going on? Why would you ask Justin to come up here?"

"Lydia, please. Just do as I say. And don't speak of this with anyone but him."

"But I—but—very well. I hate leaving you. Will you be all right?"

"I'll be fine. We'll be fine," he said quietly, knowing he had just lied to her. "Just fine."

Only as he heard the sound of Daisy moving past him on the lane did Tanner drop onto his haunches to take a closer look at the body of his cousin. He'd seen many bodies on the battlefield, too many. Bodies with no legs, no heads, pieces of bodies, and bodies that looked untouched save for a small black hole marring a jacket or a temple.

But, somehow, this was different. Thomas Harburton held no saber in one dead hand. No spent rifle laid beside him. He'd been defenseless when his attacker had robbed him of his life.

He'd died here, not elsewhere. The amount of blood told that story well enough. But what had he been doing here? The path may exist because it had been used for generations of walkers drawn by the hills, but Thomas was never a walker. He was too bulky, for one thing, and his old injury didn't allow for recreational jaunts around the countryside on foot.

At the same time, Thomas did not like to ride. He traveled the estate in a pony cart Tanner's father had provided for him, and this path wasn't wide enough for a cart.

No, if Thomas had come to this spot, he'd come for a reason. To meet someone. Someone he trusted, or else there would be a weapon somewhere.

He'd come here, and he'd waited for the person he was to meet.

Tanner got to his feet and walked the perimeter of the small clearing amid the trees, looking at Thomas, judging distances, and then walking toward one particular tree. Yes, the weeds behind the tree were bent down, as if someone had stood there.

He saw all the signs of an ambush.

Hiding from sight, waiting, only to jump out when Thomas arrived, taking the man by surprise. Grabbing the man from behind, imprisoning him against his chest with one arm as he pulled him backwards, away from the path and into the trees. As he lifted his knife and drew it deeply across the man's exposed throat, then allowed the body to drop where it was, pumping blood onto the ground with each beat of Thomas's dying heart.

"Cowardly bastard," Tanner swore softly. He'd no great love for his cousin, but nobody deserved to die this way.

The sound of hoofbeats on the path brought Tanner back to attention and he stepped onto the path just as Justin was gracefully swinging his leg up and over his mount's rump as he dismounted.

"Lydia says someone is dead," he said as he looped his mount's reins around a branch of the same tree where Tanner had secured his own horse. "And not of old age, not from the look on your face. Who is it?"

"My cousin Thomas," Tanner said with a wave of his arm toward the body lying about ten feet off the path. "Someone sliced his throat from behind."

Justin shot the cuffs on his jacket as he moved to inspect the body, stopping a good five feet from the soles of Thomas' boots. "Messy," he said without inflection. "But, then, murder is rarely neat. I rode almost entirely across country, or I could have spared Lydia this. I'm sorry. How long do you suppose he's been here?"

"I don't know," Tanner said, joining him. "I would imagine he arrived at Malvern last night. He said it was so we could be sure of our welcome."

"Ah, yes, I can see that. Welcome home, Tanner," Justin said. "Well, shall we?"

Justin didn't have to explain. Nor did Tanner. Together, they approached the body, Tanner on the left, Justin on the right.

"I don't suppose you want to take a peek in his eyes," Justin said, going down on his haunches, careful to keep his coattails from touching the ground. "Did you know that some say if you look into a dead man's eyes, you'll see the last thing he saw? I don't put much faith in that, myself."

Tanner lifted Thomas' right arm. "He's cold, and his limb moves fairly easily. He may have been out here since last night, or very early this morning."

"Well, that's good. I do hate it when they don't bend, don't you?"

"Justin, for the love of God…"

"I'm being gruesome? My apologies. Let me have a go at his pockets." He carefully unbuttoned Thomas's jacket and reached inside, somehow managing not to come in contact with any of the stiffened, blood-soaked cloth.

Tanner could see the pocket watch Thomas always wore. Moments later, Justin held the man's small purse in his palm, hefting it. They both heard the jingle of coins inside it.

"Not robbery," Justin said unnecessarily, continuing his search of the body. He performed the moves as a man who'd had practice in such things, something that would have surprised most anyone who knew him by reputation only. "I remember this fellow I came across in Toulouse a week or so before Wellington's victory," he said conversationally as he worked. "Bloody battle, and a bloody waste, since Boney had abdicated four days earlier, but you know that. At any rate, the fellow was known to have been carrying a message to the Emperor, but nobody else seemed able to locate it on the body, so he was turned over to me. Clever thing, the slim metal cylinder he'd secreted up his—ah, and what have we here?"

Tanner watched as Justin raised a velvet pouch by the strings that secured the opening.

They both got to their feet and walked some steps away from the body before Justin handed over the pouch. Tanner pulled open the strings and dumped the contents onto his palm.

"Smallish stones, but quite lovely. I've always had a fondness for diamonds set around sapphires," Justin said as the necklace glittered in the sunlight. "Apparently, so did your cousin. Although I doubt they would have flattered him."

"What was he doing with them, Justin? Stealing them? Returning them? Was he here to meet with some coconspirator? And if he did come here to meet someone, why didn't that someone at least take away the necklace? Are the jewels real, or are they paste?"

"So many questions spring to mind, I agree. I'm afraid I can only help you with that last part, and not until we get back to the house. Lydia is waiting for you."

The mention of her name turned Tanner's attention away from the jewels in his hand, the body lying on the ground behind him and the trouble that had come to Malvern thanks to both of those things. "I promised her…"

"Promised her what, my friend?" Justin asked as they mounted their horses and headed toward Malvern.

"Never mind," Tanner said, knowing he could never explain, as the quiet, uneventful life he and Lydia envisioned spending together would bore his friend to flinders within a week. "Jasmine isn't going to take this well. Thomas was her only living relative, save me, and some distant maternal aunt somewhere in the wilds of Wales. She runs a charity school for wayward females, or some such thing."

"Reformed harlots? Sounds like a jolly place, full of sermons and penance and bread without butter."

"Yes, I agree. Totally unsuitable for a sensitive young lady like Jasmine. So I suppose I'm stuck keeping her. I was going to give Thomas an allowance, send them both home. Now what in living hell am I going to do with her?"

"Perhaps she'll decide to take herself off to a nunnery."

"Once again, Justin, you're not helping."

"I never intended to. I'm only here to observe, and perhaps enjoy myself. Except that I'm not, enjoying myself, that is. Those sapphires, Tanner? I'm afraid that's all you have of the Malvern jewels, save those few bits of glass and very minor pieces you took to London. The box I located behind the portrait was empty. Everything else is gone except for a few empty cases lying on the floor. Neatness didn't seem to be a priority. In fact, I believe you were supposed to find a mess. After all, otherwise it might have been weeks or months until you'd discovered the theft."

Tanner reined in his mount, as they'd reached the scythed lawns. The entire collection numbered more than fifty pieces, some of them dating back over two hundred years. Everything was taken? Yes, of course it had been. But he had to ask anyway. "Gone? All of it? The Malvern Pride?"

"I'm sorry, but yes. So what do we have here? A theft to cover a theft? I was pondering just that when Lydia arrived, and wondering if your cousin had insisted on coming back to Malvern ahead of us to do just that. Victim of a guilty conscience, he may have felt you had all but confronted him in London. He may have panicked, believed making the rest of the jewels disappear would help to cover the fact that any more of the stones had been changed. Unless they hadn't been, and he wanted them all for himself before you returned and found a better way to lock them away. I wouldn't have needed the key, you know. Anyone with even a modicum of talent who found that portrait and opened it would have had the lockbox in his hands with very little effort. I can't imagine why your papa and ancestors didn't take more care with them. At any rate, I imagine he was going to greet you with the news that he'd discovered the theft. Except that something went fatally wrong for the man."

"You're saying that Thomas took the remainder of the jewelry, and then ran afoul of some accomplice in the theft? Whoever had been helping him replace the stones?"

"I don't think I said that precisely, but, yes, it seems feasible, as we can be certain the man's death wasn't a suicide. The Malvern Pride alone could make a man consider murder a necessary expedient."

"No reason to take the watch, the purse. Not when he had the jewels."

"A mistake, I'd say. Although why your cousin had kept the sapphires separate I can't explain. Perhaps a sentimental attachment? Then again, if the stones had already been changed out, perhaps he separated it from the real stones?"

Tanner had another thought. "Or he could have

dropped the pouch in his rush, and then stuck it in his pocket rather than chancing he could be discovered by one of the servants. He was in a hurry to meet with his accomplice, hand off the jewels, and then hie himself back to Malvern in time to play the bearer of bad news when we arrived. That way, the man who killed him wouldn't have known about the sapphires."

"Yes, I rather like that one, although we'll probably never know the truth now that old Thomas has cocked up his toes," Justin said. "Have you ever considered a life of crime, friend? I think you might have the devious brain required to be successful at it. You know, if this being the duke business doesn't work out for you."

"I'll be sure to consider it, thank you." They continued to walk the horses toward the drive, and another thought hit Tanner. "Unless the sapphires—you said they're a minor piece—were expressly left behind to prove Thomas a thief," he said, trying out the idea out loud. "Nothing of value taken from the body, but something added."

"Ah, I like that, as well, perhaps even better than the first one, although I must once again point out that we'll probably never know precisely why the necklace was in his pocket. Back to the robbery, which was successful. One thief exposed—and very dead—and the other clearly in possession of the remainder of the jewels save the sapphires, and already miles away, and riding hell for leather to the coast. Unknown, and impossible to find. Or do you plan to mount a search?"

"I'll hire some fellow from Bow Street," Tanner told

him, as he'd already come to that conclusion on his own. "I'll question the servants, make some inquiries locally, of course. But that's all. I have Lydia to protect now. I can't go haring all over the country looking for some damn stones that may very well be fakes, leaving her here alone."

"Yes. You have Lydia."

Tanner looked at his friend. "This can't touch her, Justin."

"She's more precious than any stones, you'll get no argument there. What are you thinking? What's your next step? And, whatever it is, consider me walking beside you."

They dismounted and a groom ran up to take the reins, bowing to His Grace and welcoming him home.

At last, Tanner shared his worst fears with his friend. "I'm thinking, Justin, that there was something else missing from the body. Thomas held the keys to every gate and door on this estate, and was never without them, as they were the outward sign of his authority. Malvern holds a damn sight more than those bloody jewels, Justin. I'm thinking that maybe Thomas' murderer isn't all that far away, not when he now can walk in and out of Malvern whenever the spirit moves him until we complete the massive job of replacing all the locks. Our coconspirator, and whoever may be in his employ."

"Damn. You know, Tanner, this is what comes of cutting loose our brave soldiers into a land where they can barely afford food or shelter, denying them pensions or help of any kind. It is inevitable that some will turn their talents to fleecing the rich, those who have so much, when they have so little."

"Now you sound like Rafe and Lucas, although I agree with you."

Justin put a hand on Tanner's arm, holding him in place just at the bottom of the front steps. "Events are taking a considerably ugly and confusing turn, aren't they? Before we join the ladies, let's see if we can eliminate anything, shall we? Are we still to look at what's happened today and see a conspiracy to have you wed to Jasmine, or is that over now?"

"That had all been only conjecture on our part anyway, that business about Jasmine and me. I think we can agree that plan died when Thomas was murdered. And, I think, we can also dismiss any idea that Thomas acted alone."

"I concur. We'll stay with the jewels then, and some sort of partnership, at the very least. One to steal the stones, one to sell them, have the stones replaced. But, for some unknown reason, the thieves had a falling out, and your cousin was murdered. Leaving us to ask, who is this man, this possible gang of men? Ah, wait, I believe I have one suggestion. Perhaps one of your cousin's gambling chums, one he owed a considerable sum of money?"

Tanner had thought he was beyond being shocked. "Gambling? My cousin gambled?"

"Didn't Jasmine tell you? Thomas was always sneaking off somewhere to gamble at cards, with the dice. Here on the estate, again in London. He was sometimes gone for days. To hear her tell it, your cousin was pockets-to-let, completely. Either you married her almost immediately and bailed him out of the River Tick, or he was ruined. In any event, that person or persons may have pretended to go along with him, but with an entirely different objective in mind. Invite in the devil, Tanner, and he can be counted on to show up, even with his demons in tow, and with a whole set of evil ideas you hadn't thought of on your own."

But Tanner was still attempting to picture his tight-fisted uncle as a gambler. "How blind can one man be, Justin? I had no idea Thomas played deep. But Jasmine told you this?"

"A tongue hinged at both ends, remember? Were I forced into her company for any time above a fortnight, I'd have no choice but to strangle her. But she's harmless, I suppose, unless you mind your ears bleeding from time to time."

Tanner nodded, his mind working feverishly. "What you said makes perfect sense. Why split the proceeds on the stones? Why only get them piecemeal, whenever Thomas needed funds? Why care about Thomas's plan at all? The thieves saw Malvern, and saw so much more that could be theirs. He damn well did everything but invite them in for tea."

"Yes, remove the coconspirators he so foolishly partnered with, and your cousin's plan might have worked, and there soon would have been no need for any more small thefts—or any more profit for those coconspirators. If it hadn't been for Lydia, that is. Truly an unexpected complication for him, you falling in love with her. After all, you'd been two years without a romantic attachment of any kind, and you'd taken Jasmine with you to London, so surely you were about to come up to snuff. Thomas must have felt he was closing in on his victory. He can't be faulted for that. Half of London believed the same thing."

Tanner wasn't really listening. He was still attempting to work everything out in his mind. And the more he thought, the more he realized that he had put Lydia in danger by bringing her to Malvern. He could allow Justin to come to that conclusion himself, in his own good time, while he concentrated on other things.

Justin sighed. "I'm to continue this conversation with myself? Very well. So we agree there's someone else involved in this larger plan, perhaps more than one person, perhaps an entire gang of low thieves. Whoever—*whomevers*—slit your cousin's throat when he became an impediment in some way. Perhaps he was foolish enough to tell them he wasn't going to steal any more, that his daughter was soon to be the duchess, and he no longer needed them."

"Quiet, please, Justin. I'm thinking."

"You do that. I, however, prefer to think out loud. Now, where was I? Oh, yes. Perhaps Thomas belatedly realized his mistake, and objected to having his daughter become duchess of a house that echoed in its emptiness? But, really, does the *why* of his murder matter? We're standing out here, my friend, with Lydia and Jasmine inside, and all four of us very much in the way of those who now hold the keys to every gate and door of your home. I doubt your being in residence will bother them overmuch if they decide to come calling one night soon. You wouldn't expect the thieves to return, not now that they have the jewels. Why, we'd be lambs to the slaughter, wouldn't we, murdered in our beds?

"You certainly can't be faulted for holding a boring house party, I'll say that for you. Tanner? Yoohoo. Excuse me, but I don't believe I was speaking rhetorically. Surely you have something to add, something along the lines of: *My God, man, we could be under siege at any moment and must send the women back to London, posthaste!*"

But Tanner didn't answer. He'd already passed beyond his friend's musings, and was remembering the way Lydia, on their way to Malvern, had rolled her eyes whenever Jasmine went on about whatever she seemed to prattle on about. Lydia had thought Jasmine sweet, amusing, if a little silly. In London, she had thought that. But no more, that was obvious now that he thought about the thing.

He was remembering how Jasmine had glared at Lydia when she'd walked into their private dining room at the inn on Captain Flynn's arm. Had she been glaring at Lydia—or at the man beside her?

He was remembering how Lydia had stepped in to explain that Jasmine had sustained an injury. How she'd whispered in the girl's ear in the coach, and the shocked expression that had come over Jasmine's face.

Jasmine's bruised face, poor thing.

Had Jasmine confided in Lydia, woman to woman? And, if so, what had she told her?

"Captain Flynn," he said quietly as a cold certainty gathered in his gut. He didn't have all the pieces yet, but he'd begun to see at least the outline of the puzzle. He'd been suspicious that Thomas may have sent the man to stir up trouble. Now he felt certain he'd been right.

"Captain Flynn?" Justin repeated. "Your Captain Flynn?"

"He's not my—all right, yes, my Captain Flynn. God knows I'm the idiot who invited him for supper. He knew about Fitz, about Quatre Bras, all of it. I'd already thought Thomas might have put him up to it, that business about Fitz and the ladies…"

"All right. So they were in it together, your cousin and this Flynn person. I can see how you might make that connection, Flynn as coconspirator. The man might have wanted a look at you, to size you up in some way, and used Fitz to get himself in the door. So comforting to be able to put a face to evil. But why did Flynn kill your cousin? Which one of my many very good theories most appeals to you?"

"I don't know."

"Oh, good. I was worried there for a moment that I might have gone stupid in my advancing years. Still we should probably put all this heavy thinking and theorizing to one side until you've informed Jasmine of her father's demise. You go on, and I'll round up a small party to retrieve the body. Then we'll speak again of removing the ladies to someplace safe."

Tanner looked at the closed doors to his home. Doors he'd wanted to see opened as he and Lydia approached them together, so he could watch her reaction when those doors were flung back and she saw her new home for the first time.

Thank God they'd had those moments together at the inn, on the hill above Malvern. They might be the last quiet moments they'd have together for a long time…

CHAPTER NINETEEN

LYDIA THANKED THE BUTLER as he set a lovely silver tea service on the table in the main saloon before bowing to her and to Jasmine, turning smartly on his heel, and leaving the room. Very proper, Tanner's butler, but with kind eyes. Lydia had taken to him on sight. Although he did seem to be worried about something; she wouldn't have noticed, except that a small tic had been working in the man's cheek. And the household seemed unnaturally quiet, with none of the hustle and bustle she would have expected with the master on his way home.

"He doesn't like me, you know," Jasmine said as she reached for one of the scones arranged on a small dish. "Roswell, I mean. He thinks I'm the poor relation putting on airs. Which is silly, because I'm here because Papa is the estate manager, and because Tanner wants me here. That's because Tanner is kind, and caring. It's a pity I can't love him. Oooh, these are quite good, aren't they? I think I'll have some jellied strawberry on the next one."

"Hmm?" Lydia said, her mind concentrated on listening for Tanner's arrival. There was a dead body out there. She had even caught a quick glimpse of it as she urged Daisy along the path. She'd never seen a dead body before, had never hoped to. One of the estate workers, Tanner had said. Had a tree fallen on him? Or perhaps he'd been tossed from his horse, which had then bolted and run away. She searched her mind for some reasonable explanation, but couldn't stop thinking that Tanner had looked not just serious, but rather shaken.

"I *said,* how lucky I am that Tanner doesn't love me."

Lydia shook off her thoughts and smiled at the girl, although not without effort. "Yes, how fortunate. Because he'd be doomed to disappointment, wouldn't he? Because of your Bruce Beattie."

"My—oh, I keep forgetting I told you his name. I shouldn't have done that. It was…it was our secret. You'll keep our secret, won't you? Tanner could use his influence to have him turned off, you know."

"Perhaps he should. An honorable man would have applied to your father if he wished to court you."

Jasmine's expression turned sulky. "And what good would that have done? Papa is convinced Tanner will come up to snuff, sooner or later. He has to, or Papa will soon bankrupt us with his gambling. I am under strict orders, you know, to be all that is pleasing to Tanner this week. I'm so glad the baron is here with us. You don't mind that Tanner has paired him with you, do you? I suppose you'll be the first to hear the announcement, when it comes. And, who knows, perhaps you two will have one of your own?"

Lydia tipped the silver pot in its holder and poured herself a cup of tea, surprised that her hands were steady. "Is that how you see the thing, Jasmine? That Justin and I have been invited here for each other?"

"Why, yes, of course. I've seen how the baron looks at you. He's truly smitten. What other reason could there be, since the man is Tanner's friend, and clearly *persona non grata* in London at the moment? That business about killing a man, remember? Where else could he court you? And you don't seem to mind at all that he killed someone."

"Sometimes you amaze me, Jasmine," Lydia said quietly. "But you have it all worked out in your head, don't you?"

"Oh, yes. Papa expects Tanner to propose to me within days. Why else did you think I couldn't sleep last night at the inn? Each turn of the coach wheels brought me closer to this destiny I have dreaded for nearly two years. I am only glad that you, my new friend, will be here to support me in this time of—"

"Oh, please, stop it. Just stop it," Lydia said, putting down her cup with some force. "You met your Bruce Beattie last night when you sneaked out of the inn. Are you planning an elopement, Jasmine? Or did you refuse him, having decided that being a duchess wasn't a fate more terrible than saying your farewells to a near-penniless schoolmaster? Is that why he struck you? You couldn't believe I would be so gullible as to believe that farradiddle about tripping on your hem, did you? Not with the imprint of a hand so clear on your face. Not with your slippers wet from having been out in the rain. You met your Mr. Beattie, your *lover*, and you argued. He hit you."

Jasmine's face went deathly white. "You…you promised you wouldn't say anything. In the coach, when you whispered to me that you'd seen the note in my reticule, you promised. If I was good you wouldn't say anything."

"And I won't," Lydia told her, already regretting giving in to impulse. This wasn't like her, she was never vindictive. Or was this different; was she protecting her own now? "But I find I can't keep that promise if you are going to insist on lying to me every time you open your mouth. You're not even keeping your lies straight, you've told so many of them. You don't love Tanner, you're glad he doesn't love you, and then you will marry him, because he will ask you. You make no sense."

Jasmine looked at her with wounded eyes. "But Papa *does* want me to marry Tanner. That's not a lie."

"I'm sure it's not. But all this business about believing Tanner is on the brink of asking for your hand? You know that's not true, no more than any thought that Justin and I are to be paired together this week. You know you'll never marry Tanner because he is going to—oh, let's not have this conversation. Just don't lie to me anymore. No matter what, you're Tanner's cousin, and your lies make it difficult for me to like you as I know I should."

Lydia folded her hands together in her lap. She was like an alley cat when it came to Tanner. She hadn't known she possessed so much temper, or that she couldn't control it, tamp it down…not where Tanner was concerned. Still, if she had to listen to Jasmine lie to her one more time, prattle on about marrying him while indulging in a torrid affair with her lecherous schoolmaster, why, she might not be responsible for her actions.

Jasmine burst into tears, speaking between sobs, so that she was difficult to understand. "Oh, all right, Lydia, I admit it. I've told so many lies, most of them to myself. But I can't lie to you. You're so *good,* just like Tanner, and I want to tell you the truth. I need to tell someone. I know what you were going to say. Tanner wants you, not me. I've known that for days. But when I told…when I told Br-Bruce, he said I had failed in our plan by not being nicer to Tanner, making him fall in love with me. He said I'd cost him everything."

Lydia realized she had become quite nervous, and reluctant to hear anything more. Whether it was Jasmine's tears, or the girl's wish to tell the truth, she couldn't know. But, for Tanner's sake, she would listen. "Your plan? What plan, Jasmine? I…I don't understand."

The girl sighed deeply. "But it's all so simple. Tanner was to propose to me once I'd made him feel as if he was in love with me. I can be very charming you know, and I am pretty. Much prettier than you. Oh, I'm so sorry!"

"Don't be. I asked you to tell me the truth, and the truth is the truth. Please, continue. Tanner was to propose to you…?"

"Yes. And I was to accept. Papa would be happy, beg to be dismissed from his duties because of his old injury caused by the late duke, and take himself off to gamble away the allowance Tanner would give him. He really is disgusting, my Papa, and very weak, I suppose. But he's still my father, and I must love him. Then, just before the wedding, I was to tell Tanner I simply couldn't go through with the marriage because my heart belonged to another. And then he, being such an honorable man, and loving me, wanting what is best for me, would release me from my promise. He'd settle a generous allowance on me as he had done with Papa, and Br— Bruce and I would be free to leave here forever. Together."

And then the girl actually had the audacity to smile. "We thought Paris would be a delicious place to settle. My allowance, in good English sterling, would be more than ample in Paris, which is still very poor as it recovers from the war."

Now Lydia smiled, the smile widening as the sheer ridiculousness of this idea sank into her head. "*That* was your schoolteacher's plan? Jasmine, that's ridiculous. Only a complete fool would believe such nonsense." *Beginning*, she thought, *with the idea that you can make anyone fall in love with you. Love comes unbidden, or not at all.*

Jasmine immediately took recourse to her handkerchief, sniffling. "I know. I am a fool. The plan only seemed logical when I was in his arms. Everything seemed logical when I was in his arms. You can't know what it's like to be so…so intimate. A woman needs to believe, *has* to believe, or else it's all just…dirty…and base."

"It's all right, Jasmine," Lydia said, embarrassed for the girl. "I don't think you're…base."

"Oh thank you! But…once I was in London, away from him, I began to doubt him. What had seemed so reasonable didn't seem reasonable any more. And then I finally knew it for certain, last night. I'm so ashamed."

"You believed yourself in love. I understand. When you're in love, anything seems possible."

"Then you don't blame me? He swore he loved me. And I loved him *so much*. The way he kissed me…the way he made me feel. But it was all a sham. He never loved me. He *lied* to me, Lydia, he lied to me all along. B-both of them lied to me."

Lydia looked at her sharply. "*Both* of them?"

Jasmine nodded her head furiously. "Yes. It was Papa and B-Bruce together, all along. I meant nothing to either of them. I was just a, just a—"

"Dupe?" Lydia supplied helpfully, and then felt bad again. For a moment, she'd thought Jasmine had *two* lovers. Really, the silly girl was almost impossible to follow, and some of what she'd said was very embarrassing to hear.

Once again, Jasmine nodded furiously. "It was all about the Malvern jewels, you see, and not at all about *me*. It wasn't about *either* of them loving me. No, it was always about…about those awful jewels. Papa had been stealing them, you see, replacing the stones with paste.

He'd been doing it for years, one stone at a time, to cover his gambling debts, although he said he'd only seldom done it, and with only a very few pieces."

Lydia sat back against the cushions, completely shocked. One moment they'd been speaking of false lovers, and the next they were speaking of stolen jewelry? *That's* what all this had been about all along? The famous Malvern jewels? But how, why? She had to keep Jasmine talking, that much was obvious.

"I see," she said, trying to keep her voice even. "And you knew about these…exchanges."

"That's why I couldn't bear to wear any of the pieces longer than I had to in London. I was never so relieved as when I could hand them back to Tanner each evening. I knew they might be the few that were fakes, and just knowing that made them *burn* against my skin, as if I had been the guilty one. I had to pretend I would marry Tanner so that Papa could stay on the estate, keep on stealing jewels as he needed them. And I knew what he was doing, and didn't tell Tanner. If Papa was found out, *I* could go to gaol! Br-Bruce was to be my salvation, take me away to Paris, where I'd be safe."

"Except that he never planned to take you to Paris. He was working with your father." As seemed to be the case whenever she was in Jasmine's company for too long, Lydia was developing the headache. "No, I still don't see how your Bruce Beattie fits in here, beyond the role of your lover. Oh, wait. Did he help your father with the jewels? Perhaps sell them for him?"

"Yes of course. That's how I first met Bruce, one day

when he visited the estate. Papa couldn't be seen selling jewels, now could he? I think that should be obvious to someone as intelligent as you, Lydia. Although I admit I was not so intelligent, because *I* never knew they were working together. But there was one problem, and that was the Malvern Pride, the real prize. Papa couldn't find it. All the other pieces were kept in Tanner's study, behind a portrait. But the Malvern Pride and all of the pieces that go with it weren't there. Papa didn't care, as he said it would be too dangerous to touch it, but Bruce wanted it. He wanted it badly. I…I didn't learn that, either, until last night. Until Bruce hit me."

Lydia wished Tanner could be here to listen to all of this. But if she asked Jasmine to stop now, the girl might turn mulish, and refuse to tell anyone anything else. Especially once her father was on the scene.

"Yes, why did he hit you?"

"I…I'd promised him a key. Before I left for London, actually. But I didn't give it to him. Well, I didn't leave it under the rock down at the back of the garden, the way he told me to. I mean, he loved me, I was sure of that. But he kept asking for the key, and I didn't like that. He *demanded* it. So I didn't do what he said. I can be very stubborn, you know."

Lydia's mind flashed back to the note she'd read, the one she'd found in Jasmine's reticule. The line she hadn't thought important had been the most important of them all: *Remember what you promised. The key to our future, my darling.*

"This key, Jasmine. What could Bruce Beattie have done with this key?"

"Let…let himself into Malvern, of course. With all of us gone to London and the servants going to bed early because there was no one here to care for, he felt he could sneak in at night and search for the Malvern Pride, since Papa had refused to help him." She lifted her chin in some defiance. "But if I gave him that key, and he found the Malvern Pride, then he might leave me. He *said* he loved me, but did he? Did he, really? Silly in love as I was, sometimes I felt as if the Pride was more important to him than I was. He never ceased talking about it, even…even in bed. What did it look like, had I ever seen it. On and on. So I didn't leave the key, but took it to London with me instead. I had to be sure he'd still be here when I returned."

Lydia thought she could piece things together from there. "So, once he saw your father was back at Malvern, he came to the inn where Tanner always stays, somehow got you to meet him…"

"I saw him several times. When I picked the wild-flowers, and again later that day. That's when we arranged for me to sneak outside after midnight. I told him again, I would not give him the key. I told him Tanner would not ask for my hand, that he loved you, and that we had to leave together, just the way he'd promised. That very night. And that's…that's when he admitted that he'd never loved me. He said the only way he could bed me at all was to pretend he was shoving one of his socks in my mouth to stop my incessant talking."

Lydia bit her bottom lip between her teeth. "That was

very mean of him. You…you don't have to tell me all this if you don't want to. It's very…personal."

"Oh, but I feel better, telling someone. He also said that I was silly, and stupid, and how could I believe he was interested in more than the Malvern Pride. And then, when I flung myself against him, begging him to tell me he still loved me, he pushed me away. He slapped me. It hurt very much, but not…not as much as my breaking heart."

"I'm so sorry, Jasmine." So young, so beautiful… and so very gullible. Bruce Beattie should be horse-whipped, and Thomas Harburton, as well!

"I was such a fool, Lydia, and now I'm ruined. Forever. But I didn't want him to hit me again, you can understand that, can't you? I…I gave him the key to the French doors in Tanner's study."

Lydia sprung to her feet, panic in her heart. Bruce Beattie, clearly a very bad man, a very desperate man, had a key to Tanner's study. "We have to tell Tanner, Jasmine, the moment he arrives. You do know that, don't you?"

Again, the girl nodded, then blew her nose noisily. "I may be ruined, but at least I saved Papa. He may not be the best of papas, and now he'll go to gaol for what he's done if Tanner won't forgive him. But at least I've saved him."

Lydia turned to look at her in question. "Excuse me? You *saved* your father? From what? From Bruce Beattie? Is that what you're saying?"

Jasmine wet her lips with the tip of her tongue. "Yes, of course. Last night, B-Bruce said if I didn't give him the key right then and there, he would kill Papa, just to prove that he meant what he said when he said he wanted the key. You remember, Lydia? I asked you if you gave someone what they wanted if you thought that someone still would do something they said they would do if you didn't do what they wanted? Because once they had what they wanted, they wouldn't need to do what they'd said they'd do? And you said they probably wouldn't. So I did the right thing. Finally."

Lydia's breath caught in her throat. Is that what that nonsense had been about last night? But the girl prattled on so all the time—who could listen to it all, let alone give any of it any credence?

Then another even more distressing thought hit her. Tanner had said the body belonged to one of his estate workers. Thomas Harburton was the Malvern estate manager. *Oh, God…*

Jasmine got to her feet, still dabbing at her eyes. "I…I should probably instruct Mildred not to unpack my things, shouldn't I? Once you tell Tanner what I've done, Papa and I will have to leave. You don't mind telling him, do you? I just couldn't face him with such a…a tawdry story. I…I just couldn't bear anything more. I can only hope he'll forgive Papa and me enough to simply let us go."

"Jasmine, dearest, please wait. Tanner will be here at any moment. I think…I'm certain he'll want to talk to you."

But Jasmine shook her head and kept on toward the doorway, clearly eager to be gone before Tanner arrived.

She was to be thwarted in her attempt, however, for just then Tanner appeared in the foyer, and called her name.

Lydia stayed where she was, already certain she knew what he would be saying to his cousin. Her fingertips pressed to her lips, hurting for the girl, she watched as Tanner put his hands on Jasmine's slim shoulders and spoke to her quietly.

She had a sudden remembrance of the day he had come to Grosvenor Square, to tell them all about Fitz. How unfair that he had to once again be the bearer of such sad news. Her heart ached for him.

Jasmine cried out once, before falling forward against Tanner's chest in a faint.

He looked in at Lydia, his expression one of sorrow, but also something else she could not define. Perhaps some sort of fierce protectiveness for all of them, born of Thomas's murder. She got to her feet, to go to him, to help him with Jasmine, but he shook his head as if to tell her to remain where she was.

She watched, feeling helpless, wishing she did not have to tell him what she must tell him, as he lifted Jasmine in his arms and carried her up the stairs.

CHAPTER TWENTY

"So?"

Justin removed the jeweler's loupe from his eye and tossed the necklace to Tanner, who snatched it out of the air. "Pretty glass, I'm afraid. Your cousin had been a very busy man."

Tanner stared at the stones for long moments before letting the necklace slide onto the blotter of his desk, and then got to his feet. "You know, I never even looked at the jewels since my father died, hadn't seen them worn since my mother died, and she didn't wear them often, except for the Malvern Pride. I do remember thinking in passing that they could have been hidden better, protected better, but as they'd been safe behind that portrait all these years…"

"Safe from everyone save your cousin, according to what Lydia told us. How is she, by the way?"

"She's Lydia. Calm, at least outwardly. I know she has more to tell me, but other than to say that Jasmine told her Thomas had been replacing stones in the Malvern collection and that might be why he was killed, she said she felt it necessary that Jasmine tell me the rest. She's with her now, attempting to convince her to speak to me."

"To us."

"No, Justin, I don't think so. Whatever Jasmine has to tell me, I doubt she'll say it in front of an audience."

"Oh, so now I'm relegated to an audience? I'm cut to the quick, truly." But then he smiled. "Very well, it isn't as if I'll be left at loose ends, will I? It would appear I have a perimeter to set up before dark, and armed sentries to position discreetly near every doorway, since we don't know when our killer may come calling. You go see to Lydia. Outwardly calm or not, I'm sure she needs you."

"You don't have to do that, you know. Although, from the look on your face, I think you plan to enjoy it."

"The hint of danger? I'm half alive without it, unfortunately. I might have, in a moment of madness, believed differently, but I should never have made her happy. She chose the right man."

Tanner watched his friend leave the room, on his way to round up footmen and grooms and farm workers and whoever else he could find, and station them around the large structure for the night. It wasn't something they could continue indefinitely, turning Malvern into an armed camp. But for tonight, this was the best they could do.

He got to his feet slowly, feeling as if he'd aged a decade in the past four hours, and went in search of Lydia, finally running her to ground in her own chamber.

"You may go, Sarah, thank you," she said quietly as she looked at him, and the maid curtsied, then scurried out of the room. The moment the door to the dressing room closed behind the woman, Lydia was in his arms, her cheek pressed against his chest, and he was holding her tightly, with no intention of ever letting her go.

But eventually he had to, and she looked up at him with tears standing in her lovely blue eyes. "I'm so sorry about your cousin, Tanner."

"He was a thief," he said, the words still difficult to say, even more difficult to believe. "A gambler and a thief. He stole from his own family. I won't say I ever liked the man overmuch, but I'm finding it hard to see him as other than my cousin. Lazy, and yet ambitious. Prone to whine and wheedle and play on his old injury, granted, and forever pushing a match between Jasmine and me." He shook his head as he led Lydia over to a chair beside the fire and pulled her down onto his lap. "But a thief? No."

"Jasmine says it's true," Lydia reminded him as she stroked his cheek, pressed a kiss against his forehead. "He felt forced to it, because of his gambling debts."

"And that bothers me more. I even asked Roswell about it, and he was as surprised as I was. Thomas never left the estate except to go to the village from time to time, and that during the day, on estate business. When did he have the opportunity to gamble to such excess?"

"Jasmine said he would disappear for days at a time."

"Yes, I believe I heard that from Justin as well

because she'd told him the same thing. But Roswell denies that, too. Something's wrong, Lydia. I don't know what it is, but something is wrong."

Lydia sighed, and put her cheek against his chest once more. "I'm going to say something terrible now, Tanner. And I'm ashamed of myself, because she just lost her father to a murderer. But…well, I wouldn't believe Jasmine if she told me the sky was blue."

Tanner put his hands on her shoulders and eased her away from him so that he could look at her. "I'm listening—and I don't think you said anything terrible."

"It's…it's that nothing she said to me today made any sense, not when I had a few moments to step back and truly *look* at what she said. It's just that she talks so much, and you get so weary of listening to her that you really don't listen, not for long. She lies so easily, Tanner. Even Nicole couldn't fib that well, and I always thought her extremely proficient at it. Why, she fooled our Aunt Emmaline and Rafe into thinking that each was at Ashurst with us when we actually were totally without a chaperone. For *months*, Tanner, until Charlotte finally found her out by accident. And she looked me straight in the eye and told me there were no more sugared buns, when she'd had one hidden in her reticule all along. Jasmine, that is, not Nicole."

"You don't mind if I try to sort all of that out later? What lies do you think Jasmine told you this afternoon?"

"But that's the problem. With Jasmine, how can a person be sure? Truthfully I think she's told so many different lies in just the last two days that she's now confused herself, figuratively tripping over her own tongue. She…she doesn't have the ring of innocence about her, and I may feel terrible saying that, but it must be said. If I were to believe anything she's said, I would have to believe what she told me about…her lover. I saw the note from him in her reticule, ashamed as I am to admit that I snooped, and I saw the mark on her face where he'd hit her. We all saw that."

"My cousin has a lover? Really?" Tanner held up a hand to stop Lydia from saying more, and then asked her to please go back to the beginning, and tell him everything she thought important. He never interrupted, never asked for more detail, until she at last told him the name of Jasmine's lover.

"Bruce Beattie? No, that's not possible," he told her, smiling. "We need to mark that down as another of her lies."

"But I told you, I saw the note where he asked her for the key to the French doors in your study. He signed it with his initial. He…he had very good penmanship."

"I won't comment on the penmanship. However, darling, Bruce Beattie is seventy if he's a day, and I doubt if even Mrs. Beattie considers him a wonderful lover. I think he lost his last tooth ten years ago."

Lydia sat very still, her chest rising and falling rhythmically, but each breath seemingly deeper, more agitated. "And *that* is the very last straw!" she said finally, just before hopping down off his lap and holding out her hand. "Are you coming with me?"

He got to his feet, loving the color in her face, the bright sparkle in her eyes. "I'd have to kick myself down the stairs if I said no," he told her, and allowed her to lead him into the hallway and across the corridor to Jasmine's bedchamber. "Allow me," he said, stepping past her to depress the lever and push open the door.

Lydia brushed past him without thanking him—a sure sign of her temper he believed, and one he might be prudent to note for future reference if he were ever stupid enough to provoke her out of her usual serenity.

Jasmine was seated in the middle of her bed, a silver tray on her knees, a forkful of cake frozen halfway to her mouth. "Lydia? Tanner? Is something wrong? Please say there is no more bad news. I vow, I couldn't survive anything else."

Lydia walked as she spoke, not stopping until she was standing beside the bed. "Not without a plate piled high with strawberry tarts or some such thing to bolster your courage, no, I suppose not. Give me that!"

Tanner watched as the fork was ripped from his cousin's hand just before the tray was lifted and unceremoniously handed to him.

"Here, put this somewhere. Jasmine—get out of that bed."

But Jasmine had pulled the covers up to her chin and was seemingly intent on plastering herself against the pillows. "No. You're scaring me. My papa is dead. *Murdered.* I have been grieving all afternoon. How can you be so mean to me?"

"I'm counting, Jasmine," Lydia said, hands on hips.

"One…two…you don't want me to get to three, you really don't."

The covers were flung back and Tanner caught a glimpse of his cousin's legs, bared to the knee, as she slipped off the mattress and landed feet-first on the floor, nearly falling.

"You'd have made a good Sergeant major, darling," he said softly, but when Lydia turned and glared at him, he managed to control his smile before backing up two paces.

"Who is your lover?" she asked Jasmine flatly, clearly not in the mood to tread carefully on the girl's recently bereaved sensibilities.

"But—but that was to be our secret. You *promised*." Jasmine's gaze shifted to Tanner. "She told you the name?"

"Schoolmaster Beattie, yes. As I have a healthy regard for my neck, I'm doing my best not to interfere, but I have to tell you that I don't think she believes you any more."

As if her last hope was gone with his defection, Jasmine buried her face in her hands and sobbed piteously.

Well, he'd thought it was piteously. Lydia didn't seem much impressed.

"Jasmine, your Bru—your lover probably murdered your father. We'll have his name, *now*."

"I know," Jasmine whimpered. "I know, I know. And it's all my fault, isn't it?"

"No, Jasmine, sweetheart, you couldn't have known what—" Tanner held up his hands in mock surrender when Lydia turned on him, and backed up another pace. Clearly the love of his life had been pushed beyond all endurance.

"His name, and his location. You were in bed with him. You know where he resides."

"In bed with him? You make it all sound so tawdry. I *loved* him…"

At last Lydia looked at Tanner with more than cold purpose in her eyes. Confronting Jasmine, in her recent bereavement, was not easy for her. She sighed, as if in resignation, and gathered the weeping girl into her arms. "It's all right, Jasmine. Nobody blames you for anything that happened. You were foolish, yes, but this man, this unscrupulous scoundrel, could come here now, could cause us all terrible trouble. Please, help us."

Jasmine lifted her tear-drenched face and looked at Tanner, her eyes wide. "Me? He could come here for me? He could…he could want to *kill* me?"

Tanner shrugged his shoulders, believing Lydia had found the way to get through to his cousin. If there was one thing in life Jasmine cared about, he was coming to realize, it was Jasmine. "It's possible. You know who he is."

"Oh, my God! He'll kill me, won't he? Because I know who he is. No, no, I don't want to die! Tanner, you have to help me. You have to find him, and kill him before he kills us!"

"Tell me again," Justin said as they stood hidden in the dense trees outside the small tavern in near Malvern Wells.

"I've already told you," Tanner said, peering through the branches, taking his measure of the place. It was half-past midnight.

"True. But I don't think I'll ever tire of hearing it. Wrung every last bit of information from her, did she? And all the sordid details? Tell me again about the sordid details."

"Another time," Tanner said, shaking his head. "How do you want to do this? He knows what we look like, which was probably why he showed me his face in the first place, so we can't just go walking in there. Jasmine swears he's alone, but Lydia warned me not to believe that. She's still suspicious of Jasmine."

"And if your beloved is suspicious, you're suspicious, and so am I. Why are we suspicious, hmm?"

"Because Lydia wouldn't believe Jasmine if she told her the sky was blue. And something about sugared buns, but we didn't have time to get into that. Well, damn, Justin, there he is. And he's alone. That makes things easier. I thought we might be here all night."

The baron, who had been standing with his back to a tree trunk, an unlit cheroot between his teeth, turned and peered into the clearing in front of the tavern. "And he's had a miracle, hasn't he? Heaven be praised, his sight has been restored."

Tanner watched Brice Flanagan walk out of the tavern, cautiously looking about the area with his two good eyes as he mounted the horse they'd already recognized as belonging to the man.

Without speaking again, each knowing what the

other had concluded, Tanner and Justin hurried back through the trees to where their own horses were waiting. Flanagan could have mates inside the tavern who could come to his defense. Much easier to take him on the road.

They followed at a safe distance for over a mile, Flanagan's familiarity with the road as easy as Tanner's.

"He's heading for Malvern," Justin whispered at last, unnecessarily. "Cheeky thing, isn't he?"

"Desperate is more like it," Tanner returned just as quietly. "He had to know that Jasmine would turn on him at some point. Are you ready?"

"I don't know. I almost wish to see what he's up to, don't you?"

Tanner considered this for a few moments. Was Flanagan on his way to the estate in some last bold attempt to find the Malvern Pride, that hadn't been among the stolen jewels, according to Jasmine? Was he going there to collect Jasmine, his lover? Or, yes, to kill her…

"All right," he said at last, as they slowed their horses, no longer needing to be too close to Flanagan. "I admit to some curiosity of my own. Why chance capture for the Malvern Pride? He's got the rest, he's got all of the real jewelry, enough to live handsomely on the rest of his life, damn him. Besides, nobody knows where the Pride is, remember? That's why he'd demanded the key from Jasmine, in order to conduct his own search."

"All of which brings us back to your cousin. He's already rid of Thomas. Jasmine is the only remaining loose end, the only one that could identify him. Save us, but he can't know we've been so brilliant. After all, if you called in Bow Street or anyone else, you'd be sending them after a red-haired one-eyed man with a patch. Not the best of disguises, but certainly effective."

They were on the estate now, Flanagan completely out of sight on the nearly moonless night.

Tanner's horse lifted his head, sniffing the air, and then whinnying softly.

"Over there," Justin said, pointing into the trees. "That's the fellow's mare, isn't it? He's on foot now."

"We can't stumble over him out here in the dark," Tanner said. "He'll take his time approaching, picking his place of entry."

"I'll give you odds on the doors to your study. I know that's where I plan to continue my own search in the morning. Another hidey-hole, this one much more cleverly concealed. So you're simply going to let him walk in?"

Tanner urged his mount ahead on the road, heading for the front gates rather than to ride through the trees to reach the rear of the house and gardens, and his study. He turned and grinned at his friend in the darkness. "Should we pour him a brandy, do you think?"

They left their horses tied to tree branches halfway up the drive, and traveled the rest of the way on foot, pistols at the ready in case Flanagan didn't behave as Justin thought he would. But there was little chance the man would be so bold as to try one of Thomas's keys on the front doors of Malvern.

"You put Roswell on the front doors?" Tanner said in amazement as he watched the aged butler step out from the shadows, an equally aged blunderbuss in his hands.

"He insisted, and I thought this was the safest place for him. Don't shoot, man, it's your duke."

Roswell lowered his weapon and bowed, as if greeting his master this way were an everyday occurrence. "Your Grace. May I be some humble service?"

"No, thank—yes, Roswell, if you don't mind stationing yourself at the foot of the stairs. There may be some…commotion shortly, and I would ask that you keep the ladies from coming downstairs."

"Sans this nasty thing, I believe," Justin said, deftly removing the blunderbuss from the butler's hands as they entered the foyer.

"I can't believe I'm doing this," Tanner said as they made their way down the hall after refusing Roswell's offer of candles to light their way. "Lydia's upstairs, and I've just all but invited a murderer into the house."

"Having second thoughts, are you?"

"Second thoughts, third thoughts. But if we don't get him now, I'd never sleep easily, wondering if and when he'd show up here again. Lydia understands that."

Then he held up his hand, pointing to his right, and the corridor that led to a second door to the study, one closer to the servant stairs.

Justin nodded and headed off. Tanner counted to ten, and then proceeded to the main door to what was supposed to be the duke's inner sanctum. He eased the door open, relieved to see that no fire burned in the grate, and that the only faint light in the large chamber came from the few stars in the sky outside the French doors.

But he was confident, having chosen his battlefield, and familiar with the placement of every chair, every table shrouded in darkness. He slipped into the room, staying low, having already decided that he would move to his left, and position himself in the far corner, behind a marble pedestal supporting a bust of Socrates.

He felt rather than saw Justin enter from the other side of the chamber, but even with his eyes accustomed to the darkness, he couldn't see which way his friend had gone.

It would be a devil of a thing if they ended up with Flanagan in between them, neither able to fire without fear of hitting the other one. The things you didn't think of until it was too late to change anything…

He tensed at the sound of someone moving across the slate terrace, a heel strike that couldn't be mistaken for anything else. Moments later came the sound of a key turning in the lock, and Brice Flanagan was inside the room with them.

Light a candle, light a candle, Tanner chanted inside his head. Then the man would be illuminated and it would be easy for him and Justin to step out, pistols leveled, and take the man.

But Flanagan didn't move to light a candle. He stood very still for the space of several heartbeats, and then turned toward Tanner, heading straight for the book-cases that lined the side wall.

Sliding his pistol into his waistband, Flanagan used

both hands to locate the wooden pillars that divided each expanse of books into separate sections, and then ran one hand up the third pillar, pressing on the wooden rosette that marked the fourth row of shelves.

Immediately, a small section of the shelf next to the rosette slid backwards, into the wall, and Flanagan reached into the opening with the confident air of a man who has found exactly what he'd been looking for.

Except that he hadn't.

Tanner watched the man's increasingly desperate patting and probing at the opening. Flanagan went up on tiptoe, as if to see into the dark void, now using both hands to continue his search.

"Nothing there, I'm afraid," Justin said just as Tanner was coming out from his own hiding place, as with the man's two hands occupied, there could have been no better time to take him. "I was as hopeful as you, earlier, when I discovered it. But, alas, no pretty diamonds I'm sure you were told were there. You murdered Thomas Harburton for nothing."

Flanagan had whirled about to locate the source of the taunting voice, already reaching into his waistband for his pistol as he stepped away from the bookcases.

Tanner could have shot the man. Or, as Justin seemed anxious to do, talked him to death. But Tanner wasn't an adventurous or even slightly flamboyant sort.

He merely silently stepped up behind Brice Flanagan and brought the butt of his pistol down on the back of the fellow's head, and then watched, dispassionately, as the bastard pitched unconscious to the floor.

Lydia, he was sure, would have approved.

CHAPTER TWENTY-ONE

LYDIA FELT TANNER take her hand in his as they stood outside the family mausoleum, watching as Thomas Harburton's body was carried to its last rest.

Justin had been kind enough to have taken charge of Jasmine, both in the family chapel and on the sad walk to the mausoleum, the girl leaning heavily against him, the picture of sorrow, and yet stunningly beautiful in her hastily sewn mourning black.

They'd been a sad, subdued party since Thomas's death. Jasmine had kept very much to her rooms, although she'd managed to eat everything Tanner had ordered sent up to her.

And then, this morning, just before the services, she'd startled them all with the announcement that she had decided she would very much like to go to Wales, and her late mother's sister, where she could "mourn my poor father and do penance for my own sins of the flesh. I am no better than any of those unfortunate women my aunt cares for."

Even as she sang along with the few hymns and followed in her prayer book, Lydia thought about

Jasmine's new role, the one of penitent…and the more she thought about it, the more she felt uneasy. Would she never be able to forget how easily Jasmine lied? Was she being petty, still miffed about a sugared bun?

She didn't like to think that of herself, but it had been that question that had kept her silent for two long days.

As they walked back to the house in the warm sunshine of a beautiful day, Tanner whispered in her ear. "I've missed you. Would it be selfish of me to ask you if you'd join me for a tramp through the hills this afternoon? I feel a need to clear my head, and that always seems easier to do up there."

Lydia was immediately put in mind of their last time together on a hillside overlooking Malvern. "I think I'd like that, yes," she said quietly. "Shall I wear my new boots?"

His smile was her answer.

Two hours later, the vicar still lingering over the obligatory funeral meal following the interment and fully engaged in a theological discussion with Justin, who Lydia believed to be deliberately baiting the man with his cunning questions about what form eternal damnation might take, she and Tanner were walking through the gardens, on their way to a path he knew well.

"Jasmine was to leave the key to your study beneath a rock down here, at the end of the gardens," she told him, thoughts of everything the girl had told her never far from her mind, unfortunately. "How might things have gone differently, I wonder, if she had done so before you and she left for London."

"I don't know. I suppose that's one of the questions I could ask Flanagan when I visit the gaol tomorrow. The Squire took me aside at the services, to tell me that Flanagan has been demanding to speak with me ever since he woke up, but the Squire thought I should first be allowed to bury my cousin before having to deal with his murderer."

They had moved into the shade of the trees overhanging the path that climbed slowly, but steadily. "Do you think he'll tell you where he hid the jewels?"

"In exchange for his neck? Perhaps. And I'd like to know why he didn't just take them and leave the area."

"The Malvern Pride," Lydia said as he took her hand and helped her across a section of the path crisscrossed with tree roots. "Justin believes he made your cousin tell him where it was, and then killed him."

"For not sharing it with him, yes. A falling out of thieves, almost inevitable, I suppose."

Lydia looked at him, seeing the pain in his eyes. "Tell me more about Malvern," she said, trying to divert him. "What is it like here in winter?"

He smiled, and her heart leapt.

"What is it like here in winter?" he repeated as they walked the gently meandering path that made their ascent almost unnoticeable. "Like a...like a carpet of white. The sun is low, and shines through the bare branches of the trees...and the streams sparkle in the sunlight, running clear, and icy-cold. The deer come closer. If we wake early enough, we can lie in bed and watch them feed."

He slipped an arm around her shoulders. "And if there's enough snow, I'll have the sleigh harnessed. I'll tuck you up with blankets, with a hot brick at your feet, and when the moon is full, and the night sky dancing with stars, I'll show you a wonderland that will bring tears to your eyes."

Lydia turned in his embrace, loving him so much. "It all sounds so beautiful."

"Not as beautiful as you. Malvern is where we'll live, and where we'll raise our children. But you are my world. I want these past days behind us, and damn the Malvern Pride and the rest of the jewels, damn all of it. I spoke with the vicar, Lydia. He's agreed to marry us on Friday, if you'll still have me."

"But your cousin…and Jasmine…"

"Thomas is dead, so he won't care, and I've decided to send Jasmine to her aunt, as she seems to want. I need you, Lydia, for more than stolen moments like this. I need you as my wife."

She melted against him—how could she not?—and his arms went fully around her as he took her mouth with his, a hint of desperation transferring itself to her, so that she clung to him tightly.

She was slightly breathless when he let her go, only to take her hand and grin at her. "Come on, darling. I've something to show you. Let's try out those pretty new boots."

Lifting her skirts, the better to keep up with him, she ran with him along the path until he pulled her into a thicket of bushes and wildflowers. "What's this?" she asked, looking at the small shelter nearly hidden in the greenery.

"A hunting blind," he told her. "But not today. Mind your head."

As he held back the greenery, she bent low and stepped inside, to see that someone had laid fresh blankets on the ground. She sat down, because it was impossible to really stand, and waited for him to join her.

"You did this?" she asked him, patting the blankets as she looked around her, smiled at the way small sunbeams found their way through the leafy covering, making lacy patterns everywhere. The air was redolent with the smells of wildflowers and rich, warm earth.

It was all so rustic. So very…elemental.

"Guilty as charged, yes," he said, his grin boyish, and so endearing. "I came up here before dawn. And, God help me, I spent the entirety of poor Thomas's service thinking about how I could ask you to come up here with me. Am I being selfish? Because if you—"

Lydia threw herself against him, holding his face in her hands as she kissed him, cutting off whatever else he might say. How she'd missed him these past two nights. How she'd lain awake hour after hour, longing for his touch.

There was no shyness now, no need for him to hold himself back for fear of frightening her. She told him that in the way her hands moved over him, pushing his jacket from his shoulders, fumbling with the buttons that held his trousers shut. There was only this hunger, this urgency…

"Oh God, oh, sweet Christ…" He bit down on her earlobe as she pressed her hand against him, eager to feel his arousal, glorying in his swiftly indrawn breath as she freed him, closed her hand around him.

She knew the center of her pleasure now, and wanted him to feel what she had felt. She wanted, needed, to give, as he had given to her.

"Tell me how," she said, her breathing quick and labored as a sweet, tugging tension began to blossom between her thighs. "How do I love you?"

"You don't have to…like that," he all but moaned as she slid her cupped hand up and down the soft skin that felt like velvet over the steel of his arousal. "Oh, yes, sweetness. Just like…that."

He rested his head against her chest as he stroked her nipples through the thin muslin of her gown, his touch isolating her sensations, making her doubly aware of how his touch affected her. The tug, the slight pinch of his thumbs and forefingers. She cried out with the intense, concentrated pleasure that set off small, anticipatory explosions between her legs.

She squirmed against him, her body refusing to be still, and he somehow managed to raise her gown until the thin muslin was bunched around her hips. He fingered her still throbbing flesh through the fine lawn of her undergarment, her teeth clenching as she willed the barrier gone, all barriers gone.

Her urgency transferred itself to her hand and she stroked his fullness faster, each pump of her hand more frantic somehow, until they collapsed together on the blankets, a fever of desire and *wanting* urging her on, dark thoughts coming to her…and seeming so right.

What he had done for her…she would do for him.

As her lips closed around him, as she tentatively ran her tongue over the silk of him, Tanner said her name in a way that told her that there was no world outside this secret bower for either of them. They needed only each other, all that they could give, all that they could take. There was no right, no wrong, no lingering worries…not for now, not for this moment. There was nothing in the world except the two of them, lost in the loving.

He rolled her onto her back, kneeling above her as she raised her hips and he rid her of the last barrier between them. Her thighs fell open of their own accord, a wordless invitation he took up immediately, sinking into her in one long stroke, and then holding her close, kissing her deeply, hungrily.

"Lift your legs, my darling Lydia. Wrap yourself around me. Take me in…take me in…"

She did as he said, wrapping her legs high around him, the move bringing more of him inside her, pressing their bodies close together, so that each time he withdrew, each time he filled her again, the tension between her legs grew tenfold, until she was begging him for the release that eluded her.

Until he began to move faster. Faster. She hung on tightly, certain now she would soon die from the intensity of her pleasure. "Tanner…please. *Please,* if you love me…"

It began at the very center of her. She closed her eyes tightly, simply grateful for the longed-for release of tension. But like waves hitting against the shore, the onslaught of feeling was relentless, wave after wave crashing against her, touching every part of her. Again, and again, and again, explosions of the purest delight following hard upon each other as her body throbbed against Tanner's, pulling him in, convulsing around him as he cried out in his own climax.

He collapsed against her, his breathing ragged, and she pressed frantic kisses everywhere she could touch him until, finally, reluctantly, her limbs relaxed, her heart slowed its mad pace, and she could simply hold him, a sweet lethargy overtaking her.

"We…we're getting rather good at this," he said after a long, comfortable silence, and Lydia found herself smiling, even as tears that had escaped her ran into her ears, tickling them. "We may find a bed boring."

"I don't think so," she told him as he levered himself onto his back, sliding one hand between them, to pick up hers, bring it to his lips. "I think I'm lying on more than a few stones the blankets didn't quite cushion."

"And you didn't mention that until now?"

"I didn't *care* until now," she told him as he sat up, drawing her up with him. "Do we have to go back? Couldn't we just have Roswell bring us food and fresh clothing, and stay here forever? Or at least until the first snowfall?"

"I wish we could," he said, and she heard the sincerity in his voice. And, sadly, she knew that the world was back again, and the problems they'd left behind them at Malvern.

"Mr. Flanagan is in gaol, Tanner. I'm sure he can be made to tell you where he hid the jewelry he took. And the Malvern Pride may be missing, but it hasn't been stolen. We'll find it, eventually. Justin's rather enjoying himself, looking for it."

"And Jasmine? Can I really send her off to her aunt? She just lost her father, Lydia. She may say she wants to go, but it seems wrong to me, somehow."

"Because you'd be happy to see her gone?"

He turned to her as he slid one arm into his jacket. "Yes. That's exactly why. She's without father or dowry or—"

"Virginity," Lydia said, finishing his sentence, as she was sure he didn't want to do. And then she said what she didn't want to say. "It would only be for a year, Tanner, until her mourning period is over. You could give her a dowry, and we could take her to London. She's quite beautiful, and she can be quite charming. And with the Duke of Malvern sponsoring her?"

"Only a year," he repeated as he exited the hunting blind and turned to assist Lydia. "You don't even like her, and you'd agree to her living with us for the next year?"

Lydia went up on tiptoe, and could then see the roofs of Malvern. "It's a rather large house. Justin will be leaving us soon. She could help us hunt for the Malvern Pride."

"Perhaps a month or two with her aunt?" Tanner

said. "While we travel to Ashurst for your sister's wedding, and then perhaps go on a tour of the Lake District or some such thing? She wasn't entirely blameless in all of this, you know, much as I think it was her innocence that betrayed her."

Lydia had her reservations about Jasmine's *innocence*, but Tanner was the duke, and he had obligations. She wouldn't make things difficult for him. "I think I'd like to see the Lake District with—"

Tanner's head whipped around, in the direction of the sound of a shot. "That came from Malvern," he said, taking her hand.

A second shot was fired, just as loud, just as startling.

"Pistol shots. Almost like a signal. It might be Justin, trying to summon me. Something's wrong. Lydia, you stay here. Go back inside the blind. No one will find you there. I'll come back for you once I know what's happening."

"No."

Tanner had already taken three steps away from her, obviously believing she would do as he said. Now he turned to look at her in some shock. "Lydia, please."

"I said, no. A year ago, a month ago, I would have done just as you said, Tanner. But not now. I'm coming with you. And if I slow you down, I'm sure I can find my way. After all, I just have to keep going downhill, don't I?"

"Lydia, I—oh, all right. We're wasting time." He reached back, took her hand, and they began their descent, the way not steep but made easier because of the incline they had to travel on their way up to the hunting blind.

Halfway down, they could see Roswell and two footmen coming across the scythed lawns, and Tanner changed direction, taking an intersecting path that led, not back to the gardens, but more toward the front of the large building.

Lydia, her skirts hiked high in one hand, fought breathlessness as Tanner picked up their pace, feeling almost giddy as he only barely held himself back from an all-out run.

"Roswell, I'm here!" he called out as they neared the bottom of the last small rolling stretch of hillside. "What the bloody blazes is going on?"

"Oh, Your Grace," Roswell said, holding on to his periwig, his thin cheeks flushed nearly scarlet from his exertion. "It's that man, the one you conked on the noggin the other night. He's…he's here. He's got Miss Harburton. And…and he's shot the baron."

"Sweet Jesus! Is he—"

"I don't think so, Your Grace, no. They're all in your study, Your Grace. Locked up tight inside. The man… he said to fetch you, so I—"

"Stay here," Tanner told Lydia, putting his hands on her shoulders and giving her a single shake, as if to put emphasis to his words. He turned to one of the footmen. "You, go to the stables. Have one of the grooms take my horse and ride for the doctor. Send another one for the Squire. Now! Roswell, where are my pistols?"

"I've got Jeremy loading them up for you, Your

Grace. He said what he knew how. He's…he's waiting on you just inside the Great Hall, Your Grace!" he called after Tanner, who had already begun running toward the front doors.

"Roswell, what happened?" Lydia asked the butler, her eyes following Tanner. "The man was in gaol."

"Yes, my lady. But, you see, it isn't really much of a gaol, being as how we don't need one much. And Rodney Sykes, who stays there when there's a prisoner? Well, he drinks a bit, and sleeps even more. I can't say more than that, my lady, because I don't know. There… there was a knock on the door and this fool boy here," the butler threw a quick glance at the young footman who was still standing with them, "he just opened it, and the man came strolling in bold as brass, holding a brace of pistols and demanding Miss Harburton be brought to him at once."

"Yes, you already said he's got Jasmine. Where does he have her?"

"In the master's study, my lady. She was unfortunate enough as to come down the stairs just then, and he pointed one of the pistols at her and said she needed to come with him. To the study, my lady. The baron was in there, pulling all the books off the shelves even after I asked him kindly not to, and we all heard a shot and Miss Harburton screamed and said he'd killed him and I heard the baron tell her to stop screaming, because he wasn't dead."

Lydia pressed a hand to her mouth, trying very hard not to scream herself.

"So that's when Jeremy ran to the stables and got His Grace's pistols from his coach and shot them off, hoping His Grace would hear. Jeremy was in the war, my lady, and knows just how to shoot."

Lydia looked toward the house again, to see that Tanner was gone, already inside. "What will he do? Mr. Flanagan probably thinks we have the Malvern Pride, and we don't. How will Tanner convince him?"

"I'm sure I wouldn't know. My lady, where are you going? His Grace said for you not to—"

But Lydia wasn't to be dissuaded. Not if Tanner was in danger. And Justin, as well. Why, the man might be bleeding to death even as she stood safely outside with a butler and a footman, *observing* life again, and not being a part of it.

When she entered the house one of the kitchen boys greeted her, a nasty-looking cleaver in his hand, and pointed her toward the hallway leading to Tanner's study.

"Lydia, for the love of Heaven," Tanner said when she turned the last corner, to see him standing just outside the closed doors to his study.

"What does he want?" she asked, deciding not to argue with Tanner, because she wasn't leaving, no matter what. "Surely he knows he can't just leave here again, not without everyone chasing him down. So why did he come back?"

"A good question! Why did I come back?"

Tanner and Lydia both turned their heads to look at the closed double doors.

Brice Flanagan spoke again, his Irish lilt more evident

than ever. "Come in and join us, why don't you. The door is unlocked. We're having us a small party in here. Aren't we, Jasmine, darlin'? Although, now that I'm thinking on the thing, I probably could have planned better."

"Stay out here," Tanner ordered. He stood with his back against the wall, and then reached out and opened the door closest to her. "I'm coming in, Flanagan."

"He always states the unnecessary," Lydia heard Justin say, his tone light, but not without strain. "Come on in, Tanner. Your uninvited guest is standing behind your desk, your cousin is neatly trussed to one of the chairs in front of that same desk, and I seem to be bleeding all over the other one. One saving grace, though. He's gagged dearest Jasmine. In addition, he's only got the one shot left, and if he had his druthers, I believe he'd rather shoot dear Jasmine than you anyway. Isn't that right, Flanagan?"

Lydia heard whimpering, and assumed Jasmine was trying to speak, or cry, around her gag.

She watched as Tanner disappeared into the room, and then inched as close to the door as she dared, to hear what would happen next.

"Let them go," Tanner said, and even Lydia rolled her eyes at that statement, as Flanagan laughed.

"Oh, yes, I'm sure he'll do just that," Justin drawled. "Good to see you, Tanner. Brice here has been entertaining me with the most interesting story. Do you want to tell His Grace, or shall I?"

Flanagan didn't speak, so Lydia could only imagine that he'd nodded to Justin, because the baron began to speak once more.

"'Tis a sad tale, my friend, one born of love gone very wrong, promises not kept, and, in general, things and even people not being what they were thought to be. Could you put down one of those pistols for a moment, and hand over your handkerchief? I seem to have bled all over this one. The wound isn't deep, I don't believe, but it's damnably bloody. Ah, thank you. Now, where was I?"

"Justin, for the love of Heaven…"

"Yes, that's it. For love. It was all for love. And for the Malvern jewels, of course. Even true love can't live on air, can it? Brice, you won't mind if I keep this short, will you? I seem to be feeling a tad…fuzzy."

Lydia inched closer to the open door, until she was able to push against it, slowly opening it enough that she could see Tanner's back. But she couldn't see anything else.

"Again, where was I? Ah. I suppose I should begin by telling you that your cousin, the late, lamented Thomas, was a party to absolutely nothing save wanting his daughter to marry a duke and then live off his son-in-law's largesse. He did not gamble. He did not pry stones out of the Malvern jewelry from time to time in order to pay his debts. He did, however, discover upon arriving here that his daughter, naughty puss, had taken a lover, thanks to a note delivered to him the moment he alit from his coach.

"Imagine his horror, believing you'd brought Jasmine back to Malvern in order to propose, only to learn that this lover planned to present himself to you and confess *all*, as they say in the Pennypress novels. Unless, of course, Thomas could purchase the lover's silence by meeting him in the woods with the Malvern jewels. Which he did, an act of desperation that proved to be his last act on this earth. I've come to the conclusion that the sapphires were placed on the man's body to prove he was the thief, one who'd had a falling-out with his partner in crime. Nice to have that settled in my head."

"So you're a blackmailer as well as a murderer, Flanagan," Tanner said tightly. "But you have the jewels. Why keep coming back here?"

"Fakes," Justin said, sighing. "I thought you'd have figured that out by now, my friend. There was not a genuine gem in the entire lot. Isn't that right, Brice? You'd done murder, and for what? Some bits of pretty glass. We wondered why the jewelry wasn't better protected, remember? I imagine the stones were replaced long ago. Oh, except for the Malvern Pride, which, I'm afraid, is still among the missing. Brice is certain that is real."

"My mother must have known. She rarely wore any of it. Just the Malvern Pride."

"A stone so large it would be difficult to sell and not have word get out that the Duke of Malvern was pockets-to-let. Everyone must know about the Malvern Pride," Justin said. "Who would buy such a recognizable stone? How were you going to get around that, Jasmine?"

"Jasmine?"

Lydia had said the name at the same time as Tanner.

"She said she loved me, and fool that I am, I believed her. But all she wanted was those damn stones."

"No," Lydia said, stepping into the room. Tanner grabbed her and put her behind him. But she pushed her way further into the room. "I'm fine, Tanner. As Justin said, the man only has one shot left, and I doubt he'd waste it on me. You're wrong, Mr. Flanagan. Jasmine couldn't have wanted the stones. She knew they were fakes. She told me so. Tanner? That's why she always gave them back to you after she wore them. She said they burned against her skin because she knew they weren't real, that her father had been stealing the real stones."

The look on Brice Flanagan's face was almost amusing. "Then…then why did she have me steal them?"

"A very good question, Mr. Flanagan. Perhaps we should ask her. Although I'll first warn you that she's already spun three very plausible if outrageous stories, and has even juggled bits and pieces of each so that she is at once the loving daughter, the reluctant fiancée, the betrayed innocent tricked into giving up her virginity and, lastly, a woman in fear of her life. I wouldn't be surprised if we're now to hear yet another marvelous tale."

So saying, Lydia grabbed the cloth gag and pulled it loose.

"He's lying, he's lying! I never asked him to steal anything! He made me give him the key." Jasmine twisted about as best she could, to look up at Lydia. "He hit me. You saw it, you saw how he hit me."

"I saw a mark on your cheek," Lydia said, thoughts of blue skies and sugared buns suddenly making her doubt even the things she had seen with her own eyes. "You *told* me he'd struck you. I suppose, if you were pushed to it, you could have hit yourself."

"Hit her? I never laid a hand on her," Flanagan said. "She could lie her way through the bottom of an iron pot, damn her."

"Yes, I won't disagree with you there, sir," Lydia agreed, not uncharitably. And then she considered the only other thing she had believed true. "I saw the note you wrote to her."

If Flanagan had looked confused before, he now looked totally at sea. "Note? I never wrote her any notes."

"But you asked her to remember the key. The key to your shared happiness."

"Who talks like that?" the Irishman asked, grimacing. "Lies, she tells nothing but lies! And I loved her? More fool I, that's what I say. I'm leaving. The bloody hell with the damn stone."

"I'm afraid I can't allow you to do that, Flanagan," Tanner said, raising both pistols. "You murdered my cousin."

"I worried you might remember that. He also shot me, but I think I've already forgiven him," Justin said, holding the blood-soaked handkerchief to his side. "If I might finish my little story? The man is guilty, there's no denying that. But, according to him, he only did the dirty deed so that he and Jasmine could be together. If he didn't, her father would demand that she marry you. You're madly in love with Jasmine, you know. Besotted. Our Mr. Flanagan here was equally besotted himself— what did he see in you, Jasmine? I, for one, can't imagine."

But, for once, Jasmine wasn't saying anything. She was too busy straining against the drapery cords that held her firmly in the chair.

Justin seemed to sway in his chair, and Lydia quickly went to him, taking hold of his shoulders.

"Thank you, my dear. But, as Tanner won't say it, never again cross in between two men holding pistols aimed at each other. Such moves often don't end well. Let me finish, shall we? The plan had been formulated before you took Jasmine to London, Tanner, and set into motion the moment Thomas returned to the estate. The note was delivered, the jewels were carried to the meeting place, Thomas was dispatched—Brice is very sorry for that, by the way—and Jasmine was to then beg to be sent to her aunt in Wales to recover from her bereavement. But, instead of going to Wales, she would flee whatever inn the coach stopped at, board a public coach, and rendezvous with our anxiously awaiting Romeo in Brighton. At which time, true love winning out and all of that, they would fly off to Paris on love's golden wings and begin their long-awaited happily ever after. With the Malvern Pride and all the rest of the jewelry in the collection to keep them warm."

Tanner, who had been very quiet, finally spoke. "We don't even know where the Pride is, you know. And you killed a man for glass and paste. You really are a sad case, aren't you, Flanagan?"

"I'm fairly well ashamed, yes. But I couldn't live without her. She sprinkled fairy dust all around me, blinding me to her deceitful ways."

"He's lying! Nothing happened that way!" Jasmine shouted as everyone looked at her. "It was all his idea, not mine. I tried to talk him out of killing Papa, but he wouldn't listen. He never wanted me. He wanted the jewels. He threatened to kill me, too! To hear him, you'd think all I wanted was the Malvern Pride and a way to be shed of this place."

Jasmine's eyes went wide, and she quickly shut her mouth.

But it was too late.

Lydia remembered the rosette, and the secret cubbyhole that had been revealed. It really was a clever hiding place. But if someone was really looking for it, and had the time to invest in a prolonged search…

"Excuse me," she said, just as if she'd asked to retire from the dinner table, to leave the gentlemen to their port and cigars. "I'll be back momentarily. Mr. Flanagan? With your permission?"

When he didn't answer, she turned on her heel and left the study, her steps firm and quick as she brushed past Rosswell and an entire gaggle of servants, on her way up the stairs to Jasmine's bedchamber. "Mildred," she called out as she headed for the dressing room.

"Has Miss Harburton asked you to pack her clothing for her removal to her aunt's residence?"

Mildred who appeared from the dressing room at the sound of her name, curtsied when she saw Lydia. "Yes, my lady. I'm doing that right now. And that's the last thing I'll be doing for Miss Harburton, seeing as she told me plain that I'm not to come with her when she leaves tomorrow. Just turned me off, just like that."

"You can stay with us, Mildred. My Sarah has told me you're a very good worker. There will always be a place for you here. Now, may I see the bags you've packed?"

"Yes, my lady, and thank you. I packed all but the one. Miss Harburton packed that herself, saying she couldn't trust me with her most precious possessions. As if I ever broke a single thing."

"I'm sure you haven't. I'll begin with that bag, if you don't mind."

Five minutes later, she was heading for the study once more, carrying a surprisingly heavy square, velvet-covered box containing the most beautiful necklace she'd ever seen. And not only a necklace, but two bracelets, a pair of earbobs, a large brooch, some delicate hairpins, and three rings holding stones the size of quail eggs—or so said a thoroughly impressed Mildred.

She entered the room, holding up the box, only to find a fussing Wigglesworth kneeling beside Justin, who was bare to the waist and clearly not at all embarrassed about it, and Tanner pouring out two glasses of wine.

"Where…where is Mr. Flanagan? And Jasmine?"

Tanner looked to Justin, and then shrugged his shoulders as if to say events had somehow just rolled along. "My cousin is being detained in the morning room until such time as I can arrange transport to her aunt. She did say that was where she wanted to go, remember?"

"To a home for reformed prostitutes? She never planned to go to Wales."

"No, darling, I'm sure she didn't. But that is where she's headed, just as soon as I can pen a letter of warning to her aunt. Jasmine begged me to send her off to gaol instead, but she could probably lie and wheedle her way past any warden. But not her aunt."

"How she must have hated her father, to coldly arrange to have him killed."

"She explained that. Thomas told her if she couldn't bring me up to snuff by the end of the Season, he was going to accept the vicar's request for her hand before she reached her majority in another six months. The vicar has been looking for a mother for his seven children for the past year. Thomas said marriage would mature her."

Lydia's mind conjured up a vision of the dour-faced man who had presided at Thomas's funeral. "He really would have done that? To his only daughter?"

"We'll never know, will we? I never showed the least sign of being interested in marrying her, so I imagine it was a chance Jasmine simply wasn't willing to take. If she'd only come to me, I would have found a way to help her. Instead, she found her own way. She said her way seemed much more profitable, and that once she met Flanagan, all the pieces just seemed to fall neatly into place."

"She also could have lied to you about the vicar," Lydia pointed out. "She's lied about everything else."

"That's true enough. I believed an admitted murderer more than I did your cousin, Tanner. And he wasn't even pretty. Is that the Malvern Pride you're holding, my dear?" Justin asked, and Lydia handed him the box, careful to avoid looking at him. She'd only ever seen Tanner without his shirt, and she'd not be unhappy to keep it that way.

He lifted the lid. "Ah! Magnificent." He reached into his waistcoat pocket and produced a jeweler's loupe, pressing it to his eye as he held up the necklace. "Yes. Truly magnificent. Ouch! Good God, Wigglesworth, have a care there with whatever you're doing. I'm already injured."

"And you've ruined a perfectly fine suit of clothes by bleeding all over them," Wigglesworth responded, sounding near tears. "How many times must I ask you not to do that?"

Lydia worried that she was very close to hysterical laughter. "Are either of you going to tell me where Mr. Flanagan is?"

Tanner took the box from Justin and handed him a glass of wine in return. "We let him go," he said, and then took a drink from his own glass. "Actually, we turned our backs and counted to ten, and when we turned around again, the man was gone."

"He's suffered enough, poor sot. I think he still loves

her, actually," Justin said. "Besides, it did come down to Tanner standing here with his pistol, and Brice standing over there, with his pistol, and a bad end for somebody if we didn't reach an amicable solution. I'm sure he'll be a much reformed character once he's back in Ireland, which is where I would be heading were I him."

Lydia thought about this for some moments, as Tanner watched her, a small smile playing about his lips. Almost as if he knew what she would say next.

"Then that's done, isn't it?" she said at last, because she was who she was, and she was very comfortable with who she was, and Tanner actually seemed delighted with who she was. "Roswell is waiting just outside in the hallway. Would anyone care for a cup of tea?"

EPILOGUE

THE LATE AUGUST SUN was beating down with some intensity as they all stood on the steps of the quaint white wooden church set just off the village green, and Lydia was grateful for her new bonnet and its wide brim. She was particularly fond of the sky blue ribbons that tied beneath her chin, ribbon that perfectly matched the small bit of blue ribbon pinned inside her reticule; her good luck charm that went with her everywhere.

Tanner had approved, and that meant everything to her.

They'd arrived at Ashurst Hall only yesterday morning, having begged off arriving sooner, as neither was eager to leave Malvern and the first glorious weeks of their marriage.

Nicole had greeted her with squeals and hugs and exclamations of how beautiful her twin looked, how happy she seemed. "You found just what I hoped for you, sweetheart," her sister had said. "A nice, quiet love."

Lydia smiled now, as she had smiled then, although she hadn't disabused Nicole of her assumption. But she somehow doubted that her sister's idea of a "nice, quiet love" included impassioned moments beneath the stars, or stolen hours in their favorite hunting blind…or the night Tanner had stripped them both of every scrap of clothing, picked her up so that she could wrap her legs about him, and walked the two of them into a moonlight-streaked stream.

Although he'd informed her that they needed to be more careful now, the sweet darling, ever since she'd first become nauseous upon waking in the mornings. She'd told him that Sarah had said feeling sick to her stomach was a sign that the seed had been firmly planted and assured a good pregnancy, but Tanner would take no chances with her.

Lydia reached down and took his hand in hers. He was so sweet. She loved him so very much.

"Charlotte looks well," he whispered, and Lydia looked across the expanse of steps, to where her brother and his wife stood, also holding hands. Behind them, a mobcapped nanny held the heir to the dukedom, born only a month earlier. Today was to be both a wedding and a christening, although young Rafael Fitzgerald Daughtry seemed unimpressed as he slept in the nanny's arms.

Her Aunt Emmaline's daughter had been left behind at Ashurst Hall, as she'd been awake half the night, cutting another tooth, the now Duchess of Warrington had informed them, just before she yawned behind her hand, then looked sternly at her husband as he'd put forth the notion that his wife might wish a small nap after the ceremony. The way he'd made the suggestion had Tanner chuckling quietly, and both Emmaline and Lydia had rolled their eyes…proving that some traits ran in families.

"Lucas looks terrified," Lydia commented as she looked toward her soon to be brother-in-law, and both she and Tanner smiled as they watched the bridegroom reach up and run a finger beneath his neckcloth, as if it had suddenly become too tight.

"I can't believe he let her dress him all in white," Tanner whispered. "Thank you yet again, darling, for not putting me through such hoops."

"You're very welcome. But he does look quite handsome, if somewhat uncomfortable for a man of his consequence. He really must love my sister very much."

"I gladly would have done the same for you, had you asked. And may I say again, thank God you didn't. I'd also have enjoyed hearing Justin's opinion on all of this grandeur, but part of the price he paid to return to England was to be at Prinney's beck and call if he was needed."

"I still don't understand why the Prince Regent would need him," Lydia said as a murmur began to rise among the crowd of villagers lining both sides of the grassy walk leading to the church.

"Justin is a man of many talents, none of which he'd most likely want you to know about, darling. Oh, good Lord, here she comes."

Still holding tight to Tanner's hand, Lydia leaned forward, to better see her sister as she approached.

First came the little girls, a dozen sweet, cherubic

creatures dressed all in white, long pink streamers in their hair. They danced about prettily, tossing pink rose petals in front of them as they approached—all but one obviously shy little beauty who held tightly to her basket with both hands, refusing to be parted from her petals.

That's it, sweetheart, Lydia applauded the child silently, *you hold onto what is yours. Hold on tight.*

And then Nicole appeared, riding sidesaddle atop her beloved Juliet, the mare sporting a white satin blanket and white satin ribbons braided into her mane and tail. Juliet held her head high as if proud of her appearance, and seemed to prance, her forelegs lifted high, set down delicately.

Nicole, too, was dressed all in white, her glorious coal black curls hanging loose down past her shoulders, a garland of pink roses cunningly wrapping about her head, low on her lightly freckled forehead. A veil attached to the back of the flowery ring and floated in the breeze that seemed to have agreed to appear as if on cue.

Lydia watched as a thoroughly bemused Marquess of Basingstoke came down the steps and walked over to assist Nicole from the saddle. She was close enough to see that her sister's marvelous violet eyes were awash in tears, and to hear her whispered *I love you.*

She felt Tanner's arms sliding around her waist as he gently pulled her back against him, bending his head to place a kiss on the side of her neck.

The world was beautiful. With no shadows, no

regrets, but only wonderful memories. Life was good, and to be lived every day, because every day spent with those you loved was more precious than any diamond.

And, maybe, after the ceremony, she and Tanner would find time to escape for a small nap...

* * * * *

REQUEST YOUR FREE BOOKS!

2 FREE NOVELS
FROM THE ROMANCE COLLECTION
PLUS 2 FREE GIFTS!

YES! Please send me 2 FREE novels from the Romance Collection and my 2 FREE gifts (gifts are worth about $10). After receiving them, if I don't wish to receive any more books, I can return the shipping statement marked "cancel." If I don't cancel, I will receive 4 brand-new novels every month and be billed just $5.74 per book in the U.S. or $6.24 per book in Canada. That's a saving of at least 28% off the cover price. It's quite a bargain! Shipping and handling is just 50¢ per book.* I understand that accepting the 2 free books and gifts places me under no obligation to buy anything. I can always return a shipment and cancel at any time. Even if I never buy another book, the two free books and gifts are mine to keep forever.

194/394 MDN E7NZ

Name	(PLEASE PRINT)	
Address		Apt. #
City	State/Prov.	Zip/Postal Code

Signature (if under 18, a parent or guardian must sign)

Mail to The Reader Service:
IN U.S.A.: P.O. Box 1867, Buffalo, NY 14240-1867
IN CANADA: P.O. Box 609, Fort Erie, Ontario L2A 5X3

Not valid for current subscribers to the Romance Collection
or the Romance/Suspense Collection.

Want to try two free books from another line?
Call 1-800-873-8635 or visit www.morefreebooks.com.

* Terms and prices subject to change without notice. Prices do not include applicable taxes. N.Y. residents add applicable sales tax. Canadian residents will be charged applicable provincial taxes and GST. Offer not valid in Quebec. This offer is limited to one order per household. All orders subject to approval. Credit or debit balances in a customer's account(s) may be offset by any other outstanding balance owed by or to the customer. Please allow 4 to 6 weeks for delivery. Offer available while quantities last.

Your Privacy: Harlequin Books is committed to protecting your privacy. Our Privacy Policy is available online at www.eHarlequin.com or upon request from the Reader Service. From time to time we make our lists of customers available to reputable third parties who have a product or service of interest to you. If you would prefer we not share your name and address, please check here. ☐

Help us get it right—We strive for accurate, respectful and relevant communications. To clarify or modify your communication preferences, visit us at www.ReaderService.com/consumerschoice.

MROM10R

KASEY MICHAELS

77376 HOW TO TAME A LADY ___ $7.99 U.S. ___ $8.99 CAN.
77371 HOW TO TEMPT A DUKE ___ $7.99 U.S. ___ $8.99 CAN.
77191 A MOST UNSUITABLE GROOM ___ $6.99 U.S. ___ $8.50 CAN.

(limited quantities available)

TOTAL AMOUNT $_____
POSTAGE & HANDLING $_____
($1.00 FOR 1 BOOK, 50¢ for each additional)
APPLICABLE TAXES* $_____
TOTAL PAYABLE $_____
(check or money order—please do not send cash)

To order, complete this form and send it, along with a check or money order for the total above, payable to HQN Books, to: **In the U.S.:** 3010 Walden Avenue, P.O. Box 9077, Buffalo, NY 14269-9077; **In Canada:** P.O. Box 636, Fort Erie, Ontario, L2A 5X3.

Name: _____
Address: _____ City: _____
State/Prov.: _____ Zip/Postal Code: _____
Account Number (if applicable): _____

075 CSAS

*New York residents remit applicable sales taxes.
*Canadian residents remit applicable GST and provincial taxes.

HQN™

We *are* romance™

www.HQNBooks.com

PHKM0610BL